Deep Down True

"When I wasn't inside the world of this book—because this is a book that you enter instead of merely read—I longed to be. I love it for its intensely human characters and for the way the author grants them their flaws as generously as she celebrates their daily decencies, their persistent hopefulness, their moments of personal grace."

—Marisa de los Santos, *New York Times* bestselling author of *Love Walked In* and *Belong to Me*

"Enormously readable and hugely relatable!"

—Kelly Corrigan, *New York Times* bestselling author of *The Middle Place* and *Lift*

"Engrossing, touching, and immensely satisfying. The truth shines on every page. I'd almost be willing to go back to junior high if I could sit at Juliette Fay's lunch table!"

—Beth Harbison, *New York Times* bestselling author of *Thin Rich Pretty*

And for
Shelter Me

"[Fay] does a beautiful job capturing the ebb and flow of single motherhood, from small miracles and little annoyances to the big ordeals . . . tinged with searing insight and often hilarious wry humor."　　　　—*The Boston Globe*

continued . . .

"The concerns of single motherhood after sudden tragedy come vividly to life, and as Janie learns to appreciate everyday miracles, readers will be charmed."   —*Publishers Weekly*

"Juliette Fay can hit the high notes of emotion with unexpected moments of redemption and wry humor."
     —Jacqueline Sheehan, author of *Lost & Found*

"*Shelter Me* is a richly told story that offers a keyhole into the pain and searing grief losing a loved one brings to a family. That pain is balanced against humor and the need to care-take life's day-to-day demands and relationships until one day, you realize you have the capability to love again. Fay writes with vivid dialogue and conjures up characters that feel real enough to be sitting in your kitchen."
     —Lee Woodruff, *New York Times* bestselling author of *In an Instant* and *Perfectly Imperfect*

A PENGUIN BOOK

DEEP DOWN TRUE

JULIETTE FAY's first novel, *Shelter Me*, was a 2009 Massachusetts Book Award Book of the Year, a Target 2009 Bookmarked Club selection, a Good Housekeeping Book Pick, and was chosen for the American Booksellers Association's Indie Next List. Juliette received a bachelor's degree from Boston College and a master's degree from Harvard University. She lives in Massachusetts with her husband and four children. *Deep Down True* is her second novel.

deep
down
true

Juliette Fay

PENGUIN BOOKS

PENGUIN BOOKS

Published by the Penguin Group

Penguin Group (USA) Inc., 375 Hudson Street, New York, New York 10014, U.S.A.

Penguin Group (Canada), 90 Eglinton Avenue East, Suite 700, Toronto

Ontario, Canada M4P 2Y3 (a division of Pearson Penguin Canada Inc.)

Penguin Books Ltd, 80 Strand, London WC2R ORL, England

Penguin Ireland, 25 St Stephen's Green, Dublin 2, Ireland (a division of Penguin Books Ltd)

Penguin Group (Australia), 250 Camberwell Road, Camberwell,

Victoria 3124, Australia (a division of Pearson Australia Group Pty Ltd)

Penguin Books India Pvt Ltd, II Community Centre, Panchsheel Park, New Delhi – 110 017, India

Penguin Group (NZ), 67 Apollo Drive, Rosedale, North Shore 0632,

New Zealand (a division of Pearson New Zealand Ltd)

Penguin Books (South Africa) (Pty) Ltd, 24 Sturdee Avenue,

Rosebank, Johannesburg 2196, South Africa

Penguin Books Ltd, Registered Offices:

80 Strand, London WC2R ORL, England

First published in Penguin Books 2011

1 3 5 7 9 10 8 6 4 2

PUBLISHER'S NOTE

This is a work of fiction. Names, characters, places, and incidents either are the product
of the author's imagination or are used fictitiously, and any resemblance to octual persons,
living or dead, business establishments, events, or locales is ertirely coincidental.

LIBRARY OF CONGRESS CATALOGING IN PUBLICATION DATA

Fay, Juliette.

Deep down true / Juliette Fay.

p m.

"A Pamela Dorman/Penguin book"–T. p. verso.

ISBN 978-0-14-311851-0

I. Divorced women–Fiction. 2. preteens–Fiction. 3. Domestic fiction. I. Title.

[DNLM: 1. Love stories. gsafd]

PS3606.A95D44 2011

813'.6–dc22   2010038552

Printed in the United States of America

Designed by Sabrina Bowers

For my parents,

CAROL DiGIANNI AND JOHN DACEY,

who've blazed their trails through hard times to happiness,

and whose love and enthusiasm is always a given

ACKNOWLEDGMENTS

THE FIRST FLICKERS OF *DEEP DOWN TRUE* WERE sparked at Jonas Clarke Junior High School during the years 1974–77. I still have occasional moments of post-traumatic stress from the experience. I would like to thank Rhea Nowak, Amy Smith, Jean Volante, and Alexandra Fisher, friends who never, to my knowledge, betrayed me. Thanks also to Kassia Sing, who was that all-too-rare combination of popular and nice. I'm sure there were others, but in my attempt to block out as much of that time as possible, I have inadvertently forgotten their names. My apologies and my thanks.

Thanks also to my sisters, Jennifer Dacey Allen and Kristen Dacey Iwai, the best of companions and co-conspirators, who have always known how to crack me up, even on really unfunny days. And to Linda Dacey, my stepmother, who traversed that fine line between intervening and interfering, and who quietly lobbied for a more reasonable clothing allowance for us. The life-or-death importance of this was lost on my father, being a man and being as uninterested in fashion as an otherwise socially appropriate person could possibly be.

When I tell people that middle school was the worst three years of my life, I often hear groans of agreement. As far as I can tell, it hasn't gotten any easier. Adolescents are an interesting bunch, prone to acts of both great generosity and great ferocity, and you never know which is coming at you till it's in your face. The flickers of this story were blown into flames when I first heard Rosalind Wiseman, author of *Queen Bees and Wannabes,* speak, and further fueled when I read her book. Thanks, Rosalind, for helping me make sense of the culture I so fearfully inhabited all those years ago and for unwittingly giving me guidance with the characters of *Deep Down True.*

There's the part of fiction writing that's the "dreaming up" part, and with any luck this is done alone (or at least someplace where nobody's asking for help making a bracelet out of duct tape or for rides to their friends' houses). And then there are all the other parts—reviewing, editing, fact-finding, shepherding, encouraging, deal making, publishing, promoting, selling, begging, bugging, consoling, celebrating. With any luck these are done in the company of people like:

Alison Bullock, Megan Lucier, Catherine Toro-McCue, Julia Tanen, and Anne Kuppinger, dear friends who read every scrap, often in several iterations, and gave me their unvarnished opinions while simultaneously making me feel smart and well liked. Catherine is a psychiatric nurse who had lots of good information, insights, and resources on eating disorders.

Sandra Dupuy, Tracey Palmer, and Art Hutchinson, excellent writers with whom I've spent many hours in coffee shops and on self-inflicted "retreats" challenging one another to do better.

Dr. Michael Putt, who keeps our teeth healthy and has been a wonderful consultant on everything from drill bits to dental-office politics. Dr. Paul Allen, my brother-in-law and go-to guy on what it's like to be a medical student. And Keiji Iwai, my other brother-in-law, whose photographic know-how is second only to his generosity with his time.

Patricia Campanella Daniels, a dear friend who gave me the grand tour of northeastern Connecticut and whose husband, Eric Daniels, made sure I got the sports references right.

Julia Tanen, one of my oldest friends and managing director at KCSA Strategic Communications, who tirelessly promotes my work and generously shared the depth of her personal knowledge of bulimia.

Pamela Dorman and Julie Miesionczek, editor and assistant editor, who worked so hard to get this book into the best possible shape.

Theresa Park, my agent and friend, who brilliantly stewards my career and is really fun to hang out with. And the fabulous Park Literary team of Abigail Koons, Emily Sweet, and Yahel Matalon. Amanda Cardinale, you'll be missed!

Quinn, Nick, Liam, and Brianna Fay, who have their hands full raising their father and me, and who still haven't gotten sick of my doing some "book thing" or other several times a week. Brianna has been my foreign-language consultant on teenager-speak, answering countless questions that begin with "How would you say . . . ?"

And Tom Fay, my husband and BFF, whose love, support, and endless enthusiasm for my work ("Here, sign this book, I think I can get it to Ben Affleck!") makes me feel lucky every day.

deep
down
true

CHAPTER
1

IN JEANS THAT FIT FOUR POUNDS AGO BUT NOW squeezed her in a mildly intrusive manner, Dana stood at her kitchen counter pinching foil over a tray of lasagna and waiting on hold, the phone wedged against her shoulder. Her gaze skimmed the obituaries in the local paper, but Dermott McPherson's name did not appear—not this time anyway. Mr. McPherson was the reason she'd made the lasagna, though it wasn't actually for him. He probably wasn't eating much. It was for his family, who were understandably distraught over their loved one's terminal illness. Dana didn't know them. She belonged to Comfort Food, a group who cooked for families in crisis.

When it was her turn, Dana prepared meals that would, she hoped, sustain them as hands were held and medication dispensed, bedding changed and phone calls placed. She often thought of her own mother's quick descent into a gray, fetid-smelling infirmity, with lungs that seemed to shrivel almost visibly. Dana would have appreciated a well-made meal. Nothing fancy, just something better than rubbery pizza and half-flat soda. A small connection to a world outside the thick humidity of death.

Her father's exit had been swift and clean by comparison. There'd been no hospital stays or grieving friends, or even a casket to choose. But Dana didn't like to think about that.

"Cotters Rock Dental Center," said a voice in her ear. "May I—"

Startled from her somber reverie, Dana flinched, and the phone clattered to the floor. She grabbed it up quickly. "Kendra, I'm so sorry! I hope that didn't make an awful noise in your ear."

"That's all right," said the receptionist.

"I'm so embarrassed. I really apologize."

"I'm fine. May I help you?"

"This is Dana Stellgarten. Morgan and Grady's mom? I need to make appointments for their checkups, if that's okay."

Out in the mudroom, there was a squeak of the door and the thud of a backpack dropping onto the tiles. "Excuse me for just a minute, please," Dana murmured into the phone, then covered the mouthpiece with her palm. "Morgan?" she called.

"Yeah."

"I thought you were going to Darby's."

"Well, now I'm not." Morgan appeared in the kitchen and opened the refrigerator door. She stood staring in, as if there were some movie playing that only preteens could see, in among the condiments and containers of yogurt.

"I'm so sorry, I'll have to call back," Dana said into the phone. She focused on her daughter, backlit by the refrigerator light. "The plans changed?" she asked.

"Darby didn't *feel* well." Morgan's fingers twitched abruptly into little quote marks.

"Did you reschedule for another day?"

Morgan twisted toward her mother. "No, Mom, we didn't *reschedule*. It's just hanging out. You don't reschedule hanging out."

"You seem . . . Are you angry with Darby?"

Morgan closed the refrigerator door with a thump. "I don't *get* to be angry. She didn't do anything wrong."

"How did she tell you?" Now that Morgan was in sixth grade, Dana had learned it wasn't *what* girls said to each other anymore. All the real information came from *how* they said it.

Morgan slumped into a kitchen chair, picked up a napkin, and twisted it into the shape and density of a swizzle stick. "She was standing with Kimmi, and I was like, 'Hey, I'll meet you after last period.' And she looked at Kimmi."

This was bad, Dana knew. Their eyes were their weapons now. "She looked at her?"

"Yeah. And she was like, 'Oh, yeah, um, I don't feel good. I think I should go home.' So I said, 'Are you sick?' Then she looked at Kimmi *again* and said, 'I'm fine. I just need some downtime.'"

She would rather be alone than with Morgan? thought Dana. A wave of protective anger swept over her, but she didn't show it, knowing that it would confirm Morgan's suspicions and make her feel even worse. Dana herself often needed to cling to the slim chance that things weren't quite as disheartening as they seemed. "Honey, maybe she's just overscheduled," she offered.

"We're not preschoolers, Mom." Morgan rose and went up to her room. Dana let her alone. She knew that Morgan would open a textbook and curl over the page, narrowing her focus until all that existed in the world were Figure A and Subsection B.

"I'm taking Grady to practice!" Dana called up to Morgan a little while later. She loaded Grady and all his gear into the minivan and made a detour to drop off the lasagna, Caesar salad, Italian bread, and brownies at the McPhersons' house.

"Ca' I shay inna car?" asked seven-year-old Grady, sucking on his mouth guard.

"What?" Dana struggled to pick up all the containers of food. "I could use some help here."

He yanked out the mouth guard. "I don't wanna go to the door with you. It's all, like, *sad* in there. And if a kid answers, he's gonna hate me because *my* dad's not sick and *I* don't have to wait for some lady to dump off my dinner."

Dana sighed and went to the door. No one answered. She

placed the food on the front step in the cooler labeled COMFORT
FOOD and went back to the car. As she was pulling away, a woman
in jeans and a T-shirt came out with a toddler on her hip, glanced
down at the cooler and then out toward the street. For a brief moment, she met Dana's eyes and raised a hand in thanks. Dana waved
back.

So young . . . she thought as she drove away.

Dana tried to attend as many of Grady's football practices as
she could. The coach scared her. He yelled at the unruly posse of
second-graders as if they were candidates for the Navy SEALS.
Dana wasn't used to this. Until football, Grady had been coached
mostly by weary fathers who sped down Interstate 84 removing
their ties as they drove, trying to get to practice on time. They had
no interest in yelling at other people's children—they yelled enough
at their own. They just wanted the kids to learn a few skills, have
fun, and avoid bloodying each other.

Coach Roburtin—Coach Ro, as the kids called him—espoused
a less limited philosophy. Football practice doubled as his own
workout, and he charged around the field running laps with the
boys and doing push-ups. He slapped the tops of their helmets
when they weren't listening, their little heads bobbing into their
shoulder pads, a sight that made Dana's own neck hurt. She'd heard
he was unmarried and childless, had grown up in town and played
football for Cotters Rock High. He was now a car salesman in nearby
Manchester.

"Stelly! Where's Stelly? Get your butt over here, son! Did you
come to play or knit mittens?"

"Mitten knitting" was a catchall phrase for Coach Ro, indicat-
ing anything that wasn't football. A boy ran over, his bright blue
T-shirt dangling down from under his practice jersey. That was
Grady's shirt, Dana was sure of it. Coach Ro was so busy roaring at

the boys he hadn't learned their names! Maybe Coach Ro had had his *own* helmet thumped a few too many times. Then it occurred to her—Stelly was short for Stellgarten.

"All RIGHT, now." He grabbed Grady's face mask and positioned him next to the quarterback. "Timmy's gonna take the snap. And he's gonna hand it off to YOU, and you are NOT going to drop it. You are going to run like your PANTS are on fire to the end zone! You with me?" Grady's helmet bobbed up and down. "Lemmehearyousay YES!" bawled the coach.

"YES!" came Grady's high-pitched howl.

Then the play was in motion, and the disorderly gaggle of youngsters suddenly transformed into two focused, goal-driven teams. For about six seconds. And then Grady's blockers seemed to forget they had anything else to do but ram their friends or straggle toward their water bottles. The opposing team swarmed toward Grady, who'd been running back toward his own team's goal line. One boy yanked at his practice jersey, pulling him down from behind. Then boys from both teams began leaping on top of them until there was a pile of bodies about three feet high. With Grady at the bottom. Dana let out a panicked, "Oh, my God!"

"Get up, you baboons! Get off him!" boomed Coach Ro, grabbing players by their shoulder pads and heaving them to the side. "Stelly, you okay? You're fine, right?"

Dana began to rush toward Grady but got only a step or two before a hand grasped her forearm. "You *know* you can't go to him," said the voice behind her. Dana turned to see Amy Koljian, Timmy the quarterback's mother. "Coach will wave you over if it's bad," Amy said with a knowing nod.

"But he could be hurt!" Easy for Amy to be calm. Her son was now sitting off to the side, chewing on his mouth guard like he hadn't been fed in a week.

"No parents on the field unless Coach says," Amy chided. "Grady'll be embarrassed if you go."

"Coach says?" said Dana. "Coach doesn't even know his first name!"

Amy motioned toward them. "See?" she said smugly. "He's fine." Grady was sitting up now, air heaving in and out of his little body. Dana willed him to look at her, to assure him of her presence. His helmet turned in her direction, and then he slowly got up. Coach thumped him on the shoulder. "All right, you knuckleheads, what the heck was THAT?" he yelled.

"God, I hate football," Dana breathed.

Amy chuckled beside her. "New football moms are always so skittish." Timmy was the youngest of Amy's boys, and Amy enjoyed being the superior, experienced mother.

Dana attempted a grateful smile. Grady certainly would have been embarrassed, and in the end he hadn't been terribly hurt. His spine was still intact, his teeth still fit snugly in their gums. And yet Amy's self-satisfaction made Dana want to wring her neck—or, better yet, mention the girls' night out her friend Polly was throwing, knowing that Amy was not invited.

This uncharacteristic surge of vindictiveness surprised Dana. This was not her. She never purposely hurt people's feelings. And it was the very thing she'd drilled into her children since the formation of their first friendships: Do not discuss invitations. Do not mention that Cassandra is having you over after preschool today and you might finger-paint with chocolate pudding if her mother remembered to buy some. Do not announce that you're going to Owen's birthday party at Laser Tag Rumble and you thought all the boys were asked. Don't even squeeze your host's hand behind the monkey bars at recess and whisper, "I can't wait!"

Practice was over, and Grady walked toward her—was that a limp?—grabbed her thumb, and began towing her toward the car. "Are you okay?" she asked him. "That was a heck of a pileup."

"Yeah," said Grady. "Can Travis come over tomorrow?"

"Sure, I'll call his mom when we get home."

"TRAVIS!" bellowed Grady across the parking lot. "WANNA—"

Dana clamped her hand over Grady's mouth, a lightning strike of parental correction. "What have I *told* you about that?" she murmured at him tightly.

"No one cares, Mom," he insisted, squirming away from her.

Everyone cares, she thought. *Even if they don't want to go, everyone wants to be asked.*

CHAPTER
2

THE STORY OF DANA'S DIVORCE BORED EVEN her. The lack of originality embarrassed her, and she would roll her eyes to hide her humiliation when people asked for details. "Younger woman," she would say. "*Ohhh,*" they would reply knowingly.

Of course, no dissolution of a fifteen-year marriage could be dismissed with such a simple explanation. Yes, he had been unfaithful, but Dana had forgiven him for countless things over the years, and she would have taken him back. It was Kenneth who had pushed for the divorce, saying that his love for her had never reached the same intensity he now felt for this new person. "It's my best chance for happiness," he'd told her.

Even so, he seemed disappointed in Dana's resignation to his leaving her for his twenty-nine-year-old hairdresser. Dana had exploded quite vehemently, she thought. But it soon became clear to both of them that her fury was more on behalf of their children than herself. How would they go on to have healthy, trusting relationships, she worried, if the king of their little suburban feudal system left the castle? Who would protect them from the advance of the Huns?

Dana knew all too well about living in a kingless castle, and she had promised herself it wouldn't happen to her children. Deep down she knew she had no control over the vagaries of life, but it had been comforting to pretend she had the power to keep this one heartbreak from Morgan and Grady.

Her marriage had not been completely loveless, Dana was almost certain of that. There had even been potential for the You Are the One kind of love she'd read about so often in the romance novels she couldn't get enough of. She had waited for that feeling, tried to nurture it however she could: romantic getaways, for instance, with different, yet tasteful, sexual procedures. Kenneth seemed to enjoy that very much. And she did, too, though her mind tended to wander when it involved some unusual position on her part.

And she had listened so carefully. To everything.

In the relationships she admired, both real and fictitious, the lovers were also the best of friends. They never stopped listening and offering excellent support and advice. She tried to do that. And she looked for evidence of it in Kenneth, reminding herself to be appreciative when he scolded her for not wearing a warm enough coat or suggested she might read something more literary from time to time. He was thinking of her. Offering counsel in his own way. More than she'd ever seen her own parents do for each other.

One night when she was feeling cranky and he was being particularly oblivious, she had gotten up the nerve to tell him he was not meeting her needs. His reply had been, "What needs?" Dana wasn't sure which ones, exactly, but she had them and they were unmet.

"Sorry, honey," he'd said, giving her a little one-armed hug. "I'll try to do better." Then he'd gone off to pluck a hair that had grown out like a tentacle from his otherwise smooth eyebrow.

Dana was, of course, achingly sad when the divorce papers were signed. Kenneth had insisted on taking her to lunch at a French restaurant afterward, and she'd been too dazed by the yawning abyss of her official aloneness to decline. Her hand held the fork as if it were an unfamiliar object, a tool for which she hadn't been properly trained. It slipped into the greens, the herbed tang of the olives drifting toward her, a foreign, assaulting smell. "No," she wanted to tell that smell, "go back."

She rested the fork on the plate and soothed herself by running her hand across the table linen, brushing at the sharp crumbs that had flaked from Kenneth's slice of buttered baguette. Her skin felt cold and papery brittle, as if the bread shards might pierce her and draw blood. In the manufactured dimness of the restaurant, Kenneth's face looked shadowed and bleak, as if he, too, might be contemplating the things that could cut him open.

He cleared his throat, a barely perceptible gargle accompanying the brusque cough. His allergies were acting up, and Dana almost asked him if he'd taken his antihistamine pill. But it was not her place to listen for this sound anymore, or to remind him to take his medicine. Better for her to start listening to her own sounds: the dull, unwilling thud of her pulse, the high-pitched shame of having failed at something so important and so public.

"Promise me something," she'd asked over her salade niçoise. "Please don't bring your girlfriend when you see the kids. Let them have all of you for the next couple of months at least."

"What do you mean, all of me?" he'd said, not insulted yet but ready to be. "You think I don't give the kids my full attention?"

"No, it's just . . . I want them to have as much time with you as possible." Dana was afraid that Grady and Morgan would lose their father completely, as she had lost hers. Perhaps Kenneth would be swept away by this new person, as her own father had been swept away.

"I'm only moving to Hartford," Kenneth muttered. "It's not Mars." The waiter returned to ask if they cared for dessert. Kenneth declined for them both.

Dana had muddled through those confusing, elongated months since the divorce. She found herself squinting a lot, a vain attempt to bring into sharper focus this new life of single parenting. And she noticed an edge of sharpness creeping into her tone these days. *Stay positive,* she told herself, gunning the motor of her minivan a little harder than necessary on her way to the dentist. But that barest glint of serration remained ready to strike nonetheless.

They'd been going to Dr. Sakimoto for nine years, since Morgan was three. On her first visit, Morgan had been too frightened to climb up onto the big vinyl chair by herself, so Dana had sat in it and held the shaking girl on her lap. As soon as Marie the hygienist touched her instrument to Morgan's teeth, Morgan threw up.

"Okay, sweetie, okay," Dana had soothed Morgan while trying to clean up the mess.

Dr. Sakimoto had appeared in the doorway with a roll of paper towels. "Not a problem," he'd said. Dana had expected a high, nasal voice to match his short, slightly pudgy form, but his voice was low and solid-sounding, as if it came from the heels of his shoes. "Happens all the time, doesn't it, Marie?" Marie hadn't seemed so sure of that, walking quickly from the room with her hand over her nose.

Dana kept apologizing as she cleaned and comforted Morgan.

"Just a few tossed cookies," he assured her, wiping down the chair. "A minor problem in the scheme of things. Am I right?"

"Yes," Dana had sighed. "You're right."

Morgan was almost twelve now and no longer wanted her mother anywhere near her in the dentist's office, Dana mused as she reclined in the very same chair, a paper bib clipped around her neck.

"Any change in health status?" Dr. Sakimoto asked as he studied Dana's chart, propped against his stomach. He reminded her of a birdbath: short and squat, yet with an almost visible reservoir of good humor. "New medications? Rapid weight loss or gain?" he asked.

"Yes to that last," she answered.

He glanced at her—at her face, she noticed, not at her body, where he might have tried to gauge for himself whether she'd gotten fatter or thinner. "Yes?" he said. "Loss or gain?"

"Both. I lost fifteen pounds very quickly, but I've gained back about ten."

"Were you sick?" he asked. "I hope it wasn't some fad diet."

"The Divorce Diet," she joked humorlessly. "Not a fad, exactly—more of an epidemic."

"I'm so sorry," he said gently. "How are you?"

"Okay, I guess." It appeared he was waiting for more, so she added, "I'm still flossing."

"Good," he said. "Because nothing's more important than proper dental hygiene when life starts throwing punches."

He's right, she thought. *I should be taking better care of myself. I should work out more.* But then she saw his commiserating smile. He was kidding, of course. She might still be flossing and loading the dishwasher and baking muffins for her children's class parties, but Dana knew what was different now. She'd always been able to connect with others, laugh at their quips, make them feel funny even when they weren't. These days, however, she never seemed to get the joke.

That afternoon Dana was backing her minivan out of the driveway, with Grady in the backseat bobbing his head to his favorite inappropriate music station. "Getcha, getcha down on the floor, beggin' for more . . ." the singer chanted over synthesized percussion. Dana hoped her second-grader didn't really know what he was hearing.

Suddenly there was unexpected motion in her rearview mirror. A large object—a car?—was slicing across the driveway behind her. Because its direction was reversed in the mirror, she swerved the wrong way to avoid it, then overcorrected and swerved back. Grady's football-helmeted head banged against the window as they zigzagged backward down the driveway. "Ow!" he screamed.

Dana slammed on the brakes and wrenched around in her seat. "Are you all right?"

"I'm fine," he muttered, rubbing his elbow, one of the few un-padded parts of his body.

Dana looked through the back window to see a rust-speckled orange hatchback parked by her fallen mailbox post.

"Shit!" the driver snarled through the open window, a curtain of tar-black hair obscuring the face.

Dana had a moment of fear. A curse-spewing stranger had careened onto her property. Should she even get out of the car? But Grady was already climbing out the sliding side door, heading straight for danger, as usual. Dana scrambled out after him.

"You piece of crap!" the driver, a female, was hissing at the car. She appeared to be trying to shake the steering wheel loose from its metal column. "*Uhhh!* My life *sucks.*" Dana still couldn't quite see her face, but the voice was familiar. . .

"Alder?" said Grady, leaning against the dirty car.

Dana's niece deflated, her shoulders slumping forward in defeat. "Hey, G," she muttered.

"Alder, are you okay?" fussed Dana, reaching to open the door. "Does anything hurt, sweetie? Here, let me . . ." She took Alder's elbow as the girl extricated herself from the ripped vinyl interior of the car. Alder's gray T-shirt was printed with the vague red outline of a building consumed in flames. The scribbled lettering spelled out TORCH THE HOUSE.

Dana hugged her, and Alder let herself be hugged. It had been more than a year since they'd seen each other. *August,* Dana remembered. *Ma's funeral.* The difference in Alder's appearance was startling. Her gingersnap-brown hair had been dyed black, and her clothing was bleaker than Dana ever remembered. Alder's style had always been a multihued, eclectic look. Unconventional but appealing. Now she had a wispy listlessness to her, so unlike the sturdy, straight-backed girl Dana had always adored.

"Can I live here?" Alder asked as they walked up the driveway. Dana's worried smile fell.

"Yes!" Grady said. "Definitely! Right, Mom? Right?"

Alder gave him a slow shove that sent him sideways onto the lawn. He threw himself out for extra yardage, the plastic sections of his shoulder pads clacking against each other as he landed. "Oh, man!" He laughed as he lay on the grass. "This is so awesome!"

Dana left Alder in the kitchen with a glass of sugar-free lemonade and drove Grady to practice. On the way back, she called her sister.

"I should've known she'd go to you," muttered Connie. "She blew off school again."

"The . . . uh . . . that creative . . ."

"The Summit Creativity and Awareness School. I practically had to prove she was the second coming of Salvador Dalí to get her in."

"Are you positive it's the right school? I'm sure it's great, but maybe it's not the best fit."

"Okay, enlighten me," Connie said. "What did you have in mind? Deerfield? Williston? Because she's *done* at Hamptonfield High. That place is for single-cell organisms."

Dana bit the tip of her thumb. "I heard about the trig incident."

"Trigonometry! Trigo-freaking-nometry! Like she'd *ever* have use for that. Like it *matters!*"

"Yes . . . but I don't know if it was best to force a discussion about it at Back-to-School Night."

"When else would I force a discussion about it?" demanded Connie. "All the parents and so-called teachers were *there*, Dana. The whole paramilitary establishment!"

"Well, then, uh . . ." Dana mumbled. Her sister's rants were implacable and exhausting.

"*Well, then, uh?*" Connie mimicked. "You sound like Ma! If you start using bobby pins and Charlie cologne, I'll do an intervention on you."

"I've always thought a bobby pin or two might come in handy."

Dana smiled, enjoying the rare opportunity to poke at Connie a little.

"Don't antagonize me—I'm in crisis!"

"All right," Dana acquiesced. "Does Alder say where she'd like to go to school?"

"Like she knows. And who says high school is the key to happiness anyway? It was the key to a four-year stupor for me. Besides, Alder has *talent*. If she'd ever spend more than ten minutes in the studio, she could probably have a gallery opening by the time she's eighteen!"

"Mm-hmm," Dana sympathized without actually agreeing. "Maybe it might make sense for her to stay here for a few days, until the two of you cool off." She rolled her eyes at the unlikelihood that Connie would *ever* cool off.

"Fine," said Connie. "Let her stay. Let her live out her little suburban Abercrombie & Fitch fantasy. She'll come to her senses—all six of them—soon enough."

"You're welcome," said Dana.

"Right," Connie snorted.

Dana pulled in to the driveway. Connie was right in a sense—Dana's house, snuggled in the pleasant little town of Cotters Rock, Connecticut, had seemed the embodiment of all her homey fantasies. A center-entrance Colonial, white with hunter green shutters, it had a blooming crabapple tree and a stately front door. They never used that door anymore, though. They'd used the mudroom door by the garage since Morgan had learned to walk, her little shoes always muddy, her snow boots reliably wet.

When she went in, Dana found Alder right where she'd left her, the lemonade untouched. "Did something happen?" Dana asked, settling into a chair beside her.

"Yeah, my whole fucking pathetic life happened."

"Sweetie, would you mind toning down the language just a little?"

Alder shrugged an apology.

"Your mom said you've been skipping school."

"She's driving me in*sane*."

No doubt, thought Dana. "Well . . . it would be really nice to have you around for a few days." She smiled at Alder, mentally deconstructing the hair color and the sour look. Little Alder. Smart, funny, spontaneous girl. The first baby Dana had ever held. "I've missed you."

A thin trickle of warmth flowed across the girl's face, a memory of some former happiness. "What's Cotters Rock High like?" she asked.

CHAPTER
3

"**S**HE CAN'T STAY IN *MY* ROOM," MORGAN TOLD HER mother after dinner. Alder and Grady had gone out in the yard to throw a football around. "Look at her, Mom, she's all goth! Or emo at least!"

"Emu?" asked Dana.

Morgan rolled her eyes. "Mom, that's like an *ostrich* or something. Emo is . . . It doesn't matter. She looks freakish. I'll *never* be able to sleep with her there."

Morgan had never been a good sleeper, not even in the womb, and rarely slept through the night even now. Darkness and solitude seemed to be appetizers for a full-course meal of worrying about an English test, or whether her hair would come out right in the morning, or whether Kimmi Kinnear hated her. Sleep was the trump card, and Morgan had played it.

"All right, she can stay in the TV room. But that means you and Grady *both* have to watch TV in the basement. With no fighting. You understand?" Dana bit the tip of her thumb. "I hope she won't be insulted."

"Insulted?" Morgan snorted. "She's sixteen, Mom. Trust me, she doesn't want anything to do with a stupid sixth-grader."

"Morgan, honey, you are not—"

"I know, I know." Morgan ate Grady's unfinished steak fries, her hand flying back and forth between the plate and her lips. "It's just an expression."

"Dana," said Alder, lying on the pullout couch in the TV room. She never used the more formal "Aunt Dana," just as she'd never called her mother "Mom." Connie felt the terms for "mother" were archaic and limiting. She'd taught Alder to call her Connie.

"Yes, honey." Dana tucked the bubble-gum-pink fleece blanket around Alder's sharp shoulders.

"I totally don't want to go back."

Dana sighed. "It's probably not a good idea for me to get in the middle of this."

Alder pushed the covers back and sat up. "Dana. She's insane. Come on, you *know* that."

"Your mother is very intelligent and perfectly . . . She can be difficult and stubborn, but she's your mother and she loves you. That counts."

"I'm not talking about *love*. I'm talking about that freakazoid school she sent me to. It's not even a real art school! It's all, like, 'free expression' hippie stuff. I kept telling her that, but all she cares about is creative flow, whatever *that* is. I've had it with her!" Alder shook her head in annoyance. "She doesn't get it that high school is *supposed* to be boring and pointless. And now I can't go to *my* boring, pointless high school, because I'm Trig Girl with the insane mother."

"You really want to go to high school?"

Alder sighed patiently, as if explaining the rules of Monopoly Junior to a slow-witted child. "No one *wants* to go to high school. It's high school, for godsake. But when you grow up in America, it's part of the package—like a combo meal at McDonald's. You might not want the supersize Diet Coke, but it just comes. Deal with it."

Dana pondered this as she smoothed the pink fleece. There was an unfamiliar edge to Alder that seemed recently sharpened against something jagged. The girl had never been cynical—if anything, Connie had indoctrinated her with a belief that her destiny was squarely up to her; conforming to the status quo was giving up. Might as well put on an apron and bake cupcakes for the rest of your life. "Cup-cakers," Connie would sneer about women whose lives revolved around their children's oboe lessons, their husbands' business-travel schedule, PTA fund-raisers, and hothouse yoga at the health club. Women not so very different from Dana.

Dana now felt pinpricks of concern at the sound of Alder's resignation. It could be any number of things—rebelling against her mother, or maybe some teenage hormone was joyriding around her brain, telling her to do something uncharacteristic. Maybe, thought Dana, she was just tired. Being different, constantly blazing a new trail through the obstacle course of adolescence must be exhaust-ing. "Alder, honey," she said tentatively, "are you all right?"

Alder squinted at her in a show of bafflement. "You're worried about me because I think I should be in high school? Are *you* all right?" Her teasing was a relief to Dana, who squinted back and gave her niece's hair a playful tug.

After sending Morgan and Grady off to school the next morning, Dana went to check on Alder. She was still sleeping, knees curled up, arms wrapped protectively across her chest. The delicate hol-lows beneath her eyes were a faint purplish blue, like faded bruises. She looked like she hadn't slept well in months, and Dana didn't want to wake her. She wrote a note on a pad of stationery she had from before the divorce. It said THE STELLGARTENS in jazzy script across the top, with their names—Kenneth, Dana, Morgan, Grady—written over and over as a border around the edges. Though it now gave a false impression of unity, it was handy, and Dana couldn't bring herself to get rid of it.

"Walking with Polly, back around ten. Cereal in the cabinet. Love, D," said the note.

The air was dry and cool, a classic October day in New En-gland, as Dana strode down her driveway. She and Polly hadn't been friends at first; they'd simply lived on the same street. One morning Dana had taken baby Morgan for a stroller ride, crossing Polly's driveway at the same moment Polly had come barreling down, arms swinging, having been stood up by an unreliable friend. "No commitment," Polly had huffed as she slowed to accept Dana into the current of her stride. "Everything else in her life comes first."

Well, yes, Dana had thought. *What could be less important than a walk?* Of course, she hadn't expressed this thought. "Disappointing," she'd said, heaving the stroller along a little faster, trying to prove worthy of this unexpected invitation. She hadn't lived in the neighborhood long, had quit her job as an office manager at a Hartford law firm, and was feeling friendless and bored.

"You're pretty good with a stroller," Polly had said. "The kid has a future in space travel if she gets *that* kind of ride every day."

Dana's brain crackled with pride, thankful for any sign she was doing something right. Motherhood, she was finding, was devoid of those little indicators of accomplishment and appreciation: being commended at a staff meeting, or complimented on a new pair of earrings, or invited to lunch by co-workers. None of these things, or anything remotely like them, happened now. She found herself wondering if she were any good at it.

How am I doing? she'd occasionally whisper to baby Morgan. *Are you happy you hired me?*

Dana had soon become Polly's most reliable walking partner, and eventually they started getting together in the evenings. Kenneth and Polly's husband, Victor, had clicked right away, and the four of them often had dinner together, commiserating about the trials of parenthood, chuckling over the antics of eccentric neighbors, their friendship growing more deeply rooted in the terra firma of their lives with every passing season. Ten years later, when Kenneth asked for the divorce, it had hit Polly and Victor almost as hard as it had Dana. Victor and Kenneth's friendship survived; Polly's loyalty was squarely with Dana. *What would I do without her?* Dana now wondered as she strode toward her friend's house.

Polly came down her driveway, windmilling her arms as if she were practicing the backstroke. "What a day!" she called. Though she was six inches shorter than Dana and pixielike in the delicacy of her features, she was a tough little walker, pressing their pace to the edge of comfort. Dana liked to ask Polly a philosophical or multipart question just as they reached the rise of a hill. Let Polly talk as they climbed. It was all Dana could do not to pant.

"So what's the verdict on middle school these days?" asked Polly. "Is she settled in now?"

"Pretty much," said Dana. "Did Gina ever have Ms. Cripton?"

"Kryptonite?" said Polly, her short black hair bouncing rhythmically. "Yeah, she's awful. Gina couldn't stand her. Huge collection of plastic bead necklaces. Lots of pop quizzes."

"Morgan's going to burst a blood vessel one of these days. She studies constantly because she's so worried about those stupid quizzes."

"Tell her to relax. It's only sixth grade."

"You tell her."

The women smiled at each other. Who could tell kids anything? And who was less worthy of airtime than the child's own creators? Polly knew this. Her two children, Gina and Peter, were older and had wrung several more years of worry and fury out of her. Dana envied the fact that Polly never seemed to second-guess herself as a mother. She fought with her kids, interrogated them, followed them into the high-security areas of their bedrooms, demanding access without proper clearance. She occasionally threw food at them when she was annoyed.

And for their part, Gina and Peter seemed to withstand this barrage with surprising nonchalance. Or they roared back at her, awful things that Dana hoped she would never hear from her own children. Dana had once been witness to Peter's calling Polly "a screeching bitch" right to her face. Without so much as flinching, Polly had yelled back, "And how do you think I got this way? You think I was like this before kids? Not on your ungrateful little life!"

While Dana could never be that kind of mother, she was impressed that none of them seemed too bothered by it. "Gina hates me," Polly would occasionally mention, as if commenting on a passing patch of bad weather.

As they powered down the street toward Nipmuc Pond, Dana said. "So my niece, Alder, showed up yesterday."

"Your sister Connie's girl."

"Right. Sixteen, driving some beater car I had to get towed. Knocked over my mailbox."

"Nice."

"She's a good kid. A little out there, but it's not her fault. Connie isn't exactly Carol Brady."

"What does she call us again?"

"Well, not us specifically," qualified Dana. She never liked to be the source, even secondarily, of hurt feelings.

"Yes, us *specifically*," said Polly with a smirk.

Dana smiled. What was she worried about? Polly didn't care what Connie thought. "Cupcakers."

"Love it," Polly said wryly.

Dana told her about Alder's wanting to move in. "What do you think?" she asked.

"I think you want to take her."

"I do not! I would never interfere like that!"

"Not to interfere, just to . . . I don't know . . . It's like you want to get your hands on her."

Oh, my gosh, she's right, thought Dana.

"You feel bad about how she's been raised," Polly went on, "and you want to make it up to her."

"How could I possibly do that?" Dana asked, knowing it didn't matter, knowing she loved Alder and would do anything to make her happy.

"I don't know." Polly grinned. "Cupcakes?"

After the walk, Dana called Connie on her cell phone from the driveway. She didn't want Alder to overhear the conversation in case it went badly. "So it's the beginning of second quarter," she began carefully. "What if she just stayed here until the end of it? That would be January. She'd be back for the next semester at Peak . . . Artistic . . ."

"It's not about chronological *time*, Dana, it's about being in an environment that allows the integrity of the work to flow."

"Okay, so if Alder gets . . . flowing . . . while she's here, she can scoot right back up to the Berkshires. She'd be home in an hour."

Connie was silent. Dana knew she wouldn't acquiesce—she'd determine a way for it to make sense on her own terms. "She's blocked," Connie said finally. "Change of venue could be just the thing. Maybe she'll come up with some visual commentary on the soullessness of suburbia."

"Great," said Dana, slumping in relief. "And can you send some clothes? Because she only brought two pairs of undies."

It wasn't hard to get Alder registered at Cotters Rock High; in fact, it was surprisingly easy.

"You have her birth certificate?" asked the elderly secretary in the main office. "Records from the previous school? Medical forms?"

"No, I—"

"Well, just get them in when you can."

Dana filled out paperwork while the secretary pecked slowly at her computer keyboard. "She's in the system now," said the secretary. "Tell her to come to the office when she gets to school tomorrow, and I'll give her a schedule. And don't forget to get me those records."

"She can start tomorrow?"

"Don't you want her to? Most people can't wait to get them out of the house."

When Dana got home, she told Alder, "You're all set. You start tomorrow."

Alder stared blankly out the window at the falling leaves and said, "Great."

DANA MADE PASTA FOR DINNER. FOODWISE, IT was the canvas upon which all three of them could paint their own individualized palate-pleasing pictures. Dana would heat up some marinara and a few meatballs for herself and steam a vegetable to use as a partial pasta substitute. She tried to reduce her carbohydrate intake wherever possible. Morgan would slather hers with butter and dump little snowdrifts of parmesan cheese onto it. Grady would mix his with one spoonful of peanut butter and one of ketchup.

"Whoa! What are you—the Jackson Pollock of penne?" Alder slid into her seat, wearing a black T-shirt printed with the image of an upright guitar. Its neck ran up between her breasts, ending abruptly at the top of the shirt. It was as if her face were the guitar's head.

"No," said Morgan, "he's just a pig."

Grady turned to her and opened his mouth, a wad of food sitting on his tongue.

"Gross!" yelled Morgan. "Mom! He's disgusting."

"Enough, you two," said Dana. She turned to Alder, trying not to imagine her mouth as a guitar fret and her eyes as tuning knobs. "What would you like with your pasta?"

"Oh, it doesn't matter," said Alder. "I'll just have some sauce and meatballs."

"Are you sure? I thought . . . Your mother's such a strict vegetarian . . . I assumed . . ."

A wicked grin lit Alder's features. "It'll be our little secret."

"Alder, your mother wasn't terribly thrilled about this arrangement to begin with. I certainly don't want to antagonize her by sending you back as a . . ."

"Carnivore?" Alder popped a meatball into her mouth.

"I want one, too." Grady wagged a ketchup-smeared finger at the meatballs. "What's in it?"

"It's cow." Alder pushed the bowl toward him. "Crushed cow."

Grady stabbed a meatball with his fork and studied it at eye level. "This is just like *Survivor*," he murmured. He contracted every muscle in his face as if to avoid some great threat.

"G-Man, G-Man, G-Man," chanted Alder, thumping her palm on the table.

"You don't have to if you don't want to," said Dana.

"Just *eat* it, for godsake!" said Morgan.

Alder's beat on the table picked up speed. Grady inhaled as if it would be his last breath and jammed the meatball into his mouth. Everyone froze. "Grady," Alder murmured, low and serious. "Do not—I repeat, do *not*—blow that thing out your nose." Morgan started to giggle, and Dana had to smile. "No kidding, dude. You have to chew it and swallow it, or it'll crawl right up into your nostrils. I'm telling you, it's not pretty."

Grady's jaw began to move, a look of amused horror on his face. He grabbed at his throat and squeezed his eyes shut. After a dramatic show of swallowing, he smacked his lips. "Not bad!"

Alder stabbed another meatball and waved it at him. "Round two?"

"Nah, I'm full."

Dana shot a smile of thanks at Alder. "I'm going down the street to Polly's after dinner," she told them. "She's having a little get-together."

"Do you have to?" Morgan groaned.

"Can I stay up?" said Grady.

"Well, no, I don't have to, but I want to. It's nice to have a little grown-up time every once in a while." Grown-up time was in drastically short supply since her divorce. She no longer had a husband to go out with, and it soon became clear that invitations from other couples had evaporated as well. Gatherings of women seemed to be the only social interaction she was entitled to anymore. "And no, you cannot stay up. I'll tuck you in before I leave."

"But I need help with homework," Morgan insisted.

"Bring it into the kitchen, and I'll talk you through it while I load the dishwasher."

"It's English. You have to read it and pay attention."

Dana sighed. Even when Kenneth still lived there, Morgan wanted Dana near—not necessarily to spend time with, however. Morgan spent a good portion of her evenings texting her friends or watching shows like *America's Next Top Model*. For reasons that neither of them fully understood, Morgan just wanted Dana in the building.

"I'll load the dishwasher," said Alder.

"That's so nice of you, sweetie," said Dana, "but you don't have to."

"I don't mind," said Alder. "Besides, Meatball Man here will help me, right, G?"

"What?" Grady was horrified. "I can't load the dishwasher."

"Just bring the dishes in from the table. I'll load them." No one said anything for a moment. It was as if Alder had suggested they build a wide-body jet in the backyard and fly to Greenland.

"Don't I need a bath or something?" Grady asked desperately.

"Jeez," muttered Morgan. "Somebody mark *this* day on the calendar."

Alder stood, picked up her plate and utensils, and waited for Grady to do the same. He blew a huff of resignation and followed her. Morgan excused herself to go to the bathroom, and Dana met her in her room. The English homework was not that hard, but Morgan was fidgety and irritable, sucking loudly on a LifeSaver and moaning that she didn't have a wordy brain. It was not cozy mother-daughter time. When they finished, Morgan murmured, "How long will you be gone?"

"Not that long, honey. And Alder's here if you need something."

Morgan narrowed her eyes. "Does Alder being here mean you're going out more?"

"No." But did it? Dana hadn't considered that Alder might be a benefit to the household. And yet her presence had so far had a positive effect. She'd gotten Grady to eat meat—a minor miracle (unless you counted hot dogs). And she'd gotten him to help clean up.

"She's not you, Mom," said Morgan.

"I know, sweetie. Don't worry."

Dana shucked off the wrinkled jeans and the long-sleeved T-shirt that was now speckled with tomato sauce on one sleeve. She had already planned to wear her boot-cut jeans to Polly's, but with what? What shirt would be flattering but comfortable—nice enough but not so nice as to make her look like she was trying too hard? What magical shirt would give off that elusive scent of happy-busy-smart-fun while masking the fact that she was still a bit stunned by her single status even after almost a year, that she worried about her children, particularly Morgan, and that she sometimes cried for no reason she could name? Where could she buy that perfect shirt, and what would it cost if she found it? She would pay any amount for a shirt like that. She would give her right arm.

As Dana adjusted her jewelry in the hall mirror, she caught sight of Alder sitting on the TV-room rug holding a paperback book, her gaze unfocused.

"I won't be gone too long. And I'm just up the street."

"Okay," said Alder without looking up. "Nice shirt."

Dana let herself in Polly's side door as she always did. When she walked into the living room holding a bottle of merlot, no one noticed her at first, and in that moment she was unsure. Polly was her closest friend in Cotters Rock. Of course she had other friends—college roommates, women from her old job whom she still had lunch with occasionally. These women had known her longer. But now Polly knew her best.

And possibly that made Polly her best friend, though Dana was hesitant to assign such a designation. After all, Polly, with her fiery personality and unfathomable talent for not caring what people think—Polly had loads of friends in Cotters Rock. Many were right here in this room. And not one of them happened to notice Dana as she stood in the doorway, wearing a sage linen blouse, the best shirt she could come up with for the occasion.

"There you are!" said Polly, skirting around a taller woman. She hugged Dana tightly and kissed her on the cheek. Dana handed her the merlot, and Polly grinned. "Thank God!" she whispered. "You know how I hate that crappy chardonnay they all bring."

Conversation among the women ran from politics (whether that narrow-minded member of the Board of Education could finally be voted off) to books (mostly fiction set in foreign countries governed by misogynistic regimes) to the latest bad behavior of the town's teenagers. The story that had them buzzing was that of an eighth-grade girl who'd been caught half clothed and performing oral sex on a nineteen-year-old she'd met at the Buckland Hills Mall. They were discovered in his car in the dirt parking lot at Nehantic Woods, empty bottles of hard lemonade rolling around the car floor.

The girl was known to have a somewhat troubled home life. She lived with her chain-smoking, battered-Camaro-driving mother. No father was known to be in the picture. This was immeasurably comforting to the women gathered at Polly's. This mother was not like them. They didn't smoke. They didn't drive rusty sports cars, and their children had on-site fathers, or at least fathers who took custody of them every other weekend.

And yet . . . their daughters certainly loved to spend time at the mall and were newly driven to seek out male attention of even the most appalling variety. The Internet drew them into ever-widening circles of friends of friends. They were technologically sophisticated yet naïve as slender blades of grass, oblivious to the predatory growl of the lawn mower.

"And what's with the blow job?" Jeannette with the off-kilter nose and satiny red lipstick wanted to know. "It's not enough to make out and feel each other up anymore? They have to get so . . . *personal*?"

"At least they can't get pregnant," said Polly.

"Yes, but it's just so . . . *intimate*," persisted Jeannette. "Way more than sex is. Sex you can just . . . you know . . . *do*. But putting your mouth down there . . ." Dana wondered briefly how Jeannette's marriage was doing. But she did have a point—what was normal these days? Were you supposed to read those articles in *Cosmopolitan* with titles like "The Sixteen Sex Acts That Will Make Him Thank God He's a Man" and actually follow the recipes? How hot was hot enough, and at what point did it just get weird?

The conversation about the drunken middle-schooler was winding down, but the women weren't quite ready to bury the juicy bone of scandal. Dana had had enough. She slipped off to the bathroom. Away from the relentless patter of opinions and exclamations, she leaned against the sink counter and hugged her arms across her chest.

It'll be all right, she told herself. Morgan would weather the storms of adolescence just as she herself had. Morgan might be immature at times, but she wasn't stupid. She couldn't possibly wander so far from what Dana had tried to give her, a list of which might take up several typed pages but basically boiled down to . . . a sense of herself . . . the knowledge that she existed, and that this was a good thing, and that she should make all reasonable attempts to continue doing so. It was the basis of motherhood, after all, to keep one's offspring from ceasing to exist.

Dana checked her mascara and found herself thinking for the

millionth time since her own adolescence that if her vaguely hazel eyes had some actual color—a definitive brown or green or blue— maybe that would distract from what was wrong with her. Which was nothing, really. Her nose was straight, her skin was clear. Yet she couldn't seem to forgive herself the colorlessness of her eyes, the pallidness of her hair, or her no-longer-teenage figure.

And there had always been some small, irrational sense she had of waiting. That if she were patient and good and responsible, someday she would wake up and everything wrong with her would have been replaced—with real colors or more delicate proportions. Dana sometimes had to remind herself that no different corporeal form would magically emerge some day . . . This was it.

When the last guests left, Dana helped Polly tidy up. "Denise finally fired that horrible nanny," Polly reported, gathering damp cocktail napkins and sticky dessert plates. "Don't know why it took her so long."

"It's hard to fire people. Whenever I had to, I nearly had a nervous breakdown."

"Let me guess. It was usually some secretary who was . . . oh, like embezzling from the petty-cash box, right?" Polly smirked. "You're so nice it'd have to be something that bad or worse!"

"I'm not that nice," Dana said defensively, knowing that Polly generally used the word to mean nice-boring, or nice-pushover, or nice-but-not-too-smart.

"Right. Can you take this bag of trash out to the garage? Be careful, I think it's leaking."

Dana held out her hand for the trash. Polly laughed and let the bag drop back into the can. "See what I'm talking about?"

And maybe Polly was right. Maybe if Dana's best friend in Cotters Rock asked her to handle a leaking garbage bag, Dana should say, *Carry your own damn trash.* But she loved Polly, and she felt that Polly loved her. And what was a little garbage between friends?

When the cleanup was finished, Polly reached up to give her a hug. Polly's hugs were tight and serious, and Dana had the sensation of being claimed for Polly's tribe, a ritual of belonging that was both comforting and a bit alarming in its finality.

"Thanks for staying," Polly said. "I guess this is what it's like having a sister." Then she laughed and released her arms. "Well, maybe not *your* sister . . . but the kind I always wished I had." Polly was like that. She could go from who-cares to I-love-you in the flutter of an eyelash. Dana let the sweetness of the comment fill her and keep her warm for the brisk walk home.

D ANA HAD LEARNED TO SLEEP ALONE LONG BE-
fore her divorce. Kenneth had frequent sales trips, and early in
their marriage she worried that something would happen to him. On
his occasional overseas trips, she wouldn't sleep a wink, imagining
his plane crashing into the ocean, his broken body floating facedown
in the darkened waves. The nightmares about her father were always
worse then. But Kenneth invariably returned, and over time Dana
learned to relax.

She could almost pinpoint when the affair had begun—two years
ago the sales trips had gotten longer. Before then, he'd made a much
bigger deal of how good it was to be home, sleeping in his own bed,
with his wife and his favorite pillow. He had a thing for that pillow.
Dana had been able to overlook most of Kenneth's idiosyncrasies—
his intense aversion to amusement parks, for instance.

But the bliss that settled the features of his face as he laid his
travel-weary head on that pillow . . . it got under Dana's skin in the
strangest way. As if he were happier to see *it* than *her*. She tossed it
in the closet when he traveled but always had it back on the bed
when he came home. Stupid pillow. Stupid her for wasting energy
hating an inanimate object.

That pillow was long gone. It had left with the first carload of
Kenneth's things when he moved out. Dana was happy for that at
least. She'd been having some sugar-free lemonade when that pillow went out the door, tucked under her soon-to-be-ex-husband's

arm. She raised her glass to it, and for a moment she actually smiled to herself, enjoying the pointless victory as she lost the war.

Dana was awakened by motion in the house. There was no actual sound, but the air seemed to flow in the wrong direction under her bedroom door. Then the doorknob turned and a faint glow from the little plastic night-light in the hallway spilled around the shape of a figure. Too large to be a child but too short for an adult.

Morgan. She slid under the covers on her father's former side. "Dreams?" murmured Dana.

"Haven't slept yet."

"Oh, honey," Dana sighed. Why couldn't Morgan just lay herself down, let her body rest, and descend into blankness? No one needed blankness more than Morgan these days and no one was getting less of it than her.

"Do you ever miss Dad?" asked Morgan.

Miss Dad? What was the right answer to this preteen riddle? "You don't need to worry about that, sweetie."

"I just wondered," Morgan whispered.

"Well . . ." Dana stalled. She'd had two glasses of wine at Polly's. Couldn't she take this particular pop quiz in the morning?

"Well, *do* you?"

"Um . . . in a way."

"What way?"

"I guess I miss having a husband." This was true. Better to stick with the truth, or a close cousin thereof. Morgan got irritable when Dana gave what she called "Tooth Fairy answers."

"What do you miss exactly?"

Yes, what exactly? Help with the kids, an extra hand with the house and yard work, having an escort to dinners and parties. Sex. Someone to talk to. More things than she liked to admit.

"It was nice having his help. It's harder to do it all myself."

"You don't feel lonely?"

Lonely. Dana didn't even like to think of the word. Despite the fact that she rarely had a moment alone, she often felt she'd been sentenced to solitary confinement.

"Well, do you?"

"Sometimes, yes."

"Do you think you'll ever get married again?"

Dana could barely see Morgan in the dark. It was as if her own mind were questioning her. "Maybe someday. But I don't think about it very much."

"Why not?"

Because the chances weren't good. Men her age were going for younger women. A forty-five-year-old—even without kids—was a hard sell these days. And now that she did have children, her standards were higher. Not for herself but for Morgan and Grady. What she said was, "Just too busy, I guess."

"Is Polly your best friend?"

"She's a very dear friend . . ."

"Is she your best, though?"

"I guess maybe she is. She's very good to me." What was Morgan getting at? Why all this concern with her mother's social life?

"Do you think she'd ever, like, turn on you?"

"Why do you ask?"

"I don't know . . . I don't think Darby and me are friends anymore," Morgan's voice was lower and more strained now. "She doesn't even, like, answer when I say hi."

"Are you sure she hears you?"

Morgan gave a derisive little snort. "Everyone hears everything, Mom. It's middle school. We pay attention to stuff like that."

"Well, then maybe she's not a very good friend, and you're better off without her."

A soft hiss of resignation sifted over the pillow. "You don't get it."

"Explain it to me, then."

"Everyone's like that. Everyone's ignoring *some*one. If I'm better off without Darby, I'm better off with no friends at all." And there it was. The loneliness dilemma. Some things could be overlooked, and some things could be forgiven. And then there were the things that *had* to be forgiven no matter how bad they were, because otherwise the choice was solitary confinement. Hard enough at forty-five. Impossible at twelve.

"It's like Bubble Wrap," said Morgan. "We're all like pieces of Bubble Wrap. And every day a few more bubbles get popped. If you're lucky, it's only one or two. But if it's bad, and everyone ignores you and talks about you behind your back, it's like hundreds. Then what've you got?"

"What?"

"Just a piece of useless plastic. Might as well throw it away."

Lying there in the darkened bedroom, Dana reached out to stroke Morgan's fine, silky hair. And she could think of no rebuttal to the girl's contention, because there was none. She was right. And the stakes seemed higher than in years past, the pressure more intense than ever to be that perfect, precisely casual girl. To be above reproach. But the mountains of societal reproach had risen so high, how could anyone manage to surmount them?

"I love you, Morgan," was all Dana could think of to say. "Daddy and I love you so much."

"I know," Morgan sighed, curled in the comforting obscurity of her mother's bed. "Thanks."

When Dana woke the next morning, Morgan was gone. Dana had a moment of panic imagining that she'd slipped away and done herself some unspecified harm. She knew it wasn't true, but she slid quickly from beneath the covers and got up all the same. Better to be standing when thoughts like that came. Lying down, you were just too vulnerable to their fungal spread.

She padded quickly down the hall and peeked past the half-open door of the bathroom. Morgan was there, already dressed. She was studying herself in the mirror, pressing a finger into the tiny speed bump of tummy that had sprouted up about six months ago. Dana had noticed it, too, and had started offering apple slices and carrots with low-fat dip instead of Morgan's usual toast with butter and honey after school. Morgan maintained the silence Dana had initiated on the subject and nibbled penitently at the vegetation.

Dana watched Morgan now poke at the benign layer of flesh as if it did not belong to her, as if it were some alien life-form or pale-toned leech sucking something out of her that she needed. It was the way Dana herself jabbed at her own thighs when she sat on the edge of the tub to draw a bath for Grady and noticed her legs spreading on the cold white porcelain.

Morgan poked her stomach again, and a look of hopelessness passed across her face.

Bubble Wrap, thought Dana. Popping before her very eyes.

CHAPTER

6

"DID I HEAR COACH RO CALLING YOU STELLY?"
Dana asked Grady that afternoon.

"Yeah," he said, chewing on a dried apricot. It was the only way to get him to eat fruit.

"Do you like that? I've never heard you called that before."

"Kinda yes and kinda no," Grady picked a piece of apricot out of his teeth. "It's fun to have a nickname . . . but Stelly sounds like Stella. Kinda like a girl's name."

"If you don't want him to call you that, you can ask him politely to use your real name."

Grady shrugged. "I don't care that much. Not enough to act like a baby about it anyway."

"It's not babyish to want to be called by your actual name, Grady." But he was done with the subject and went up to his room to work on his latest Lego creation.

That night, after football practice, Dana approached Coach Ro as he stuffed equipment into a black duffel. "Do you have a minute?" she asked. He had one knee down as if genuflecting before the altar of the duffel. Even from a squat he was intimidating.

"Sure," he said, still ramming footballs and plastic cones into the bag. When he looked up and saw Dana, he stopped, the brown clipboard in his hand arresting in midair. There was a corner missing from the clipboard, she noticed, as if someone had taken a bite out of it.

"Well, first I wanted to thank you for coaching." Dana smiled, hoping her friendliness would soften him. "You're doing a wonderful job, and I know the boys aren't always easy!"

Coach Ro nodded. "Some of them really need the discipline, that's for sure." He stuffed the clipboard into the bag and yanked on the zipper to close it. When he stood and squared himself, he was a good head taller than she. "You're Stelly's mom," he said. "You're always here."

"Well, I try to get to the practices as much as I can. And I wanted to mention—"

"That's good. Football's kind of scary to some of them. Parents showing up gives them courage."

"They're so busy knocking each other over, they barely seem to notice."

"They notice," he said.

Dana glanced over at Grady, squatting on the ground apparently waiting for something. Then another boy came running up and tried to leapfrog over him but couldn't quite make it past Grady's helmet. He slid down off Grady's back, clutching himself between the legs. The other boys laughed, and Dana could hear one of them say, "Right in the nuts!"

Coach Ro chuckled. "That's why God invented athletic cups."

Dana smiled tentatively. "I just wanted to ask . . . if you don't mind . . . I think Grady would rather be called by his real name. Not Stelly."

"He asked me to call him Stelly." Coach Ro slung the duffel over his shoulder and turned toward the parking lot. Laying his free hand on Dana's shoulder blade, he guided her to walk with him. The feel of his big, thick-fingered hand lingering on her back flustered her.

"He told you . . . ?"

"Well, you know, with a name like Grady . . ." Coach Ro said, as if it were obvious. "How come his father's never here? Work late?"

"Well, yes . . . He's a . . ." *What was he again?* "He's in sales, and he travels a lot." *And what was wrong with the name Grady?* "Also . . . he lives in Hartford now. He doesn't . . . We don't . . ." Coach Ro was looking at her, waiting patiently for her to knit her tangled words into actual sentences, and this, too, was distracting. "We're divorced."

His ears slid a few millimeters back into his sandy blond crew cut. "Huh." After a beat he continued. "So you don't care if I call him Stelly, right? It's good for a kid to have a nickname."

Yes, okay, a nickname like Buddy or Chip or even G, as Alder called him. But Stelly?

Coach turned to go, calling over his shoulder, "Keep coming to practice. It's good, you being here." He turned back, gave her a smile and a wave. Then he bumped into the fender of his massive black pickup and almost toppled over. His eyes darted toward her to see if she'd noticed. Dana quickly averted her gaze so as not to compound his embarrassment.

When she corralled Grady from his leapfrogging teammates, she muttered at him, "Why did you *ask* him to call you Stelly?"

He shrugged and handed her his helmet. "Just sounded cooler than Grady."

Morgan had gone to a friend's house after school. Well, not a friend, exactly, but a girl who, like Morgan, played cello in the middle-school orchestra. Morgan hadn't been able to master the piece for an upcoming concert and had been pestering Dana for help.

"But, sweetheart, I keep telling you I don't read music!" Dana had said rather vehemently last week. "It's like asking me to teach you . . . I don't know . . . boxing."

She had offered to get a tutor, but Morgan had said, "Forget it. No way is some, like, musical genius coming over here to tell me how bad I am. I already *know* how bad I am."

Dana was stumped. It was hopeless. Then Morgan mentioned this morning that she was going over to this girl's house to practice and could Dana drop the cello off after school. Problem solved.

"You help them too much," Kenneth often said. But he wasn't here to see the tears and frustration, just like he wasn't there when some big-muscled coach started calling his son Stelly. Kenneth could just keep his advice to himself.

The silence of the house was marred by something, Dana noticed, as she pasted peanut butter and ketchup into a sandwich for Grady. There was a humming sound the house made, a faint chorus of electrified sighing from the refrigerator, the furnace, and several lesser appliances. But there was a strange vibration interjecting itself into the usual household hum. And where was Alder?

Dana walked down the hall to the TV room. Papers and books were strewn around as if they'd been tossed from a low-flying aircraft. She wondered briefly if someone had broken in. But Morgan's and Grady's rooms were often messy. Grady's sometimes looked vandalized.

Still, something was wrong. Dana heard the faintest little gasping sound and discovered Alder sitting with her knees to her chest, wedged between the far end of the couch and the wall. She'd obviously been crying and was trying mightily to stop. Dana crouched into the corner with her and reached for the girl. "Alder, sweetie!" she murmured. "What happened?"

Alder fell against her and allowed herself to be hugged. "It's stupid . . . It's nothing . . . I'm just hormonal."

Dana stroked Alder's flat black hair. It was something, of course. Something had detonated this minor madness in her niece. Having curled into the smallest possible surface area herself more than once in the past year, Dana felt like the Queen of Stupid-Nothing-Hormonal. "When did this start?" she asked.

"I don't know. An hour ago, maybe." Alder wiped her nose on the hem of her T-shirt.

"You must be exhausted, honey. Did someone call? Did your mother—"

"No, it wasn't her," Alder muttered. "I was doing this stupid writing assignment, and I just started thinking too much."

"What were you thinking about?" asked Dana.

"Something I don't want to think about. Or talk about." Her face looked so dark. Dana was used to Morgan's moods, but Alder had always seemed untroubled by the ordinary snares of girlhood. It was as if she'd been born with an internal Geiger counter, strangely perceptive to the difference between life's mere surface rumblings and the real threat of a plate shift.

"Okay." Dana squeezed Alder's hand and helped her rise out of the tiny space that had contained her. "But if you change your mind, you can come talk to me anytime—day or night, okay? I'm always here if you need me."

"I know," said Alder. "You're like that."

On Friday, Morgan had a dentist appointment. She and Dana sat in the waiting room, each reading a *People* magazine. Morgan's had a picture on the cover of a teenage superstar who'd passed out in the back of a limousine with a bottle of Grey Goose in her lap and the window open, to the delight of the paparazzi. The smaller inset picture showed the star and her mother retreating from a courthouse. The mother held her hand up, as if her little palm and fingers could fend off the assault of shouting reporters and the rapid fire of Uzi-size cameras. The girl cringed against her mother, looking ashen. *And average,* Dana realized. This millionaire teenager, undoubtedly recognized in any tar-paper shack in any Third World country, looked like she'd been plucked at random from a high-school field-hockey team somewhere.

Dana wanted to ask Morgan what she thought of this girl. Was it satisfying to see someone who presumably had everything plummet to the bottom of the social soup just like anyone else? Or did Morgan see, as Dana did, that somewhere behind the overpriced clothes and the capped teeth, the girl was a real person, with real pain, and was far too young to be abusing herself like this? But Morgan's eyes flicked across the pages, soaking in every detail, and

Dana knew interrupting her would provoke nothing more than an irritated shrug.

Dana's glance fell to the magazine in her own hands. It featured an older actress on the cover, hands on narrow hips, victorious smile exaggerated by high-gloss lipstick. The inset picture was grainy and showed her stepping off a curb clutching a plastic grocery bag. She wore sweatpants and an oversize coat that billowed out to one side, making her seem large and ragged. The caption read, "Back in a Size Two, I'm Me Again!"

Dana remembered this actress as the cute, bouncy one from a 1980s sitcom. A comeback of sorts. And Dana was happy for her, if a little bit jealous. *Size two,* she thought. *I'd be happy with a size eight.* But then it occurred to her: *Comeback to what?* The woman's career hadn't been revived. She was just thinner.

The waiting-room door opened, and Marie the hygienist said, "Morgan, we're ready for you now." With effort, Morgan gave Marie a polite half smile, an attempt to cloak her anxiety. Dana wanted to give her some indication of motherly encouragement, but she knew the rules. Parental affection prohibited, except under cover of utter privacy and, if possible, darkness.

Dana was soon bored by the shimmering starlets and hunky boy-men whose names she didn't recognize. She closed her eyes, rested her head against the back of the chair, and ran through a mental checklist. *Get paper goods for Morgan's party . . . Have car cleaned—floor has more crumbs than a cracker factory . . . Grady's game on Sunday . . .* Football. Coach Ro. That perked-up look he gave when she said she was divorced. The squareness of him, the warm, frying-pan-size hand on her back . . . *Taller than Kenneth and broader, though not quite as handsome . . . but nice enough . . . and warm enough . . .*

"Mrs. Stellgarten?" said a deep voice.

Dana's eyes fluttered, and she sat straight up. "Mmm?" she muttered, "Yes?"

Dr. Sakimoto's face wavered before her. "I hate to wake you," he said. "You look so serene."

"Oh!" She passed a hand across her lips to make sure she hadn't drooled. "I was just—"

"It's Friday," he said, smiling. "Who doesn't need a nap? Sometimes I go into my office and close my eyes—I'm out like a light. Marie has to throw something at me."

Dana sighed. Dr. Sakimoto had such a talent for putting people at ease. "Is her appointment over already?" she asked.

"No, not quite." His face settled into a strangely pensive state. "Would you come to my office for a quick chat?"

Dana rose and followed him. Something was wrong. Dr. Sakimoto never called her into the office. *The insurance,* she thought. Kenneth was always trying to "get the best bang for the buck." It was so like him to change their coverage and not tell her.

"Please, have a seat. This one's more comfortable," he said pointing to an upholstered chair with a pale green paisley pattern. *It's the bad-news chair!* Dana realized. Meant to cushion the blow of unpaid bills or the necessity of a root canal. He seated himself in the other chair, a battered Windsor with the stain worn down on the arms. "Mrs. Stellgarten," he began.

"Please call me Dana," she said, realizing she'd never bothered to give him the right to this familiarity in all the years she'd known him. It was only now, with some obvious unpleasantness in the offing, that she was taking him into her circle of friendship, in the unlikely event it would provide some small protection from . . . whatever this was.

The smooth skin around his brown eyes crinkled warmly. "Dana it is, then." He took a breath. "So. I'm seeing a change in Morgan's enamel that worries me a little." He seemed to be waiting for her consent to go on, or perhaps giving her a moment to prepare herself.

"Okay . . ." she said.

"Tooth enamel, it's kind of like glass—very smooth, especially at Morgan's age. All those adult teeth are fairly new, so they should be in pretty good shape. What I'm seeing with Morgan is the beginning of some erosion, especially on the backs of her front teeth and the insides of her molars." He paused again. "Dana, this pattern of erosion—it's consistent with purging."

For the briefest moment, Dana's brain blocked his meaning. *Purging,* her brain mollified her, *getting rid of stuff you didn't need was a good thing, right?* But then it came to her in small pieces. Apparently Morgan was getting rid of something she needed.

"Could there be some other reason for this . . . pattern?" Dana asked tightly, trying to stanch the steady flow of panic that was seeping into her chest.

"A very reasonable question." He nodded. "For instance, constantly sucking on something acidic, like lemons, or chewing sticky candy causes enamel to deteriorate."

Morgan didn't like lemons and preferred chocolate to chewy candy. But in that moment, the fact that something else—anything else—might explain this came as a relief.

"Dana," he said gently. "Candy degrades enamel in very specific places, mostly the crowns. And lemon tends to erode the fronts of the teeth, not the insides. It wasn't either of those things."

"I would know," Dana insisted, pressing the words from her lips in an even flow, trying desperately not to reveal the panic that was now filling her head like rushing water. "I would certainly know if she were . . . doing . . . that."

"You are a very concerned, conscientious parent. Anyone can see that. And teenage girls can be incredibly secretive. Believe me, I had my own to deal with."

Dr. Sakimoto was a father? Dana clung to this distraction like a life jacket. "How old are they?"

"I have two daughters—a college sophomore and one in medical school."

"That's wonderful! What kind of medicine is she pursuing?"

"Undecided," he said. "Dana, we need to think about getting Morgan to stop purging. I can give you a list of resources. . . ."

Purging. That word would never be the same to her again. "No," she said, unable to take in any more information. "Not right now."

There was a knock on the door, and Marie's voice, raised slightly, said, "Morgan's all set." Dana ejected herself from the bad-news chair and fairly lunged for the exit.

On the car ride home, Morgan flipped open the vanity mirror and ran her tongue across her teeth. "I just love when they're all smooth and clean," she said. "It's like you get to start over with a whole new set of teeth."

But you don't, Dana wanted to say. *The body you're born in is the one you die in.* Driving home with her possibly bulimic daughter, Dana realized she could no longer indulge in that fantasy about waking up with upgraded parts. There were no do-overs. Ruined teeth would never be new, a middle-aged body would never be young again, a collapsed marriage would never go back to the point before you knew it was over.

As she pulled in to the safety of her own driveway, Dana could hear her mother's raspy voice saying, *You play the hand you're dealt.* Then Ma would glance at her husband sitting in the far corner of the couch staring blankly in the direction of the television, and take another drag of courage from her Marlboro Light.

CHAPTER
7

THE ISSUE OF WHAT TO DO NEXT.
Should she talk to Morgan now? And say what, exactly? "Please stop making yourself vomit, honey. It's ruining your teeth"? Or maybe, "WHAT COULD YOU POSSIBLY BE THINKING?" Or should she be honest and say, "I'm so sorry that I've obviously failed you in some massive, bottomless, irretrievable way"?

No, probably not.

Dana had spent the last twelve years feeding her children. Within moments of their births, she had nursed them. Since then she'd spent hours of every day planning, buying, preparing, and offering meals to them. She'd imitated a wide variety of vehicles as she drove spoonfuls to their lips, and always asked the direction in which their sandwiches should be cut, because they would refuse to eat squares when they wanted triangles. She'd had countless conversations with other mothers about what and when to feed them and what to do when they refused to eat anything but buttered saltines. She'd learned to have a certain amount of high-calorie, nonnutritious snacks on hand, because other kids were less likely to come over if there wasn't anything "good" to eat.

Vomiting all that effort back up was inconceivable to her, a conversation she didn't know how to begin. She should tell Kenneth, she knew. Yet food had been *her* job. And it was hard to imagine calling her ex-husband, who had chosen some other, somehow better woman instead of her, and say, "You were right about me, I'm inferior. A factory second as a wife and a mother."

Dana didn't call Kenneth. Locked in her room, she called Polly, possibly her best friend, the only one she trusted not to make her feel even worse. "Hey, do you have a minute?" Then she started to cry in soft, gulping gasps, and Polly said, "Take all the time you need, I'm right here."

In pieces, Dana got it out. Polly was skeptical. "Morgan's too sensible for that. She's a good, smart girl. How does this guy know for sure?" Dana explained how Dr. Sakimoto had ruled out other causes. Polly didn't buy it. "How many bulimics do you think they have in China, huh? Not that many, I'm guessing. So how much experience could he have?"

"China?"

"Sure, isn't he Chinese?"

"Um, I'm pretty sure Sakimoto is a Japanese name. And his first name is Anthony, so maybe he's part something else, too."

"Does he have an accent?"

"Somewhere between Boston and New York. Sort of Rhode Islandish."

"Oh," said Polly. "Well, still. I don't believe it. I've known that kid since she was in diapers. She's eaten over here hundreds of times. She's not a puker."

Dana sighed. Polly was so reassuring. Not inasmuch as she was right. The more Dana thought about it, the more she saw that it might be true. Morgan often raced to the bathroom after dinner and sucked on breath mints in the evening. She'd gained weight and was disgusted with herself.

But Polly's disbelief was comforting nonetheless. Polly had taken a particular shine to Morgan right from the beginning. While Dana bemoaned Morgan's moods and stubbornness, Polly admired them. "So she's headstrong," Polly would say. "It'll serve her well." As a little girl, Morgan would "run away" to Polly's house when she'd been denied her inalienable right to jump from an upper limb of the crabapple tree in the front yard or have a cell phone in third grade. The two of them had reveled in being in cahoots against Dana. Then Polly would gently set her straight, and Morgan would come home full of Nilla Wafers and newfound compliance. So if Polly, with all her motherly confidence, hadn't seen it and didn't even accept it in the face of dental evidence, Dana felt she had permission to loathe herself a little less completely.

At dinner Dana's eyes were lowered toward her green beans, but she didn't actually see them as she severed them into smaller and smaller pieces. Her peripheral vision, and every last one of her brain cells, was focused on Morgan's plate. There went a piece of chicken, then a forkful of rice. The fork dropped onto the plate when Morgan stopped to tell Grady to quit jumping around like a hyperactive hamster. "I swear you need medication," she grumbled. Dana waited for the fork to rise from the plate again, but it lay there, abandoned.

"Do we have to go to Dad's?"

Dana stopped mincing her green beans and looked up.

"Mom, hello? Are you, like, with us?" Morgan asked.

"What? Yes." Dana glanced around the table. They were all looking at her.

"Yes you're here?" said Morgan. "Or yes we have to go to Dad's?"

"Yes to both. Why wouldn't you want to go to Dad's?"

Grady and Morgan looked at each other. Grady sat down and started to eat his rice. Morgan sighed. "It's just not that fun. You know, since Tina moved in. It's kind of boring."

Tina *moved in*? Instinctively Dana's face froze, every muscle held hostage by the need to seem calm in the midst of panic. *Nobody move*, she ordered those muscles. *Nobody take a breath.* Her mind sped through a list of acceptable responses, sifting for the one with the fewest possible implications. "Why is that boring?"

Grady huffed, unable to keep quiet. "Because! She's, you know, a *girl*, and she's a *grown-up*. And she wants to play *board games*! She bought Trouble, the one with the popping thing in the middle so if you're three years old you won't lose the dice? It's so BORING and DUMB!"

Dana sifted for another vanilla-flavored response. "I guess she thought you'd like it."

"Dad wants us to spend time with her," said Morgan. "He wants us to like her, and it's kind of . . . I don't know. Exhausting."

"I see." And Dana did see. The very thought of it wore her out completely. She was aware that Kenneth's new girlfriend had started dropping by during the kids' weekend visits over the summer. He'd been seeing her for . . . Dana guessed it was about two years now. So she wasn't really the "new" girlfriend. She was old. Not in age, of course. But she was probably closing in on thirty, that magic number when, for most women, being single loses its shine. Funny how all that had gotten past Dana until this very moment. This day of all days. This bad-news, screwed-up, nerve-shredding day. *Damn him,* she thought. *I do not need this now.*

"Well," she said, "that seems like something you should take up with your father."

"Couldn't you talk to him?" asked Morgan.

I would do anything for you, thought Dana. She let the air escape from its imprisonment in her lungs. "No, sweetie, I can't. Dad's in charge in Hartford. I'm only in charge here. At our house." The doorbell rang. No one rose to answer it. "Grady, are you packed?"

"Oops!" Grady jumped up, jostling the table, and ran to his room.

"Go open the door for Dad," Dana said to Morgan.

"Can you? I forgot something in my room."

"I'll get it," offered Alder.

"Thanks, sweetie, but I'll do it," Dana said, rising and moving toward the mudroom. The doorbell rang again, and she thought, *If he rings that thing one more time . . .* She didn't know what she'd do, but it would not be friendly. "It's unlocked," she told him irritably when she pulled the door toward her. "It wasn't even closed all the way."

"I . . . I didn't . . ." he stammered, surprised. During their marriage he'd often joked that she was intractably pleasant, even to telemarketers. "I shouldn't just barge in," he said. "I don't live here anymore."

"I'm well aware of that fact. You live in Hartford now. With Tina, apparently." There was a tingling in her fingers that made her want to grab something and squeeze hard. Not just because of the live-in girlfriend or the ringing doorbell, or even the fact that her daughter was apparently undoing all her efforts at nourishment. This rage seemed prehistoric in origin, and if she wasn't careful, she might just grasp Kenneth in a tender place—the throat, perhaps, or somewhere south of that—and dig in. Kenneth's fingers kneaded at his jacket cuffs, and trepidation stung at his cheeks. After all these years, had she somehow managed to intimidate him?

"I should have told you about that," he spouted. "I meant to, and then things seemed to come up. But the kids really like her, I think."

Dana snorted sarcastically. This was different, having Kenneth on the defensive. This felt good. "Whether they like her or not is not my problem. But in the future you need to inform me of big changes like this. They ask me about it, and I should be prepared to answer, not caught off guard like some insignificant . . . I need to be kept apprised, you understand?"

"Yes," he said, eyes cast to his shoes. "Yes, absolutely."

When he left with the kids, Dana pondered her confrontation with Kenneth. She'd so rarely ever taken him to task like that. It was the highlight of her day, she realized. *How pathetic.*

CHAPTER
8

SATURDAY PASSED IN A HAZE OF THINKING ABOUT
Morgan's problem, then trying not to obsess about it, then chas-
tising herself for not facing the issue, all the while drinking what
must have amounted to a gallon of sugar-free lemonade. By the afternoon her stomach hurt. She forced herself to find an eating-disorders
Web site, but before she'd read more than a paragraph, she got thirsty
again and went for another glass of her painkiller of choice.

The one thing she was able to accomplish was preparing a meal
for the McPhersons. "Alder?" she called as she swaddled a loaf of
sourdough bread in foil. "Sweetie, I have to drop off this dinner. I'll
be back in fifteen minutes!"

When Dana approached the small ranch-style house, she double-
checked the number on the mailbox, because it seemed like the
wrong building. It looked tidier, less sad than the other time she'd
been here. The lawn was mowed, she realized, and the shrubs had
been trimmed. She juggled the foil pan of chicken tetrazzini and the
shopping bag that contained the rest of the McPhersons' dinner and
rang the doorbell. Footsteps sounded, and Dana took a step back
from the door, organizing her features into a mildly pleasant (but not
overly happy) look.

The woman she'd seen the last time, tall and slack-shouldered,
opened the screen door. Though she was likely only in her mid-
thirties, lines of tension were creased between her eyebrows. She
drew a breath and generated a smile. "This must be dinner!"

"It sure is," said Dana. "Can I bring it in for you?"

The woman opened the screen. "Oh, watch the suitcase!" she said as Dana nearly tripped over it. "My brother came to help out for a few days, but he's heading back tonight." Her voice tightened at the mention of this imminent abandonment. "He's got his own family, of course."

Dana put the food on a small side table by the door. "He must be good company."

She nodded. "He took the kids to the playground for one last swing on the swings before he leaves."

"How many do you have?"

"Three," she said. "My oldest is six, then four, and the baby is almost two."

Oh, God, thought Dana, *three little ones and a dying husband.* "You must be busy!" she said, trying to keep the conversation light.

"Yeah, a bit." The woman managed to smile back. "The oldest is pretty well behaved, but my daughter, she can wear you down without even breaking a sweat. And the little one is just into trouble like all toddlers are. I'm lucky my husband's around to help."

Lucky? She acted as if her husband were on vacation instead of fighting for his life. "Has he been sick long?" Dana asked.

"Just a few months." The woman's face darkened. "They say it's aggressive, but I know he's going to beat it. He'll be one for the case studies." She took a quick breath. "He has to be."

Vicarious sorrow pinched at Dana. She felt her chin begin to tremble and attempted a smile to control it. She reached her hand out to the woman's forearm, knowing it was possibly the exact wrong thing to do but unable to stop herself. "There's plenty here," she said, trying to keep her voice even. "Not that you're probably all that hungry . . ."

"Not much. The kids will have some," the woman said. She patted Dana's hand. "But thank you. It just feels good to have it here."

As Dana drove back home, letting tears drip off her chin, the streetlights came on. *It gets dark so early now,* she thought. *Seems like nighttime lasts for days.*

Grady had a football game on Sunday morning, and Kenneth planned to meet Dana there with the kids. She and Alder arrived a few minutes early.

"Stelly's mom! Dana!" Coach Ro was motioning her toward him with his clipboard. It was strange to hear him calling her name. Did he know all the parents' names?

"You can go on up to the stands," she said to Alder. "I'll be right there."

Coach Ro seemed to be watching her as she came toward him. "I knew you'd be here," he said. "Would you mind . . . Can you do MPR?"

"MPR?" she asked. He talked to her like she knew his language.

"Minimum play requirements. You see who's on the field for each play and mark off their numbers on this sheet. Each kid has to be in at least eight plays per half or I get in trouble with the league." He handed her the clipboard. "You're on the field with us—best seat in the house!"

Except she never got to sit, since the job required skittering up and down the sidelines, trying to make out jersey numbers, which were folded like skirt pleats across the boys' chests and jammed into their skintight pants. Each play lasted about ten seconds before someone went the wrong way, or the catch was missed, or the ball carrier was mobbed by a swarm of opposing players. Coach Ro motioned players on and off the field, adjusted chin straps, and tied flapping shoelaces. "Ow! That's too tight!" one boy complained. "It'll loosen up," Coach snapped.

Dana followed his lead, corralling players who were wandering too far up the sidelines and reminding them about good sportsmanship when they howled at bad plays. At halftime Coach Ro opened a container of sliced oranges, placed it in the grass, and let the kids crawl over each other like newborn piglets to get at them. He took Dana's elbow and guided her away from the jostling boys. "How'm I doing? Everyone getting a fair shake?"

She sighed. "I'll be honest, I'm just not sure. The numbers are so hard to see, and they never stop moving. I'm amazed you can tell who's who under their helmets."

"What good's a coach if he doesn't know his players? Parents like you helping out—that makes it easier. Hey," he said, giving her shoulder a playful poke, "you're pretty good out there yourself, corralling them and telling them to stop messing around. We make an excellent team." His cheery blue-eyed gaze rested on her a few seconds too long, and she turned away toward the boys.

"Oh, now, stop that, please!" she called as another orange rind flew through the air. "Peels in the trash basket, boys, that's where they go!"

The second half was easier because she'd memorized some of the player numbers by differences in their uniforms. Number nine had duct tape across his shoe; the one who adjusted his athletic cup almost constantly was number sixteen. When Coach Ro wasn't organizing his players, he stationed himself by Dana, his elbow brushing against her shoulder, pointing out who was who. There was something impressive about him. He was energetic and fairly successful at teaching a bunch of seven-year-olds such a complicated game.

"Why do you do this?" she asked. "You don't even have a child on the team."

He smiled and shook his head. "I just love this game. And I miss playing. Me and a bunch of guys play touch football when they don't have stuff to do with their families and such." He ran a hand over his crew cut. "But it's *touch*. It's a whole different sport. I just love the idea of what these little guys have ahead of them—years of the real thing. Tackle football."

Years of this? she thought with a jolt. Years of watching people crash into her son at full speed as she prayed for all the pieces of his tender little body to remain correctly situated? *Maybe he'll take up tennis,* she hoped without much conviction.

"What about you?" he asked. "You ever play any sports?"

"I played basketball in middle school," she offered weakly.

"I knew you were athletic—I can always tell." He put his fingers around her upper arm and said, "Tense up." Her biceps contracted of its own accord. "There you go! That's a good strong arm. Nice triceps, too. Most women don't have that. You work out?"

"Um . . . a little . . ." she stammered.

"Coach!" bellowed the referee suddenly. "You got too many players here!"

Coach Ro jogged onto the field, yelling, "Ben, I told you, you're offense!"

Without quite knowing why, Dana turned to gaze up at the stands. Morgan was talking to Alder, her hands flicking this way and that. Alder put a hand over her mouth in sympathetic horror. Kenneth, however, was staring straight at Dana. Even at this distance, she could tell he was on high alert. In broad daylight, in plain view, practically *onstage,* another man had been touching her in a surprisingly familiar way, unmistakably appreciating her body. It was a visual for which Kenneth was clearly unprepared, and his shock was absolutely delicious. Dana turned back to the field, studying the clipboard so no one could see her grin.

At the end of the game, Coach Ro made all the kids say, "Thank you Mrs. Stellgarten," which they drawled in unconvincing unison.

"Thanks." He grinned, patting the back of her shoulder. "You're a real asset on the field."

That night, after Grady had recounted every moment of the game as if she hadn't been standing right there on the sideline, and Morgan had listed the many ways in which Tina was boring, including her light blue furniture that had replaced Kenneth's in the condo, Dana went downstairs to fold sheets in the hall by the linen closet.

The phone rang, and Alder answered it. "Jack somebody," she said, bringing the phone to Dana.

"Hello?" Dana cradled the phone against her ear as she stacked towels.

"Hey there, Dana, it's Jack Roburtin."

"Hi," she said brightly, hoping a face would come to her to match the familiar voice.

"That was some game today."

Coach Ro, thought Dana, relieved to have figured it out. "It certainly was," she said, though she'd been so busy making checkmarks she wasn't really sure how they'd played.

"Those boys have come a long way since August," he went on. "Their discipline's improving, and I saw some excellent play execution out there today—I know you did, too."

"They were just great." She had the strange sensation that he was about to offer to sell her the team. She recalled that he was a car salesman over at Manchester Motors.

"And thanks again for all your help. I feel I control them pretty well, but it always helps to have a woman around—a mom," he corrected himself, "to make them feel at home and secure."

"It's nice of you to call and say so."

"Yes, well, uh . . . I didn't just call for that. I wanted to . . . Well, at first I thought I'd hold off during the season. I *am* Stelly's coach. As you know."

Yes, she was fairly clear on this point—what on earth was he getting at? "You're doing a wonderful job," she assured him.

"Thanks. Thanks a lot." He took a breath and exhaled noisily into his receiver. "So . . . it would be good to get together sometime. Like I said, I was half thinking I shouldn't ask until after the play-offs. You know, so it wouldn't look funny to the other parents. Like I might give Stelly more playing time or something. But I wouldn't do that. That's not the kind of coach I am."

A date? Was he asking her on a date? "Oh!" she said. "No, you wouldn't . . ."

"And then I thought, hey—it's none of their business! We're not in the military, it's not like there's some law against . . . what's it called . . . "

"Fraternizing," Dana said. She sat down on the floor, unfolded sheets lying around her like snowdrifts. How long had it been since she'd been asked out on a date? Since Kenneth, of course. And that had been eighteen years ago.

"Right! And I don't feel like waiting four weeks to ask you out. Who knows—maybe you'd be going with someone else by then and I'd have lost my chance. Oh, but . . ." His voice went low all of a sudden. "Are you seeing anyone? Because I'm not the kind of guy to horn in."

Dana almost laughed. Seeing someone? Not hardly! His little pokes and arm squeezes were the first physical contact she'd had with a man since her marriage had imploded. It was embarrassing how such piddling crumbs of flirtation had made her pulse race. "No, I . . . I'm available."

"Well, that's great! So I was thinking maybe Saturday."

This was the point of decision. This was yes or no. . . .

"If you're not interested, that's fine," he said quickly. "No hard feelings."

Her mind flicked to Kenneth's look of horror in the stands, then to his condo, where Tina's light blue furniture now roamed freely, dominating the landscape.

"I'm interested," she said. "I'd be very happy to go out with you."

"Yeah?"

"Yes." As soon as the word was out of her mouth, she was second-guessing herself. How well did she know this man? Was she even attracted to him? He was good-looking—tall and muscular and blue-eyed. Though his eyes were so close together as to be located almost on the bridge of his nose. And he yelled a lot. Which was probably just a coaching thing. Still . . .

"This weekend isn't the best, though," she said quickly. "I have the kids, and I tend to make social plans on the weekends they're with their father." This was true, but the sad fact was she rarely had any plans at all on the weekends.

"Oh." He sounded disappointed. "That's about two weeks from now."

She offered an apologetic sigh. "I'm sorry."

"No, that's fine. Really! It's nothing to worry about. Let's call it for that Saturday, and I'll give you a jingle in a week or so with some details. How's that for a plan?"

"Great." That gave her two whole weeks to process all this—two weeks to worry, she realized. "And thanks for asking."

"Thanks for saying yes!"

When the call ended, Dana put her hand over her mouth and squeezed but couldn't subdue a wide grin. She had gone from Unwanted to Wanted in the course of a phone call!

Alder appeared and leaned in the doorjamb, crossing her arms. "He asked you out," she said.

Dana picked up a towel to fold. "I guess he did. Grady's coach—that one from the—"

"Yeah, I know. The huge guy who kept touching you."

The skin prickled along Dana's scalp. "Was it that obvious? Because I wouldn't want people to think I was purposely . . . or that, you know, we weren't focusing on the game . . ."

Alder shrugged. "Nobody thought anything. Besides, who cares?"

I do! thought Dana. But she knew that was the wrong answer. Why did it matter what anyone else thought? "Should I have said no? He seems like a very nice man."

Alder shrugged again, picked up a washcloth, folded it, and set it on the stack in the linen closet. "He's a guy," she said, and went back into the TV room and turned out the light.

CHAPTER
9

A COUPLE OF NIGHTS LATER, DANA WAS SETTLING into bed when the phone rang. The caller ID read STELL-GARTEN, K. *I hope he knows he can't talk to the kids at this hour,* she thought, and wondered if he might be calling to ask about Coach Ro and that little scene at the game last Sunday.

"Hi," he said. It was neutral enough, but Dana now knew for sure that something was bothering him. The tone was too low, as if that one note rang a whole minor chord.

"What's up?" She tried not to smile in case he could tell and think she was gloating.

He took a breath, seemed about to say something but exhaled instead. "Well, I was hoping things would turn around," he began.

Things, she thought. Maybe he and Tina were having trouble. Satisfaction glinted through her like something gold-plated, followed by a twinge of guilt. *Don't build your happiness on the unhappiness of others,* she told herself. She'd seen that on the tag of a tea bag once.

"I didn't know if you'd heard, or read it in the paper," he said.

"The paper?" Had there been some sort of altercation between them? Had the police been called? In all the years of their marriage, he'd never even yelled very loudly.

"Yes, Dick Portman—you remember him. The CFO. The grand jury indicted him." Dana had seen him at company parties. His shirt cuffs were frayed, and he didn't seem to be spending much on dry cleaning. He was the chief financial officer. She just thought he was frugal.

"Indicted?" she asked. This was not about Tina, then. This was legitimately bad.

"It was in the paper for the whole damned business world to see. God, what an idiot. For a guy who spent his life tracking money, he certainly had no idea of how to cover his *own* tracks."

"Oh, my gosh," she murmured.

"Yes, well, the company can get back on its feet—the feds say he didn't spend much of it, poor bastard. Appears he was just squirreling it away."

"That's a relief," she said. But it wasn't really. Clearly there was more to it.

"Oh, right," he said with an edge of sarcasm, "it's all fine and dandy. Except that I'm in *sales*, Dana. How the hell can I sell the product when it looks like the inmates are running the asylum? Who'll buy from us now? I wouldn't, I'll tell you that."

"It's hurting your commissions," she realized.

"Of course it is!" He wasn't angry at her, she knew, but he needed to rail at someone. That had always been her job, to let him get things off his chest. *Where's Tina?* Dana wondered. Why wasn't Tina the one on the business end of his anger?

"Anyway," he muttered, reining himself back in. "It'll get better. We'll put this behind us, put some safeguards in place, and we'll be back on the A-list."

"Good," she said. "It's important to take the long view."

"True." He paused. "But listen, it's going to be a little tight for a while. Right now my income is nearly half what it was back when the divorce mediator came up with the support amount. I won't be able to kick in what I normally do."

Dana sat straight up. *Kick in?* He wasn't just kicking in. He was the sole source of support for the household. "But how can I possibly—"

"I know," he cut her off. "I feel terrible. But six months, a year from now, it'll be back to normal. With all the guys leaving for other companies, there'll be a lot of accounts to pick up."

"But what am I supposed to do until then?"

"I guess you'll have to tighten up a little. For instance, it's nice to take Alder in, she's a good kid and all, but this really isn't the time to have another mouth to feed."

"She doesn't eat that much, and she's—"

"I'm just saying, you could cut some costs. Also, I think it might be time to . . . you know . . ."

"What?" she was starting to feel frantic. "Time to what?"

"You weren't going to stay home forever—Grady's in second grade. What could you possibly be doing with all that time and no kids around? How can there be that many dishes to wash?"

It wasn't as if working were a foreign concept to her. She'd begun to think about finding something part-time a year ago. But then her marriage had disintegrated, and suddenly her responsibilities had doubled. Emotional exhaustion alone had sent her crawling beaten to her bed every night. Thoughts of outside work had flown from her mind.

But what shocked her was that he didn't see how *he personally* had made her life immeasurably harder. He seemed to think she dithered around all day, spritzing the plants and reorganizing the Tupperware lids. This house, this family, *was* her business, and she'd had her *own* downturn, called my-husband-left-me-for-another-woman. Dana had received a promotion as a result: she was now CEO, CFO, and COO combined. She was so angered and hurt by his utter lack of understanding that she could only sputter, "Kenneth, if you think for *one minute* that I'm just sitting around—"

"No," he placated her, "I didn't mean it like that. I'm sorry if you took it the wrong way."

"If *I* took it . . . if *I* . . ."

"Dana, stop for a moment and think. It's not unreasonable to ask you to start contributing."

She hung up on him. Dana had never hung up on anyone in her life, but her finger came out and stabbed at the little button, and she threw the phone onto the carpet so hard that the back came off and the battery popped out.

Start contributing, he said. START contributing! As if until now she had simply been along for the ride. And what a ride it had been. *Oh, yes,* she ranted to herself, *I've been LUCKY, haven't I? Married to a man with the emotional intelligence of ALGAE! Left for some firm-skinned CHILD with bad taste in FURNITURE! And NOW!* she thought. *NOW I have to muddle along with less money and put up with insulting comments about my time-management skills!* Dana threw off the down comforter and slid her feet into her slippers. *Washing DISHES!* she fumed, gliding past her children's bedrooms. *He has no IDEA of what it takes to run this house and take care of his children . . . No idea about ANYTHING . . .*

And that was it, really. It wasn't that she was so busy with the house and the kids that she couldn't manage a part-time job—something with mother's hours, perhaps, though those jobs tended to be low-paying and boring. No, it was the realization that the man she'd vowed to love until death had never really understood or appreciated her.

The emptiness that lived in the basement of her stomach expanded like a bellows, and her slippered feet took her to the refrigerator. Yogurt, almonds, apples, she tried to tell herself. *No, those aren't enough.* Potatoes, oil, salt . . . *Yes.* And before she had another thought, home fries were sizzling in a pan on the stove, the smell like a drug, like crispy golden consolation.

A memory of her mother flickered through Dana's mind. Standing over a pan, frying something—hot dogs in butter, possibly, or liver and onions—pungent, prickly smells infiltrating the house. An ash hanging from the end of her cigarette, the secret glow of the ember visible only when her mother dragged heavily on the filtered end. Her mother always dragged heavily.

Ma was lonely, Dana realized. Daddy came home after work and sat on the couch. He might have known her way back when they first got married, but eventually he didn't seem to know anyone. Only the interior of his own body, compressed into the couch like a sunken ship.

Dana poured herself a glass of sugar-free lemonade and filled a cereal bowl with the fried potatoes. She sat down and ate and was consoled. She knew this false sense of pain relief would turn to self-recrimination as soon as the last morsel reached her lips. But for these few moments, it was a reprieve. And that was all she hoped for.

The next morning Alder was running late and slammed around the kitchen, muttering to herself before racing to catch the bus. Morgan grumbled at Dana that there was only one frozen waffle left and why hadn't she bought more, since they were obviously running out. Grady came in wearing shorts and a basketball shirt, the shiny polyester glimmering under the kitchen lights.

"It's too cold for that outfit today," said Dana, still weary from her late-night fight with Kenneth and subsequent cooking project. "How about some pants and a long-sleeved shirt?"

"I'm not cold," said Grady. He grabbed the Lucky Charms from the cereal cabinet and began to rummage for his favorite plastic bowl with the integrated straw.

"Grady, honey, it's about forty-five degrees out. You're going to freeze if you wear that."

"No I'm not." Cereal spilled around the edges of his bowl as he poured.

"Grady, I'm asking you to change your clothes." Dana could feel her temper rising. She stepped closer to his chair, hands on her hips.

"No." He ate, scrutinizing the Lucky Charms box as though it held the secret to making a shot from half court. If he'd stopped to look at her, had given the slightest indication that he was considering her point, she would have let it go. But his utter indifference to her request, an indifference both he and Morgan (and Kenneth!) had shown on countless occasions—this time it made her snap. She slammed her hand on the table. "I said change your clothes!"

Grady flinched, dropping his spoon with a clatter onto the table. "I'll wear a jacket, okay?" he murmured meekly. "I'll zip it all the way, I promise."

It was his tone, more than his vow to zip up, that made her back down. She had scared him. It wasn't like her to yell, and the hand slamming, that was just . . . well, she didn't even know. It was as if her arm were attached to a string someone else was pulling.

She glanced at Morgan, standing by the toaster, waiting for her frozen waffle to pop. Morgan had been watching her, and when the lever sprang up on the toaster, she didn't seem to notice.

"Your waffle's done," said Dana. Morgan turned then and flicked it out and onto a plate.

They were late, and Dana had to drive them. As she pulled in to the middle-school drop-off lane, Morgan said, "You've got the list, right?"

"List?"

"For the party store. You said you were going today."

"Oh, right." Dana had completely forgotten her promise to pick up the paper goods for Morgan's birthday party. Ten girls would be descending on them the next night, and Dana hadn't had a chance to get to the Party On! store. *Too busy washing dishes,* she grumbled to herself.

"Mom, you have to get them today, because if they're not right, you have to take them back tomorrow and get something else. You promised."

"I know," said Dana, feeling that bitter edge rising in her voice. "I said I would, and I will."

She pulled up to the curb, and Morgan opened the passenger-side door. "Have a good day, sweetie."

"Not likely," said Morgan. She slammed the door and merged into the flow of backpacks.

After Dana dropped Grady off, fleece jacket zipped up to his chin, she returned to the house to get the list for the party store. *I have to get this car cleaned out today,* she told herself. Cheez-It crumbs were sprinkled across the floor mats like orange sawdust. She ran into the house, leaving the car door open. Then the phone rang several times, and she found herself answering e-mails and throwing in a load of laundry before she managed to return to the car.

As she backed down the driveway, something brushed against her ankle. Instinctively she pulled her feet up. When the car began to move quickly down the incline of the driveway, she stomped on the brake and jerked to a stop. *I'm losing my mind,* she thought. She drove to Party On!, and as she pulled in to the parking lot, she felt it again, that sense that something was crawling around the floor of her car.

Then there was a blur of motion, and the thing jumped onto her lap. A chipmunk. With an oddly orange tinge to its face.

"AAHHH!" Dana screamed, swerving by a streetlight pole at the edge of the parking lot. She stomped on the brake again, her body heaved forward, and her upper lip banged into the steering wheel. She wrenched the car into park, opened the door, and leaped out onto the asphalt, screaming, hands swiping at her thighs as if the creature were still attached to her lap. With adrenaline humming through her veins, it was a few seconds before her nervous system registered that she was no longer in danger of imminent destruction.

She heard laughter and looked up. Two small children were hopping around slapping at their thighs and laughing as if they'd never seen anything so funny. "Ahhhh!" one yelled, waving his little hands in the air.

Beside them stood a woman holding a dozen helium balloons. "Okay, everyone into the car now," she barked, and slid back the minivan door.

"Ahhhhh!" yelled the kids, falling into each other in hysterics.

"I said NOW!" She hustled them into the minivan, and squealed out of the parking lot.

Those kids are definitely not buckled in, thought Dana. Then it occurred to her that *she'd* been the reason for the woman's swift departure. *Dear God,* she realized with horror, *she must have thought I was some sort of druggie.*

After a few moments of standing there wondering what on earth to do next, Dana cautiously opened all the car doors. She reached in and pressed the horn. A moment later the vicious, possibly rabid chipmunk skittered out toward some bushes by the side of the lot. Dana quickly closed the doors and locked the car.

She tried to act normal as she strode through Party On! looking for happy-face paper goods while her knees quivered and her upper lip throbbed from its collision with the steering wheel. When she got to the cash register, she tried to smile pleasantly but ended up grimacing in pain.

"Dude, you know you're bleeding, right?" said the clerk, his beard growing in patches around his acne.

Dana put her fingers to her upper lip, which felt oddly swollen. Her fingers were bloody when she looked at them. "Oh," she breathed. "I banged my mouth."

"Is that why you were going psycho out in the lot?"

"You saw that?"

"Yeah, we all heard it and went over to the window." He bobbed his head and chuckled at the memory. "But what was the deal with honking the horn?" he asked. "That was, like, *sick.*"

Dana shook her head. "Please," she implored him, "just ring it up."

DANA WAS ABLE TO CONTROL HER EMOTIONS until she was back in the car, and then humiliation settled on her like crows on roadkill. The tears came when she tried to switch lanes. That's when she saw that the passenger-side mirror was hanging from a thin red wire exposed like an artery. Apparently she hadn't entirely missed that light pole. The mirror banged against the door panel when she made turns. Every clank made her cry harder.

When she got home, she yanked the swinging mirror from the door panel. *What do you do with an amputated auto part?* she wondered, eventually stuffing it at the back of the coat closet. She went to the bathroom and carefully rolled her lip up with her thumbs. There was a small gash on the inside, and her front tooth had been chipped—a triangular piece was missing.

Good Lord, she thought, *I look like a* Hee Haw *character,* and she started to cry again.

Finally she was steady enough to form a plan. Morgan's party was the following night, and she couldn't offer the guests chips and cheesy dip through broken teeth. Much as she hated to face Dr. Sakimoto again, she dialed the number. She would tell him she was working on the purging issue. That's all she would need to say, that she was working on it.

No one picked up the phone, nor did an answering machine

come on. Sucking on a Popsicle to ice her lip, Dana called again, with the same results. *Well, this is ridiculous,* she thought. Someone had to be there. She decided they must be having phone problems and got in her car, checking first for rodents lurking under the seats.

When she pushed on the heavy glass door and entered the office, there was no one behind the reception desk, but there were people in the waiting room. The phone seemed ready to ring out of its cradle. "Where is everyone?" she asked an elderly gentleman.

"The place is practically abandoned!" he yelled, as if the ringing phone were a foghorn. "Ahh, I've had about enough of this." He struggled out of his seat and left.

The only remaining occupants were a young mother and a preschooler sitting on her lap. The little girl looked unhappy, and the mother was whispering in her ear. "But I don't want to," insisted the girl loudly. The mother whispered again. The girl answered, "I don't care if they all fall out. I'll just eat mashed potatoes forever!" And she began to cry.

The mother sighed. "I know it's only ten o'clock," she said to Dana as she rose to leave, jostling the girl onto her hip, "but it's already been a *really* long day."

For you and me both, thought Dana, now alone in the waiting room. The phone began to ring again. "Oh, for Pete's sake," she muttered, and went to the receptionist desk. Reaching over the high counter for the phone, she picked up the receiver. "Hello, Cotters Rock Dental Center."

"Yeah, I got this bill here, and it can't be right. I'm saying to my wife, this just can't be right. And I'm just going to call this dentist guy up and check it out, because you never know if someone typed the wrong number, or something of that nature . . ."

He seemed to have a lot on his mind, and Dana let him go on for a while, her tongue flicking across the broken tooth. Finally she said, "It sounds like you have a question about your bill."

"Yes!" he said. "I do!"

"I'm just helping out at the moment, so why don't you give me your name and number and I'll have a member of the staff get back to you in a timely manner. Would that be all right?"

That was just fine with him, and he thanked her several times. He was satisfied. Dana remembered what that was like—listening carefully to a problem and providing an answer that was satisfactory. She remembered what it was like to have people say thank you.

As soon as she leaned back over the counter to put the phone down, it rang again. She opened the door to the left of the counter that led back to the operatories and Dr. Sakimoto's office and heard the high-pitched whine of a drill. "Hello?" she called tentatively.

"Be right with you!" called Dr. Sakimoto. His voice sounded harried.

Poor guy, she thought. Where was his staff? She went around to the reception desk to see if she could put the answering machine on, but it was a more complicated system than the one at her old job. Dana sank into the vinyl swivel chair. She'd had a chair like this. Back when people appreciated her. By the time she'd answered four or five calls, taken messages in her careful handwriting, and tidied up the desk area, a patient emerged from the office behind her. "Oh," he said, the right side of his mouth drooping like an unwatered plant. "You came in."

"I'm just helping out," she told him. "A staff member will call to schedule your next appointment." He smiled at her with the unanesthetized half of his face and went out through the heavy glass door. Dana turned to find Dr. Sakimoto leaning in the doorway.

"So," he said, motioning to her with his chin, his voice warm with humor. "I've known you for years, and I had *no idea* you were my fairy godmother. How'd I miss that?"

Dana grinned up at him. "Oh, I just can't stand the sound of a ringing phone. Why didn't you put the answering machine on?"

"I don't know *how,* if you can believe it! My receptionist, Kendra, went home with a stomach bug this morning, and Marie has the day off. I didn't want to bother them." He caught sight of the cracked tooth. "How the heck did you do that?"

She sighed. "It's so embarrassing, I can't even say it. Besides, you have all these people to call back." She handed him the list of messages.

"I'll call tonight, after hours." He glanced at the waiting room. "And it appears you're my only customer at the moment." She followed him into one of the operatories and sat in the exam chair. "Come on," he goaded her. "I could use a good story. How'd you do it?"

"You're going to think I'm some sort of . . ."

"What? Some sort of normal human being? Everyone slips on a banana peel now and then." Still she hesitated. "Okay," he said, and seemed to be letting her off the hook. He leaned his head from side to side, stretching his neck muscles. It reminded Dana of a boxer entering a ring. "You know," he said, "it's not like you'd shock me. I have plenty of embarrassing stories, too."

She sighed. "Bet you can't beat *this* one."

"Bet I can. I've got a ripsnorter. Want to hear it?"

"Yes!" She was desperate, she realized, to be reminded that she wasn't the only person who'd ever made a raving idiot of herself in public.

"All right. This one time . . ." He glanced at her and grinned. "I'd gotten up the nerve to ask out this woman I liked. And to my surprise she said yes, so I wanted to take her somewhere really nice. I picked this upscale restaurant—the PolytechnicON20—you know it?"

"Oh, yes, Kenneth and I went there once. Beautiful. And the food was fantastic."

"Right. Well, I put on my best suit and drove over to her house. It was winter, very cold, so I wanted to be considerate and leave the car running with the heat on. I get out of the car, and just as the door closes—you know, when you hear the latch go *ca-chunk*?—I see the button on the door is down." He shook his head. "I locked myself out with the car running."

"That's terrible," said Dana, secretly disappointed. It was embarrassing, but nowhere near as bad as her own story.

"That's nothing," he said, his hand batting the air. She hadn't noticed this before, that he talked with his hands. Until now most of their conversations had occurred with his fingers in her mouth. "So I'm thinking I'll call one of my daughters to bring me a spare set of keys," he went on. "Maybe she could get there before this woman even noticed. I go to reach into my suit pocket for my cell phone, and that's when I realize I've caught the side of the jacket in the car door. So I start pulling and tugging"—he pantomimed this for her—"and I wrench so hard that I split the seam of my best suit jacket, right up to the armpit!"

Dana started to laugh. "Oh, no!"

"And why won't the jacket come out?" Dr. Sakimoto continued, his hands going up as if to implore the gods. "Because the cell phone is stuck in the pocket on the other side of the door! But wait, it gets even better . . .

"So she comes out, and by this time I've wiggled out of the jacket, and I'm standing there in the freezing cold with my silk tie flapping in the breeze. And I try to be all nonchalant about it, like this happens all the time and if she could just get me a coat hanger, I could pop the button out. No worries, we'll still make our reservation.

"Well, the *one thing* that went right is the button popped up quickly. But there was still the problem of the jacket. I had nothing but my shirt and tie, which looked silly in the winter and seemed too casual. There wasn't time to go home and get another, so she insists—*insists*, mind you—that I wear one of her dead husband's jackets."

"Her husband was dead?"

"Yes, he'd been dead for three years, and she still had all his clothes." He gave her a glance that said, *We both know what that means*. . . . "So I wear this horrible old jacket, which is too long and too narrow and clearly hadn't been dry-cleaned since it was last worn. I looked like a little boy dressing up in his daddy's suit, with the arms flapping this way and that. A total nightmare.

"And to make matters *worse*, she has herself a little trip down memory lane with the jacket! Goes on and on about all the times he wore it, and where they went, and how much fun they had. One glass of wine was not enough, not for this evening, no way. So I order another, and the waiter sets it down before me, and I go to reach for it . . . but the sleeve is too long, and I forget to push it up as I'd been doing all evening like a five-year-old, and I knock the glass over!" His hands began to wind in circles toward his chest. "I see it coming toward me like it's in slow motion, and I know in another nanosecond I'm about to be doused with red wine. And all I can think is, 'No, this can't be happening. It's not believable.' Can you believe it, even now?"

"No!" Dana breathed. "And you did it to yourself!"

"Yes!" he said, pointing at her. "Thank you—that's the most important part. If the waiter had done it, that'd be bad, but it wouldn't have been my fault. This *was* my fault. It was *all me!*"

"She got upset, didn't she?" asked Dana.

"She began to cry—loudly. I had to throw some cash at the waiter and practically carry her out. I got her home, and of course I said I would have the jacket dry-cleaned." His voice went falsetto. "'No,' she says, 'it's not really his anymore. Just throw it away.'"

"Oh, Dr. Sakimoto, that is just about the worst date story I've ever heard!"

"Please call me Tony," he said with a satisfied grin. "Now that you know my most embarrassing moment, it's weird to be so formal." He clasped his hands together, "Okay, are you going to tell me how you busted this tooth, or should I just shut up and get to work?"

Dana sighed. Of course she had to tell him now. Part of her wanted to, she realized. He would laugh, and his laughter would dilute her shame, and it would seem just a little less mortifying the next time she thought of it. "Well, my son, Grady, he loves Cheez-Its. . . ."

By the time she was imitating the pimply clerk saying, "Dude, you know you're bleeding, right?" Tony Sakimoto was shaking with hilarity. Finally their laughter subsided, and they sighed themselves to composure. "Thank you for telling me," he said. "Until now it's been a hell of a day."

"For me, too." She nodded, relieved. Now that she'd confessed, the sin of her indecorousness was absolved.

Tony examined the tooth and took X-rays, after which he told her, "Well, this is one of those times the glass is half full *and* half empty." Dana felt her shoulders tense as he went on. "There doesn't appear to be any nerve damage, so you won't need a root canal. But the chip is just large enough that I'm afraid a filling wouldn't hold for very long. We're going to have to put a temporary on today, and have you come back for a veneer."

Is that covered by insurance? was all Dana could think. And if not, how much would it be? But she didn't ask. He was having a hard enough day without considering her money worries.

Like a commentator murmuring at a golf tournament, he told her what he was doing at each step. "I'm smoothing these little rough pieces of enamel your steering wheel left behind . . . Now, where is that three-thirty bur?" he muttered to himself. Metal instruments clinked as he rooted around. The drill spun out its *zeeeeee!* sound off and on like a tiny siren as he buffed the newly composed fill. "This polishing paste," he said. "It's made with crushed diamonds. You've got diamonds in your mouth right now." His gaze flicked up to her eyes. "Go tell *that* to those goons at the party store." When he bent toward her, she could smell peppermint as he exhaled, with a faint undercurrent of aftershave.

"Now I take an impression of the tooth to create the veneer." When he was done, he handed her the mirror. She couldn't see very clearly without her reading glasses, but it seemed fine. "I can't even tell!" she said truthfully.

"Yeah." He grinned as he yanked at his latex gloves and tossed them in the trash. "I'm pretty good with a chip, if I do say." He gave her follow-up instructions. "No nail biting. And chew hard stuff with your back teeth."

"Thanks for taking me so quickly," said Dana.

"Don't thank me." He ducked into his office for a moment, then walked her out to the waiting room. "Thank my receptionist and hygienist for being out and all those patients for leaving. Sometimes a good thing comes when everything else falls apart."

He handed her a sheet of paper with some names and phone numbers. "Association for the Prevention of Eating Disorders" blared out at her from the list. "I'm sure you're already working on it," he said, "but just in case you needed some further resources." Then he reached for the ringing phone. "Cotters Rock Dental," he said into the receiver. "Speaking . . ." He rolled his eyes at her. "Yes, I'm a regular one-man band today . . ."

THE COLLISION DEDUCTIBLE ON THE CAR WAS A thousand dollars. Dana called the insurance agency to confirm that there'd been a mistake. The agent, a woman with a practiced customer-relations brand of charm, told her, "We'll get to the bottom of this in a jiff!"

We'll get to the bottom of this, and we'll find the deductible is only two hundred fifty dollars, Dana told herself. She'd set up the coverage herself and would never have agreed to such a large deductible. Kenneth was the one who thought bad things would never happen. "Insurance companies make their millions off people like you," he'd often told Dana.

People like me, she brooded as she waited on hold. *People who sideswipe light poles and chip teeth and act like a lunatic in public . . . we need insurance.*

The breezy voice of the agent came back on the line. "Apparently Mr. Stellgarten increased the deductible about a year ago. He preferred a lower premium."

"*He* preferred?" said Dana. "But it's *my car!*"

"He's listed as the primary policyholder," said the agent, downshifting to a friendly-but-firm tone. "If he instructs me to change the coverage, I'm bound by law to make that adjustment. You might want to discuss this with him." Dana called several repair shops instead. The lowest estimate for the replacement mirror was almost five hundred dollars.

The front door opened, and Morgan came into the kitchen, studying the package of paper plates Dana had left in the mudroom. "Did they have any that weren't so, like, *happy*?" she said.

Dana sighed, feeling certain that a return trip to Party On! was in her future. "Happy-face plates, honey. That's what you asked for. They're happy."

Morgan shrugged. "Okay."

"Okay? You like them?"

"Well, I'm not going to frame them or anything. They're just paper plates, Mom. No one will care that much." She sank down into a chair next to Dana. "What happened to your lip?"

Dana told Morgan the story, and Morgan interjected regularly with mortified gasps of, "Oh, my *God*, Mom! You were scared of a chipmunk?" and "Oh, my *God*, Mom! They all saw you?" When Dana got to the part about chipping her tooth, Morgan said, "Let me see." Dana rolled up her lip, and Morgan leaned close, running her tongue across her own teeth. "Did it hurt a lot?"

"A little," said Dana. "You think it looks okay? It's just temporary. I have to go back for a veneer next week."

"Smile," said Morgan, leaning back to get a fuller view. Dana smiled, her lips pulling taut across her face. Morgan started to giggle.

"What?" said Dana.

"I just can't believe a cute little *chipmunk* made you freak out!"

"He wasn't cute, he was horrible—his face was orange!"

"Whatever you say." Morgan laughed. "At least your hair looks good. Are you using a new conditioner or something?" She reached her hand out to stroke her mother's hair, shifting it to one side, then the other. "It's shinier. It almost looks like Kimmi's."

Then Morgan began to recount the cogent facts of her day, the most important of which always revolved around lunch. She'd been thinking about sitting with the popular girls, because she'd helped one of them make an ecosystem terrarium in science. "She didn't get it that the dirt goes in first, not the little plant." But Morgan couldn't catch her eye to see if she would move over. "It would've looked like I was squeezing in, not just sitting down, you know, normally."

But then Darby called out to her, "Hey, nice shirt!" and they laughed really hard, because it reminded them of the time they bought the same shirt in different colors. The clerk at Hollister was really cute, but he had a little snot in his nose and it made him look totally disgusting. Morgan and Darby told all this to Kimmi Kinnear, who'd had that very same thing happen once, only it was her brother, who's not cute at all, but girls seem to like him for some dumb reason.

"It was so funny, Mom, and it was really good, because I was sitting *between* Kimmi and Darby, so they couldn't turn away from me."

"Why would they turn away from you?"

"I don't know. Kids do it all the time. You're with someone, then somebody else comes over and says to the person you're with, 'I have to tell you something!' and they turn away."

"But that's not right. If they need to speak privately, they shouldn't do it in the middle of a crowded lunchroom."

"Mom, I know, but that's what they do."

"Well, I certainly hope *you* don't."

"Not that much," said Morgan wistfully. "I can never think of anything good enough to say."

Grady banged through the door and unloaded his backpack, jacket, baseball mitt, and spongy Nerf football onto the mudroom floor like so much fill dirt dropping from a backhoe. "How was school?" Dana asked.

"Good." He shrugged, as if the question were meaningless. "Can you move your car? I'm gonna skateboard in the driveway."

"Okay, but you have to use knee and elbow pads—Please don't give me a face," she said, stopping him mid-whine. "I only want you to be safe."

She had just parked out on the street when another car pulled up, an avocado green station wagon with graffiti scrawled across the door panels. Music throbbing from the car cut out suddenly in the middle of a barrage of pulsing, unintelligible words.

Alder was on the passenger side and leaned over to hug the driver, then sprang from the car, which started to roll before the door was completely shut. The driver leaned out her window and screamed, "CALL ME LATER!" Dana caught a fleeting glance: a girl with short, spiky black hair and rings of eyeliner that seemed to creep down to her cheekbones.

Alder cocked her head as she took in the sight of Dana's puffy lip. "Tough day?" she said.

Dana was still processing the green station wagon and its loud, blackened occupant. "You have a new friend," she said, hoping she sounded happy about this development.

"Maybe," said Alder, and she started for the house.

When the kids were in bed, Dana pulled the dental-insurance binder from the desk in Kenneth's office, a square little room on the first floor he'd claimed when they bought the house. On the wall by the desk, he had taped the children's pictures and notes. "TO DADY," one declared in uncertain crayon, "A BG LLYN." Dana had written in pencil along the bottom, "a big lion." It was drawn in slashes of orange, with red for the tongue, teeth, and eyes. Inexplicably, its tail was green. Under the Scotch tape at the four corners, the paper was several shades lighter.

"Dad, Your The Best!" gushed a pink-and-purple birthday card from Morgan. It was almost two years since she'd written it, the most recent addition to the wall. Now the collection served as a sort of two-dimensional time capsule from the days when his fathering was a daily occurrence.

Why didn't he bring their pictures with him when he moved out? Dana wondered, saddened and a little annoyed. Should she take them down? If she did, would it be a harsh indicator of his removal from their lives? But if she didn't, their arrested development would become more and more blatant. Which was worse?

Through the open door, she heard Alder say, "Connie." The silence after that one brief utterance seemed to go on for minutes.

"Are you done?" Alder said, annoyed. More silence. Then, "Fine, just let me know when it's my turn to talk . . . How you *look*? When have you ever cared how you look to other people? . . . It's *Dana*, for godsake. She's, like, the least judgmental person on the planet. She loves *every*body." The words seemed complimentary, but the tone was not. Dana frowned.

"I'm fine . . ." Alder went on. "Yeah, despite all that, life here is totally great . . . Well, you don't– . . . You don't– . . . Could you stop interrupting me for once? . . . Okay, I just called to say could you *please* have my car fixed? . . . Because it's not her responsibility, and besides, she can't afford it . . . Because I just *know* . . . You say I'm so intuitive, and you're all proud of it until I pick up on something you don't feel like knowing . . . No, it *is* true . . . Like the time you were dating that chiropractor guy? I told you he was a loser . . . Okay, whatever. Can you please get my car fixed? . . . I'm asking you nicely . . . Nice *does too* count for something . . . Forget it, then . . . Good night, Mother . . . No, I'm calling you that because you're my *actual mother* . . . Good night."

B Y FIVE O'CLOCK ON FRIDAY, MORGAN HAD HUNG streamers in the dining room, taken them down because they looked babyish, and put them back up because the room looked boring without them. She was thinking of removing them again because boring was better than babyish when Alder strode past. Morgan flagged her down with, "Did you have streamers at your twelfth birthday party?"

"Oh . . . um, no. Connie doesn't do store-bought stuff. She thinks it's unimaginative."

"Well, what did you have, then?"

"She let me and my friends paint anything we wanted on the living-room wall. But she got kind of disgusted with all the rainbows and 'Girls Rule,' and she painted it over the next day."

Morgan glanced at the streamers. "These look bad, don't they?"

"They're okay." After a moment Alder said, "I like those china cups your mom has with the handles that curl up at the bottom. When we'd come here for holidays, she'd always use them."

"You haven't been here for a long time. Since Grandma died, I think."

Alder's eyes went unfocussed for a moment. "Yeah," she said.

"Are you going to be around tonight?" Morgan asked hopefully as she yanked at the streamers.

"No, I'm hanging with a friend."

"Does Mom know?"

"Yep," said Alder. And then she was gone.

At 5:20 the doorbell rang. Morgan gave her already sparkly lips one more dab of gloss and ran for the door. Dana knew to stay put, straightening the napkins and adjusting the teacups.

"Hi!" Darby's breathless voice sounded from the mudroom. "I came early!"

"I was hoping you would! 'Cause I'm, like—" A high-pitched squeal erupted from Morgan.

"I knew you wanted me to! Also, here!" There was a rustle of paper. "Do you love it? Isn't it so sophisticated?"

"Totally! Here, do the thingy. I'm so excited my hands are shaking!"

The girls ran into the dining room, matching manic grins electrifying their faces. "Mom, look!" The necklace had a rhinestone-encrusted heart with a tiny pink bead in the middle.

"Isn't that pretty," said Dana, smiling more about the girls' excitement than the necklace.

"It's my first piece of real jewelry!" said Morgan. She turned to Darby. "Now I have to change my shirt—help me pick something." The girls sprinted for the stairway.

Dana thought about her mother's pearl pendant, which she'd given Morgan when she'd turned ten. That was real jewelry. This sparkly heart would be broken, lost, or considered boring in six months. But she was happy for Morgan's excitement, however impermanent it might be.

The party was a success, at least as far as the guests knew. They arrived emitting squeals of social bliss, which subsided and erupted throughout the evening—when the pizza arrived, drinking Sprite from Dana's heirloom teacups, and when Tracey laughed so hard the

Sprite came out her nose. They went to Morgan's bedroom, where they gave one another new hairdos and plastered themselves with strawberry-kiwi-smelling glitter. Two came down for another bowl of popcorn, then scurried back up to the inner sanctum of girlitude. No one traveled alone.

Dana was on her way to ask if they were ready for the cake when she heard two girls whispering to each other on the second-floor landing.

"Can you believe Kimmi came?"

"She didn't commit till the last day of the RSVP."

"Do you think she felt . . . you know—what's the word—*sorry* for Morgan?"

"Because her parents split up? No, that was, like, months ago."

"Why would she come, then? There aren't even any boys here."

"No clue."

"Maybe she thinks Morgan's, like . . ."

"Even though she gets all awkward sometimes."

The tinny thumping of a ringtone sounded, and one of the girls giggled and said, "It's Jason. Should I text him back?"

"Tell him we're too busy partying to talk."

Dana heard the door to Morgan's room open and voices wafting out in ribbons of sound: "No way!" and "Eww!" and "I SAW it!" Then the door closed again. Dana didn't go up. They'd let her know when they wanted cake.

And they did, swarming down the stairs, a glittered, made-up flock of motion and drama. They were starving, they said, though several girls ate only a bite. Morgan had a lick or two of the bright pink frosting and pronounced herself stuffed. It was dark by then, and they decided to play manhunt in the woods behind the house, rising like startled birds from the table, swooping toward the mudroom, and grabbing their fleece North Face jackets and Ugg boots.

Grady gaped at them as they buzzed by on their way into the cool, dark yard. "They're playing manhunt like *that*?" he asked Dana. "Everybody can see that sparkle junk a mile away."

Dana was about to return some washed teacups to the safety of the china closet in the dining room. From the shadow of the hallway, she saw Morgan and stopped short, stunned. Morgan was systematically eating all the leftover cake from the other girls' plates. She barely chewed but seemed to swallow each sugary lump whole. It was the practiced economy that shocked Dana most of all, each movement like a surgical strike on unsuspecting prey.

Morgan gathered the plates and strode toward the doorway. When she caught sight of her mother, she flicked a finger to the corner of her mouth, pushing a crumb between her lips. "I was just cleaning up," she said, and put the pile of plates on the kitchen counter. Before Dana could respond, Morgan zipped her jacket and headed back outside.

The party went on. No longer satisfied with racing through the darkened corners of the yard, the girls went to the basement. Morgan ejected Grady, and they took turns playing a video dance game, howling with hilarity at one another's gyrations. Grady stomped upstairs, declared his sister a buttface, and Dana let him watch TV in Alder's room.

Dana sat down at the kitchen table. At last she had a moment to think. It wasn't so much thoughts, but images that came to her. Morgan pretending to be full in front of her friends, then bringing forkful after forkful to her mouth, expressionless. Expressionless! She had seemed so happy with the party. What would make her do that?

I know my own daughter, Dana told herself. This thought hovered around until it seemed like a taunt, as if someone were in her head mimicking her with her own words.

The front door opened and shut. Dana looked up at the clock, thankful it was only eight. She hadn't set a curfew for Alder, because she had no idea what a reasonable time was these days. Besides,

Alder had always seemed so mature, needing such constraints as much as she might need a bib or a pacifier.

As Alder moved across the kitchen, Dana noticed a difference in her gait. Her joints seemed less tightly hinged. "Hey . . ." She grinned at Dana. "We're so . . . we're just so . . . hungry!" Her eyes alighted on the remaining birthday cake "Can I have it?" she asked.

"Of course," said Dana, rising. "I'll cut you a piece."

"That's okay." She picked up the cake plate and started for the mudroom. "I'll be home . . . I don't know . . . later. But not too, too late, okay, Dana?" The word "Dana" came out slowly, as if hyphenated. "Bye," she added, and the door slammed behind her.

Oh my God, what do I do? Dana thought, but the avocado station wagon was gone before she could organize her thoughts and act. *I'm not ready to parent a teenager . . . Maybe Kenneth was right.* She considered calling her sister but knew that Connie would be disgusted with her—for taking it either too seriously or not seriously enough. Dana could imagine her saying, *Kids get high, don't freak out,* as easily as *How could you let her leave the house!*

It wasn't that Dana had never seen anyone high before. At the University of Connecticut, she had tried marijuana while dating a boy named Billy who never went a day without it. He once demonstrated at a party how taking a bong hit while standing on your head gave you the most massive head rush. Dana smoked only the very thin joints he rolled especially for her. He called them "dolly doobies," and he loved the way her face scrunched up when she tried to inhale.

Billy wasn't remotely her type. But he'd pursued her with a determination she found compelling in someone who seemed so completely lacking in any other form of ambition. He was cute and popular and intelligent in a wasteful sort of way. And people's reactions to seeing them together gave her private shudders of delight. She hoped it made them consider there might be more to her than a nice smile and an A-minus average.

Eventually they broke up, because their relationship never normalized. Dana wanted to understand him but never quite did. Meanwhile, every time she smoked a "dolly doobie," she became certain that people were conspiring to steal her carefully written class notes. Without them she was sure she would flunk out, become unemployable, and have to clip free trial coupons in order to eat. "Keep your hands off my notebooks," she would tell Billy and his friends in a haze of smoke, as they laughed at her in convulsive gasps, "and clip your *own* coupons."

In retrospect her foray into the world of pot smoking had been silly and harmless. But now, with her beloved niece wandering around high in the darkened town of Cotters Rock, the possibilities for disaster seemed countless. Dana dialed the phone.

"Is it over yet?" Polly wanted to know. "Did you survive?"

"Survive?" asked Dana.

"Isn't Morgan's party tonight?"

"Oh, right. But listen, I need your advice on something." Dana barely knew where to begin. "Do ... did ... have you ever had to deal with kids smoking pot? Not your kids, of course, necessarily ... but, you know, maybe their friends?"

"Are those girls smoking pot at Morgan's party?" Polly was immediately furious on Dana's behalf. "Because you'd better call up all those parents *right this minute* and—"

"Not Morgan's friends. But I think Alder might have been ... possibly a little bit ... high. She came in a few minutes ago and left again so quickly I didn't react fast enough. She's not even mine, Polly, and I have no idea what to do."

"All right, first you call her and tell her to get her little butt home."

"I don't know where she is," Dana was embarrassed to admit. "And she doesn't have a cell phone."

"She's sixteen and she doesn't have a cell phone? What is she— Amish?"

"I should have gotten her one," Dana chastised herself. "I don't know what I was thinking."

"Stop that! You're nice enough to take the kid in, and if she comes without accessories, well, that's your sister's department."

"I don't even know her friend's name! How could I be so irresponsible?"

"Do you want me to come over?"

It was tempting. Polly's signature certainty was such a comfort it was almost as good as home fries. But Dana knew it could also be a liability. "Oh, Polly, that's so nice of you—but I think maybe I should give this one a try myself and see how it goes."

As the call ended, the doorbell rang, and Dana hurried toward the mudroom, knowing that Alder would never ring the bell but hoping all the same it was her. When she opened the door, a woman stood on the porch. She had shoulder-length auburn hair that fell away from her face in such a casually perfect way it reminded Dana of a magazine ad. She wore a tight-fitting blue-striped T-shirt above her low-rise jeans. Morgan had the same shirt in purple.

"Nora Kinnear," said the woman, glancing into the mudroom. "I'm here to pick up Kimmi?"

"Oh, yes, come right in! Nice to meet you. I'm Dana, Morgan's mom."

Nora Kinnear followed her into the house but lingered in the mudroom strewn with fleece jackets and muddy boots. "I'll wait here for her," she murmured.

The scuff marks on the mudroom walls from lacrosse sticks, art projects, and flying shoes seemed suddenly very noticeable to Dana, and she had a momentary notion that she should have had it repainted before the party. "I'll just run and get her," she said.

The girls trooped up the stairs, escorting Kimmi to the door. She had caramel blond hair that seemed to glint even indoors and a sprinkling of freckles across her nose that maximized her cuteness without looking overly ethnic. "This was *so, so* fun!" she said to Morgan. "Thanks for inviting me. I hope you have the best birthday *ever*." And she laid her long, thin arms—younger copies of her mother's, Dana realized—around Morgan's neck for a brief, airy embrace.

Morgan said nothing for a moment, her eyes wide. Then she cooed, "Thanks for coming. See you at lunch Monday?"

In quick succession the other girls were picked up, and then Dana and Morgan were alone in the mudroom. Morgan slumped against her mother.

"Was it fun?" asked Dana, cupping a hand around her daughter's flushed cheek. *I know you,* she said silently. *I know my daughter.*

"It was a total blast. And Kimmi was really, like, *next* to me the whole night—it was almost weird! Like when we played manhunt, she hid with me and sat in my lap! I think Darby's mad."

"She's probably worried she'll get left out. Make sure you're extra nice to her at school."

Dana's hand remained on Morgan's cheek, stroking it with her thumb. Something needed to be said, but Dana had no idea of how to begin. *I saw you stuffing your face with other people's leftovers, and I just wanted to know . . .* What exactly? What was the key question?

Morgan heaved a dramatic sigh and smiled wanly.

"Time for bed," said Dana, hating herself for the relief she felt. She would talk to Morgan tomorrow, she vowed, when they were both more alert.

It was eleven o'clock when Alder came in with the empty cake plate and handed it to Dana, faint stripes of pink frosting running across the ceramic finish. It appeared to have been licked. "Sorry," she said, her eyes clear and focused.

Dana released a breath she'd held captive all night. "Are you okay?"

"Yeah. I don't usually do that." Alder got a glass, filled it with water, and drank the whole thing down. She filled the glass again and turned to lean her back against the counter.

"I was *so worried* about you, honey." Dana struggled to keep her voice from breaking.

"I know. It was bad, and I knew that, but I just couldn't sort of . . . control it. If you need to punish me or anything, go for it."

"I don't want to *punish* you, Alder. I want you to be safe and healthy!"

Alder's chin dropped down to her chest. "Really, *really* sorry," she whispered.

"Okay." Dana sighed. "All right." Perhaps there was more to say, something else she should do, but if there was, she couldn't think what. "Just please don't do it again."

"I won't. And I'm seriously sorry," Alder said, squinting at the glass dangling in her hand. "Hey." She looked up at Dana. "Did you ever kiss a girl? Not like a peck, I mean a real kiss."

"Uh . . ." Dana's brain seemed to lurch around inside her skull. Was Alder really asking . . . ?

"You don't have to tell me if you did," Alder said quickly. "It's kind of . . . different, and I just wondered if you ever had."

"Well, I'm certainly very fond of some of my friends, and I guess I don't think there's anything wrong with . . . But I can't say I ever wanted to . . ."

"Yeah," said Alder. "I didn't think so." She put her glass in the dishwasher. "God, I'm tired," she said, and headed for her room.

I should call Connie, Dana kept thinking as she climbed the stairs. But it was late, probably too late, and for that she was thankful. The light was on in Grady's room, and she realized she'd forgotten about him completely. He was lying across his mattress, a *Star Wars* spaceship in one limp hand, C-3PO in the other. His pants were off, but he still wore his shirt, socks, and boxers. Dana set the toys on his dresser and slid him under the covers. She picked up the dirt-smeared pants to put them in the bathroom hamper.

When she opened the bathroom door, a smell hit her—

something like sweetened parmesan cheese. She recognized the
odor almost immediately. Someone had thrown up, and the stomach contents had not been pungent like hot dogs or sour like yogurt. It had been sweet. Like cake. Dana looked in the toilet bowl
and noticed flecks of something unnaturally pink inside the rim.
Frosting. There was no doubt about it.

———————————⟨∞⟩———————————

DANA LAY IN HER BED THAT NIGHT TRYING TO snatch at sleep, but she couldn't power down from the anxiety that had mounted all evening. It was certain now—she could no longer wish it away. Morgan binging and purging. Alder smoking pot with a nameless junk-car-driving possible lesbian. Even Grady, putting himself to bed like a motherless child.

These were indicators. Big flashing neon signs of Dana's ineptitude at the most important job she'd ever have. How had this happened? Hadn't she once been competent? Her reviews as an office manager had always been glowing. Her grades had always been good. Yet her marriage had failed, and the children in her care were troubled. (Well, Grady seemed fine, but who knew how long that would last if she neglected him as she had tonight?)

And now I have to get a job, she told herself. *I have to solve all these problems while earning an income.* The tears came, a welcome release. It was the only reasonable response, and it was comforting that this one thing, her sadness, still worked. The sobbing wore her out, and she slipped into a merciful torpor.

Ma, said a voice. It was her own voice, calling out in their old house in Watertown, Massachusetts, the two-family with the landlady living upstairs. *Ma!* she called again, running through the kitchen, out the back door to the tiny yard. So small, and yet complete. The swing set and the sandbox and the fort she used to play house in, which leaned up against the detached garage, two-byfours and plywood their father had nailed into place before he'd slipped away from them into the empty shell of his sad, quiet world.

Her mother was sitting on one of the swings drifting back and forth, guiding the gentle motion with bare toes dug into the grass below. "Ma," Dana called to her. "I can fix it!"

Her mother glanced up, face lit with surprise. "You can?"

"Yes!" said Dana. "There are these pills now." Her shorts hung straight down from her waist, no womanly hips to impede her little hand as it wiggled into the pocket to find the cool, round tablets. "See!"

"Those are just pebbles," said her mother. "Pebbles won't fix him. They won't fix anything."

"No, Ma, they're pills. They'll bring him back to us. Make him take them!"

"He's too sad," said her mother, who settled back onto the swing and started to pump. "He won't let go of his darkness. Throw those pebbles away and swing with me."

"Ma, please!"

As her mother picked up speed, swinging higher and higher, a baby's cry came from the house. "All your sister does is squawk and squawk," muttered Ma. "You get her this time."

"Ma, make Dad take the pills!"

"Take them yourself." And the swing flew off the swing set, sailing high up into the sky until, like a balloon let loose from the bunch, her mother floated out of sight.

The ringing of the phone woke Dana, partly dissipating the haunting ache of desertion.

"Please tell me you are *not* still in bed!"

"Not really," said Dana, raking her fingers through the snarls in her hair.

"Get your butt up and get over here!" commanded Polly playfully. "I need a walk!"

Dana pulled on her sport pants and a long-sleeved T-shirt. On her way downstairs, she peeked into Morgan's bedroom. The girl was curled around her squishy pillow, fashioned to look like an oversize Hershey bar, her breaths coming in slow, even passes.

Dana went downstairs, following the sound of voices to the kitchen. "Just smack it on the side of the bowl, G," Alder was saying.

"I can't. It'll come out all ewwy and disgusting." Grady's voice now.

"You want scrambled eggs, you gotta do it. I'll cook them, but you have to crack them."

"Good morning," said Dana. "What's going on here—a cooking class?"

Grady held out an egg to her. "Mom, you do it."

"Polly wants to walk," she said, ignoring the egg. "Is everything okay here?"

"G'head. It's a beautiful day," said Alder. Out the kitchen window, the sky was a perturbed gray.

"You're sure?" asked Dana. "I'll make it a short one."

"Totally. Go." As Dana went into the mudroom to find her sneakers, she heard Alder say, "Jeez, what do you think is *in* there—monkey brains? Just do it."

A crack sounded, and Grady said, "GROSS!"

Alder laughed. "There's worse things than that, G."

Dana set off down her driveway. Her lungs fully expanded, taking in the dank chill of the air and a sense of relief to be away from the house and the events of the previous evening.

Polly soon joined her. "I was worried about you last night. How did it end up with Alder?"

"She apologized."

"*Apologized?*" Polly was shaking her head. "They usually deny it. Or they say it was in the brownies and they didn't know."

"No, she took full responsibility. But I still didn't get to the bottom of this new friend of hers." Dana wanted to ask Polly about the kiss—did kids experiment so freely with that kind of thing these days? But it was too personal; Alder was hers now—for the time being anyway—and protecting her niece from amateur analysis overrode her need for reassurance.

"You know," said Polly, "the thing about teenage girls is, they change friends about every twenty minutes. You'd be amazed. They try them on like jeans in a department store. They might wear them for a while, but they generally don't keep them for long if the fit isn't good."

"So you think I should trust her?"

"Well, that's another thing altogether. There should be a different word for when a parent lets out the leash a little. It's trust, but it's trust in a thing that's so changeable you barely can stand it, and you have to keep all your fingers and toes crossed." They swung onto a side road that skirted Nipmuc Pond. A heron flew out from the shallows, its narrow gray wings flapping hard until it was safely aloft. "But the party was good?" said Polly. "Morgan was happy?"

"I guess," Dana sighed. "One of the girls, Kimmi Kinnear, gave her a lot of attention. All the other girls follow Kimmi around like she's got a treasure map or something. So I guess that makes it a success, when the popular girl chooses you."

Polly brightened. "Oh, yeah, she's Nora's girl. You know Nora?"

"I met her for the first time when she picked up Kimmi from the party."

"She's a hot ticket. She's the marketing director for that new chain at Evergreen Mall—Perfectua Couture. You've heard of it, right? It's very *in*." Polly's eyes glimmered with interest, which surprised Dana. Polly wasn't usually so taken with people's résumés. "She runs my book group—very selective about who joins. She's got a thing about 'group dynamics,' which is smart when you think about it. One obnoxious person can ruin a whole evening."

"How can anyone be obnoxious about books?"

"Oh, please, like it's about the *books*. It's a chance to get out of the house, drink wine, and gab!" Polly smirked. "I think Victor has a little bit of a crush on her."

"Victor your husband?"

"Yes, Victor my husband! How many Victors do you know?"

"But doesn't that bother you?"

"Nah, who cares? We all have innocent little crushes from time to time." Polly flicked her hand. "Enough about that. Tell me about the party."

Dana could feel the hopelessness welling at the thought of it. She described watching Morgan eat the other girls' cake and the sight of the frosting in the toilet bowl.

"Well, maybe her stomach was upset," said Polly. "You don't know for a fact that she stuck her finger down her throat."

Dana stopped walking, and after another step Polly stopped, too. The two women looked at each other. Polly went first. "That was the wrong thing to say, wasn't it?" she asked.

Dana nodded. Her head hurt and her eyes stung.

"I don't want to believe it," murmured Polly. "I love that kid."

Dana turned to look out over the lake. An old aluminum rowboat bobbed at the end of a nearby dock. She wanted to get in and row.

"Okay," Polly said softly. "She's doing it. How do we help her?"

Dana shrugged. A gust of wind came across the lake and nudged a tear from her eyelid.

"This is not you," said Polly. "This is not your fault. You're a fantastic mother, kind and patient . . . Jeez, you're so patient you make glaciers look like they're in a hurry!"

"I don't know what to do," breathed Dana. "I can't even . . ."

"You get her some help, is what. Start by calling the guidance counselor at school. You didn't cause this problem, and you can't fix it by yourself."

Dana brushed the tears off her face. "Don't tell anyone, okay? Not even Victor. He and Kenneth are such close friends, and I have to broach this with him my own way."

"Of course," said Polly as they turned to continue their walk. "Not a peep."

—————

When Dana got home, Alder was sitting on the floor in the TV room doing homework. She looked up, rolled her eyes dramatically, and pretended to snap her pencil in frustration when Dana peeked in. Dana smiled back. Grady was in the basement watching a particularly screechy cartoon. Dana turned the volume down and went up the two flights of stairs to Morgan's room.

The light was still off, but Dana could see Morgan's hand moving in the dimness. It was sliding slowly up and down the Hershey-themed pillow, stroking it as if it were a small scared animal.

I do that, Dana realized. *I run my hand across things as if I'm soothing them, but really I'm soothing myself.* She went over and sat on the edge of the bed.

"What is it," said Morgan.

"Nothing. I just wanted to talk with you."

"About what?"

"Sweetie, did you get sick last night?"

Morgan didn't answer for a minute. "No," she said finally, but without conviction, as if she were trying out the answer to see if it would work.

Keep going, Dana told herself. *Keep moving toward an answer.* "I think maybe you did," she said. "I think maybe you ate too much cake and it didn't feel good."

"I didn't eat that much," Morgan murmured.

Dana knew it would be hard to get Morgan to admit to purging, and yet she was still surprised. It wasn't so long ago that Morgan had told her everything. She had to approach her daughter from a different angle now, and, offered a version of a true story she and Polly had worked out on their walk. "I knew this girl in my dorm at UConn," she said. "She used to put her finger down her throat when she ate too much. She was worried about her weight."

Morgan closed her eyes and pulled the pillow closer, as if to drift back to sleep. Her words were almost inaudible. "Did it work?"

"Not really. She'd lose a few pounds and then gain it back. On top of being really bad for you, it's not a very effective diet."

"At least she didn't get fatter."

"No, but people started avoiding her. No one wanted to be around someone who did that."

"She should've kept it to herself."

"She did, but people found out. There aren't many secrets in this world that don't get found out eventually."

Morgan's eyes opened, and she glanced at her mother.

Dana pushed herself to form the words in her head, to make them real and solid enough to say. "Morgan, I think you're making yourself throw up."

Morgan didn't answer.

Dana went on. "I need you to just tell me."

After a minute, Morgan sat up. "I have to pee," she said, and crawled out over the pillow.

"I'm going to keep asking you about this," said Dana as she watched Morgan retreat from the room. *Patient as a glacier,* she told herself.

That night they all stayed in and watched a movie together, though it was Saturday and the phone rang with offers. In a succession of calls from the still-unnamed friend, Alder reiterated her intention to "hang home." Dana was relieved not to have to worry about her whereabouts or state of consciousness. She didn't think to ground Alder until Alder essentially grounded herself.

Darby called, inviting Morgan for a sleepover, but Morgan declined with vague excuses. "No," she said to Darby, "she's not . . . I would tell you . . . Of course I would invite you, too, but we're not getting together . . . I swear I haven't talked to Kimmi since yesterday . . ."

Timmy Koljian invited Grady to go to Kreamy Kones. "No thanks," said Grady, and hung up.

"Why did you say no?" Dana admonished him. "You love Kreamy Kones."

"Timmy's annoying," said Grady. "Do we have any heavy popcorn?"

"Heavy?"

"Yeah, not that light stuff. The kind that has all the butter so it weighs a ton."

They watched an action-adventure movie about an archaeologist racing to find a treasure hidden by a Civil War hero. Grady twitched in his seat as if he were trying to beat the bad guys to the loot, too. Morgan didn't appear to be watching all that much. Alder laughed a lot, mostly at Grady.

They all went willingly to bed after the credits rolled. It was ten o'clock, and Dana knew Kenneth would be up, probably reading the latest bestseller about the 114 habits of highly successful salesmen or the like. Though she dreaded it, she knew she had to tell him about Morgan. She kissed the kids good night, closed her bedroom door, and dialed.

"Yuh?" said a woman's voice, breathy, as if she'd been exercising.

"Excuse me, I'm so sorry," said Dana, at first thinking she had misdialed. In the next moment, it dawned on her: *Tina.* "I'm trying to reach Kenneth Stellgarten," she said coldly.

"Kenny," muttered the woman, "it's for you."

Dana heard fabric rustling, then whispers: "What? No!" and "Just *take* it."

Kenneth cleared his throat, a juicy hawking sound indicating he hadn't been taking his allergy medicine. "Can I help you?" he said irritably.

"It's Dana." The archness of her tone surprised even her. "Call me when you have a minute to talk about our daughter." She hit the "off" button.

"Uhhh!" She shuddered in disgust. An image came to her, unbidden, of how Kenneth used to wrap himself around her after sex, his

breath blowing on her neck like a bellows until it made her chilly. But it wasn't Dana in the image. It was this Tina.

She flinched again, her shoulders clenching up around her neck. In a second she was out of bed and heading downstairs. She flipped on the kitchen light and poured herself a glass of sugar-free lemonade. *Why did she pick up the phone? You don't answer when you're still panting from . . . And "Kenny"! He made me call him Kenneth for years, and she gets to call him KENNY!*

Dana picked at the remnants of the "heavy" popcorn she had virtuously avoided all evening. The salty richness of it settled her. Kenneth was sleeping with another woman—this was not news, she told herself. (Though why he had chosen someone who would be so coarse as to answer a phone practically mid-coitus was beyond her.) What bothered her more, she had to admit, was the fact that he had someone and she didn't.

Not yet anyway. Her date with Coach Ro was coming up next weekend, and who knew if that might be the start of something? And if they liked each other, how soon would it be before they might spend the night together? Never with the kids around, of course, but possibly on weekends when they were with their father. What would it be like to be with someone new? She hadn't slept with anyone but Kenneth in almost twenty years. There had been several before that, but when she thought about it now, it seemed as if she were remembering a story about some other woman. Not her. Not this present-day, problem-laden single mother.

Billy the pothead came to mind. He had been very nice to her, surprisingly sweet and considerate, at least on the nights he wasn't giggly and stupid from having partied too much. *Too bad about him,* she found herself thinking. *He was a pretty good boyfriend about fifty percent of the time.* Maybe Jack would be like the good half of Billy. He seemed to find her appealing, and he had a way of standing close, touching her without crossing the line to intrusiveness.

How would it be for that line to disappear completely? For him to be granted full access, with nothing between her body and those hands? A pleasing ache began to throb as she imagined the scene, his closeness, his wanting her . . .

A moment later Alder came padding into the kitchen. When she saw the flush in Dana's cheeks, her eyebrows flicked up a fraction of an inch. Dana grabbed the sponge and began wiping the clean countertop. "I hope I didn't wake you, sweetie," she said, following her industrious hand as it moved down the Formica.

"No, I wasn't sleeping." Alder took out a glass and ran the water, holding a finger under the stream to gauge the temperature. "I was thinking about last night. I kind of freaked you out."

"Well, I've seen people high before," said Dana, slightly put off by the idea that Alder might think her a complete innocent. "I just didn't expect it from you."

"I told Jet—"

Jet, thought Dana. *That's the girl's name.*

"I told her I'm not getting high anymore. I have to keep clear about things." She took another sip of water. "Oh, and also it bugged you. Which is totally understandable and all."

"Okay, well . . . that's good," said Dana, not missing the fact that Alder didn't seem terribly motivated by her aunt's concern over the matter. "There are so many nice kids to spend time with, honey. I'm sure you can find some who aren't into drugs."

"Jet's not *into* drugs. We just wanted to . . . I don't even know. It was there, and we smoked it. But I'm not doing it anymore, and she said she won't either." Alder's gaze became more purposeful as she looked at her aunt. "She's the only friend I have right now. I'm not ditching her just because we did something stupid one time."

"It sounds like. . ." Dana hesitated, ". . . maybe you're interested in being more than friends."

Alder pinched her lips together, but a little grin popped out all the same. "Actually," she said, "this is so lame, but we kind of got our signals crossed on that one."

"What do you mean?"

"Jet's not one of those kids people, like, *notice.* Or if they do, it's not in a good way. I guess she was surprised I wanted to hang out with her, and she thought . . ." Alder let out a little chuckle. "She thought I was . . . you know . . . *into* her. So she kissed me. And I kissed her back because . . . I don't know. I guess I thought it was worth a try."

"But if she's not gay, why would she . . . ?"

The amusement on Alder's face faded. "People want to be liked. They do things or go along with stuff because they're afraid they'll get shut out if they don't." The pale green of her eyes seemed darker, like clouded sea glass. Then she shrugged. "Anyway, thanks for, you know, hanging in there. I'll keep it together better from now on." Alder gave her a quick hug and went back to bed.

The wind had kept up all day, and Dana could hear the creaking of tree branches out in the yard. Suddenly there was a crack followed by a resounding thump. She parted the curtain and looked out. At the edge of the yard near the streetlight lay a large amputated bough. *Nature's pruning,* her mother would have said. At least now Dana didn't have to pay a landscaping company to come and trim it; the wind had done it for her. *A free service,* she realized. *The only one I'm likely to get.*

CHAPTER
14

KENNETH WAS UP IN THE STANDS WHEN THEY GOT to Grady's football game the next morning. He didn't usually come when it wasn't his weekend with the kids, so Dana suspected that last night's phone call had made an impression.

She wasn't responsible for recording the minimum play requirements; Amy Koljian, Timmy the quarterback's mother, had been given the duty. But when Dana walked Grady over to the sidelines and adjusted his helmet, Coach Ro came and stood beside her, remarking on how lucky they were that the clouds had cleared and the field had dried out. A perfect day for football. "Hope it's this nice *next* weekend," he murmured, nudging her conspiratorially.

Dana smiled and nodded, hoping that Amy Koljian hadn't picked up on Coach's secretive tone. Or the fact that he was standing just a little too close. Avoiding his gaze, Dana fussed with Grady's helmet strap. "Okay, honey, I'll be right up in the stands."

Grady spit out his mouth guard. "With Dad?" he asked. Coach Ro stiffened.

"And Morgan. Yes, I'll be up there with both of them." She glanced briefly at Coach, "Have a good game!" she chimed and strode quickly away.

"How come Alder gets to stay home and I have to come?" Morgan whined as soon as Dana was seated next to her.

"She's still catching up on all the work she's missed, honey, I told you that. And you come to Grady's games—just like he goes to

your concerts—because we're a family. We support one another."
Dana had given this speech so many times it came out as if it were
prerecorded. Besides, she was distracted by Kenneth, sitting on
Morgan's opposite side, clutching with the hems of his jacket
sleeves as if he were undergoing a Senate inquiry.

"I couldn't care *less* if he comes to my concerts," insisted Morgan. "In fact, I'd prefer if he *didn't*. You always sit up front, and I can
see him chewing on his shirt collar or picking his nose, and it makes
me mess up. I swear, I would actually play *better* if you left him at
home!"

"Morgan, please. Enough."

"Dad, do you think this is fair? Grady doesn't even know I'm
here. He can barely see through the bars in the stupid helmet. He
probably can't tell if *you're* here either."

"He knows we're here, Morgan," said Kenneth. "And don't fight
with your mother about it."

Morgan let out a frustrated groan. "Can I at least get a hot
chocolate?"

Kenneth pulled some bills from his wallet and said, "Get some
for Mom and me, too."

"I don't care for any, thanks," said Dana. When was the last
time he'd bought her a fattening beverage like hot chocolate? He
always assumed she wanted diet soda or bottled water.

"Something else, then?" he asked.

"No thanks, I'm fine."

Morgan glanced at her mother. Then she made her way down
the sparsely populated stands, hopping from one seat to the next.

"I'm sorry about last night," Kenneth said quickly. "That was
not . . . There was no intention to . . ."

Dana stared straight ahead. "I'm very concerned about Morgan," she murmured. There was no one sitting near them, but she
kept her voice low anyway. Kenneth leaned toward her, sliding a
few inches closer on the bench.

"Why?" he said. Worry swelled in his voice, but Dana knew

there was relief, too, for the change in subject matter. She gave a brief synopsis: the eroded enamel, the bingeing on cake, the evidence of vomit in the bathroom, and, most important, Morgan's lack of denial.

"How are you going to handle it?" Kenneth asked.

"How are *we* going to handle it," she corrected him. "I'm not the only parent here, Kenneth."

"I know that," he grumbled. "I just meant that you always seem to have a plan. You're good at figuring these things out."

He thinks I'm good at this? Dana let that sink in a moment. "I'm going to call the school counselor tomorrow. And Dr. Sakimoto gave me a list of resources. But we have to work *together* on this. Don't go getting distracted by the rest of your life."

"Of course not!" he retorted. Morgan was starting to make her way up the stands toward them. "You just need to keep me up to speed. That's all I'm asking. I'm her father," he added.

"Yes, I *know*," muttered Dana.

Morgan stepped up to their bench holding two Styrofoam cups of hot chocolate and handed her father one. "Can you shove over a little?" she said, taking her former spot between her parents. She held out the other cup to Dana. "We can share," she said. "You have the first sip."

The next morning, after the kids left, Dana called the middle school and asked to speak to the guidance counselor, Mr. Kresgee. "I'm Morgan Stellgarten's mom? She's in sixth grade?"

"Oh, yes, Morgan, yes." His voice had a nasal twang to it. "I haven't clicked with that crop of kiddos yet—they've only been here a month. But I will. I have a knack for it."

Dana wasn't sure what to make of his self-proclaimed knack, but she soldiered on, telling him her concerns. It hurt just to say the words, but Mr. Kresgee responded with avuncular kindness. "There's quite a number of kiddos with this problem," he said. "I'll invite her for a little heart-to-heart, and we'll see where she's at."

When Dana hung up the phone, she felt a sense of dread. She'd just told a stranger that her daughter had an eating disorder. *He's a professional,* she reminded herself. *He knows what to do a lot better than I do.*

Reluctantly she pulled out the sheet Dr. Sakimoto had given her, titled simply "Resources." Subheadings included "Orthodontia," "Dental Anxiety," and "Other Important Concerns." She poured a glass of sugar-free lemonade, went into Kenneth's office—*her* office, she reminded herself—and started with the National Eating Disorders Association Web site, clicking around, following links to new sites as well.

"Bulimia is a cyclical pattern of behaviors, rather than just one action," declared one Web site. "In a typical scenario, the bulimic's shame about her body causes her to restrict food intake. But eventually her hunger grows so strong that she overeats, sometimes several thousand calories at a time. The shame at having lost control and the anxiety about gaining weight make her desperate to undo her actions, so she purges. In the short term, it makes her feel better, but eventually the purging also causes shame and anxiety, creating a tension that drives her to overeat again."

Shame, Dana realized. *It's all about shame.* The thought bounced around her brain like a pinball, ricocheting against sore spots she barely knew she had.

Another Web site explained, "Bulimics aren't always thin. The huge intake of calories during bingeing can be partially offset by purging, but it is a relatively inefficient means of weight loss."

She clicked on the link to a page of suggestions for parents. The first point seemed to blink out at her from the screen: "Be aware of your feelings about your own body. Don't communicate dissatisfaction with your shape to your children. This leads them to believe they should be self-critical, too." Dana was certainly dissatisfied with her shape, as well as several other of her physical attributes. She didn't talk about it—why bore others with your insecurities? But had she somehow "communicated" this dissatisfaction to Morgan? Morgan was a perceptive girl; how was Dana supposed to counteract this subtle transference of information? Sing her own praises? Lie?

At lunchtime she went into the kitchen and microwaved a potato, careful as always not to take too much butter. But from what she had read that morning, she didn't want to "restrict" herself either. *Where's the line?* she wondered. *How much is enough but not too much?*

Dana was scrubbing a hardened spill of applesauce in the refrigerator when Morgan came home from school, saying, ". . . so annoying how she's like OHMYGOD every ten seconds, like everything on the planet needs an exclamation point or something."

"I *know.*" This second voice wasn't immediately recognizable. "Most stuff is so boring it's not even worth *mentioning.*"

"Just throw your jacket on the bench," said Morgan. "We're supposed to hang them up, but we never do." The girls came into the kitchen. "Mom," said Morgan with a look of veiled pride, "this is Kimmi."

"Of course!" Dana said brightly. Morgan narrowed her eyes. Dana dialed back her smile. "From the party. How are you?"

"Fine," said Kimmi. "How are *you*?" Dana noticed that she held her lips slightly parted, which had the effect of sucking in her cheeks.

"Are you girls hungry?" Dana asked, immediately second-guessing herself. Should food be the first thing she mentioned? Probably not. And yet the Web sites said to promote healthy eating . . .

"Um," said Morgan, waiting for Kimmi's response.

"No thanks," Kimmi said. "I don't really like to eat between meals."

"Let's go up to my room," said Morgan, and the girls headed for the stairs.

A moment later the phone rang.

"Uh, hi . . . Is this the . . . Is this where . . . I'm looking for Alder Garrett. Is she, you know . . . there?" The voice was low and full, but the stammering made him sound as if he were about fourteen. Dana grinned. It was cute, this young man's nervousness. Maybe he was calling to ask Alder for a date. Maybe now she would stop hanging around with Jet, the pot smoker.

"She's not home from school yet," she told him. "Can I take your name and have her call you back?"

"Oh." The caller took a moment to consider what to do next, letting out a prizewinning string of "uh"s and "um"s. Finally he decided to employ some actual words. "Did she ever get a cell phone?"

"Unfortunately not," said Dana.

"Stubborn." He chuckled to himself. "Okay, yeah. Could you tell her E called? It's Ethan really, but she calls me E. And, um . . . could you tell her—ask her—to call me?"

"She has your number?"

"Yeah," he sighed, though Dana wasn't sure whether it was happy or sad. "She knows it by heart."

Dana prepared dinner that night as if dieticians, rather than children, would be eating it. She broiled fillet of sole, topped with a smattering of butter and bread crumbs—with doubtful hope she had chosen the most eating-disorder-aware quantities of each. She also made brown rice, spinach salad, steamed green beans, and glazed carrots.

"What's with all the vegetables?" Morgan asked.

"Just trying to eat healthy," said Dana. "Have as much as you want."

"That's easy," said Grady. "I'll have zero."

"Grady," Dana said wearily, "you don't have to eat a whole serving, but at least please have a bite."

He snorted. "Why?"

"Because . . ."

"Because *why*?"

"Because you'll never know if you like something if you don't try it." Dana could feel her voice getting tight. "And because I worked hard to make this meal—the least you could do is show a little gratitude."

"But I don't *like* it. Why should I be all gratitudey for stuff I don't even *like*?"

Before Dana could answer, Alder claimed the airspace over the table. "There's this kid at school who skateboards everywhere. I mean, like, *everywhere*. The thing's practically glued to his feet."

Grady looked over at her, suspicious but interested. "Really?"

"No lie." Alder took a big bite of sole. She glanced at Dana, nodding her appreciation.

"What can he do?" challenged Grady.

"All kinds of stuff." She took in a forkful of green beans and let out a little grunt of approval.

"Can he land a seven-twenty?"

"What, when they spin around twice? I don't know. Maybe. Jet says he hangs out at Glastonbury Skate Park. Maybe when I get my car fixed, I'll take you to watch him sometime."

"That'd be *sick*," murmured Grady.

"Eat a green bean and I'll get you a peanut-butter-and-ketchup sandwich." Alder looked over at Dana for confirmation that this would be acceptable. Dana shrugged her consent. She had made too much of it, she could see that now. Trying to do the right thing, she had done precisely the wrong thing.

Grady reached for the green bean Alder held out. He made a face as he chewed. "Disgusting," he said, and swallowed it.

When Alder returned to the table with the sandwich, Dana insisted, "At least say thank you."

He simpered in a high voice, *"Thank you, Alder."*

"Welcome, G," she simpered back.

"Oh, Alder, that reminds me," said Dana. "Someone called for you. Ethan, but you call him E?" She pressed the back of her fork against some stray bread crumbs. "He wants you to call."

Alder stopped chewing. Her elbows clamped in at her sides as if to buttress her ribs. She swallowed the lump of food in her mouth. "What'd he want?"

Dana puzzled at Alder's reaction. "He didn't say."

Staring down at her plate, Alder shook her head. "Anyone want these carrots?" she asked. "I took too much."

CHAPTER
15

AT BEDTIME DANA WENT UP TO MORGAN'S ROOM. She wanted to ask if Mr. Kresgee had had his promised "heart-to-heart," but she didn't want to open a can of worms prematurely. She would wait until he called, or until Morgan brought it up.

Morgan sat back against the pillows, studying a copy of *Cosmopolitan* magazine. "Where'd that come from?" Dana asked as she sat down on the bed.

"Kimmi brought it over. Her mom has a subscription."

"I don't know how I feel about that," Dana warned. "*Cosmo* runs some pretty racy articles."

"All that sex stuff? That's for freaks. We just like the fashions." Morgan flipped through the thick, glossy pages. "Like here," she said, laying the tome out before her mother, smoothing the paper reverently. "See how these jeans are cut way low but they don't make her hips look big? Kimmi says they're really flattering. I definitely want a pair of these!"

Dana studied the picture. The young model was impossibly thin, yet not emaciated. Her full breasts seemed to be trying to escape the scant tank top, and her arms were narrow but toned with sinewy muscle. How could anyone look this good? "Honey," said Dana, "I'm sure this girl is pretty in real life, but I have to guess this photo's been touched up."

Morgan studied the picture again. "No," she countered. "She's just super skinny."

"Yes, but think about it—do you know anyone who looks like this?" Dana summoned facts she'd just learned from "Photoshopping Us into a Panic: How the Media Tricks Us into Hating Ourselves," an article she'd read online. "With computers now they can make a girl thinner or tanner or make her eyes bluer with a few keystrokes. There probably isn't a photo in here that hasn't been altered in some way."

"Well, still . . ." said Morgan uncertainly. "Can I get the jeans?"

Dana squinted at the tiny paragraph on the bottom of the page. "Is that right?" she asked. "Does it say two hundred and fifty-four dollars? I can't tell without my glasses."

"Yeah." Morgan sighed, defeated.

"Wow. Maybe we should figure out a way to *sell* them instead of buy them, huh?"

Morgan crossed her arms over her ribs, pressing in on herself as if to impose martial law on her anarchical body parts. Her chin trembled. "Why do I have to look so . . . like *this*?" she quavered. "I'm so *ugly*." Tears slid down her cheeks.

"No, Morgan," Dana soothed, reaching out to hold her. "You're beautiful, honey."

"I'm *disgusting*." Morgan's weeping escalated. "You don't even know how bad it is! You're pretty, so everyone likes you!"

No I'm not and *No they don't* were the first responses that leaped to Dana's mind. Instead she said, "I'm glad you think I'm pretty, sweetheart, but if people only like me for that, then they aren't real friends, now, are they?"

Morgan groaned. "You don't think being pretty matters because you don't think you *are* pretty. You think people like you for *you*."

Hard as it was to hear her own daughter call her a social simpleton, the comment stung even more for the drop of truth it contained. And now there was confirmation that not only did Morgan know of her mother's insecurities but in Morgan's mind they were baseless.

"Hey," Dana said, pulling back so they faced each other. "Being pretty might get people interested in you, but it's not what lasting relationships are based on." She squinted in frustration. "And I don't like hearing you say the only reason people like me is because of my looks. That makes me sound brainless *and* friendless."

Morgan sniffled loudly and reached for the box of tissues on her bedside table. "Sorry," she muttered.

"Okay," said Dana. She smoothed a tendril of hair off her daughter's damp cheek. "Listen, sweetie. You don't love me for what I look like any more than I love you for what you look like. We love each other because we do, and that will never go away."

"I guess," whispered Morgan.

"You are so *loved,* Morgan, and for all the right reasons. Not for what jeans you wear or how you look in them, okay?"

"Okay." Morgan's eyes drooped, and she lay back on the pillows. Dana pulled the covers up and tucked them tight. She kissed Morgan's cheeks and landed a last kiss on her forehead. "Cozy-sweet dreams," she whispered, and turned off the light.

She knew she had gotten off easy, that Morgan was tired and willing to be talked out of an industrial-size fit of self-pity. But Dana felt some small relief at having begun what she knew would be a long, hard swim against the social imperative to be perfect. It was better, at least, than waiting to get washed farther downstream.

On her way to bed, Dana took a detour downstairs to the TV room. Alder was lying on the pullout couch, her face blank, the pink fleece blanket tossed haphazardly across her narrow frame. Her fingers worried at a piece of the hem.

"Just came down to say good night," Dana ventured from the door.

Alder's fingers went still. She gave her aunt a brief, wan smile. "Good night," she murmured.

"Alder?"

"Yeah."

"You didn't seem too happy to get a call from Ethan."

"Not much," said Alder.

Dana wanted to come into the room, sit on the bed, straighten the covers. But she sensed it was better not to intrude as she tried to glean a little information about her niece's social life. "Is he in one of your classes?"

"What?" said Alder, turning her head toward Dana as if just noticing her. "No, I don't know him from here. He's from . . . before."

"Was he unkind to you?"

Alder considered this for a moment. Her fingers began to work the hem of the blanket again. "Unkind," she murmured.

Dana felt weak as she sensed the depth of the girl's sadness. She wanted so badly to come into the room, but Alder's manner locked her out. "Alder," Dana whispered from the doorway. "I'm here if you want to tell me."

Alder nodded and closed her eyes.

The following afternoon Dana went to Cotters Rock Dental in hopes of convincing Dr. Sakimoto to accept a payment plan. She had no idea what his policies were, but he had given her the impression of a man willing to consider alternatives. And though she'd been wrong about people before, imagining kindness when there was in fact very little, she hoped she was right this time.

There was a new person seated at the reception desk, bent over, squinting at a magazine of some kind. Dana could see the salt-and-pepper roots in her brassy red hair.

"Half a sec," said the woman, not looking up. "Now, what am I supposed to make of *that*?" she muttered to herself. Glancing finally at Dana, she hoisted up a set of knitting needles tangled in yarn. "Does that look right to you?"

"It looks like the start of something . . ." offered Dana.

The woman studied the shapeless loops. "You think?"

What kind of receptionist are *you*? Dana thought irritably. "Um, is Dr. Sakimoto running late?"

"Oh, you have plenty of time." The woman smirked, pushing her brittle hair off her face. "It's a mess back there. He's one of those *micro*managers. I've temped long enough to know when someone's going all micro on me. I figured out yesterday to just let him do it all himself. Brought my knitting to keep me busy. Go on back if you want to," she offered smugly.

Dana gave her an incredulous stare. *Never in all my years of managing temps . . .* But this was not her business. Dana went down the hallway and clicked her fingernails hesitantly against the office door.

"*What.*"

Dana pushed the door open. Dr. Sakimoto was behind his desk, hunching forward toward his computer screen. "Oh, for godsake," he muttered as he rose to greet her. "Dana, I am so sorry. I've got the receptionist from hell out there, and I'm trying to do all the billing myself. Please forgive the chaos. Let's take care of that tooth, shall we?"

"Do you think we could talk for a minute first?"

"Certainly." He motioned to the upholstered chair where she'd learned of Morgan's purging.

"Oh, we don't need to sit down," she said quickly. "I know how busy you are."

"You, Mrs. Stellgarten, have got to be my most considerate patient," he said, smiling warmly. "Take all the time you need."

Dana hitched the strap of her purse back up to her shoulder and held on to it, gripping the soft leather as she described her "present, temporary circumstances."

"Please don't apologize," he said, almost before she'd finished. "Of course I'll do a payment plan. And trust me, you won't be the first. Ask my bookkeeper—he's ready to kill me." He led her into the operatory by his office. In the next room, she could hear Marie the hygienist gently admonishing a patient, "Floss is your friend, you know . . ."

"Your receptionist, Kendra—she must have a really terrible case of that stomach bug," Dana said as she slid back into the enormous vinyl chair.

Dr. Sakimoto chuckled. "Actually, she has a very wonderful case of a bun in the oven."

"She's pregnant? She's so young—I didn't even know she was married!"

Silently he raised his eyebrows at her as he snapped on his latex gloves.

"*Ohhh,*" murmured Dana. "Is she . . . Will she be okay?"

"She's got some sorting out to do, but she's very happy, telling the whole world about it." He clipped the bib around her neck and tucked a stray lock of hair behind her shoulder.

"But why isn't she here now?" asked Dana.

He let out an aggravated groan. "She can't take the smells! That's why she was tossing her cookies, not the bug. So she's on medical leave until the nausea subsides." He gently raised her upper lip to examine the temporary on her tooth, then turned to organize his instruments.

"I don't mean to butt in . . ." ventured Dana.

"Be my guest."

"That temp out there is very unprofessional. I don't think I ever had one who was that bad."

"She's an unmitigated disaster—honestly, she's killing me. You've hired temps?"

"Well, not recently, but years ago I managed a legal office in Hartford, and I used temps sometimes. If I'd had one like her, I would have requested someone else. I'm sure you can ask the supervisor at the agency for someone more . . . skilled."

Dr. Sakimoto listened to her, a tube of numbing gel in his hand, his brown eyes blinking slowly as he took this in. "Hold on," he said. "What about you?"

Dana shifted in the chair. "Well, it's really not my place to speak to her supervisor . . ."

"No!" He waved her off with laugh. "I mean, you temping!

You've obviously got the skills, and you've got your financial setback. Plus, you'd really be helping me out. One more day with Brassy Betty out there and I'll end up on the eleven-o'clock news."

"Oh, I don't know . . ." Dana shook her head. How could this work? It was a full-time job. Who would be home for the kids in the afternoon? With Morgan in her present state, she needed adult supervision now more than ever.

"Think about it," he urged her. "It would solve both our problems."

The guilt she felt at turning him down soon trickled toward indignation. How could he ask her to do this, knowing everything she was dealing with? He continued to chat amiably as he worked, but all she could think about was the pressure she now felt to solve his problem and his insistence that it would solve hers, too. How did he know what was best for her? She knew it was unreasonable, but her anger swelled nonetheless.

"Now, this is what we call a try-in," he was saying. "The veneer is placed with a little glycerin so you can make sure you're happy with it before it goes in permanently." He lowered the chair and held out a hand mirror. "Go over by the window so you can see it in natural light."

Looking in the mirror, all she saw were the worry lines carved between her pale brows, and her temper flared. "It doesn't look right," she said.

"No?" he said, coming up beside her. "Let's have a peek." He was an inch or so shorter than she, an effect that was amplified by his scrunching down and squinting up at her mouth as he gently pressed back her upper lip. "What's off about it?" he asked.

"I don't know . . . The color's wrong." She heard the bitterness in her tone, the absence of courtesy, and it made her even angrier. It was *his* fault she felt like a shrew.

"You think?" he asked mildly.

She glared into the mirror to avoid his gaze and tapped at the tooth. "This one's a different shade from the others."

"Dana," he said, the corners of his mouth tensing to avoid a smile. "That's your real tooth. The other one's the veneer."

She turned to stare blindly out the window, willing her unfounded fury back into its cage.

"Hey," Dr. Sakimoto murmured. "That wacko temp of mine is not your problem. You've got enough on your mind right now. And you've got to do what's best for you."

His understanding surprised her, and it served to tame her anger. "You were right about Morgan," she said finally. "She's purging."

"Yeah." He nodded.

"She won't admit it."

"She's ashamed. We all hide what we're ashamed of."

Of course we do, she thought. And yet this secret was out—to her dentist, of all people. She pulled air into her lungs and let it go. "The tooth is fine," she said.

"It's gorgeous," he agreed, motioning her toward the exam chair, "if I do say so myself."

CHAPTER
16

"ODE TO JOY" WAS ONE OF THE FIRST PIECES MOR-
gan had learned when she'd taken up the cello two years
ago. After practicing endlessly, she'd performed it for her parents.
Dana's memory was vivid: Morgan's frown of concentration as she
struggled to hit every note correctly and the bloom of pride once
she'd finished and looked up to find her mother's reaction. This was
replaced by mild disgust as she glanced at her father, a hint of uncharacteristic dampness welling in his eyes.

"Dad," Morgan had chided, "your allergies are out of control!"

Helpless to respond, Kenneth had looked to Dana. A glance
had passed between them then, a rare instance of pure and perfect
communication. *Yes,* that glance said, *she's real. This beautiful, talented, human manifestation of life's grace is real, and she came from us.*

Kenneth had reached over and squeezed Dana's hand so hard
she thought her pinkie might break, but she didn't care. She squeezed
back and said, "Morgan, could you get Daddy a tissue?"

"Looks like he needs a whole *box,*" Morgan had muttered as she
left the room.

Kenneth had pulled Dana into a quick but forceful embrace.
"Thank you," he whispered. It seemed to be the thank-you she'd
been waiting for her whole married life—a thank-you for everything,
all of it. "Thank *you,*" she'd whispered back.

The undiluted purity of that moment stayed with them long
after Morgan had returned with the tissues and they'd showered her

with praise and affection. For weeks they were more considerate and more attracted to each other than they'd been in years. He would call her during the day just to see what she was up to, and she made every single one of his favorite meals. They were affectionate during the day, passionate at night.

Eventually it faded. Their conversations slipped back into a simple conveyance of information: the septic system was due to be pumped; Grady had poison ivy again. They went to bed at different times rather than together for the purpose of intimacy. With a leaden sadness, Dana realized this return to a businesslike relationship hadn't surprised her. She knew then that they would never achieve the kind of indelible love she'd hoped for all those years ago. Apparently Kenneth had come to the same conclusion. It was soon thereafter, Dana later calculated, that he'd taken up with Tina.

But rather than a reminder of failure, "Ode to Joy" had become an overture of hope in Dana's mind. That feeling of utter connection was possible; if she had achieved it once for those few brief weeks with Kenneth, she might someday be granted another chance. Maybe next time it would take.

Dana had assigned the "Ode to Joy" ringtone to Morgan's incoming calls. It rang on Dana's cell phone as she pulled out of the dental-office parking lot. The call was brief. "Can I go to Kimmi's?" Morgan shouted from the noisy school bus.

"Sure. What time should I pick you up?"

"I can't hear you! I'll call you from Kimmi's!"

As she approached her house, Dana could see the avocado green station wagon in her driveway. She had a momentary inclination to keep driving, maybe surprise Grady by picking him up at school. But Grady loved the bus ride home with its reliable rowdiness. Besides, this girl Jet was just another teenager, Dana reminded herself, not a member of some suburban drug ring. *You can handle this,* she insisted. *Go meet Alder's friend.*

The girls were in the kitchen, Jet on her cell phone, eating from a can of salted almonds. "No way," she said into the phone as she crunched on the nuts. "Nuh-uh!" Alder nudged her, and she raised a hand and a quick glance to Dana, a faux-casual gesture that came off as impertinent and uncertain at the same time. Dana smiled and turned to Alder. "How was school?"

She shrugged. "Schoolish."

Jet fired another almond into her mouth and said, "I hope you told him he was a freak."

Dana tried to focus on Alder. "Do you feel like you're all caught up in your classes?"

"Hmm?" said Alder, distracted. "More or less." She nudged Jet again.

Jet held up a finger to indicate she'd be off in a minute. "I didn't say that, and I *wouldn't* say that, and I'm so *done* with this," and she snapped the phone shut.

"Jet, this is my Aunt Dana," Alder said, corralling Jet's attention before it wandered off again.

"Hi, Aunt Dana." Jet grinned a little too brightly.

"Can I get you something to drink, Jet?" said Dana. "Those almonds are pretty salty."

Jet glanced to Alder for interpretation, then said, "Uh, sure. Do you have any Red Bull?"

"Red Bull?" asked Dana, startled. Wasn't that something musicians and celebrities drank? She couldn't remember if it contained alcohol.

Alder laughed. "It's one of those energy drinks with like a ton of caffeine in it." She turned to Jet and gave her a little whack on the arm. "And no, my aunt does not stock Red Bull for her kids, Jet. She's a responsible adult."

Jet gave a sly smile. "She doesn't *look* that responsible." This was clearly a compliment. "I bet she has a private stash somewhere."

"Please," Alder snorted. "If she had a private stash, it wouldn't be Red Bull, for godsake."

"What would it be, then?" challenged Jet.

Dana's skin prickled with anxiety—what *would* her private stash be?

Alder slung her arm around Dana's shoulder. "That's *her* business."

Jet's phone began to ring, a thumping, intrusive sound, and she checked the caller ID. "Yeah, I don't think so," she told it. "Oh, shit—" Quick look to Dana. "Shoot! I gotta go. Walk me out?" She hooked her arm in Alder's. To Dana she said, "Nice to finally meet you."

"Nice to finally meet you, too," said Dana.

From the mudroom Dana heard Jet's loud whisper. "See, I was good!"

"Shut up," murmured Alder. "What were you—raised by wolves?"

"You've met my mother!" Jet let out a howl, and they laughed as the door slammed behind them. Alder had left her sweatshirt on the kitchen counter, and Dana walked it back to the TV room. The corner of a piece of paper peeked out from behind an end table where Alder had stacked her homework. Dana tugged out the paper and recognized Alder's handwriting.

> I might be going blind.
> Blind to the bold defiance of rogue color,
> Blind to the fearless play of shadow and light,
> Blind to the hand that aches to create,
> Severed from beauty.
>
> But also blind, mercifully blind
> To the dirty sameness of brushes in a crowded jar,
> To the angry smell of the mistreated palette,
> To the careless violation of the virgin canvas.
> I'm stricken by the gift of sightlessness.

Dana quickly tucked it back behind the end table, but the words continued to bubble up in her mind. *Blind . . . the careless vio-*

lation of the virgin canvas . . . and the memory of Alder's distraught face when she'd declared that Ethan boy unkind. These concerns sprang to the forefront when the phone rang just after they sat down for dinner. Morgan hopped up to get it.

"Please don't answer the phone while we're eating," said Dana.

"Maybe it's important." Morgan reached for the receiver. "Let me just check the caller ID."

"Morgan, please, I've asked you before not to—"

"'Osgood, E,'" she read. "Who's *that*?"

Alder called out sharply, "Don't!"

But Morgan had already hit the "talk" button and was saying, "Hello? . . . Yes, she's here." She held out the phone to Alder, whose face had gone dark with anger. Dana couldn't remember ever seeing such a look of fury from her niece. Apparently neither had Morgan. *Sorry!* she mouthed.

After a moment Alder took the phone. She stood up and strode out of the dining room. "Ethan," she snapped as she was leaving, and then, "Don't call me that, and don't . . ." She was quickly out of hearing range.

"I feel so *bad*," said Morgan, her face pinched in shame.

Grady chimed in, "She looked like her skin was gonna peel back and it would be all like gears and motors and stuff and she would maybe bite your body in half!"

"Shut up!" Morgan's hand lashed out to smack him.

Grady lunged sideways off his chair to evade her and landed on the floor with his feet up in the air. "Ow!" he yelled. *"Mommm!"*

"That's enough!" said Dana. "Grady, please get up and finish your dinner."

"But I don't—"

"Fine!" said Dana, her temper rising. "Just go get in the tub." He sprinted from the room, and Dana turned to Morgan, angrier at her daughter than she could ever remember feeling. How could Morgan be so inconsiderate? "I hope you know you owe her an apology," Dana snapped.

Morgan's eyes were shiny, and the corners of her mouth sank downward. "I *know,* okay?" Tears wiggled loose from her lids as she ran out, feet hammering up the stairs to her room. A door slammed. Dana let loose a frustrated sigh and surveyed the table, remains of the highly nutritious, half-eaten meal dotting the landscape. How did it all fall apart so fast? How did everyone go from fine to miserable in a matter of moments?

Grady had overfilled the tub, and Dana was about to scold him about it when she realized it wasn't actually full of water; soap bubbles took up about half its depth. Grady pasted some onto his chin. "I got a beard!" he giggled at her. "I'm a man!"

She offered a weary smile. "Don't forget your feet," she told him, and went to Morgan's room.

Morgan was sitting on her bed, back against the wall, clutching the Hershey pillow. Her jaw clenched as she worked to stave off future tears. "It was an *accident,*" she growled.

"I know." Dana moved a layer of clothing off Morgan's desk chair and sat down. "But, sweetie, you need to listen."

"I do listen!"

"This time you didn't," Dana said gently. "I asked you not to answer it, and so did Alder. You need to pay more attention to the people around you and not just do whatever pops into your head."

"If you want me to feel bad, you got your wish, okay? How should *I* know she didn't want to talk to that guy?" Morgan's eyes began to leak. "Does she *hate* me now?"

Dana got up and sat on the bed next to Morgan, wrapping her arms around her. The girl toppled sideways into her mother's lap like a felled tree. "No," soothed Dana. "Alder's not like that. Just think about the best apology you can give, and give it. Then it will be over."

They sat there for a few minutes, Morgan's upper half curled into the safe haven of her mother's lap. She took a breath and murmured, "And I'm not doing that throwing-up thing. I did for a while, but I stopped."

Dana felt a surge of hope. Maybe the problem had solved itself! But suspicion needled at her. "When?" she asked. "When did you stop?"

"About a month ago."

A lie. Or at least a distortion of the truth. "Well, I'd like to know a little more about that."

"Not now, Mom, okay?" Morgan sniffled pitifully. "I feel bad already." For good measure she added, "And I've got a test on photosynthesis tomorrow I haven't studied enough for."

Dana let it go. The admission, however flawed, had been made, and she could use it to sand down Morgan's resistance until the truth peeked through.

When Dana went downstairs, Alder was sitting cross-legged on the couch, working on math problems. She looked up when Dana came in, then went back to squinting at the textbook in front of her. "Sorry I lost it," she muttered. "Is Morgan freaked out?"

"She feels pretty bad. But I'm more concerned about you at the moment. How'd it go?"

"Good," said Alder, glancing up from her homework again. "I've been wanting to tell him what an utter waste of bodily organs he is, and I finally got the chance. It was great." Her eyes were dull and lightless; they dared Dana to contradict her.

"Okay," said Dana. But she remained unconvinced.

Late that night, with the house mercifully quiet, Dana sat in the office writing checks. There was enough to pay the bills this month, but she'd charged the repair of the sideview mirror to her credit card. That payment would be waiting for her a mere thirty days from now at the end of November—which was when she would start buying Christmas gifts, so December's bill would be higher, too.

Even worse, Kenneth's alimony check was substantially lower

than the approved amount. *I should call my lawyer,* she thought. But then she'd have to *pay* the lawyer and the mediator, and very possibly Kenneth would be able to prove that his income had dropped, and she'd end up with what he'd just given her. Except she'd be poorer for the expenses she'd incurred trying to get him to pay more.

I need a job.

That business with Dr. Sakimoto—what was that? she chided herself. He'd *offered* her a job, for Pete's sake, and she'd acted like he was forcing her to bungee-jump off Travelers Tower.

He's probably a great boss, she thought. Better than the senior partner at her old law firm, who could barely stay awake when she updated him on staffing or supplies but harangued her like a three-year-old when the lightbulb in his office wasn't bright enough.

Maybe she wouldn't have to work full-time for Dr. Sakimoto. And what if she could find someone to help out on the afternoons when she did have to work? Alder would help. But Morgan's situation was delicate; Alder couldn't be expected to police her the way a parent would. The phone on the desk rang, and Dana reached to answer it.

"It's me," said Kenneth. "I'm calling about Morgan." Dana leaned back in the chair. Kenneth rarely took the lead on anything pertaining to the kids. This would be interesting. "I've located a psychiatrist," he said, "a specialist in the field for over twenty years, and he admits to Connecticut Children's Medical Center if that becomes—"

"Excuse me—"

"—necessary. His credentials are excellent, and—"

"Excuse me, Kenneth, but let's just discuss this a minute." She put her feet down from the desk and sat up. "Morgan did finally admit to purging, but she says she's stopped—though I don't fully believe that. I called her guidance counselor, and he's going to talk to her. I think hauling her into a psychiatrist's office before we've even—"

"I'm not suggesting *hauling* her anywhere. But we've got to get ahead of this thing before—"

"And you think I'm ignoring it, waiting around for her to develop holes in her esophagus?"

"Well . . ." Kenneth blustered. "No, of course not . . ."

"I just don't think Morgan's ready for psychiatry," she insisted. "We need a clearer picture of what's happening, and I think we should wait to hear what the guidance counselor says."

There was silence at the other end of the line. She knew he was deciding whether to concede. "I'm trying to be supportive," he grumbled finally.

"And I appreciate it," she said.

A thought popped into her head then, only a half-formed notion, but she felt compelled to explore it. "How's work?" she asked.

"Same," he said. "We're in a holding pattern until this embezzlement thing dies down."

"Well, there may be some good news on this end. I've been offered a job." She bit the tip of her thumb for a moment. "I was thinking maybe you could help out with the kids a couple of afternoons a week. You know, just till business picks up again."

Kenneth let out an astounded laugh. "You're kidding, right? Dana, I have to work! Not just when I feel like it—all the time. I can't just *not show up* on a regular basis!"

"I'm not doing this for kicks, Kenneth," she said, her temper starting to flare. "*You* were the one who told me to get a job, so I—"

"Not a *full-time* job—just mother's hours, while the kids are at school."

Just mother's hours. Not a real job, not anything that would disrupt his dandy little life. Dana's jaw went tight with fury. "Well, I'm *sorry* it's not the right kind of job to suit you," she snapped, "but picking up hours at Kreamy Kones isn't going to cut it. If you want me to *contribute,* as you say, then the least you could do is be with them so I *can.*"

"Don't you tell *me*—" Kenneth seethed. "I have provided for this family for fifteen years! And what's *happened* to you? You used to be this sweet . . . You used to be so *nice!*"

"Well, I'm *not* anymore!" she yelled, and poked at the "off" button on the receiver. It was the second time in two weeks she'd hung up on him. Maybe he was right—she certainly didn't feel as nice as she used to. With a wisp of a smile, she realized, *Polly would be so proud.*

CHAPTER
17

T HE BRIGHTLY LIT PRODUCE SECTION OF STOP & Shop seemed festive and inviting after the somber cold of the late-October night. Customers dwindled as closing time neared, but Dana was still picking out pears, trying to decide between organic and "conventional." Could she afford organic? Would just a little pesticide be such an awful thing?

As she stood squinting at the yellow-green fruit, Dana's peripheral vision caught someone looking in her direction. When she glanced up, it took her a moment to put a name to the face: Nora Kinnear, Kimmi's mother. Oddly enough, her gaze was directed to Dana's feet. Dana looked down to see that she still wore the ragged sneakers she used for yard work. Before heading to the store, she'd remembered to exchange her dusty sweatshirt for a clean fleece jacket. But the sneakers—grizzled with dirt, threads unraveling at the toe—had come along for the ride.

"Dana, right?"

Dana glanced up to the elegant composure of Nora's face and felt her stomach go hollow. "Oh, hi!" she said. "Isn't this a great time to shop? We practically have the place to ourselves."

"I always shop at night," said Nora. Her cropped gray leather jacket was half zipped, revealing the bony ridge of her clavicle. "I work during the day."

"Oh, that's right. At that new store in the Evergreen Mall. Perfectua."

Nora smiled indulgently. "I'm the marketing director, so I don't actually work *at* the store. I'm at the corporate offices."

"That must be . . ." *What?* wondered Dana desperately. *What must it be?* ". . . exciting."

Nora gave a little shrug. "It's fun." She leaned slightly forward, inviting Dana into her confidence. "But at the end of the day, it's just work, you know?"

Dana nodded. She did know. Or at least she used to know. Twelve years ago when she'd last held a job. "So the girls seem to be getting along," she said brightly.

"Thick as thieves," said Nora, her fingers slipping into the front of the cart to align the straps of her Coach purse. "Your Margot is just a sweetheart."

"Um, it's Morgan, and it's so nice how they make new friends at this age, isn't it? I'm glad they found each other. Kimmi's a great kid." *Is she a great kid?* Dana had no idea.

"Girls, though. Not easy." The layers of Nora's short, mahogany-colored hair slid back and forth as she shook her head. "Are you around this weekend?" she said suddenly. "We're having a little get-together. Love to have you join us."

"Oh, let me think," said Dana, tapping her lips, feigning a calendar logjammed with activities. Then it came to her. She *did* have plans. "I'm going out Saturday night." Disappointment swelled in her: so many weekends without invitations, and now she had to turn one down.

"No, it's Friday. Just a little happy hour after work . . . or whatever you"—Nora wiggled her slim fingers—"do. Come by around seven—and bring your daughter to keep Kimmi company." She was taking a step back now, inching her cart toward the pumpkins and butternut squash.

Dana wanted to ask what she could bring—an appetizer or a dessert, maybe—but she would've had to raise her voice. *A happy hour,* she thought. *I could definitely use one of those.*

She finished her shopping and pulled in to the checkout line.

The woman in front of her was trying to calm a little girl sitting in the child seat of the cart, facing Dana. "Lolly, we're almost done," the woman was saying. "Just hang in there for a few more minutes, and then we'll—"

"Don't call me that!" the girl growled, her cheeks ruddy and damp. "Lolly's a baby name! I'm not a baby!" *About four,* Dana guessed. Almost too big for the cart.

The man in front of them had a mountain of groceries on the conveyor belt. "That price isn't right," he drawled at the checkout clerk. "Those are two for one."

The clerk flicked a switch, and a light began to blink above them. "Hector!" called the clerk. "Price check!" No one answered. "Hector!" The light continued to flash.

Dana could see only the weary mother's back, but she could hear her mutter, "Oh, God, please . . ." The girl began to twist in her seat, reaching out for the gum and candy. "No, Lolly—" The mother caught her hand just as she swiped a box of Twix bars onto the floor.

"Hey there," Dana crooned to the girl as the mother crouched to pick up the candy. She grabbed a banana out of her own cart and held it up to her ear. "Just a second," she told Lolly, "I've got a call coming in." It was a game she'd played with her own children often enough when a grocery trip had outlasted their patience. Lolly glared at Dana. "Hello," said Dana into the banana. She made a face. "Well, that's the silliest thing I've ever heard!"

Lolly's glare softened into fascination, so Dana continued. "There's no one named Lolly here." The girl's face went wide with surprise.

The mother was just replacing the fallen box of candy and turned to see who was saying her daughter's name. They recognized each other immediately—it was Mrs. McPherson.

"I'm sorry I can't talk to you right now," Dana told her, "I'm on a call." She pretended to listen intently to the banana. "Well, I'll check. But I'm sure she's not here." She looked at the girl. "You're not Lolly McPherson, are you?"

"Yes! Laura Jean McPherson! But *she* calls me Lolly." She pointed an accusing little finger at her mother.

"Well, it must be because you're so sweet," said Dana, catching Mrs. McPherson's quick eye roll. She handed the banana to Laura. "When you're done talking, could you peel it for me? I'm a little hungry." Mrs. McPherson actually laughed.

Laura held the banana to her ear. "Hello?" she said, joining in the gag. "That's too silly! Stop calling me!" and she hung up, landing the banana on her thigh. She laughed and looked up at Dana for approval, and Dana giggled back. The price check completed, the clerk was ringing up the man's groceries again.

Mrs. McPherson sighed. "Thank you," she murmured to Dana. "I was getting ready to take her and just leave the groceries here." Laura entertained herself with repeated hang-ups on her banana phone as Mrs. McPherson began unloading her cart. "I wouldn't usually bring her out so late, but she was giving me such a hard time about going to bed, and my husband's too weak to handle her these days. The minute she turned four, she got so stubborn!"

"My daughter's pretty stubborn, too," Dana commiserated. "And she's twelve, so she doesn't fit in the cart anymore."

"I'm in trouble when that day comes." Mrs. McPherson shook her head. "I always shop at night so I don't have to bring them. I can't imagine what single mothers do without a husband to hold down the fort."

Dana didn't know how to respond at first. It was as if Mrs. McPherson were talking about something that would never apply to her.

"Actually," said Dana, "I'm a single mom myself—divorced. It's tough, but you get used to it." She immediately regretted using the word "you," having meant it only in the general sense.

"Oh, I'm sorry, I didn't mean . . ." said Mrs. McPherson, embarrassed.

"No, it's fine," Dana assured her, relieved that the other woman hadn't noticed her gaffe.

"And you cook dinners for us on top of it all!"

"I like to," said Dana. "I really do."

The bags were loaded in the cart, and Laura handed her the banana. "It's for you." She grinned.

Dana took it and said, "I'm sorry, Mr. President, but I can't talk to you now. Please call back later." She waved to Laura as her mother wheeled her out.

While Dana was driving home, her cell phone rang. "Hey there," said a deep voice. "It's Jack. I called the house, and your daughter said you were out. But I didn't leave a message with her, just in case."

"In case?"

"In case you hadn't told the kids about us."

Us, thought Dana. The word hummed like a warm breath in her ear. "Good thinking."

"So I pulled Grady's emergency contact form from my football folder to get your cell number." He laughed and added, "Course, it's a misuse of official information. But what the heck, right? Live dangerously!"

Dana chuckled appreciatively. "Well, now you have it," she said, a hint of coyness creeping into her voice, "so you don't have to go stealing it next time."

"That's right," he teased back. "It's all mine, now."

This is flirting, she thought. *I am actually flirting!*

Jack presented his plan for their date: he'd gotten two tickets to Saturday's UConn football game. "Because I know how much you love football." The certainty in his voice made her wonder momentarily if he might be right. "I'll be by to grab you around three," he was saying.

"Sounds great!" she said. "I went to UConn, you know."

"No kidding!" Then he gave a little sigh. "I know I'm supposed to act cool, but I gotta tell you, I am really excited about this. It's been a long time since I met someone who gave me that feeling of . . . you know . . ."

Connection?

"Of just being really *pumped*. You are one special lady, and it's going to be great."

Dana wasn't asleep when Morgan came into the soft blackness of her bedroom, but just at the edge of consciousness, when sensible thoughts take unexpected turns. *The lawn mower needs servicing. I'll get Alder to help me put it in the back of the minivan, and then I'll raise the sail and let the wind take me out across the pond . . .*

Sheets rustling, bed creaking, a pillow being pushed up next to hers. "Mom?"

"Nuh?" snorted Dana, her head twitching in the direction of Morgan's voice.

"Mom, I feel bad."

"Okay," Dana muttered numbly.

"I shouldn't have lied to you."

"Lied?" said Dana. She was awake now.

"About the barfing." A hand slid onto Dana's forearm and pulled at the loose skin around her elbow. "I should have told you."

Dana shifted onto her side to face Morgan. A pale sliver of light sifted in around the door and cast itself across the girl's face. "Tell me now," she murmured.

"It's just . . . I just feel so fat sometimes."

But you're not! Dana wanted to say. *You're beautiful!* Yet she knew there was no traction in that approach. When had a mother's good opinion of her daughter's looks ever counted? *Facts,* Dana told herself. *Start with those.* "When did it start?" she asked.

"April vacation, when it got so hot and we had to go out and buy all new shorts because last year's didn't fit me. Remember that?"

Dana had only a vague image of it. The divorce had just been finalized, and she'd been in an almost constant state of distraction by the terrifying realization of her aloneness. The only thing she remembered was a similar look of terror on Morgan's face in the dressing room as she realized she was two sizes bigger. "Yes, but, sweetie, you're not done growing yet. Of course you need bigger clothes than you wore a year ago."

"Mom, stop, okay? Don't always give, like, *answers*."

Dana sighed. *Shut up, she's telling me. Just listen to her saying senseless things and keep my mouth shut.*

"So a lot of girls do it, and I tried it," Morgan said.

"A lot of girls?"

"Well, some. Or some girls just eat a peach or maybe a bag of chips for lunch. The baked kind."

"*Where* did you try it?"

"Here. You were at the lawyer's, signing stuff with Dad, and Grady was . . . I don't know, somewhere. I came home and ate a whole thing of ice cream. It was butter pecan, and I knew you wouldn't notice because it was Dad's favorite, left over from when he lived with us. There was, like, snow all over the top, but I scraped it off and pigged out." The image of Morgan sitting alone with her father's freezer-burned ice cream was heartbreaking to Dana.

Oblivious to this, Morgan went on, "I felt so sick I thought I was going to barf, but I didn't. And I was kind of disappointed, because I wanted all that ice cream *out*. You know how that feels? When you eat too much and you just want it *out*?"

Of course she did. All too well. "Yes," Dana whispered. "I do."

"So I went in the bathroom and put my finger down my throat. It's gross, and it kinda hurts. But afterward I felt way better. And . . . I don't know . . . mature. Because you weren't home, and neither was Dad, of course. But I handled it. I solved it myself, like Dad always says to."

Dana was glad Morgan couldn't see her face. *I could honestly kill him,* she thought, though she wasn't sure whom she blamed more— Kenneth or herself.

"But I stopped," said Morgan. "It was sort of taking over. I'd wake up and think about when to do it and what I'd eat and stuff. It was really distracting, so I stopped about a month ago."

And there it was—the lie Dana had somehow known was waiting for her. "Morgan," she said, "did you throw up the night of your party? I'm asking you to be honest with me."

There was no answer at first. "Yeah," she said finally.

"Honey, *why*?"

"I was just really worried the party would bomb and everyone would think I was a freak."

"But it *didn't* bomb. It went really well."

"I know, but just because something isn't bombing now, that doesn't mean it won't completely bomb a minute from now."

This was true, of course. Bombs dropped out of thin air all the time. Or just sat there ticking.

Morgan promised she was done with purging. It was behind her. And besides, she insisted, everything was going really well now. She was almost best friends with one of the most popular girls in school. Everyone liked her. Everything was fine.

D R. SAKIMOTO WAS ANSWERING HIS OWN PHONE. When Dana called the next morning, his distinctive baritone, with that oddly casual grumble to it, said, "Cotters Rock Dental, can I help you?"

"Tony?" she said, surprising herself. When had she gotten so comfortable calling him Tony?

"Yes?"

"It's Dana Stellgarten."

"Dana," he said with obvious delight. "Don't tell me your tooth is acting up. That was some of my best work."

"No, it's fine. Great, really." She dabbed the tip of her tongue at the tooth, realizing she'd hardly given it a second thought. "Actually, I, uh . . . I was calling to ask if you were still interested in my help—temporarily—as a receptionist."

"You're kidding me."

"Well, no, I'm not . . . but if you've already—"

"This is terrific!" he said. "You are completely making my day."

"I hope your day won't get unmade when you find out I can only manage part-time . . ."

"Dana, you're a single mom with young kids at home. I figured full-time wasn't in the cards."

Yes! thought Dana, giving the kitchen table a soundless little slap.

The conversation that ensued was measured by bits of negotiation interspersed with his now-familiar banter. "Be sure to bring your knitting," he told her. "Or whatever hobby you have."

"Pottery," she quipped. "I'll just clear a space for my wheel in the waiting room."

The compensation he offered was reasonable, and he felt he could manage with her leaving at three o'clock most days if she was willing to handle any straggling issues the following morning. However, on Wednesdays he worked from noon until eight, and he hoped she could find a way to get the kids covered for that one day each week.

"Oh, I can manage that," Dana said, though she had no idea how. Despite this hitch, Dana felt a tingle of victory. She had done it. As of Monday morning, she would officially be employed.

"Dad, *please!*" begged Morgan. She faced him in the dining room that night, dressed in her coolest jeans and skimpiest shirt. "Mom'll drive me to your house. Kimmi's *waiting* for me!"

Kenneth struggled to leash his features into a false composure, but the clenching of his molars made his temples throb with fury. "Mom should have checked with me first about that—"

"Morgan," Dana warned, "I told you it was only if Dad didn't mind."

"—but since she didn't feel the need," Kenneth continued, "*I* have to be the bad guy."

"Oh, my God, Dad, *why*? I'll be with you the *whole weekend*. And I'll be extra cooperative—I won't fight with Grady or ignore Tina, I promise. But you *have* to let me go to Kimmi's!"

Kenneth shot Dana a murderous look. "Morgan." His voice strained for patience. "It's Tina's birthday today. She's turning thirty, and she really wants it to be special. Special means *all four* of us together to celebrate her birthday. It is *not* optional."

Morgan turned to Dana and wailed, *"Mom!"*

"Sweetie, I had no idea Dad had plans. We should've checked with him before—"

"I HATE YOU BOTH!" screamed Morgan, and she stomped out of the room.

Kenneth pulled himself to his full height. "Do you have any idea of how badly you've undermined me? She's going to mope all night now and ruin Tina's birthday. I have half a mind to let her go to her damned friend's house, just to keep her from hurting Tina's feelings!"

Dana felt bad, but not about the potential ruin of Kenneth's evening. There was a tiny alarm going off in the back of her mind: *Tina is turning thirty, and she's insisting on spending her birthday with Kenneth AND his children?* "All four of us," he'd said. That's what special means. *That's what special* used *to mean,* thought Dana. *Except I was one of the four.*

"It was an accident," she told him dryly. "That's all I can say." Then she went out to the backyard, where Morgan held her arms wrapped around herself, weeping with fury and self-pity.

"And I can't believe you told Mr. Kresgee!" Morgan wailed.

So she'd finally talked with the guidance counselor. "Honey, I was worried about you," said Dana. "I needed to make sure you were okay."

"Mom, he came to get me in the lunchroom. *At lunchtime,*" she hissed. "I almost *died.*"

Dana could only imagine how embarrassing it must have been to be singled out so publicly. How could a school counselor be that clueless? "Did it help, at least?" she asked, knowing the answer before she'd finished asking the question.

Morgan shuddered at the memory. "He wears corduroys and he smells like mustard. I am *never* talking to him again."

Finally Morgan calmed down, and Kenneth herded both kids out to his car. And as much as Dana missed them on their weekends away, the quiet that settled over the house was a welcome relief. She trudged upstairs to get ready for Nora Kinnear's cocktail party, but nothing in her closet seemed right. She tried on every pair of pants she owned, finally deciding on the black jeans. *Jeans, casual,* she told herself. *Black, not too casual.* Finding the right shirt was hopeless, so that took much less time. The smell of beef stew met her at the bottom of the stairs—dinner for the McPhersons! In all the fuss with Kenneth and Morgan, she had nearly forgotten. Thankfully, the crusty bread, buttered peas, and apple crumb cake were already packaged up.

Alder and Jet were sprawled on the couch in the TV room, heads resting on opposite ends, feet fighting playfully for position in the middle. Dana interrupted a snickering disagreement over which horror film was the stupidest when she popped her head in to say she was leaving. "The number for the Kinnears is on the pad in the kitchen, and you know my cell number."

"Have fun," said Alder, reaching over to yank the clicker out of Jet's hand.

"Yeah," Jet giggled and heaved a pillow at Alder. "Have a boatload of it."

The McPhersons lived in the opposite direction from the Kinnears, in a little neighborhood where the houses were smaller and seemed to elbow one another for every inch of yard space. As much as she'd enjoyed seeing Mrs. McPherson and her daughter in the grocery store, Dana hoped no one would answer the door so she could make a quick drop.

The beef stew had leaked out of the pan and smeared her fingers when she picked it up. She hung the bag of side dishes from her wrist and carried the stew with her fingertips, rang the doorbell with her elbow, and silently counted to ten. She would leave the meal in the Comfort Food cooler on the front step if she finished before anyone answered. *One . . . two . . .*

The knob began to twist back and forth, and then there was a thumping sound. The person on the other side was knocking, as if he or she were the one trying to get in. "Mama!" called a thin little voice. "Ma-maaaa! Da door's locked!" The door began to shudder as the knob was rhythmically yanked from the other side.

Someone called from farther away, the words getting clearer as they approached. ". . . a minute! I can only do sixteen things at once." The door opened, and Mrs. McPherson was behind it, swinging a chubby toddler onto her hip.

"I'm so sorry I'm late," said Dana.

"No! Please, it's fine. It's so nice of you to come at all." Mrs. McPherson gave a shy smile and opened the screen door. She looked calmer than the other times Dana had seen her. Her eyes crinkled pleasantly; she seemed almost hopeful. "We always love Mrs. Stellgarten's meals, don't we, Monkey Man?" she said to the toddler, giving him a squeeze that made him giggle.

"Please—call me Dana."

"Well, Dana, I have to admit you're our favorite," she said over her shoulder as she led the way into the kitchen. "Not that we don't appreciate every meal people bring, of course." She plopped the little boy onto the tan Formica counter, mottled with faint stains. "But yours get the most points around this house, that's for sure."

Dana set down the stew on the kitchen table between the Magic Markers and scattered pieces of construction paper. "That's a lot more than I get from my own family," she said with a sigh.

"Naturally." Mrs. McPherson gave a sardonic grin, hip against the counter, her body a barricade to keep the little boy from falling.

Dana smiled back. "I don't know your first name," she said.

"Mary Ellen."

Dana held out her upturned hands, sticky with stew, and said, "Could I . . . ?" Mary Ellen turned on the water in the sink, adjusting it to warm. "How is he?" Dana murmured, rinsing her hands, wondering where in the house Mr. McPherson was.

The little boy squirmed against his mother, she swung him down off the counter, and he ran out of the kitchen. "Better," she said, handing Dana a dish towel. "They said he wouldn't be, but I didn't believe it. I told him he had to keep fighting, and it's finally paying off."

Dana wondered at this—the volunteer coordinator at Comfort Food had said Mr. McPherson was terminal. Was Mary Ellen right? Or was she in denial? Dana shuddered at the thought of how hard it would hit if the latter were true. "Is there anything else you need? Food shopping? Errands?"

Mary Ellen smiled gratefully. "That's so generous, but we just need to get through this so things can get back to normal. Please just keep bringing those yummy dinners. We always love it when it's Mrs. Stellgarten's night."

The Kinnears lived down one of those meandering side roads where even the smaller houses sat on enormous lots. As it turned out, it hadn't been necessary to squint at the numbers on the mailboxes to gauge how much farther to go. The Kinnear house was at the end, its driveway veering sharply off the cul-de-sac as if to snub its nose at the houses tethered closer to the street.

Dana parked behind a red Hummer and had half a thought to go home and change into nicer clothes. But she took a breath and walked up the driveway, clutching her little purse and a rather expensive bottle of cabernet, the label adorned with a print of the French countryside.

The house was smaller than she expected, given the length of the driveway. But it was well lit, carefully landscaped, and seemed to radiate a strange, almost visible heat through the large bay window. The silvery hum of jazz music beckoned her into the house.

Standing on the front porch, Dana wondered whether to ring the doorbell. The dark-paneled door was not quite closed. Was this a tacit invitation to push it open, or had someone neglected to shut it all the way? Dana rang the bell. She waited several minutes before someone came.

"It's open!" a man called as he yanked open the door. "Everyone knows to just come the hell in . . ." He was tall, well over six feet, and had short black hair that glittered silver here and there. His pink oxford shirt was rolled at the cuffs and open at the neck, though it bore the telltale wrinkles of having been recently constrained by a tie. The shirt was tucked into faded, unbelted, perfectly fitting jeans. "Friend of Nora's?" he speculated, hanging a hand over the top of the door. "Or are you lost in the woods, little girl?"

The cocky smile, the languid stance, his weight balanced on one leg while the other rested loosely—it was completely familiar to Dana. It was what some men did, particularly good-looking men, when they wanted to flirt a little, to establish themselves as the lead dog whose pack you might be invited to join. Dana handled the situation as she knew she was required to, by flirting mildly but by no means indicating a rejection of such an offer, if it were to be made. "Just on my way to grandmother's house." She smiled, holding up the bottle of wine. "Grandma likes a nice glass of red in the evening."

A sly, appreciative grin. He stepped out of the doorway finally and beckoned her in. "We'll text Granny and tell her not to wait up."

Dana introduced herself. "Our daughters are friends," she added, offering her hand to shake.

He accepted it and held it for an extra second. "Darby's mom?"

"No, Morgan's."

"Oh . . . Right! Morgan." It was clear he didn't know Morgan, but Dana took no offense. The fathers rarely kept up with their kids' rapidly rotating social worlds. "I'm Carter." He guided her down a pomegranate-red hallway hung with small charcoal sketches in enormous black frames, toward the jazz music and the loud hum of voices in the thrall of human contact.

Carter Kinnear made sure her hand was wrapped safely around the stem of a wineglass before releasing her into the uncharted waters of the party. Dana glanced around, noting a vaguely familiar face or two.

"Dana?" said a voice behind her.

Dana turned and reached out for a hug. "I am *so* glad to see you," she murmured into Polly's ear. "I barely know anyone!"

"I didn't realize you and Nora had hit it off so fast," said Polly, her grip a little looser than usual. "You should have told me." Then, as an afterthought, "You could've come with us."

"'Us'? Victor's here, too?"

Polly gave an eye roll. "Sniffing around the hostess with the mostess." Dana followed her gaze across the room. Victor was leaning against a granite countertop as Nora Kinnear talked, her long fingers pointing to herself and then away and then back again. His eyes never left her face as he took a swig from his beer. Nora must have sensed Polly's and Dana's attention, because she glanced toward them and quickly extricated herself. Victor gave Dana a wave as Nora made her way over.

"I'm so glad you came!" she said, her hands lighting on Dana's back as she leaned in for Dana to peck her on the cheek. "Polly always mentions you at book group, and I thought, 'She sounds interesting, I'll have to get to know her better.'"

Dana smiled, grateful for this gesture of acceptance. But as she glanced at Polly, something seemed slightly off. There was a tension behind Polly's smile, a subtle uneasiness that surprised Dana. Nora chatted blithely about how well Morgan and Kimmi got along, how they must have eaten half the batter of the brownies they made, laughing so hard they dropped the bowl. Dana explained Morgan's absence and apologized for the change in plans.

"Oh, Kimmi will understand. We've talked about how complicated it gets when parents split. Anyway, she has Devynne up there with her now, so she's got nothing to mope about." Her gaze skimming the room, Nora said suddenly, "Dana, you don't know Beth

Getman, do you? You've got to meet her. You two have so much in common." Steering Dana away, Nora said over her shoulder, "Pol, you don't mind if I steal her for a minute, right?" Then they were weaving through the crowd, stopping for Nora to introduce Dana to various friends. They never did catch up to the elusive Beth Getman, and Dana didn't talk to Polly again for the rest of the party.

Occasionally she saw her across the room, and it seemed to Dana as if Polly were watching her, or possibly watching Nora, who was always at her side, bestowing her with the gifts of new acquaintances. Why hadn't Nora included Polly? Dana kept meaning to circle around to her, but the opportunity never presented itself.

Hours later, as she made her way back down the driveway, feeling as if she'd gotten a good grade on a test she hadn't studied for, Dana gave her beaded clutch a little squeeze. She had made new friends—with people who didn't know her as half of Kenneth-and-Dana, or even as his duped ex-wife. She had soloed, and though it didn't feel quite as good as arriving on the arm of a man who loved her, it made her feel sharp and audacious and, oddly enough, just a little bit dangerous.

JACK GRIPPED HER HAND AND PRESSED FASTER down the sidewalk; her leather-soled mules slapped the cement, sending tremors into her ankles. Propelled toward Rentschler Field, she heard the aggregated buzz of forty thousand voices greeting friends, buying UConn sweatshirts, or excusing themselves as they made their way across the stands. Though she had graduated from UConn twenty-odd years earlier, it was Dana's first time at "The Rent," as Jack referred to it. In her day, football was played at Memorial Stadium, and she felt suddenly sentimental for her college days, which had seemed so full of drama at the time but were a cakewalk compared to her life now. Jack towed her along toward their seats, his enormous hand gripping hers, compressing her knuckles uncomfortably against one another. And yet she felt thrilled to be so explicitly claimed. *This one's taken,* he seemed to say with that hand. *She's with me.*

Once they were seated, Jack slid closer to Dana, pressing her toward the aisle. "Cold?" he asked as he rubbed her back.

"A little," she admitted.

"Wait till the game starts." He grinned. "That'll get your blood flowing."

Her feelings toward football could hardly be called passionate, but what was the harm? Dana was used to adjusting her own opinions to make room for others'. She *wanted* to like what he liked, and that was almost as good as actually liking it.

From her seat on the aisle, she saw a man and a little boy climbing the stairs hand in hand. "This one?" the boy asked at every row. "Is this our seats?"

"No, buddy," the man answered each time. "A little farther up." Dana found herself studying the man's face. He seemed familiar somehow. Suddenly he was staring back. "Dana!" he said.

"Oh, my God!" It was Billy, her college boyfriend. He looked older, of course, and weathered in ways she wouldn't have expected. But he was clear-eyed, and she noticed a wedding ring glinting on his finger just before he leaned down to hug her.

"You're a sight," he murmured in her ear. The embrace went a fraction of a second too long.

"Jack Roburtin," said a slightly peevish voice beside her. Jack's huge hand came out in front of her, momentarily obscuring her view.

"Bill Waterman, nice to meet you." He gave Jack's hand a double pump and stepped back into the aisle, putting a respectable distance between himself and Dana.

"Bill and I were classmates," Dana said quickly. "Where'd we meet? Freshman Spanish?"

"Yeah." He aimed his response at Jack. "At like eight-thirty in the morning. I wasn't *hablo*-ing too much español at that hour, if you know what I mean."

"Or any other hour," Dana teased.

"She got me through," he told Jack. "I got a C-minus, but I passed. *That* class anyway."

"Not much of a student, huh?" said Jack. His eyes wandered out onto the field, not waiting for the answer. His fingers slid onto Dana's and wriggled into an embrace.

Billy's gaze turned back to her. "No, not much." As he studied her face, she had a brief memory of his hands in her hair, his lips grazing her eyebrows.

Embarrassed, she turned her attention to the boy. "You like football?" she said brightly.

"Yeah!" he said. "Well, I never seen a game before, but I think so. I got a helmet!"

"You do? You're lucky—*my* son didn't get a helmet until just this year, and he's seven."

"I'm four and three-quarters! And I'm getting a hot dog, but I don't have to eat it all. And cotton candy!"

Billy rubbed the top of his little buzz cut, and the boy wrapped his arms around his father's thigh. "Okay, Sean-o, we better get to our seats." He took one last glance at Dana. "Great to see you," he said.

"He's beautiful," she murmured. *Good for you,* she wanted to say. Billy steered the boy up the stairs.

"Oh, COME ON!" Jack suddenly yelled toward the field. "You call that a KICKOFF?"

At halftime Jack huffed an aggravated sigh. He'd talked almost incessantly, coaching the game from his seat high above the sidelines, punctuated by shouts of, "OH, yeah! THAT'S what I'm talking 'bout!" or "It's called BLOCKING, for cryin' out loud! Quit the TAP DANCING!"

"When you think about the scholarships these jerks are getting," he now muttered, arms reaching up, stretching the tension out of his spine, "it makes you want to beat 'em with a stick."

"Come on, Jack," she chided playfully. "They're just kids. They're trying."

"You're right." He smiled indulgently. "But there's a difference between *trying* and *winning.* And if you don't have the mental toughness to kick some butt and win, you shouldn't be playing the game, is all I'm saying." He stood up. "Hungry? I'll run and get us some snacks. I gotta hit the head anyway." He climbed past her into the aisle and was gone before she realized he hadn't asked what she wanted. But there was something nice about his choosing things for her. Kenneth always insisted *she* get the food, so he wouldn't have to listen to any remarks if he didn't get just the right thing, he said. *Stop thinking about Kenneth,* she admonished herself.

"Hey, Dana." She turned to see Billy and Sean sitting two rows up. He motioned for her to come sit with them. "My curiosity's getting the best of me." He grinned as she squeezed in next to him. "What've you been doing the past twenty years?" She told him about Morgan and Grady and the temporary addition of Alder. "You always had a soft spot for the lost and lonely," he said. "If I were sixteen and mixed up, I'd find my way to your house, too." His smile faded a little. "And Jack's your husband?"

"Oh, he's . . . well, he's my date, I guess."

"You guess? You're not sure?" He laughed. "Because I'm pretty sure *he's* sure."

"*Uhh!*" she groaned. "I'm not used to this! It's my first date since the divorce, and I barely remember how to do it."

"Oh, you're a smart girl," he teased. "You'll get the hang of it. I felt the same after my divorce. But I finally met the right one and was ready to . . . you know . . . be the guy."

"The guy?"

"I was just hanging out for years . . . Well, *you* know that. But I finally got my act together and was ready to step up for once." He put an arm around Sean, who was happily licking at his stick of cotton candy. "I should've tried it sooner."

She grinned at him. "You're going to hate me for saying this . . . but I'm proud of you."

"Hey, you're Dana—you're unhatable." He gazed at her a moment. "So you like this guy?"

"Yeah . . ." she said. "He's Grady's football coach. You should see him with the boys—he's wonderful."

"Great." Billy nodded. *What are you doing with this loser?* is how it sounded in her head. She stiffened and looked out over the crowd. "He's nice," she said. "It feels good to be wanted."

He patted her knee, drawing her attention to him again. "Isn't *that* the truth." It was an apology, she knew. "You better get back," he told her. "I think Jack figured out we were more than just study partners."

"It's so good to see you." She sighed. "And meet your little pal here. Bye, Sean."

"Bye," said Sean, revealing the wad of melting pink fluff in his mouth.

Billy watched her rise. "Hang in there," he said. "Stay true."

True, she ruminated, waiting for Jack to return. *To what, exactly?*

The UConn Huskies did not win. "Spanked," Jack muttered derisively as they drove home.

"Where do the boys play tomorrow?" Dana asked.

"They don't play again till next Saturday. Coach'll have them busting their butts this week. Notre Dame is strong on defense, but their QB's recovering from a groin pull, so they'll—"

"No, *our* boys," said Dana. "Where are *you* coaching tomorrow?"

Jack blinked, reeling himself back to his own life. "Oh, yeah. Vernon." They talked about the game and a bet he had with a co-worker that he could sell more Ford F-150s by Christmas. Soon they were pulling in to her driveway. He unbuckled his seat belt and turned toward her, his hand resting on the back of her seat. "This was great," he said, grinning. "But I knew it would be."

"It was really fun," she agreed. The way his gaze kept flicking from her eyes to her lips made her heart pound as if it were trying to find an emergency exit.

"I feel really comfortable with you, you know?" he said. "Some women make you want to puff up the truth so you'll sound better. But you're not like that." A finger leaned out from the hand on her seat back and traced the curve of her cheek. "God, you're pretty." His face came closer, the blue of his eyes a darker, oceanic color in the dimness of the truck's cab.

With all his attention focused on her, Dana had a rare moment of feeling wonderfully lucky. *This is a good man,* she thought. Perhaps not as urbane as Kenneth, nor as insightful as Billy. But unlike them, he hadn't allowed other women or drugs to lure him away. Jack wanted *her.*

Now lightly kissing the corners of her mouth, Jack murmured, "You taste good." Gently, then more insistently, he probed deeper, a slow, sensual escalation.

I'm being kissed! she thought. *When was the last time . . . ? New Year's Eve . . . Polly and Victor's party . . . Kenneth patting my back as he gave me his last kiss . . .* This was so much better. Jack was a good kisser, but, more important, there was so much wanting behind it. She put her hand out to Jack's shoulder, and he nibbled her ear. "Let's go inside," he breathed.

Dana froze.

"Whoa, hey," he said. "It's fine."

"No, it's just—"

"Seriously, no biggie."

"Alder's home, and I wouldn't feel right . . ." Alder was sleeping over at Jet's. The house was empty. "Also, I'm not really—"

"Course not. My bad." He arranged himself back into his seat and slapped his hands on the steering wheel. "So when can I see you again?" He grinned and wagged a finger at her. "And don't say two weeks from now, because there is no *way* I can wait that long."

Wanted, wanted, wanted . . . the thought reverberated in her chest. "No," she said. "Neither can I."

H ER ALARM WAS SET FOR SIX-FIFTEEN ON MON-
day morning, but Dana was wide awake by a quarter to five.
Seamless, she kept thinking. *The kids should barely be aware that I'm
working now.* By seven she was in the kitchen making breakfast,
wearing an apron printed with the word MANGIA! to shield her
work clothes. Grady straggled in, his pajama top hanging off one
shoulder.

"Pancakes or waffles?" she asked.

"What day is it?" His half-lidded eyes squinted in her direction.

"Monday."

"Is there school?"

"Of course there is. Monday's a school day—you know that,
silly."

"We only get pancakes on weekends."

"Well, I got up early, and I just felt like making them. So which
is it—pancakes or waffles?"

"Toast," he said, slumping onto a kitchen chair and scratching
his neck. "We had pancakes at Dad and Tina's yesterday. He puts all
those chocolate chips in them."

Dana stared at the bowl of pancake batter. "Sounds like you
had a fun weekend." She poured Grady a glass of orange juice.

"It was awesome." He slurped at the juice. A drip ran down his
chin, and he wiped it on the shoulder of his pajama top. "We went
to Dad's health club, just him and me, and we had races in the pool

where you could only use one arm and stuff. I beat him fourteen times. No, *fifteen*."

"Where was Morgan?" Dana asked. *He better not have left her at his apartment to wander around on the Internet,* she thought, loading the toaster and slamming down the knob.

"Her and Tina went shopping in the West End."

He can't cover the bills, but they can go shopping in the West End? Dana fumed. *Boy, is he in for a phone call.*

"But it was so dumb," said Grady. "They didn't even buy anything! They just *looked* at stuff. What's the point of *that*?" He slumped further in his seat. "I don't want to go to school. I hate it."

"No you don't, honey," she said. "School's fun. Especially recess, right?"

"I hate it. Especially recess."

Dana was waiting outside the heavy glass exterior door of Cotters Rock Dental Center when Tony arrived with the keys, blue medical scrubs peeking through his unzipped leather bomber jacket. "You're early." He smiled warmly as he unlocked the door. "No surprise."

They completed her employment forms and went over how to find files, submit claims, and the like. "I had Marie give me the lowdown on this crazy phone system," Tony said, leaning over her as she sat in the swivel chair behind the desk. That strange scent he had, the commingling of mint and musky aftershave, drifted by her. "You practically need a pilot's license to operate it," he joked. "She comes in at eight-thirty if we can't make it behave."

The little bell that hung from the handle of the office door jingled, and a man in a business suit came in. He removed his Bluetooth earpiece, pocketing it as he approached the desk.

"Can I help you?" said Dana. Tony patted her on the shoulder and went back to his office.

At a quarter to twelve, Marie the hygienist came into the reception-ist area with a take-out menu from Nelly's Deli. "Do you mind or-dering?" she asked Dana. "Tony gets a veggie sub, no onions, and an iced tea. Just tell him when the delivery guy shows."

"Sure. And what are you having?"

"Nothing. I take my run during the lunch hour." Marie turned to leave, her posture light-pole straight. "Switch over to the answer-ing service right at noon. Otherwise you'll never escape."

Dana was eating her yogurt when Tony's lunch arrived. He came out and handed the delivery man some bills. Turning to Dana, he said, "Hey, you started without me."

"Oh, sorry—I figured it might be a working lunch."

"Nah," he said. "Come and join me." She followed him to the kitchenette at the back of the office, and they sat at the little wooden café table. Searching for something to say, she asked about the fil-ing system, though she'd already figured it out. Soon she'd ex-hausted all work-related subject matter, and there was a silence that lingered for several moments. Tony dabbed his mouth with a nap-kin. "So," he said. "How was your weekend?"

"Uh, great. How was yours?"

"Very nice, I gotta say." He stretched back in his chair.

"Anything in particular?"

"Well, since you asked . . ." He gave a little lopsided grin. "My daughter Lizzie was home from college, and I was a little nervous because my . . . friend was visiting. Martine lives in New York, and the two of them had never crossed paths before."

"How'd it go?"

"Surprisingly well." He nodded. "I don't scare too easily, but there's nothing to put fear in my heart like the girls giving my dates the once-over. It should be the opposite, right? I'm their father—they should be worried about *my* good opinion, I keep telling them." His face warmed with barely concealed pride. "But they never buy it. Their mother raised them well."

Dana smiled. "I'm sure you had a little something to do with it."

"A smidge, I guess. But you know mothers and daughters—it's a fight to the end, practically. All the while you love each other within an inch of your lives. It's a wonder any of you survive."

He's right, she thought. *I'm still not sure if I'll make it.*

"Their mother sounds pretty impressive." Dana said, wondering where the woman was now. Were they divorced? Would Kenneth speak so highly of *her* to a stranger?

"She was durable." Though he was still smiling, his voice had taken on a faint pinch of bitterness. "I used to say it was her best weapon—she could outlast them. Turns out she wasn't as durable as I thought, though."

His face barely changed, but the air in the room seemed suddenly charged with his sadness, and it stung Dana as surely as if she'd touched an exposed wire. A sound slipped out when she dared to exhale, a barely perceptible, *"Oh."*

"Bone cancer," he said. "Five years ago."

"Tony, I'm so sorry."

"Thanks." He nodded. "I still miss her."

"She sounds very special."

"Top shelf," he murmured. After a moment he asked, "So what about you? What did you do this weekend?"

Drawn in by the confidence he'd shared, Dana replied without thinking, "Well, I had a date."

"Yeah? And?"

"No, it was nothing. Just a football game."

"You like this guy?" It was the same question Billy had asked. Why was everyone so nosy?

"He seems nice enough." She shrugged, busying herself with wiping a drip on the side of her yogurt container. "First date, hard to tell."

"Sometimes," he said. "Other times you click from the start. But you're right, it's good to keep the jury out for a while, see how it goes."

She checked her watch. "It's almost one," she said, thankful for an excuse to stop talking about her tenuous love life. "I'd better get out there."

Dana was staring at a package of boneless chicken breasts, their damp pinkness lying exposed in the shallow Styrofoam tray. She was trying to decide whether to grill them or bake them when the phone rang. "Hello," she said, frowning at the chicken.

"It's me. And I'm about done with your little suburban exchange program."

Dana smiled. There was something strangely comforting about the dependability of her sister's sharp edges. She hazarded a playful rebuttal: "But she's just getting the hang of the language—she's almost fluent in entitled whining."

"Oh, I'll *bet*."

"Don't worry," Dana said, bringing the phone into the mudroom for privacy. "I haven't taken her to the mall even once. She's still yours."

"So what the hell is she *doing* there! It's been four fucking weeks!"

"Jeez, it has, hasn't it?" said Dana. It was the end of September when Alder had come slamming into her mailbox, and now it was almost November. "You must really miss her."

"*Yes,* I miss her—she's my goddamned *kid*! Like *you* wouldn't miss *your* kids. You'd be having a nervous breakdown after twenty minutes."

"My kids go to their father every other weekend, Connie," Dana said matter-of-factly, "so I'm a little more used to it than you give me credit for."

"Oh, all right—you're a separation all-star." Connie had a way of conceding a point while simultaneously implying there really was no point to begin with. "Either way, you still have my kid."

"Safe and sound. Actually, she stayed after school for help with a science lab, but want me to have her call you?"

Connie was uncharacteristically silent for a moment. "She's pissed at me."

"About not fixing her car?"

"Well, yeah, *that*," as if it were too obvious to bother mentioning. "But there's something else, and I don't know what. It's bugging the shit out of me."

"When did it start?"

"Hell if I know. Two, three months ago, maybe? At first I thought she was blocked and taking it out on me. She's got about six half-finished canvases lying at the bottom of the basement stairs where she threw them." Another aggravated sigh. "But then she never . . . you know . . . surfaced. She's not a moody kid, Dana. She gets pissy sometimes, but she always snaps out of it."

Dana sat down on the tile floor. The two sisters were quiet for a moment, silently contemplating their favorite sixteen-year-old. Dana considered whether to tell Connie about Alder's getting high but decided against it; Alder had promised it wouldn't happen again, and Dana trusted her. Best to focus on the more pressing matter. "You know about Ethan, right?" she said.

Connie knew that Ethan had stopped showing up sometime during the summer and then had left for college in Vermont. Dana told her about his phone calls and Alder's raging response.

"He called here, and I gave him your number. Miserable little prick," muttered Connie. "She *adored* that kid—they were best friends. He must have done something completely heinous for her to act like that."

"She won't tell me."

"*Make* her tell you."

"And how am I supposed to do that, Connie? Bribe her with Gummi Bears?"

"Like you always *used* to? Don't think I didn't know about that, by the way."

"I didn't bribe her. I gave them to her."

"So you could get her addicted to sugar and chemicals, like *you* are?"

"No, Connie. Just because she liked them."

Connie gave a little snort, her signal that the subject matter was no longer worthy of her attention. "You really should have called me, Dana."

"I know." Dana bit the tip of her thumb. "It just seemed like she might be getting a break from it here. I was afraid you might make her go home."

"Now *you're* the one not giving *me* any credit!"

"I'm really sorry." They agreed to keep in better touch, and Dana was just saying, "Bye Connie," when Alder came in the door. She gave Dana a worried look, then wrapped her arms around Dana's waist. "I can still stay, right?" she whispered.

"Of course, sweetie." Dana hugged her back. "As long as you need."

CHAPTER
21

MORGAN HAD GONE TO KIMMI'S HOUSE AFTER school and stayed for dinner. Dana now traveled through the twilit town to retrieve her. The cul-de-sac seemed strangely quiet, denuded of the late-model cars that had populated it during the party only a few nights ago. Dana walked up the winding driveway, car keys jangling against one another as the ring swung from her tensed finger.

Pressing the doorbell, she ran a hand through her hair, fingers snagging on the tiny knots that had spun themselves over the course of the day. The brush in her car had disappeared again, likely ending up in Morgan's backpack. She wished she had one brush that was always there for emergencies such as this, but did mothers have anything that belonged only to them? Dana certainly didn't. *There's no such thing as "mine,"* she thought, standing there waiting to be granted entrance. *Everything I own is up for grabs.*

Nora opened the door, her glance gliding over Dana like water over smooth rocks in a streambed. "You look nice—some sort of appointment?"

"Oh, thanks. No, I started a new job today and haven't had a chance to change."

"New job!" Nora ushered Dana into the pomegranate-colored foyer. "Good for you! Where?"

"Oh, no." Dana waved away Nora's excitement. "It's nothing. I picked up a few hours at my dentist's office. His receptionist needed a sudden leave of absence, and he was desperate." This was not a lie, Dana told herself; it was just an incomplete list of who was in need of what.

"Oh." Nora's smile remained bright while her enthusiasm receded. "Well, aren't you a team player, jumping in like that! He's lucky to have a patient with time on her hands."

Dana quickly moved the conversation away from her omission. "The tough thing is," she confided, "all my work clothes are so out of date. I feel like a throwback to the last century."

"Well, you told the right person." Nora gave her a playful little poke. "We have to go shopping at my store! I would *love* to help you pick out some things."

"Oh, my gosh, that is so nice," said Dana, hoping her horror didn't show. Even a few items at such an expensive store would decimate her budget. "But I don't want to bother you."

"Please?" begged Nora. "I love to dress people. Kimmi's like my own personal Barbie doll!"

To Dana's relief the girls chose this moment to come racing down the stairs, giggling, bumping shoulders. Morgan caught sight of her mother, and her face fell. "Mom, we're not finished!"

"Hello to you, too," said Dana. "Finished with what?"

Kimmi cut in. "We got this amazing recipe off Epicurious for these super-gooey bars with, like, chocolate and marshmallows and junk!" she gushed. "They're almost cooked!"

"I didn't know you two were making sweets again," said Nora, her polite-for-company smile tightening. "That sounds like a lot of calories."

Kimmi rolled her eyes. "We're only having one. I'll give Dad the rest to take into the office."

"Well, Dad can take them *all* into the office, because Morgan has to go home now. Besides, I don't want sweets sitting in your stomach all night." Nora turned to Dana with a commiserating smile. "They just don't understand how fast that stuff goes to the thighs, like we do."

Dana understood all too well, her own thighs hosting plenty of morsels she shouldn't have eaten. But she didn't like Nora talking to the girls this way. Morgan's list of worries was far too long already. "Morgan, can you go round up your things?" she said.

"You know," said Nora when the girls were out of earshot, "we don't have to shop. We should just go out for a glass of wine some night." Her face fell into a strange blankness that, for the briefest moment, reminded Dana of her father. "I feel like I don't really *know* anyone in this town," said Nora. "All we do is breeze by each other at parties or dropping our kids off at ballet or whatever." She gave an uncertain smile. "You want to?" she asked. "Go out some night?"

This unexpected sadness from Nora felt so familiar to Dana. "I'd love to," she said.

"I knew you would." Nora sighed. "You get it. Polly always says that about you."

On the ride home, Morgan gave the play-by-play of her day. She'd sat with Kimmi at lunch, of course, and Darby tried to sit between them, but Kimmi hung her arm around Morgan's neck and the two of them almost fell off the bench. "We laughed so hard our stomach muscles went all spastic!" She warmed her hands against the vent on the dashboard. "Then Toby came over to talk to me *alone*." Toby wanted her to ask Kimmi if Jason asked her out, would she say yes. Morgan immediately relayed this to Kimmi, who mouthed, *Oh, my GOD,* and said, "Tell him I'll get back to him." Then they ran to the girls' room, and Kimmi kept pinching herself because she couldn't believe the hottest kid in the grade liked her. They still hadn't come up with an answer yet.

In science class Darby wanted to be Morgan's partner for quizzing each other on the constellations, but Devynne asked her first, and even though Morgan was a little scared of Devynne ("She can be wicked mean"), Morgan decided to give her a chance, because she's really good friends with Kimmi. Devynne invited Morgan to the party she was having on Friday for Halloween. "But she told me not to tell anyone, because it's totally NL." Morgan leaned back in the car seat, toed off her boots, and put her sock-clad feet up to the heating vent.

"What's NL?" asked Dana.

"No losers."

The next morning Dana glanced into Grady's room on her way to the shower. He was sitting on the floor amid a thin layer of boy mulch: Matchbox cars, their paint chipped from multiple crashes; empty cereal boxes cut open and taped together to make a hangar for his small fleet of planes; clothes he'd stripped off and left where he'd been standing, like puddles of fabric.

"How'd you sleep, sweetie?" Dana asked as he rebuilt a dismembered Lego spaceship.

He slid the spaceship into the cereal-box aircraft hangar and looked up at her. "Can I have pancakes this morning? Like, a lot of them? I need to build up my muscles."

"Oh, sweetie, I think we might be a little late for that. I can make them tomorrow morning—on Wednesdays I don't have to go in to work so early."

"But I need them today!"

Dana glanced up at the *Star Wars* clock, where Yoda's misshapen green arms told her it was seven-fifteen. "Oh my gosh—the bus will be here in twenty minutes! Get dressed and eat breakfast, quick as you can!" And she raced toward the shower.

Once she was dressed, Dana hurried downstairs, her little zippered bag of cosmetics in hand. There were three stoplights between her house and Cotters Rock Dental, and she planned to apply her makeup at each of them. In the kitchen Alder was spreading pumpkin butter on toast and Grady was eating Rice Krispies, the milk a mysterious tan color.

"What's in your cereal?" Dana reached into the refrigerator for the container of yogurt.

"She-up," he answered around a large mouthful.

"Syrup," translated Alder. "My idea."

"What in the world for?"

"He was bugged because he couldn't have pancakes, but really he only wants the syrup, so . . ." She pinched her fingers and twisted her wrist, a pantomime of pouring. "Just a little," she added.

Morgan blew into the kitchen at a sprint, reached past her mother, and grabbed three plums from the vegetable drawer. "Can Kimmi come over?" She said it so quickly it sounded like one long word. Dana was still attempting to decode it when Morgan bolted for the mudroom. "Bye!" she yelled. Seconds later the front door slammed.

"I'll come home right after school," said Alder, who seemed to be pondering something that didn't suit her. "I'm pretty much caught up."

"Is everything okay?" Dana asked. "You look worried about something."

Alder shrugged. "There's always something to worry about if you look hard enough."

At lunch Tony told her about his older daughter's first cadaver in medical school. She'd named him Smitty, after a boy who had teased her throughout high school for being klutzy. "Spazimoto," he'd dubbed her, and he always seemed to be there to clap and congratulate her when she dropped her lunch tray or tripped over the edge of a carpet runner.

"My gentle little Abby sliced that boy six ways to Sunday!" Tony laughed, and Dana had giggled along with him, savoring the idea of the girl's symbolic retribution.

But the concerned look on Alder's face that morning felt

strangely ominous to Dana, and she couldn't quite settle in. When her cell phone vibrated in her pocket at a quarter to three, she wrestled it out of her pocket, certain it was bad news. "Hello?" she said anxiously.

"Hey there, beautiful."

Dana exhaled. "Jack."

"Expecting someone else?" he joked. "If you're waiting for a better offer, I can get off the line."

"No," she reassured him. "I'm a little jumpy today for some reason. How are you?"

He was just fine. He'd booked a trip to Tampa to visit his mother for Thanksgiving, and the Patriots had played well on Sunday, even with some key players missing. "You can't buy games like that," he told her. "When a bunch of guys who shouldn't win do anyway, it's like God wants everyone to be happy."

Everyone but the fans of the opposing team, Dana thought. "Listen, Jack, thanks so much for calling, but I really should chat later. I'm at work now, and if a patient walks in—"

"Working? I thought you were a home mom."

"Remember I told you I was starting a new job? At my dentist's office?"

"Oh . . . right," he said, his voice laced with disappointment. "Well, I guess you can't go to breakfast tomorrow. I'm working the evening shift at the dealership so I thought maybe we could grab a bite at Hebron Diner."

"Oh, I can do that—I don't have to be in till noon. That would be perfect!"

They made plans to meet the next morning. Dana grinned as she finished her work. *Don't be an idiot,* she chided herself, but the grin would not go away.

Sometimes she imagined little scenarios of their relationship becoming more intimate, thinking about it at odd times like when she was taking her makeup off at night. She would look in the mirror at her pink-scrubbed cheeks, a headband holding her hair away from her face like a young girl's, and she would think, *This is how he'll see me, just me, nothing else.*

However, the fantasy that slipped around in her mind, emerging and receding at her whim, was a completely different thing from actually doing it. With Jack. In real time. She was well aware that she could not simply put Jack back into her imaginary box if she felt like it once things were under way.

It was a quarter past three by the time she went out to her car, only to find that while ruminating about imaginary sex versus actual sex she'd left her keys on her desk. She was followed back into the office by a woman with a crutch and eyebrows pinched into furrows. She waved a bill at Dana like some sort of primitive weapon. "I hope you don't expect me to *pay* this!" the woman warned.

Although Dana promised to sort it out the next day, the woman refused to let the bill out of her possession and insisted on following Dana to the copy machine, hobbling ruefully down the hallway, to ensure that it was not "switched" with a less incriminating document. By the time Dana was back in the parking lot, it was three-thirty, and she had a moment of panic. How easily she had let her three-o'clock quitting time slide another half hour. And what could happen in thirty whole minutes with children at home unsupervised? Anything. Anything could happen.

When Dana got home, Grady was shooting a basketball toward the hoop on the garage. He slammed the ball against the pavement, dodging back and forth as if to evade sniper fire. He grimaced, snatched up the ball, and heaved it upward. It ricocheted off the rim and shot back, narrowly missing his head as it flew past him. Dana saw his face turn momentarily violent in exasperation.

She glanced to the house. The kitchen curtains were pulled back, and Alder was visible behind the crosshatched windowpanes. Her chair was turned sideways so she could see out the window to her left and attend to the books on the kitchen table to her right. Grady repeated his swerving and dribbling.

"Hi, sweetie," Dana said. "Sorry I'm late. You got home all right?"

"Huh? Yeah." He stopped, arched, and thrust the ball at the basket again. It hit the backboard, bounced across the rim, and leaped out. "Shit!" Grady muttered.

"Hey!" warned Dana. "We don't use that kind of—"

"*Sorry.*" His back was turned as he retrieved the ball, but she knew he was rolling his eyes. It was his eye-rolling tone.

"All right. Well, come in the house and we'll get started on your homework."

"Don't have any."

"Mrs. Cataldo didn't give any homework?" Mrs. Cataldo always gave homework, even on Fridays. And this was Tuesday.

"I did it already. At school." He dribbled faster, then sprang up and lurched toward the basket, released the ball, and stumbled backward as his feet hit the asphalt. The ball dropped through the hoop.

"Nice one!" said Dana, waiting for his stony expression to crack open in pride. But he just grabbed at the bouncing ball and began to dribble around the driveway again.

Dana went into the house, dropped her purse, and toed off her work shoes. A sweet, buttery smell wafted toward her as she rounded the corner into the kitchen.

"Hi," she said to Alder, whose homework covered the table. "How come you're in here?"

Alder jiggled her hand, tapping her pencil against a notebook. "Just being visible."

Dana filled the teakettle with water. "Want some tea? It's getting so chilly. I need something to warm me up." Alder shook her head, the eraser end of the pencil bobbing more slowly as her gaze darted out to the driveway. Dana sank down into a chair across from her and peered out the window, too. "Does he seem grouchy to you?" she asked.

"Yeah," said Alder. "Something's bugging him."

"Maybe because I'm working?"

Alder shrugged. A buzz sounded from the stove, and she got up and shut it off. Striding a few steps out of the kitchen to the bottom of the stairs, she called, "Morgan! They're done!" Then she gathered up her schoolwork and retreated to her room.

The girls skittered into the kitchen, simultaneously greeting Dana and jostling each other for oven mitts. Dana chatted with them as they slid the oatmeal cookies onto baking racks. Each girl took one, tossing the steaming gems back and forth between their hands to avoid being burned. When Dana called out the window for Grady to come in and have one, he said he had to practice more. She made a mental note to check in with him at bedtime and see if she could get to the bottom of his sour mood.

As she went up to her room to change out of her work clothes, Dana reflected that she'd been wrong to be so worried. No tragedy had struck—at least nothing more serious than a few missed baskets. Tomorrow was Wednesday, and she'd be at work until eight o'clock. Morgan would go to Kimmi's, and Amy Koljian had agreed to have Grady over to play with Timmy. Barring the unforeseen snafu, everything would work out just fine.

"TELL ME ABOUT YOUR DATE!" POLLY COMMANDED as she and Dana strode down the street, thankful to get their walk in before the granite-gray cloud cover burst. Dana told her everything, including the slightly embarrassing end of the evening. Then she recounted the breakfast she'd just returned from, how the waitress had tried to flirt with Jack and he'd ignored it, and round two of the kissing session that had occurred in her driveway in broad daylight.

"Well, he's an idiot if he thinks he can get in your pants that easy. I don't care how good of a kisser he is. I mean, come on, where does he think you live—the Playboy Mansion?"

Dana put two fingers up behind her head and said breathily, "Hi, I'm Fluffy!"

They lapsed into a fit of giggles and had to slow down, Polly clutching Dana's arm and choking out, "If you make me wet my new yoga pants, you're gonna wash them!"

Once they picked up speed again, Polly said, "No, really. Are you gonna sleep with this guy?"

"I don't know!" Dana groaned. "I like him, and I'm attracted to him, and I certainly don't want to sleep alone for the rest of my life. But, God, I'm just so *nervous!*"

"Yeah, and what if he turns creepy, like he wants to do it to the tune of the UConn fight song or something?" Polly started to warble, *"UConn Husky, symbol of might to the foe . . ."*

"Oh, thanks! Just what I needed—more things to freak out about!"

"You'll be fine," said Polly. "And it could turn out unbelievably great. Maybe this guy realizes how lucky he is and wants to treat you like a princess. You're a catch, Dana. Don't forget that. *You* are the catch."

"We all caught up for the moment?" Tony asked her that afternoon, resting a hand on the back of her desk chair as he peered at her computer screen.

"Yeah, you know you have this little dead spot in your schedule where nothing seems to be happening." Dana tapped the top of her pen against the screen. "Do you want me to adjust that when I make new appointments?"

"God no!" He chuckled. "That's the buffer zone. Usually I'm making up for an appointment that went over or taking someone who shows up early. But every once in a while . . ." He closed his eyes and gave a little snore, "I get a nap! Just give a shout when the next appointment shows."

She thought he was joking, but later when she nudged open his door, he was sitting in the big upholstered chair, head resting against the seat back. His face did not have that slack, recently expired look that people often have when they sleep sitting up, and Dana thought he might be meditating. But when she whispered his name, he didn't stir. "Tony," she called more insistently. Again nothing. She crossed the room and laid her hand on his arm. His eyelids fluttered open, and he smiled up at her as if he were waking from the closing scene of a wonderful dream.

"Sorry," she whispered, and left him to collect himself before his next patient.

As she drove out of the office parking lot that night, she wondered what he'd been smiling about, what vision could have caused such a contented look. And she wondered if they'd ever be close enough friends someday that she might be able to ask him.

Amy Koljian greeted Dana at the door when she arrived to pick up Grady. "They're watching TV," she said. "I hope you don't mind."

"No, of course not." Dana gave a grateful smile. She didn't care if his brain had turned to applesauce as he watched commercials for child-size battle gear and nutritionally vacant microwave snacks. He'd been supervised by an adult. He was safe.

"They had a hard time agreeing on what to do," Amy explained with a regretful sigh. "They just wore me out with the bickering, so I caved."

Bickering? Grady didn't bicker with his friends. "I'm sorry," said Dana, surprised. "I hope Grady wasn't being difficult."

Amy shrugged and gave her head a little shake that said, *Who knows?*—but without actually indicating that Grady *wasn't* being difficult. She inhaled dramatically as if to comment, thought better of it, and exhaled. Then she took another quick breath. "Well, I just wondered if Grady might be put off by Timmy's success. You know, at football. Coach Ro kind of favors him."

This annoyed Dana on two fronts: Jack was perfectly fair with the boys, and Grady might not be the best player on the team, but he certainly contributed. "Oh, I don't think Jack particularly favors anyone. Quarterbacking is a high-profile position." She added quickly, "And Timmy's great at it."

"Jack?" said Amy. "Is that his first name? I don't think I've ever heard it before."

Dana could have kicked herself. "It's on the team Web site," she said, but it had taken her an extra second to respond, and she was sure that in that time Amy had begun constructing her own idea of how Dana had gotten so familiar with the coach's personal details. "I'll just go round up Grady," she said, and moved toward the family room, from which a televised child's voice commanded, *"Try it! It's awesome!"*

They thanked Amy—Dana profusely, Grady tepidly—and went to pick up Morgan. In the car she asked him about the play date. Her questions degenerated from open to cross-examining the more he evaded her. When they pulled into the Kinnears' driveway, she turned to look at him. "Grady, I know you said that everything's fine when we talked last night, but it doesn't seem fine. And if you don't want to talk about it, I can't make you, but I can't have you behaving badly at other people's houses, okay?" He shrugged and looked away. She hoped that whatever it was, it would pass quickly and without further reason to defend him to the likes of that superior Amy Koljian.

Dana got out of the car and went up to the house to retrieve Morgan. After they had said their good-byes and stepped out onto the Kinnears' front porch, Nora opened the door again and murmured a strangely furtive, *"Dana."* When Dana turned, she saw the pinching tension around Nora's eyes. "Let's go for that glass of wine tonight."

Dana was torn. She felt sympathy for Nora, who seemed to have some hidden sadness, despite all her professional, financial, and social success. And it was flattering—Nora could ask anyone, and the answer would be yes, and not necessarily for the right reasons. There were plenty who would have exulted in the unhappiness of the popular girl. Maybe that was why Nora wanted her, Dana supposed, because she could be trusted. "I'm sorry," she said. "I haven't seen the kids all day. How about tomorrow night?"

They made a plan to meet at Keeney's Lakeside Tavern at nine o'clock the next evening, and Nora seemed grateful. "Indebted" was the word she used, and it reverberated in Dana's mind as she drove home.

———

At work the next day, Dana planned to call Grady's teacher around lunchtime to see if there was anything going on at school that might be causing this funk he was in. Was he having trouble with his work? Was he being picked on? Her cell phone rang a few minutes before the lunch hour, and Mrs. Cataldo was on the other end of the line, as if she had read Dana's mind.

"No emergency!" Mrs. Cataldo sang out, her words trilling in a manufactured levity that made Dana cringe. Maybe no bones had been broken, but something was up if the teacher was calling in the middle of the day, her voice coated in sweetness like caramel on an apple. "I'm just calling to check in," said Mrs. Cataldo, "see how things are going at home."

"I was actually going to call you in a few minutes and see if everything's okay at school."

"Isn't that a funny coincidence!" chirped Mrs. Cataldo. "Let me tell you what I'm seeing here." Her description made Dana's chest ache. Quarreling with friends, shoving in the lunch line, tipping out of his chair and causing a commotion. "And he's been insisting on staying in at recess. He says he needs to get his homework done because he's too busy after school."

"Well, that's strange," said Dana. "Unless he has a play date, he has plenty of time after school. I have a new job, but it's just part-time, and I'm almost always home to help him."

"*Ohhh,*" Mrs. Cataldo said sagely. "A new job."

Dana felt her face go hot. *Yes,* she wanted to say, *I went back to work because my husband left me, then his commissions dropped off and we were going broke. So I found a job that hardly affects the children at all, and I'm KILLING myself to make it all go smoothly. So don't you dare insinuate . . .*

"Thanks so much for calling," she said to Mrs. Cataldo. "I'll talk to Grady's dad, and we'll work on it from our end. Let's check in next week, okay?"

They said good-bye and Dana dropped the cell phone on her

desk. She took a deep, cleansing breath, the kind they talked about in labor-and-delivery classes, as if the excruciating pain of child-birth could simply be blown out of the body on a gust of carbon dioxide. But the ache in her chest stayed firmly embedded behind her solar plexus.

"Am I eating alone?" Tony's low voice sounded from the kitchenette at the back of the office.

"Be right there!" she called, but she didn't get up. Tears formed in the corners of her eyes. She had to leak just a little before anyone saw her.

Suddenly he was there in the doorway. "Hey," he said gently, questioningly.

"I'm sorry . . . I shouldn't be . . ." She picked up the end of her scarf that fell in a lariat around her neck and dabbed at the drips on her cheeks.

"What's this about?" he murmured.

She shook her head in aggravation. *Stop crying,* she told herself. *Stop right now.*

He moved toward her and reached for her hand, his warm tan fingers curling around hers and drawing her up out of her chair. "Let's go into my office in case someone comes in," he said, and led her to the overstuffed upholstered chair. He drew the wooden chair up beside her and sat down, reaching across to his desk for a box of tissues.

She blew her nose—a juicy, messy sound—and muttered, "This is so embarrassing."

"I spend my day in people's *mouths,*" he said, smiling. "You think a nose blow grosses me out? Besides, someday it might be *me* crying to *you,* and *I'll* be the one honking like a congested goose."

A quick laugh erupted from her then, and she felt better. She told him about the call from Mrs. Cataldo.

"Okay, first of all, I thought the generation of teachers who blamed the mother for everything would've retired by now," he said.

"And second of all, it doesn't make any sense that the sole reason for Grady's being out of whack is your part-time job. I mean, maybe there's no reason at all. Sometimes we just get in a funk for a few days, and then we snap out of it."

"But Grady's not a moody kid," she said. "This seems like something more."

"And if you say it is, then it is, because no one knows him better than you. But you can't just immediately assume it's all your fault, Dana. It's not your job to keep them from ever being sad or angry. It's your job to help them deal with it when it happens."

She nodded. Of course he was right. She fingered the soft, thin scarf, the ends now damp from her tears. "But it hurts when they hurt."

He patted her knee. "And what kind of mother would you be if it didn't?" He leaned back in his chair. "You know, let me suggest something. It's just an idea. But I'm remembering that after Ingrid died, of course my girls were completely miserable. We cried every day. Every single day for months. Then they stopped crying quite so much and slowly got back into the swing of their lives—middle school, high school, it's all very compelling, right? But about six months later, Lizzie, the younger one, started crying all over again. I couldn't for the life of me figure out why—and neither could she! Finally we figured it out together. It was almost the end of school, and she couldn't imagine what summer would be like without Mom. How would she know where to go and what to do without Mom to help her organize it? Who would ditch everything and take them to the beach while I was at work?"

Tony's eyes got a little shiny then, and Dana felt another tear slide from the corner of her eye. But it didn't embarrass her the way its predecessors had. A commiserating tear was nothing to be ashamed of. "So," she said, "maybe Grady's just feeling it again, that Kenneth's not living with us anymore."

"Maybe." He shrugged. "Hard to say. I'm sure you'll figure it out."

"Thank you," she said, and she wanted to say more, but he was getting up and it seemed as if the opportunity had passed. "I guess we'd better have our lunch," she said.

"Yeah, nothing like a good cry to work up an appetite." He wagged his finger at her. "And listen, don't cry in the reception area anymore, okay? People will think I'm mistreating you. Do all your crying in here with me."

At nine that night, Dana pulled her car in to the parking lot of Keeney's Lakeside Tavern. Grady and Morgan were in bed, and she'd left Alder in the kitchen finishing her homework. Gazing out over the shadowy waters of Nipmuc Pond, she realized she hadn't been there since Victor's birthday several years ago. Polly had surprised him by having all his friends waiting for him in the wooden booths. Victor loved the place, and he and Kenneth used to go often to have a beer and watch a game in the bar. Dana wondered if that was still the case, now that Kenneth lived in Hartford. With Tina.

Nora pulled up in her little silver BMW and seemed to emerge almost before it had come to a complete stop. "God, it's so great to be *out*!" she said as she clutched Dana against her. The buttery softness of her leather jacket smelled like the interior of a foreign car misted with perfume. She planted a light kiss on Dana's cheek and steered her toward the door of Keeney's.

Dana could feel the interest from the sparsely populated room as they entered. The volume of the general murmuring rose slightly, and she heard the word "wives" and a burst of laughter from a group of men at a booth by the windows who all seemed to have dressed from the same REI catalog.

Nora ignored it and told the bartender, "Two Amstels, please." Turning to Dana, she asked, "That okay with you?" It was fine with Dana—beer was cheaper than wine and lasted longer.

They made their way to a booth away from the other patrons and chatted about their daughters' plan for Halloween. Dana admitted she was sad not to have Morgan trick-or-treating in her own neighborhood for the first time. "Though I know she'll have a great time with Kimmi up by your house," she added.

"Oh, I know," Nora sympathized. "A little piece of your heart tears loose when they start doing things on their own."

Their conversation tumbled congenially over a variety of matters. There was the upcoming sixth-grade dance. And the confusing grading practices of the Spanish teacher. ("It's not her fault," said Dana. "I don't think she speaks that much English.") Then Kimmi's insistence on getting a puppy for Christmas. ("Over my dead body," said Nora. "There's no smell I hate worse than a wet dog.")

For Dana there was a delicious sense of having been admitted to an exclusive club, the membership fee waived by the club's president. Dana could feel herself warming to the honor, her responses growing looser and more confident as they talked. Almost an hour had passed before she realized that their beers were empty, and it was her turn to get the next round.

Nora took a long sip from the new beer. "You know why I like this place?" she said. "It's real. It's a cruddy old tavern, and it's not trying to be hipper or younger than it is. I'm so sick of that crap, aren't you? You know, how everyone our age is starting to dress too young? You can get away with it in your thirties, but not once you cross that steel bridge into Fortyland." She laughed humorlessly. "No *way*."

Dana was stumped as to how to respond. While she didn't think Nora dressed *too* young, she certainly seemed abreast of the latest fashions, with her cropped leather jacket and designer jeans. Also, Dana didn't feel that "everyone" was doing it. Yes, there were a few women trying far too hard to present themselves as fresh and hip, and this was clear in the way they talked and dressed and entered every room as if it were some sort of stalled frat party where people were just waiting for them to arrive so the good times could roll. But most people responded to these women as if they *were* the main attraction. And if that's what you said you were, and everyone seemed to agree, then what was the harm?

"It is kind of annoying. I just wish I could pull it off myself," Dana joked, trying to inject a little levity.

"No you don't—*trust* me." Nora's thumbnail worried the metallic edge of the beer bottle label. "It takes way too much effort, and it's pathetic, and it doesn't really work anyway. The husband still wants the newer model."

She's right, thought Dana, and a vague sense of futility began to lap at the edge of her newfound confidence. She looked down at her hands, resting idly on the table. Her skin was dry, scored with tiny white lines like threads across her knuckles.

"*You* know better than anyone," Nora said, anger sparking in her tone. "It doesn't even matter if they aren't as pretty as you. It's just that they're new. And you're not." She scraped harder at the label until an edge peeled off. "And you can't compete with that."

So Nora knew about Kenneth's infidelity. *Polly must've told her,* thought Dana, and the idea sent a prickle of anger across her skin. *It doesn't matter,* Dana told herself, *everyone knows.* But Nora seemed to have some personal experience of it. Dana glanced up into her sullen gaze. "Carter . . . ?" she asked.

Nora looked out the window to the night-blackened surface of Nipmuc Pond. "Not that there's any proof," she said. "No satin thongs in his suit pockets or anything."

"Then why do you think . . . ?"

"Because the guy's a hound!" Nora said irritably. "He was a hound when I married him, and I was an idiot because I thought I was so *all that,* he'd never want anything else. He picked *me.* I won. I'm the lucky fucking winner of a *hound.*"

Dana's hands felt cold; she slid them between her knees to warm them. And she was suddenly so tired. She wanted to lie down right there on the dusty floor of Keeney's or walk out the door and into the murky waters of Nipmuc Pond and submerge herself in blackness. Nora's anger and despair amplified her own. Men left. It had always been so in her life. Apparently it was a universal truth.

Nora patted the table to get Dana's attention. "Hey," she said.

"I apologize. I just killed a nice evening. Two friends getting together for some girl time."

"No, it just—"

"Sucks."

"Yeah," Dana admitted. "It does."

"And that's why women are as strong as they are and why we have such great friendships. Because we don't fool around on each other." Nora laughed, and the sound sent a breath of relief through Dana. "Well, that's not true. There's plenty of *biatches* in this town who'd be happy to stab you in the back. But not you." Nora grinned. "Polly always says you have a pure heart."

Dana laughed. "She does not!"

"Well, something like that anyway. True heart or true blue . . . grand ol' flag . . . Halls of Montezuma." Nora's grin was so wide she could barely make her lips pucker around the rim of her beer bottle to take another gulp.

"Very funny," said Dana, feeling her hands warm up again.

Nora finished her swig and let her bottle land heavily on the table. "You're the Top Gun of friendship, that's what you are!"

CHAPTER

23

WHEN THE ALARM WENT OFF AT SIX THE NEXT morning, Dana felt as if she were being defibrillated. Her body tensed against the attack, hand striking out to subdue the rogue appliance. It had been a late night.

Not all that *late,* she told herself. Eleven forty-five was only slightly beyond the point of tame, even for a school night. It was probably the third beer that had made her put her pajama top on backward when she got home—she noticed this as she rose and caught sight of herself in the mirror over the bureau. She knew she had not gotten drunk. Three beers was only one past her usual limit, though it was true that without Kenneth to accompany her to dinner parties or the occasional restaurant her opportunities for maintaining a respectable tolerance for alcohol had dwindled. She had gotten a little silly, maybe. Drunk, no. Definitely not.

She did remember laughing and telling Nora things about Kenneth that weren't flattering, such as his love affair with his pillow. She had mimicked him in a child's voice, calling it a "wittle piddow," throwing Nora into such a fit of giggles that the group of men had looked over at them.

"Oh, turn around," Nora had chided. "Haven't you ever heard people laugh before?" Startled, the men had immediately looked away, causing another round of barely controlled snickering from the women.

Now, as Dana stood in the shower with the hot stream of water eroding her sluggishness, she remembered that her cell phone had rung twice during the later part of the evening—first it was Kenneth, then Jack. Both times Dana had checked to be sure it wasn't a call from home, then made a show of silencing the ring, to Nora's grinning approval. At the time it felt careless and wild. Now she wondered what they'd been calling about. She'd check messages on her way to work.

Once dressed, Dana went to see that the kids were up. Morgan was at her desk, back taut with focus as she leaned over a textbook, scribbling into a spiral-bound notebook to her right.

"I thought you told me your homework was done before I let you watch TV last night."

Morgan didn't look up. Her hand continued to jerk across the notebook page. "It is. This is just social studies. There's a test next week."

"Okay, well, come down for breakfast soon—a real breakfast, not just plums, okay?"

Grady was still asleep, lying facedown on his bed, his mouth open, saliva darkening a spot on his pillow. When she called his name, his eyes flew open and he grunted, "Uh?"

"Time to get up, sweetie."

Grady rolled off his bed, landing in a crouch on the carpet. Then he stood up and scratched his side. "Did Dad talk to you? Can I go?"

"Go where?"

"To his house to trick-or-treat."

"I thought you were going with Farruk and Travis!"

Grady groaned and sat down on his bed. "He was supposed to talk to you!"

"Well, he may have called, but I was in the middle of something and couldn't pick up."

"In the middle of what?" Grady squinted at her suspiciously.

"Hold on," she said, wagging a finger at him. "What happened to Farruk and Travis? Because you can't just cancel on them for no good—"

"*They* canceled on *me!*"

"What? Why?"

"Because they're BUTTHOLES! And I hate them, and I'm going to DAD'S!" Grady flopped backward onto his bed and pulled the *Star Wars* coverlet over his face, his muffled sobs fierce and desperate.

She knelt next to the bed. "Okay," she soothed, patting his exposed stomach. He flinched away from her. "Grady? Can you come out of there so we can talk about this?"

"*No!*"

"Well, I've got a plan, but I can't tell it to a bedspread, now, can I? I'm not talking to a Jedi about this plan—I need to talk to *you*."

He peeked out from under the coverlet, Obi-Wan Kenobi's wrinkled hand spread across his cheek. "What."

"Here it is. While you're at school, I'll talk to Dad and we'll sort everything out, okay?"

"I am NOT trick-or-treating with those buttholes, so don't think you can make me!"

"Grady, I'm not thrilled about that word you keep using, so if you want my help, you'll have to find some other way to say you don't like them."

"I HATE them!"

"What is this about? How come they canceled?"

"Just call Dad," he grumbled, sitting up again. "I already told him everything."

When Dana checked her cell-phone messages, she found that Jack hadn't left one and she didn't bother to listen to Kenneth's. She had only a ten-minute drive to get a hold of him, and she knew his message would have no information. Kenneth hated voice mail, tended to say "Um" a lot, and got off as quickly as he could. He'd once admitted to her that it was his only shortcoming as a salesman—he could not leave a compelling message. Dana called his cell phone, assuming that he'd be on his way to work.

"Hello?" said a woman's voice, tentatively, as if she were already regretting the decision to answer. Dana's first instinct was to hang up and call Kenneth's work number. But she needed to get to the bottom of this trick-or-treat problem quickly—in the next nine and a half minutes, if possible; otherwise she'd have to wait until her lunch break.

"Hello?" the woman's voice came at her again. "Are you there?"

"Yes, I'm here," Dana retorted. "May I speak to Kenneth, please?"

"Yeah, uh . . . he's in the men's room. You want to hold on? Or he could call back when he's done."

Done? In some *men's room* at seven forty-five in the morning? Where the heck was he anyway?

"I swear I'll have him call you," insisted the woman. "This is . . . this is Tina, by the way."

You're not "by the way," thought Dana. *You're right in the middle of everything.*

"Jeez, where *is* he?" muttered Tina. "He doesn't usually take this long unless he's—"

A snort of disgust erupted from Dana. Did this Tina actually think she didn't know how long her husband of fifteen years took in the bathroom? Or that she'd care to discuss this personal and mildly revolting information with his mistress?

"Oh, ick. I'm sorry," said Tina. "That was super inappropriate."

Dana sat at the first traffic light, right hand gripping the wheel as if she might rip it from the steering column, left hand holding the cell phone a few inches from her ear. *Okay,* she counseled herself. *Calm down and drive carefully. You can NOT afford another accident.*

"Uh, Dana?" came the voice again, squeaky with worry. "I know you don't want to talk to me, and personally, I can't blame you. I'd be way pissed if I was you. But since Ken seems to have fallen in or something, do you want me to just tell you about the Grady thing?"

Damn *straight* she was pissed. The bimbo seemed to get that at least. "Yes, just tell me," Dana snapped. "I have to get to work."

"Okay, well, Grady's been calling a lot. Sometimes he yells at Kenny and says mean stuff, like he's cheap because he doesn't coach any of Grady's teams—which isn't true, it's just because it's not baseball season, and you and I both know that's the only sport Ken has any *clue* about. Or he'll cry and say he hates school, and all the kids are buttholes, and why can't he just go to work with Ken." Tina let out a whispery sigh. She sounded perplexed, even concerned. "It's like he's not sure if he hates his dad or loves him, you know?"

The pain in Dana's chest, growing steadily as Tina spoke, now pressed against her lungs. *"Oh,"* she said.

"I know it," Tina said. "Poor little guy."

An image emerged in Dana's mind of Grady as a baby. He'd woken from a nap while she was vacuuming. She hadn't heard him babbling to himself, nor had she heard the babbling turn plaintive, then desperate. By the time she'd turned off the vacuum, Grady's screams were frantic. She'd rushed up the stairs, whisking him out of his crib, cuddling him and crooning her apology. But he had arched his back and refused to be consoled. He continued to yell at her, his little pink tongue quivering in his wide-open mouth. "It's over," she'd kept saying. "You're safe now, sweetie. I've got you."

But it wasn't over for him until *he* determined it was over. Not then and not now.

"Um, Dana? It's my turn, I gotta go. Just call back when you decide about tonight. I won't answer, I promise. Kenny's all broken up about this, by the way."

Good, thought Dana, turning in to the office parking lot. *I hope he hates himself for it.* But before she could respond, Tina said, "The nurse is waiting. Bye." And the call ended.

Dana sat behind the steering wheel, the engine silent now, Tina's words echoing inside her chest. Oak leaves, brittle and lifeless, skittered across the parking lot, swept along by the late-October breeze.

Poor little guy.

Grady, her funny, unpredictable boy. She'd had no idea that Kenneth's leaving had affected him so profoundly. How had she missed it?

It's like he's not sure if he hates his dad or loves him.

Dana slammed her hands against the steering wheel. *Goddamn you, Kenneth!* But goddamn him for what? For leaving, yes, but people left—Dana knew that all too well. Sometimes they left even though they continued to sit right there in the same room. Which was worse, in a way, because you had to watch them leaving you over and over every day.

If she agreed to let Grady have Halloween in Hartford with Kenneth (and how could she not?), she would be alone. Morgan would be with Kimmi, Alder would probably be off with that Jet, and Dana would be left to hand out candy and scare off teenagers from tossing toilet paper through the crabapple tree as they'd once done years ago. The very thought of it depressed her.

There was movement in the periphery of her vision—Tony walking toward the door of the building, his wide shoulders hunched against the cold. One side of the leather bomber jacket flapped out, and the wind pressed his blue scrubs against the slight protrusion of his stomach. He was about five feet six inches tall, she guessed.

He caught sight of her sitting in her minivan, gazed at her for a moment, and then cocked his head toward the glass door as if inviting her to join him. She got out of the car.

"And how's my completely indispensable receptionist this morning?"

She tried to smile. "Hanging in there."

"Yeah?" He unlocked the door and held it open for her. "Because for a minute there, I thought you might be planning to greet our patients in the parking lot today."

"It's a thought," she said, shrugging off her jacket. "I could offer valet service."

"I'm all for improving the patient experience," he said, smiling, "but I prefer to have you in the building. Someone to call 911 in case I drill my hand or something." He stopped before going into his office. "Seriously—everything okay?"

The bell on the glass door jingled. She nodded to him. "Thanks for asking." And she went to her desk to greet the first patient.

Her cell phone rang around nine. It was Kenneth, but she didn't answer. The waiting room was full of patients, and she knew it would be a tense conversation. Not because she'd have to give up Grady for Halloween; she'd reconciled herself to that. It was the call with Tina that had her feeling brittle and desiccated, as if she were made out of straw. Tina was real for her now, no longer Kenneth's Imaginary Girlfriend. Before today she might as well have been Kenneth's pillow—comforting, perhaps, but without any actual human qualities.

Dana accepted that she was someone's ex-wife, the first Mrs. Stellgarten and not likely the last. But there was suddenly a clearer sense of her own obsolescence layered onto that. How would she talk to Kenneth, how would she even seem recognizable to herself, now that she was so obviously just a figment of his past?

At lunchtime she listened to the messages he'd left on her cell phone. The one from last night was short (despite being riddled with "um"s and "uh"s) and merely alluded to a situation they should discuss. The second message began with an intake of breath and then, "Dana," as if he were confirming her name to some anonymous third party. "I didn't mean for her to . . . uh . . . I should have told you myself that Grady was, um . . . and I apologize for that. So would you please call so we can discuss it? . . . This is Kenneth."

No kidding, she thought. *I know who you are, for Pete's sake.* His discomfort soothed her. It sounded so much like her own. This made it a little easier to dial his cell phone for the second time that day.

"Hi," he said tentatively, and before she could respond, he added, "I really didn't . . ."

"I know," she said. "Let's just talk about Grady."

Afterward, Dana took her lunch to the kitchenette, where Tony sat with his half-eaten sub and a bottle of iced tea. She knew she would tell him about Grady—he already knew part of the story. But she surprised herself by also recounting her first conversation with Kenneth's girlfriend.

"Sounds young," Tony said.

"She just turned thirty last week."

"Even younger than that," he said, raising his eyebrows. And he was right, she realized, smiling at the suggestion of Tina's immaturity. Tony smiled back, gave a little shrug, and added, "But hey—that's *his* problem."

D ANA HAD JUST RIPPED OPEN A PACKET OF SPLENDA and was dusting the steaming surface of her tea with it when Morgan came in. "I thought you were going to Kimmi's," she said, surprised.

"Yeah, um, I was . . ." Morgan's hands were tucked up into the cuffs of her fleece jacket, and her shoulders were hunched as if the afternoon chill had followed her into the house. "I just wanted to get in a little cello. I'm way behind on that piece for the concert."

The holiday strings concert was six weeks away, and Dana was tempted to point that out, but Morgan was already moving toward the stairs. Soon a melodic humming punctuated by random moments of silence drifted down.

She's nervous about something, Dana realized. Morgan was not a very good musician, and she regularly complained about pieces being boring or too hard. In fact, she'd told her parents last fall she was quitting. But then Kenneth had moved out after New Year's, and the cello had stayed.

The mudroom door opened and slammed, and Grady came loping into the kitchen without even taking off his backpack. "Can I go?" he asked. "To Dad and Tina's?"

"Dad and I talked about it, and he'll pick you up at four-thirty," she said, removing the backpack from his shoulders. "He'll bring you back in the morning. Why don't you put your skeleton costume by the door so you don't forget it."

"I'm doing the ninja costume from last year. That skeleton one's stupid." He shrugged off his jacket and let it slip to the floor as he crossed the kitchen toward the cabinet with the snacks.

"What? Two weeks ago you were begging me for it. You thought it was the coolest thing ever." Dana picked up the jacket and draped it over the back of a chair. Grady started to climb onto the counter, but she nudged him down and reached into the cabinet for the Cheez-Its.

He plunged his hand into the box, then tilted his face upward and released about half the handful into his mouth. "Skeletons are for babies," he said as he crunched. "They would've made fun of me."

"No they wouldn't. Lots of kids do skeletons. Besides, that costume was expensive, and I can't return it now."

"Well, they already *did* make fun of me," said Grady, jamming the rest of the crackers into his mouth. "A lot."

Dana studied him. "What did they say?"

He didn't answer her for a second; then he blurted out, "They said I was *already* a skeleton, but I was like a skeleton *without bones*! And then they pretended they couldn't see me for the rest of recess!" He slammed the Cheez-Its box onto the table. It tipped over, and little orange squares splayed out across the tabletop.

"Oh, Grady." She reached for him, and he buried his face against her stomach. "That was a mean thing to say. You are definitely *not* a skeleton without bones."

"Can we move?" he begged, his voice muffled against her sweater. "I hate it here."

"Is that why you don't want to trick-or-treat with Travis and Farruk?"

"No, they're just jerks! My whole school is full of jerks, and it *bugs* me, that's all!"

Fighting with friends, Grady's teacher had said. He was sour and irritable from missing his dad, and his friends weren't putting up with it.

"You know what I think?" she said.

"What?"

"I think you need something to get your mind off this," she coaxed. "And I can't wait one more minute to find out what happens in *Rowan of Rin*."

He looked up at her finally, chin resting against her stomach, his eyelashes sparkling with dampness. "I don't want to *read*," he said, groaning.

"How about if I read and you just listen?"

He wiped his nose on the sleeve of his shirt and considered her offer. "That could work," he conceded. "When's Dad coming again?"

"Four-thirty. Go get the book."

By ten of five, Grady had been picked up by Kenneth, and Dana had driven Morgan to Kimmi's house. Alder called to say that she and Jet had plans to see the *Rocky Horror Picture Show* at the Goodwin Street Cinema in East Hartford. "What are *you* doing?" she asked.

Dana explained the whereabouts of Grady and Morgan. "So I'll be here, handing out candy."

"By yourself."

"With my book, which I haven't had a chance to read in weeks." She tried to put a good spin on it. "It'll be nice to have a little time to myself."

"I could come back and hang with you. I really don't mind."

"No, sweetie, go have fun. I'll be happy as a clam here with my book." But then Dana had a thought: Was Alder looking for an out? Was this code for "Make me come home"? She murmured quickly, "Unless you *want* me to tell you to stay in. You can blame it on me if it helps."

"Oh, that's so sweet," Alder said, in that way she had of making Dana feel like an adorable toddler. "But actually, I think I'm better off distracted. I had a really good Halloween last year, and if I think about it too much, I'll get all . . . you know."

At five-fifteen, with the last rays of light simmering at the edges of the treetops, the doorbell rang for the first time. Two ballerinas, a firefighter, and a raccoon. The raccoon costume was beautiful, clearly made by a seamstress who knew how to tackle fake fur. "Quite a costume," Dana remarked, catching the young mother's eye as she doled out 3 Musketeers bars to the children.

"My mother-in-law," muttered the woman with a quick eye roll. "It's dry-clean-only."

Dana offered a sympathetic laugh and said, "Oh, for Pete's sake." The woman smiled back—relieved, it seemed, to be understood at last.

Probably got into a snit with her husband about it, Dana thought as the children chimed out their prompted thank-yous and took off for the next house. She returned to the kitchen to read her book, wishing her husband-related snits were as simple as an interfering mother-in-law.

But apparently the book did not want to be read. She usually loved science-fiction romances, loved imagining herself in a place and time so disconnected from her own. There were always riddles to be solved and antagonists to be outsmarted. But though the odds were stacked against them, the lovers always discovered the one scenario that would unite them in the end. And the love scenes were quite satisfying in their level of detail. *Just enough to make you feel as if you yourself were being made love to by a powerful yet kind intergalactic warrior,* Dana often thought, *but not so much that you were forced to visualize his "throbbing member."*

Handsome warrior or no, however, Dana couldn't make herself attend to the story. Her thoughts drifted to Grady. A skeleton with no bones—what was that supposed to mean? And how had he gotten to a point with his friends that they were calling him names and pretending he wasn't there? Her own father had never coached her basketball team, or even gone to a game, but it hadn't made her angry or inclined to fight with her friends. To the contrary, it was even more important to stay on good terms, despite the ebb and flow of petty disagreements and betrayals.

Connie, though—she bounced in and out of friendships as if it were a contact sport. Everyone was eventually determined to be stupid or annoying, though she did seem to put up with the ones who were entertaining a while longer than most. Dana assumed this was also the case with Alder's father, but, having no idea who that was, she couldn't be sure.

After quitting art school, Connie had waited tables at Durgin Park in Boston, a restaurant known for its surly staff, where her snide remarks were appreciated as part of the "experience." Her scrupulously stashed tips had funded an extended trip to Europe.

Dana had almost lost touch with her then. Connie called occasionally (though never on holidays and birthdays, when you *wanted* her to call). Soon after she left, Dana had gotten married and immersed herself in creating a home life that conformed to her ideals of wedded happiness. It was easier to have Connie out of the picture—she had a way of letting you know your ideals were crap. "So how's it going over there in White-Picket-Fenceville?" she asked during one of her infrequent international calls. "Has it all fallen to shit yet?"

But soon thereafter Connie had come home pregnant. And strangely sad. And even more strangely quiet.

"She's all inside herself," their mother had said. "For once."

Connie had moved back into the house in Watertown, Massachusetts, where they'd grown up. Their father was gone, and it was good for their mother to have a baby to care for. Dana took every opportunity to visit. It was unanimously agreed that Alder was a miracle of a child. Smart and funny, with an uncanny knack for making each of them feel uniquely adored.

And now that beatific child had shoe-polish-black hair (though it did seem to be growing out a little) and had to be distracted from remembering the good Halloween she'd had last year.

The doorbell rang throughout the evening as Dana tried unsuccessfully to read her book. Each time, she made enthusiastic comments about costumes, doled out candy, and checked to see if anyone was lurking around with rolls of toilet paper, eyeing her trees. No one ever was.

The doorbell rang again when she was in the bathroom, and she had to wash her hands quickly and call out, "Coming! Be right there!" as it chimed several times more. She grabbed the plastic witch's cauldron of candy and yanked open the door. Expecting to look down into the faces of little treat beggars, she was taken aback when the only face on her porch towered above her.

"Trick or treat, beautiful," said Jack Roburtin. A set of red velvet devil horns stood erect from his sandy blond crew cut.

"Jack!" she said with astonishment that bordered on horror.

"I know." He grinned. "I'm a little early, but I couldn't wait." He stepped into the mudroom and closed the door behind him. "I was so psyched you didn't call," he added.

"I didn't . . . call?"

His right arm, which had been tucked behind his back, now brought forth a Whitman's Sampler of chocolates. "Bet I'm the only trick-or-treater who brought his own treat," he said.

"Oh, that is so . . ." she said appreciatively as she took the small box. "But did we . . . ? I don't remember talking about—"

"No," he said. "The phone message. I called your cell last night, because I'm trying to be discreet and everything." Dana had been at Keeney's with Nora, and she'd shut off the ring. "But you didn't answer, so I figured the best thing was to leave a message on your voice mail at home. Don't worry, though, I was planning to hang up if one of the kids answered."

She'd forgotten to check the messages when she got home. "I have to admit I never did get the message, Jack. What'd it say?"

"That I'd plan to come over around nine unless I heard from you. I figured your ex would have the kids." He scanned her for confirmation. "Oh, wait—does he? Did I mess up?"

"No, it's fine," she said. "As it turns out, none of them are home right now."

"Excellent!" he said. "Then you won't mind if I give you a

little . . ." He leaned over and kissed her cheek. It was tender and soft, and when he finished, he whispered into her ear, "Your skin is the best." His arm circled her waist and drew her to him so that her stomach rested against his. He wanted to kiss her lips, she knew that. She tilted her face up to his.

There was a thumping sound, and for a second she thought it was his heart hammering against her chest. In the next moment, the thumping was louder—footsteps coming up her porch steps. The doorbell rang.

"Don't answer it," Jack whispered.

"I have to," she murmured apologetically, tugging herself out of his grasp. "It's Halloween."

She shooed him into the main part of the house, out of sight of the costumed throng. The group was bigger, older, and their costumes were more haphazard. Most of them simply wore their sports uniforms. A few were hoboes. One was Tinker Bell, but she was clearly only in it for the way the outfit showed off her shape. "Happy Halloween!" called a boy's voice from the back. "If you're sick of answering the door, we can just take the rest of the candy off your hands." The group guffawed their approval.

"That's *very* thoughtful of you," Dana said with a knowing smile as she tossed pieces of candy into their pillowcases, "but I don't want the next group of kids to go away disappointed."

"There's no one out anymore!"

"Just in case," she said and closed the door.

She found Jack sitting in the living room, one arm stretched out along the back of the couch. It was clear that he meant for her to sit next to him, beneath the shelter of that arm. As she did so, something in her resisted. It was the devil horns. They made him look silly. *Like an overgrown boy,* she thought. She reached up, tugged them off, and tossed them onto the coffee table.

"Hey," he said, feigning anger. "My costume!"

"You're too handsome to be a devil." This was true. He certainly was attractive, with those smoky blue eyes. "And who wants to kiss the Prince of Darkness?" She smiled. "Not me."

He smiled back, puffed up a little from the compliment. "Now, where were we . . . ?" he murmured as his arm behind her began to pull her in for a kiss. It was a good kiss. He was a good kisser. But all Dana could think was, *"Now, where were we"? Who says stuff like that anymore?* She found herself drawing back, and as she did, something across the room caught her eye. She turned to look and realized that it wasn't actually in the room—it was out the window. A white ball of some kind was being thrown in her yard. Toilet paper.

"They're doing it!" she said. "They're throwing—"

Jack followed her gaze, and in the next moment he was up off the couch and dashing out of the room. "Son of a—" she heard him mutter.

Then he was in the front yard. Through the window she could see him cutting off the escape route of one of the boys as the others ran from the property. Without actually touching him, Jack was using his intimidating size to corral the boy, shaking a finger at him and pointing to the trees. ". . . NO RESPECT . . ." she could hear him say, and then he was pointing to the house and yelling, ". . . ALL ALONE . . ." and ". . . IF I EVER . . ."

He stood there, arms crossed over his expansive chest, and supervised the boy's removal of the toilet paper from the crabapple tree. Dana was astonished. And enormously thankful.

The phone rang. "Yeah?" she answered, still watching Jack and the boy.

"Mom?"

"Oh, Morgan," she said. "Are you done trick-or-treating?"

"Whoa, that was weird. You never say 'Yeah' when you answer the phone."

"Well, I . . . Where are you?"

"At Kimmi's," she said. "Can I sleep over? Also, can we just quick go over to Devynne's? She lives up the street."

"Sure, sweetie. Do you need me to drop off some pajamas?" Jack was pointing to pieces of toilet paper on the lawn now.

"Kimmi'll lend me some. I don't have to go to Devynne's if you don't want me to. I can just stay here and listen to Kimmi's iPod."

The boy was holding out the flimsy pieces of paper to Jack. Jack was waving him off, gesturing to him to put them in his own pocket. "Is Kimmi's mother okay with you two going?"

"Um, well . . . yeah."

"Then I'm fine with it. But don't stay too late, okay?"

"No," Morgan said quickly. "Kimmi promised we'd only go for a few minutes."

"Sounds good." The boy was leaving now, and Jack was walking back toward the house. "I'll pick you up in the morning, then. Love you, Morgan."

"Bye, Mom."

When Jack walked into the living room, his cheeks were pink with cold. Dana reached out to put her hands on them. "That was amazing," she said.

Jack reached up to her wrists. He pulled one hand down to his mouth and kissed her palm. "Hey," he said with a proud little grin, "no one TPs *my* girl's house."

And then she was up on her tiptoes to kiss him, pressing herself against him, wanting to be claimed by him. His thick, powerful arms drew her in tight, his hands running up and down her back. She kneaded her fingers into the rope of muscle across his shoulders. He kissed her harder, and his teeth clacked against hers, a momentary snag in the silky feel of wanting him.

He unbuttoned her blouse; she responded in kind, untucking his polo shirt and pulling it off. He had a handsome face, yes, but this was nothing in comparison to the masterpiece that was his chest. Smooth, unmarked skin, chiseled pectorals, and a navel anchored like a perfect little boat among the gentle swells of his abdominal muscles. Dana's fingers traced across the magnificent chest. A gratified growl rumbled from his throat, and she knew she had delivered a signal, and the signal had been received and decoded, and that sex would happen in the very near future. And that was fine with her.

She did feel a tingle of anxiety about how it would go, and what it would imply, and what would happen afterward. But mostly she thought, *It's time. Time to be claimed by someone new.*

A few minutes later, she was naked (or mostly naked—her socks were still on and her bra hung by one strap from her shoulder). The soft nap of the couch fabric pulsed against her from below, as Jack Roburtin did the same from above. *Kenneth and I never had sex on the couch,* she mused. *We were never in so much of a hurry that we couldn't wait till we got to the bedroom.*

And she wondered if she should be insulted that Jack Roburtin had a condom so handy he barely had to break away for more than a moment to reach it. But at least she wouldn't have to worry that she was, at that very moment, contracting AIDS or, God forbid, getting pregnant.

Might Alder walk in? She'd said they were going to an eight-o'clock movie, and it couldn't be much past nine. Plus, East Hartford was twenty minutes away. Probably safe on that score.

Dana knew she should be focusing more. She would never achieve a climax if she didn't, and she was certain Jack would be disappointed if there was no tangible, audible evidence that she was enjoying herself. No matter how many times she'd tried to assure Kenneth that it didn't indicate some failure on his part, he tended to sulk if she didn't hit the high note.

And yet it was like reading that book: her mind kept wandering around like a hummingbird, flitting from one thought to another. Maybe she had adult-onset attention deficit disorder.

For Pete's sake, focus! she told herself. *Pay attention!*

What she noticed was that Jack's cologne, pleasant at normal distances, was a little overpowering with her nose so close to his neck. His hand cradled her head, and she thought that was nice. His protectiveness was very appealing, and the more she thought about that—the way he'd handled that awful toilet-paper-throwing boy, his voice saying, *IF I EVER*—the more aroused she became. Eventually she was able to achieve her goal, just moments before Jack exploded with groans that signified his satisfaction.

Phew! she thought. *Just in the nick of time.*

She and Jack lay on the couch together. She was on the outside edge facing the windows as he curled around her from behind. "Was this too soon?" he asked.

"No," she said. "It was just right."

"I can't stop thinking about you, Dana. I think about you all the time."

It took her a moment to know how to respond, but before the silence turned awkward, she said, "I feel so comfortable with you."

This was true, she realized. She'd spent so much time trying to be a good wife and mother, puzzling out what each member of her family needed from her. But she never found herself doing that with Jack. He seemed only to want to be with her, and though her presence wasn't always easy to provide, she didn't think about it much.

Eventually they put their clothes back on, averting their eyes modestly from the other's buttoning and zipping and buckling.

"Alder will be back any minute," she said, generating a little sigh of regret.

"I should probably get out of here, then, huh?"

"Well . . ."

"But we'll see each other on Sunday. It's the last game of the season," he reminded her.

They kissed good night. And then he left. Dana took a shower, put on pajamas, and got into bed. When Alder came in, she was reading her book.

"How'd it go?" Alder asked, studying her.

"Fine. How about you? Were you distracted enough?"

"As much as I could be, I guess."

"Were you with Ethan last year?" Dana probed gently.

Alder slumped down onto the side of Dana's bed. "Yeah. We went as Franny and Zooey."

"The brother and sister from the J. D. Salinger story?"

Alder nodded. "No one got it. Not one person could guess. I never even told anyone until now." Her jaw tightened. "Asshole probably did. Probably told everyone." Dana reached out and stroked the back of Alder's hand. "I'm glad I'm here," Alder said wearily. "But being anywhere kinda sucks right now." She turned her palm upward, and Dana continued to run her fingertips across it.

Dana wanted to say something, but everything that came to her sounded hollow and false. She watched Alder stare into middle space and continued to stroke her upturned hand. After a minute the tension in the girl's face seemed to ebb, and her shoulders slid a little lower into their sockets. Alder gave Dana's hand a gentle squeeze, rose, and left the room. Soon Dana heard the water run in the bathroom downstairs, then the bleating of the springs on the pullout couch.

She propped her book against her bent knees and began to read with renewed focus, as if it were important, as if it might solve something, even though she knew it would not.

"CAN WE DO THE ROUTE THAT GOES BY VILLAGE Donuts?" Dana asked Polly on their walk the next day. "I've been craving a latte since the moment I woke up this morning."

"Yeah, nobody smokes anymore," teased Polly. "They just have a post-sex coffee drink."

Dana groaned. "Do you think I jumped the gun? I've only been dating the guy for a week!"

"I lay the blame squarely on Tina."

"*What?* Why?" said Dana, startled into breaking stride. "I mean, I'm all for blaming Tina—as far as I'm concerned, she's responsible for global warming, world hunger, and athlete's foot."

"Right." Polly grinned. "And for turning you into a sex-crazed dental receptionist."

"No, really," said Dana, slowing to look at Polly. "I don't want her to be the reason for *anything* I do. I can barely stand that she exists."

"Exactly. She's . . . she's like"—Polly squinted in concentration—"like a *factor* out there. And you were kind of pretending she wasn't."

"I was not!"

"Yeah, and then when she turned out to be real, you threw caution down the garbage disposal and slept with your boyfriend. It breaks that last tie with Kenneth. Makes a ton of sense."

"Polly!"

"What? I'm serious."

"I do not base my personal decisions—or *any* decisions—on the existence of that bimbo!"

Polly pursed her lips, unconvinced. "Okay, new subject. How's Morgan doing?"

Dana took a few more irritated strides, then sighed. She could never stay mad at Polly. "She's better, I think. This friendship with Kimmi Kinnear has given her a lot of confidence. She doesn't seem to feel the need to . . . you know . . ."

"Puke."

They didn't talk for a few moments, the thought of their beloved Morgan heaving up the contents of her stomach sobering them into silence. "She definitely seems happier now," Dana said finally. "She slept over at Kimmi's last night. And went to a party in the neighborhood—some girl in their class named Devynne."

"What's the last name?" asked Polly. "Maybe I know them."

"Oh, I never got a last name. I figured if Nora was okay with it, they must be a good family."

"So you didn't call and speak to the parents? Because you really ought to do that, you know. Sometimes the parents are completely out of the loop."

"In sixth grade? Isn't that more of a high-school thing?"

"Well, yes and no," said Polly. She told a story about her son, Peter, going to a friend's house to watch a *Stargate* marathon one Saturday afternoon when he was in middle school. "It was still daylight, for crying out loud!" said Polly. The parents were at a sibling's track meet and were gone for hours, never suspecting that a bunch of preteen boys were sampling their Grand Marnier and peach schnapps.

"How did you find out about it?"

"One of the boys threw up chunks of red, and they thought he was about to die and called 911." Polly gave an exasperated head shake as they arrived at Village Donuts. "Turns out he'd used the booze to wash down a jar of maraschino cherries. He was a straight-A student, too! It's amazing how dumb these very bright kids can be." They ordered their coffee and sat at one of the faux-wood booths, sipping down their drinks before going back out into the stinging breeze.

"Well, I'm sure everything went fine," said Dana. "I called over there this morning, and the girls were still asleep. Nora would have told me if anything had happened."

Polly took another sip and gazed out the window. "I'm sure she probably would," she said.

On her way to the Kinnears' to retrieve Morgan, Dana called Kenneth. The evening had gone well, he said. They'd gone house to house in the West End, passing UConn Law School in their travels. "He loved seeing the law students wandering around in crazy getups." Kenneth chuckled. "This one guy was SpongeBob SquarePants, and he actually had about a hundred yellow sponges stuck to him. Grady couldn't get over it."

"I'm just wondering when you're bringing him back," said Dana.

"Oh, well, maybe I should hang on to him until his game tomorrow. I'll be coming to Cotters Rock for that anyway. Saves me a trip."

Tomorrow? thought Dana. *I let you take him for a night—Halloween, no less—and you keep him for the whole weekend? I don't think so.*

"What does *Grady* want to do?" she said, biting back the urge to add that she didn't give a flying fig about saving him a trip. Grady was already in his swim trunks, Kenneth reported. Dana could hear him in the background muttering, "Come *on,* Dad!" They were on their way to the health club. Dana talked to Grady briefly, his answers monosyllabic and impatient.

She was about to hang up when Kenneth got back on the phone. "Just one more thing . . ." he said, sounding as if he were gathering his courage to deliver something unpleasant. "I'm bringing Tina to Grady's football game tomorrow."

"No you're not," she warned.

"Yeah," he said. "I am. It's the last game of the season, and he wants her to see him play."

"Goddamn it, Kenneth . . . god*damn it*."

"I know," he said. "If it helps, I'm not exactly looking forward to it either."

"No, it *doesn't* help!" she yelled. "Nothing helps!"

Kenneth was quiet for a moment. Then he murmured, "Tina's not going anywhere, Dana. Trust me on that one. She's here, and we have to do this, and we have to make it look normal for the kids' sake."

For the kids' sake? The kids would have been better off if their father hadn't screwed around with his goddamned lady barber *and left the family!* she thought. Her breath rushed in and out of her mouth. Kenneth knew enough to keep his own shut.

"Fine," she muttered.

"We'll keep it brief."

"Yes," she said, pulling in to the Kinnears' driveway. "Do that."

When Nora opened the front door, she said, "They're still sleeping, can you believe it?"

"What time did they go to bed?" asked Dana, still rattled from the conversation with Kenneth.

"Oh, who knows!" Nora fluttered her long fingers and started up the stairs. "Those two could talk the oxygen out of a spaceship." She turned back toward Dana, still standing below in the foyer. "Well, come on," she said, grinning mischievously. "I have a present for you."

Dana followed her up to a large master bedroom swathed in hues of gold and cream: lemon- and butter-colored striped wallpaper, sheer ivory swag curtains, a king-size bed loaded with a satiny amber down comforter shot with threads of gold and mustard. Nora disappeared, apparently swallowed whole by her own decor, but then she emerged from a walk-in closet. She held out a gold- and black-checked shopping bag with PERFECTUA printed in red up one side. "Okay, it's not a true gift-gift because I got it at work, but when I saw it on the samples rack, I knew it was meant for you."

Dana carefully removed the tissue-swaddled item. It was a blouse, a creamy champagne color. The collar was wider than she usually wore and came to sharp points. The cuffs were long and tight, with three small, flat mother-of-pearl buttons at each wrist. Darts running up from the bottom hem to each breast emphasized a narrow waist and ample chest. The tiny tag inside the collar said simply PERFECTUA—SOIE.

"This is so . . . It's . . . Are you sure?" Dana stammered.

"Sure?" said Nora, as if the word were unfamiliar to her. "Of course I'm sure. Try it on." She crossed her arms over her narrow rib cage and waited.

For a moment Dana didn't know what to do. Was she supposed to disrobe in front of Nora? Nora wasn't moving, and she wasn't offering the privacy of her bathroom, so Dana pulled her gray cabled turtleneck over her head, her upper half now clothed only in her worst, most stretched-out purple bra.

"You'd wear a different bra, of course," said Nora, "but raw silk covers pretty well anyway."

Dana put on the shirt, careful not to let her fingernails snag the delicate material. As she buttoned up the front, Nora adeptly did the buttons at her wrists and flipped the cuffs back. Squinting critically at the blouse, she adjusted the shoulders and fussed with the collar, sliding her fingers down the tips so they hung in perfect symmetry. Then she pivoted Dana until she was facing an enormous mirror hung over a low chest of drawers.

"Brilliant," she breathed. Dana wasn't sure if she was referring to herself or the shirt.

The two women spent several moments gushing to each other about the shirt's utter perfection: how it could be worn with dressy jeans or a floor-length skirt, how its color accented Dana's sandy blond hair, how its cut was so subtly flattering that no one would ever say, "How flattering"—people would simply think you looked *that good.*

All the while Dana kept thinking, *I will never be able to reciprocate with anything nearly as perfect.* The fact that Nora had paid nothing for the blouse didn't factor in. She felt shaky knowing that one day Nora would see that Dana's gift-giving capabilities would never measure up.

"Mom?" Morgan was standing in the doorway staring at her. "Whose is that?" she asked.

"Well . . . it's . . ."

"It's hers!" trilled Nora. "Just a tiny little gift from the shop. Isn't your mother gorgeous?"

"Uh," muttered Morgan. "Yeah. Mom, are we leaving soon? I have a bunch of studying to do for social studies. I have to, like, *know* China."

Dana noticed how pale she looked; her lips seemed bloodless. "Sure, sweetie. Why don't you go gather up your stuff."

Morgan held up a plastic shopping bag with her costume in it. "Good to go," she said, and, glancing at Nora, "Thanks for having me." Then she turned and walked back down the hallway.

On the ride home, Dana asked Morgan about her night, but Morgan wasn't very talkative. "I'm really tired," she said. "I think we slept for about a minute and a half."

"Why didn't you go to bed if you were so tired?"

"Because Kimmi didn't want to, and it's her house."

At a stoplight Dana slowed the car to a halt. "Morgan," she said, turning to face her, "if you wanted to go to bed, you should've just nicely told her so and went."

Morgan looked at her, the fog of weariness clearing momentarily. "Right," she said. "Like *you* would ever go against the host."

Dana was stunned. "I would go against the host if the host was being unreasonable," she insisted.

"You say that, but you wouldn't. You're, like, *seriously* polite, Mom. You would go along with it."

The traffic light changed to green, and Dana had to face front. Morgan leaned back against the headrest and closed her eyes.

Tina, thought Dana as soon as she opened her eyes on Sunday morning.

And, *She better not try to be too friendly.*

And, *What do you wear to meet the woman who destroyed your marriage?*

They parked in the lot by the high-school football field, but neither Morgan nor Alder got out. They waited for Dana to open her door first. She had told them on the ride over.

"Dad's bringing Tina," was all she'd said, and she hoped it sounded like no big deal.

Apparently she hadn't pulled it off. They'd been silent for the remaining few minutes of the trip and now flanked her like body-guards as the three of them walked to the field. Kenneth and Tina were standing by the chain-link fence, just behind the home team's bench. Kenneth was handing a water bottle over the fence to Grady, who took it and trotted back to his teammates.

Let's get this the hell over with, Dana thought, and headed straight toward them. "Why don't you girls go on up and get seats," she said. "I'm just going to say a quick hello."

"I will, too," said Morgan.

Alder hung an arm around Morgan. "Come on, girlfriend," she said, and steered her in the direction of the stands.

Kenneth saw her first; his posture straightened, and his fingers began to clench at his jacket sleeves. He leaned briefly toward Tina, who glanced over her shoulder at Dana, then turned away. Beyond them, Jack Roburtin was giving the team his customary pregame pep talk.

"And I don't wanna see anyone knitting mittens out there!" he was bawling at them. "You got that? Lemmehearyousay YES!"

Yes! thought Dana. *No mitten knitting.* And then she was steps away and Kenneth was introducing them, as if she and Tina had no prior knowledge of each other, as if they didn't know *exactly* who the other person was. "Nice to meet you," said Dana.

"Real nice to meet you, too," said Tina, holding out her hand to shake, then thinking better of it and pulling back. But by that time Dana had responded by extending her own hand, and Tina had to reach out again to grasp it. Her face turned red and splotchy. She had long brown hair that fell away from her face in wisps. It was fine and thin, like a child's. She had gray eyes and a small upturned nose. She was petite, shorter than Dana by several inches, with narrow shoulders. Dana couldn't see much of her figure, because she was wearing a calf-length, baby blue down coat.

Behind them, Coach Ro yelled, "Two laps, double time!"

"Grady's been telling me all about his team," said Tina, her eyelids flickering nervously. "He's totally proud about it."

Dana was aware of someone approaching, but she couldn't take her eyes off Tina. *It doesn't even matter if they aren't as pretty as you,* Nora had said. *It's just that they're new. And you're not.*

"Hey there, beautiful." Jack Roburtin was standing on the other side of the fence. He reached over to land a beefy hand on her shoulder, seeming to Dana as if he were doing an impression of a peacock, flaring his pectoral muscles for lack of a tail. He turned to Kenneth and grinned cockily. "We're definitely going to win, now that I've got my good-luck charm here."

Dana almost laughed out loud, and for the briefest moment she wished desperately that someone else were there to confirm that this bizarre scene—Tina with her puffy coat and pug nose, Kenneth pinching at his jacket sleeves in abject discomfort, Jack with his cartoonlike posturing—was actually taking place. *This is happening,* she told herself, biting the inside of her lip to keep from laughing. *These people are real.*

"I'm going to head up into the stands now," she told them. To Tina she said, "I'm sure I'll see you again." Then she smiled at Jack. "Good luck, Coach."

"Thanks much." He pitched her an intimate little wink and added, "I'll call you tonight."

"Sounds good." And she went to join Morgan and Alder.

The girls watched as she approached, studying her as if she were some exotic bird that might fly off into the clouds at any second. She took up a spot in between them. Morgan eyed her for a moment, and Dana put her arm around her and gave a little squeeze.

"Impressive," murmured Alder.

"Thanks," Dana whispered and turned to watch the game.

DRIVING TO WORK ON FRIDAY, WITH AN AGGRES-sive rain dropping like countless tiny paratroopers onto the roof of her car, Dana felt calmer and more hopeful than she had felt in months.

The week had been virtually without incident. Grady's conceit over his game-winning run into the end zone on Sunday had cooled slightly and by Monday morning was evident only in a slight swagger after he catapulted himself out of her minivan at school. A boy Dana didn't recognize screamed, "Stelly!" and ran at him full throttle, knocking them both to the grass on impact. Grady gave him a happy cuff to the chest as they got up, and they ambled along shouldering into each other as they headed toward the playground.

On Tuesday night Kenneth had called to say he anticipated a light schedule on Wednesday and would be by to spend time with the kids while she worked late. He left shortly before she got home around eight-fifteen, and she found that Grady and Morgan had done their homework and eaten dinner. They were playing the Wii in the basement, not entirely amicably but without any obvious pinching, shoving, baiting remarks, or snatching at each other's controller. When Dana walked in, Grady leaned over to Morgan and whispered in her ear. Morgan gave an indulgent smile and nodded.

Apparently Alder had left with Jet just before Kenneth arrived and had returned after his departure. "Having their dad at the house again was sort of a little fantasy for them," Alder later explained to

Dana. "If I was here, too, it would have been like casting Amy Wine-house in *High School Musical*. Totally ruins the effect."

Dana was *almost* successful at not asking what Kenneth had given them for dinner, but when she tucked Grady in that night, the question seemed to grow legs and sneak out on its own.

"Chicken nuggets," he said, rolling back and forth in his *Star Wars* comforter until his lower half was satisfactorily encapsulated in fabric Jedi. "In the microwave instead of the toaster oven like you make, but I ate them anyway," he said, pleased with himself. "And an apple."

"Cut up?"

"No he just handed it to me."

"Did you eat it?"

"Yeah," Grady snorted sarcastically. "Like *that* would happen."

She threw the blanket up over his head and tickled him until he giggled like the little boy he was. Then she pulled the blanket back down under his chin and cupped his cheeks with both hands. He grinned up at her, and she realized it was the calmest, happiest look she'd seen on his face in a long time. "Was it good to have Dad here?" she murmured, not wanting the answer to matter as much as she knew it would.

"Yeah," he sighed. The grin quickly downgraded as he added, "Before he came, when we were waiting for him, Morgan said, 'Remember, this is a *visit*. It's not like when he used to come home from work and he lived here. So don't get all sad when he leaves.'"

Morgan knew how much this meant to him, Dana realized. "Were you sad?" she asked Grady.

"A little," he admitted. "I kinda almost forgot about the leaving part. But then she gave me the look. You know, like"—Grady tilted his head and raised his eyebrows—"and I remembered."

"And you felt better?"

"Yeah." He rubbed his cheek up against her hand. "Well, no, but then she let me be King Boo in Mario Kart." He shifted onto his side, and his knees slid up toward his belly.

"That was pretty nice of her," said Dana.

"Yeah, she's nice sometimes . . ." His eyelids drooped and his voice trailed off. "But not that much . . ."

Dana kissed him good night and went to Morgan's room; she was sitting in bed with an earth-science textbook propped on her knees. "How was it tonight?" Dana asked.

Morgan shrugged. "A little weird . . . but okay. Is he going to do that a lot?"

"I don't know. It depends on his work schedule, I guess. What were you and Grady whispering about when I came in?"

"Nothing big. Dad brought us a bag of Twizzlers, and Grady didn't want me to tell you."

"Why not?"

"I don't know. I think he just wanted to have a secret about Dad. Like it would kind of keep the feeling of him being here."

Dana smiled. "Thanks for being a good big sister." Morgan shrugged nonchalantly, but a proud little grin lit her face all the same.

Dana reached for the textbook; Morgan hung on to it for a moment but then released it, and Dana set it to rest on the floor. "When you were little, you used to do this funny thing." She tapped Morgan's hip, and Morgan slid over to make room. "You always wanted to bring a book to bed with you."

"Which one?"

"Oh, different ones." Dana ran a finger over the downy strands along Morgan's hairline. "For a while it was *Barnyard Dance* . . . Let's see, you loved *The Seven Silly Eaters*. I think the biggest hit was probably *Goodnight Moon*."

"Yeah," she murmured, sliding down into her covers. "I remember that . . . The old lady whispering hush. It was so . . ." Contentment softened the tension around her eyes.

The memory of a book, Dana mused as she turned off the light and headed out of the room. *Wouldn't life be so easy if that's all we needed to feel comforted?*

And now, with the windshield wipers flinging themselves frantically against the watery onslaught and thunder crashing against nearby hills, Dana cradled this tiny memory of her two contented children—both happy at the same time, no less!

In the office restroom, she leaned over to run the hand dryer across the rain-dampened ends of her hair before taking up her post out front. The warm air blew on her neck and down her blouse. It smoothed away the gooseflesh on her arms and made her smile secretly to herself.

"Dana." Tony's voice came from the hallway. "We've got patients stacking up out there. You almost done?"

A prickle of shame ran over her. "Sorry!" she called, and scooted out to her desk. He was squinting at a file and didn't look up as she passed.

The phone rang and rang. Patients came in like refugees, shaking drops from their jackets and umbrellas, dampening the upholstery and the air. They left bracing themselves to face the strobes of thunder bursting amid the downpour.

"Dana!" called Tony from his office at about eleven-thirty. She cut short the parting pleasantries with a patient and hastened to his door.

"United Dental changed their policy on sealants—did I forget to tell you that?"

"Oh, I . . . I don't think you mentioned it, but—"

"It's my fault," he muttered, waving off her impending apology. "Can you resubmit these?" He handed off the bills as he turned back to his computer screen. She took them and left.

Marie came out to the reception desk to herd the next patient to the operatory. Before opening the door to the waiting room, she caught Dana's eye, tipped her head toward Tony's office, and murmured, "Don't take it personally. He's just in a mood."

Dana gave her a relieved smile. "I thought it was me!"

"If it's you, you'll know it." Marie opened the door. "Mr. Kranefus?"

An elderly gentleman pressed his hands down on the arms of his chair, levering himself to a standing position. "This seems distinctly unsafe," he grumbled at Marie as he slowly approached. "One is not supposed to use electrical appliances in a thunderstorm."

"The building is grounded, Mr. Kranefus," Marie informed him. "Dr. Sakimoto would never subject you to undue—"

There was a boom of thunder that seemed designed to rattle their rib cages, and then they were in darkness, the only light a gray cast filtering meekly in through the big glass exterior door. Another thunderous explosion lit up the office with a cold flash, briefly illuminating Dana behind her desk, Marie in the doorway, and Mr. Kranefus with his hands clasped before him. "Thanks be to the Almighty," he whispered.

Marie helped him on with his coat and handed him his slightly misshapen fedora. He was gone by the time Tony came out of his office, cell phone pressed to his ear, saying, "Okay . . . all right . . . Tell them to stay safe out there." He snapped the phone shut. "Blown transformer—the whole block's out," he told them. "I'm thinking we cancel the rest of the appointments." He said this as if he were putting it to a vote, and they nodded their assent.

Dana used her cell phone to call the afternoon's patients while Tony and Marie stowed equipment and gathered up instruments for sterilization. Marie left as Dana made her last call.

"I got through to most of them," she told Tony when he came to her desk with his jacket on. "But there are three or four who only got messages."

"No worries," he said. "I was planning to come back after lunch anyway. I've got a camping lantern in my trunk, so I can get through the pile of paperwork that's been dogging me for weeks. And if somebody shows, I can let them know what happened."

"You're going out for lunch?"

"Yeah, you want to join me? I figured I'd head over to Keeney's for a burger. Seriously, why don't you come?" He gave her an encouraging smile, but she could see the weariness behind it, and a sort of melancholy. Something was off. Maybe he needed company.

She had second thoughts as she followed him by car down the storm-battered streets toward Nipmuc Pond. She shouldn't be spending money when she had a perfectly good yogurt, an apple, and a little bag of carrots sitting on the passenger seat next to her. *Too late to back out now,* she told herself. Besides, a burger sounded so good.

"This is on me, by the way," Tony said as they took a table by the expanse of windows.

"Absolutely not."

"Absolutely *yes,*" he insisted. "I'm the one who dragged you down here to eat greasy tavern food. Anyway, I'll claim it as a business expense. We'll say it's"—he squinted up at the rafters—"it's your two-week review."

"Oh, really." She smirked. "Well, how'm I doing?"

"Excellent." He smiled back. Then he looked at the menu and asked, "What're you having?"

Their burgers came, and they chatted amiably, conversation wending around kids and patients and work. "By the way," he said. "Don't try to be friends with Marie."

"Why not?"

"Marie is not about her day job. Don't get me wrong—she's a great hygienist. Thorough, efficient, the whole package. But I'm convinced she has some sort of alternative lifestyle going, and work is just something she has to do so she can go back to it afterward. She will not befriend you, so don't take it like it's some sort of failure on your part."

This evoked such a variety of questions that Dana didn't know which to begin with. What kind of alternative lifestyle? Why can't she have friends at work and have her other life, too? But what came out was, "What makes you think I would take it as a personal failure?"

He gazed out over the rain-pitted surface of Nipmuc Pond, attempting unsuccessfully to suppress a smile. "Come on," he said, turning back to her. "You like to be friends with everyone."

"No I don't." This was patently false, so she followed it with, "And what's wrong with that?"

"Nothing," he said. "It just doesn't work with someone like Marie, that's all."

Dana narrowed her eyes at him, and he let out a quick burst of laughter. "Well," she said, "I guess you're in a better mood now. Even if it is at my expense."

His smile faded, and he said, "I was kind of a jerk today, wasn't I?"

"Not really . . . You just seemed like you had something on your mind."

He made a little grunt of acknowledgment. "I got a call from Abby last night."

"Your daughter in medical school?"

"Yeah. Vanderbilt. Way the hell in Nashville." He tossed the french fry he was holding back onto his plate. "Why'd I ever let her go so far away that I'd need a damned plane ticket to get to her?"

"What happened? Is she okay?"

Tony described the phone call he'd received late the previous night. Abby was sitting folded into the closet of a comatose patient's room, crying in a whisper to him that she couldn't take it one more minute. It was too hard and too demoralizing and if she had to manually disimpact one more constipated elderly patient, she was going to bash in her own skull with a bedpan. "She's certain the interns sit around thinking up nasty things to make the med students do."

"Poor thing," Dana commiserated.

"It's so frustrating, because I know if I could just *be there*—give her some TLC and a decent meal—I could make about half of it go away! Most of what she eats is from the damned vending machines, and now she has pimples for the first time in her life." Tony's hands reached out as if to hold his beloved daughter's cheeks. "That beautiful glowing face with pimples—I can't imagine it!"

Dana felt her throat tighten. Possibly because she'd so rarely seen Kenneth show the same depth of emotion with Morgan and Grady . . . But no, it wasn't that. It was her own face she imagined in those loving hands, attached not to Tony or Kenneth . . . but to her own father.

Dad. In her mind it was almost a plea. *Daddy, reach for me.*

But he never had and never would, though it didn't keep her from wanting it, even now. Even in her forties, with her own children to care for, she would've given almost anything to feel her father's hands caressing her cheeks, to see such selfless concern for her happiness in his gaze. The tension in her throat swelled up into her jaw. She pressed her lips together to subdue it.

Tony's hands lowered onto the table, and she realized he was watching her. It was embarrassing, being caught speechless like this. She had to respond, so she took a breath to level herself and murmured, "You're such a good dad."

Then it was his turn to be bashful, giving a little one-shoulder shrug and saying, "I don't know about that . . ."

"Of course you are," she said quietly. "Anyone can see it."

"I just miss them." He picked up his fork and moved the last few french fries around the chipped plate. "They're their own people now. They've gone out into the world to do good things and find good people to be with." He looked up at Dana. "But sometimes—God, do I *miss* them." His face was calm, but the sadness was so palpable that Dana felt as if it belonged to her.

And staring back across the table at him, over the condiments and cold remains of lunch, she felt she could see the expanse of his fatherhood—the exuberant, giddy joy, the soul-chilling worry, flashes of anger and laughter, puzzlement and surprise, a love so elemental and indelible that it was written in his every cell. She nodded and barely managed to stop herself from reaching out to give his hand a squeeze—of recognition, or solidarity, or maybe it was sympathy. Morgan and Grady were still with her, after all, and she could no more fathom their being gone than she could imagine her own death.

The intensity of the moment caught Dana off guard, and she pulled herself back from it, turning to watch a birch tree bent low over the pond. The surface of the water, in constant motion from the pelting rain, seemed to make endless attempts to jump up and touch the dangling leaves. She glanced back at him with a less intimate smile. He followed her lead.

"So," he said, tossing his crumpled napkin onto his plate. "What's up for the weekend?"

It was Kenneth's turn for the kids, she told him, and Alder had joined the Wilderness Club at school. She'd be hiking Mount Frissell, the highest peak in Connecticut, on Sunday.

"And now I know what everyone in your family is doing this weekend except *you*," he teased.

"Oh, not much. Catching up on all the stuff that doesn't get done during the week anymore," she said mildly. "Also, I have a date."

"Oh?" Tony nodded encouragingly. "Same guy as before?"

"Same guy." She shrugged, wishing she hadn't mentioned it. It felt strangely uncomfortable to talk to Tony about Jack.

Tony didn't take the hint. "So you must like this guy," he probed genially. He asked how they'd met and where they'd gone on dates. "And what do you like about him? What's your favorite quality?"

"Well," said Dana, struggling to come up with something other than, *He really likes me.* "He's very . . . positive. When there's something he enjoys, he goes for it. He doesn't overanalyze."

"Good," Tony said, nodding. "And what do you like *least* about him? That's harder, I bet."

It wasn't actually that hard. *He's kind of a bull in a china shop,* she almost said. But that didn't sound very nice. And she certainly wasn't going to mention how entertained he was by making the reflected light from his watch crystal flick around a room, especially when she talked for too long.

"Well, I suppose he's a little on the boyish side," she finally admitted.

"Boyish?" said Tony with a wave of his hand. "If *that's* the worst you can come up with . . . Gimme a for-instance. What's so boyish it bothers you?"

She didn't like the way Tony dismissed her concern so easily. "Okay," she said, crossing her arms, "he likes to run over things with his truck. Like, if there's a soda can or a piece of trash in the road, he'll swerve to hit it. And then when he does, he says, 'Two points!'"

Tony was quiet for a moment. "Really?" he said. "I guess I could see how that could be kind of . . . But, hey, it's not *that* bad—and every guy's got his stupid little habits, right?"

Oh, really, she wanted to say. *What are yours?* But then the waitress came with the check, and she realized she didn't want to know about Tony's faults. She didn't want anything to ruin the image of him wishing so desperately he could hold his daughter's face in his empty hands.

CHAPTER

27

WITH MORGAN AND GRADY AT KENNETH'S FOR the weekend, Dana filled Saturday with errands, house-cleaning, shrub pruning, returning phone calls, and an overdue oil and filter change for the minivan. To her dismay, all of this was accomplished by midafternoon.

Relax, she told herself. *Get your book.* But there was a notion circling on the horizon of her consciousness that the house was too quiet and somehow it might get stuck that way if she didn't keep moving. She went to her closet and reviewed everything hanger by hanger. *Too small . . . Keep . . . Completely out of fashion . . . Keep . . . Old but comfortable . . . What was I thinking? . . . Keep . . .* She was bundling up the outcasts to take to Goodwill when Alder came in.

"Wow, did *you* sleep late," said Dana.

"I was up in the middle of the night for a while." Alder raked her two-toned hair—bike-tire black on the ends, gingerbread brown at the part—into a messy nest at the back of her head and secured it with an elastic band. "Can we go shopping? My underwear's all stretched out."

Dana was happy to have another activity, another problem to work on that was easily solved. As they drove to the Buckland Hills Mall, she thought of Connie's dire prediction that her daughter would be swept up into—what had she called it?—a little suburban, Abercrombie & Fitch fantasy. But Alder didn't seem the least bit spellbound by it.

"What store do you want to go to?" Dana asked. "Or we can shop around if you want."

Alder blew her warm breath at the window and wiped jagged switchbacks into the condensation with her finger. "I don't really care. Wherever's cheapest."

They ended up at Macy's, and Dana took the opportunity to purchase a lacy ivory bra from the clearance rack to go with her new blouse. Alder met her at the register with a three-pack from one of the displays. "No color?" asked Dana. "They have some really cute prints on that table."

Alder squinched up her face and shrugged. As they walked through the parking lot toward the car, Alder muttered suddenly, "God, this place is depressing. Look at it—it's just a wasteland of dirty asphalt."

She had a point. The shops inside the mall were saturated with color and enticing images. By comparison, the parking lot was dismal and smelled of exhaust. "You're right," Dana said, unlocking the minivan. "Most people wouldn't notice, but you—you're a noticer."

"Wish I wasn't." She heaved a long sigh, letting the air hiss through her lips. "And now you're going to ask what's wrong, because I'm acting like a cranky two-year-old. But I can't stop. You know, when you're being an idiot—you *know* it, but you can't stop? There should be a button on the side of our heads like they have on hair-dryer plugs."

"A reset button?"

"Yeah, and if you knew you were doing it but you couldn't, like, reach or something, your friend could push the button for you and save you from your own stupidity."

"I could probably use one of those," Dana mused. "I bet that would come in very handy." She pulled out onto Buckland Street. "So, um . . . anything in particular bothering you?"

Alder shrugged. "Where are we going?"

"Just a quick detour." Dana thought keeping Alder in the car a little longer might help to draw her out. She turned onto Tolland Turnpike and headed toward a park she knew of.

Alder pulled her legs up and crossed them on the seat. She didn't say anything for a while, until she muttered, "I don't want to go home for Thanksgiving."

Thanksgiving? Dana hadn't thought that far ahead, though it was only two weeks away. "Why not?" she asked.

Alder let out another hiss of a sigh. "Because E . . . Ethan will be back from college."

"Are you worried about seeing him?"

"I guess." Alder uncrossed her legs and set her feet down, then recrossed them back up on the seat. "Or not seeing him."

Dana nodded. "So you don't want to see him, but if you're both home, he might try to call you again. Or"—she shot a quick glance at Alder—"maybe you're worried he *won't* try to call." She turned onto a side road. "Because maybe he's over it. And you're not yet."

Alder's lip trembled, and a tear leaked out of the corner of her eye. "Did you ever hate somebody so much you wanted to kill *yourself*?" she breathed.

Dana pulled in to a small dirt parking lot by the side of the road. "Alder, honey. You don't have to tell me what happened—but I hope you've told someone."

Alder shook her head, and the tear flung itself off her chin and onto her sweatshirt. Dana reached out and ran her knuckles over the wet cheek. "It seems like a lot for one person to hold on to all by herself," she said. "Might feel better if you had some help."

Alder said nothing. Tears flew down her face faster now, and Dana let her hand rest on Alder's shoulder, waiting for her to be cried out enough to talk.

As she waited, Dana mused about the disastrous ending to her own high-school romance. She had dated Jim Cain her senior year, but they'd broken up that summer, agreeing that long-distance relationships never worked out. Dana had been relieved. She couldn't wait to get to UConn and be a whole new person, a person of her own making, whose mother didn't exhale clichés with the smoke from her Marlboro Lights, whose sister didn't think the entire world was intractably inane, and whose father wasn't . . . gone.

There had been a giant party at Chuck Traveleski's house that last weekend before everyone left for college, and Chuck had come up to her and said, "I always wanted to kiss you, but I never had the 'nads to ask." He had greasy red hair that he combed straight forward into his eyes. But he was a generally nice guy and had been kind enough to risk his parents' property and wrath by hosting the most unpredictable party of their young lives. How could she say no?

You'd never go against the host, Morgan had said. And maybe she was right, because Dana had allowed it. But Chuck's kiss went on too long, as if he'd figured out how to start the procedure but never considered how to end it.

Ex-boyfriend Jim had provided some help in that area. He pulled Chuck off her and attempted to punch him but was too drunk to do more than push poor Chuck onto the ground. Then he turned to Dana with his face screwed up into a horrible grimace of rage and tears, and screamed, "YOU BROKE MY HEART!" He'd ripped open the front of his lime green Lacoste shirt and wailed, "See? It's BROKEN!"

Dana had spent the remainder of the evening conferring with her girlfriends about getting back together with Jim for just one night, apologizing to Chuck, and meeting with Jim's emissaries, who were just as drunk as he was. Eventually they all went home and didn't see each other again until Thanksgiving, by which time it didn't matter in the least. They were college students. They barely recognized themselves or each other.

Dana peered at Alder, still crumpled and staring through the windshield, tears dripping slower now. "Should we go back to the house?" Dana whispered. Alder shook her head no. Dana slid her hand from Alder's shoulder down to her wrist. She took Alder's hand in her own, and Alder squeezed back. They would continue to wait.

Dana gazed out to the stand of pine trees just beyond the parking area. There were wooden picnic tables slightly misshapen by the beginning stages of rot. She and Kenneth had brought the kids here from time to time to eat sandwiches and feed the ducks that lived in the shallows of the adjacent stream. *Kenneth,* she thought. *He was the only one who broke my heart.*

She'd dated after college, but no one she'd felt that strongly about until she met Kenneth. He'd had the whole package: smart, handsome, gainfully employed, not living with his parents, funny but also serious. Serious at the right times, like when they'd been dating for two and a half years and it was time, as her mother had so unceremoniously told her, to "fish or cut bait."

And so they'd gotten married, and moved to a pleasant house in a pleasant suburb, and had children. Dana's mind flashed to a visit they'd made to this spot, years ago. Morgan's face, still round and plump with the vestiges of babyhood, was drawn with worry because they were out of bread and some of the ducks hadn't gotten a turn.

"You really should have brought more," Kenneth had groused at Dana.

Who cares what you think? Dana remembered silently retorting.

And then last January he had broken her heart. She glanced at Alder, pale and tear-streaked, staring hollow-eyed out the window, and thought, *But it didn't look like this.*

Dana had been horror-struck when Kenneth ended the marriage. But her heart? Was it that or her neatly arranged life that had been hacked apart with a dull knife and then hastily sewn back together with visible seams and hanging threads? Alder's anguish was clearly so deeply personal it seemed to vibrate through her body like blasts from a sonic boom.

"Did you ever hate anyone *that much*?" Alder whispered, her voice hoarse as if she'd recently been screaming. "Did you ever feel so . . ."

"Betrayed?" said Dana. "No, honey, I don't think I ever did. Not like you seem to."

"Not even Kenneth?"

Dana wondered how much to say. Alder was in adult-size pain and yet was still a young girl. "Well," said Dana finally, "things weren't really right with us for a while. I was very upset, don't get me wrong. But I don't think I felt quite as . . . attacked by an ally as you seem to feel."

Tears rose again in Alder's lower lids. "He was my *best friend*. The best one I ever had."

"You loved him." Dana stroked the hair off Alder's damp cheeks. "And you trusted him."

Alder's hands flew to cover her face, as if she were about to lose pieces of herself that she would never get back. Her weeping was ragged and painful-sounding. She rocked back and forth against the car seat. *"Ahh!"* she keened. *"Ahhh!"* It went on and on, and it scared Dana. *What if she's having a nervous breakdown?* she thought. *What if I'm sitting here doing nothing, watching her lose her mind?*

She kept her hand on Alder's arm, not sure if the weeping girl could even perceive it but wanting nonetheless to remind her that she wasn't alone. Dana herself had so often felt as if she were wandering the craters of some forgotten moon, orbiting a distant planet. She needed to keep Alder tethered to the earth, to a place where she was loved and wanted and where her pain mattered to someone, even if it was just an aunt with problems of her own.

The rocking slowed and came to a stop; the harsh keening trailed off into sobs. Dana slid her hand up to the back of Alder's neck and gently pulsed her fingers against the straining muscles.

"Oh, sweetie," she murmured. "Sweet, sweet girl."

Alder's hands slid down from her face and dropped into her lap. "I'm so . . . fucking . . . *stupid*."

"No, baby," soothed Dana. "You're just human. We all get caught off guard sometimes."

"Not me." Alder glanced at her for the first time. "I notice stuff–

things other people don't pick up on. Connie says it's the artist in me, always watching."

Dana wasn't sure how to respond to this. It was true, Alder was very perceptive, the epitome of an old soul. But did she really believe she'd be able to see the truth in every situation?

"Like Jet," said Alder, running the back of her hand under her dripping chin. "Everyone sees this weird girl with too much eyeliner and a shitbox car and a mother who doesn't even *pretend* to try to keep track of her. But she's good inside. And I think she's going to do good things—not like soon, but someday."

"Have you ever told her this?"

Alder shrugged and inhaled a sniffle. "A little." She looked over at the pine trees. "You have to be careful how much you say. It weirds people out."

True enough, thought Dana. Her hand rose up to the back of Alder's head, her fingers smoothing out the tension in the girl's scalp. Alder closed her eyes and took a normal-size breath. "So . . ." said Dana. "This betrayal from Ethan. You didn't see it coming." Alder's head shake was so subtle that Dana sensed it more with her hand than with her eyes. "And that compounds the misery, because you think you should've been able to." An all-but-imperceptible nod from Alder. "And you don't want to tell anyone because . . . ?"

Alder's chest rose with an influx of air, then sank even deeper into her frame. "Because words are stupid. They're like those plastic letters with the magnets that little kids stick on the fridge. If I spell it out, it's like trying to say something you can't spell with plastic." She glanced at Dana to see if she understood. Dana didn't fully, but she nodded, wanting to keep Alder talking.

"But I guess not saying anything wasn't really working that well either." Alder sighed and gazed out at the rotting picnic tables. "He was in my world-civ class because he, like, flunked it or something when he had mono freshman year and they wouldn't let him graduate without it."

She had taken an interest in him right away, she told Dana, not for any obvious reason that she could name but just because, sitting sluggishly at his battered desk three seats up and one row over, he'd seemed thoughtful and good. "He used to come to the studio during his free periods and do these wicked-cheesy watercolors." Ethan knew he had no talent for art, she said, and he didn't care. She loved that about him.

And though she was a freshman and he was a senior, they soon became inseparable. "We were, you know, those weird kids who never do sports or clubs or dances or anything else the school throws at you." Her chin seemed to quaver for a moment. "It was just totally . . . easy."

"But you weren't boyfriend and girlfriend," said Dana. Alder's gaze dropped slightly, and she shook her head. "Did you want to be?" asked Dana.

"I liked him," admitted Alder, her voice small. "But he didn't really think of me that way." Though his lack of romantic interest in her was disappointing, mostly she was just happy to have someone she could be completely herself with.

She seemed relieved to talk about him, as Dana suspected she might. It made sense to cry yourself hoarse and want to do violence to someone who'd hurt you. What didn't make sense, but was somehow just as compelling, was to remember the time before the moment of betrayal. Ethan had known all there was to know about her, and that warm, silky comfort of being known and loved, though no longer existent, was somehow no less real.

"Alder," Dana said gently, "what happened?"

Alder's jaw went tight. "He wanted—" She clenched her molars and started again. "He didn't want to be a virgin when he got to college. But he didn't want some lame hookup . . . so he asked me. He said I didn't have to," she added quickly. "He was totally embarrassed even bringing it up."

Because he was smart enough to see how badly it could hurt you, thought Dana.

"How did it go?" she asked, trying to keep her voice even and light.

Alder's eyes filled again. "Totally great," she whispered. "Especially afterward, when we were lying there all . . . like every single piece of us was connected." She made a little gasp for air, but it wasn't enough to keep her from crying again. "You know how that feels? When your minds and bodies are, like, *merged*?"

Dana wasn't sure if she did know. "Did you see each other after that?" she asked.

"No," Alder choked out between sobs. "He didn't . . . He said he needed to . . . spend time with his other friends and his family before he left for . . . I tried to . . . but he *wouldn't*." She turned to Dana, her face awash, eyes begging for some possible explanation. "He wouldn't see me—not even to say good-bye!"

That goddamned fucking little bastard, thought Dana.

She leaned across the console of cup holders between their seats and put her arms around the brokenhearted girl. "Oh, sweetie," she murmured. "Not fair. Not fair at all."

"He's a piece of shit!" wailed Alder.

"Yes, he is," Dana soothed, stroking her hair. "He is a massive, fly-covered piece of shit."

Alder pulled back and looked up at her aunt.

"What?" said Dana. "I'm agreeing with you."

"Yeah, but you don't usually say . . ."

"Oh, please." Dana rolled her eyes. "If there were ever a time for swear words, this is it." She held Alder's chin with one hand and wiped her cheeks with the other. "You got sucker-punched by the one person you expected to stand by you—and you gave up your virginity in the bargain! I'm thinking worse words than *that,* I promise you."

Alder stared at her aunt and allowed her face to be wiped like a baby's after a first attempt at self-feeding. The tears slowed, and her mouth softened, one side curling almost imperceptibly at the corner. "I'm sick of sitting in this car," she said.

Dana reached for the door handle. "We should keep the doors open." She grinned over at Alder. "Your mother would say we need to let the bad energy out."

"My mother is the mayor of Crazytown," Alder muttered.

"Maybe," said Dana. "But it couldn't hurt."

Leaving the car doors ajar like the wings of an enormous metal dragonfly, they walked over to the stream and followed it a little ways to a low dam. Amber-colored water poured over the algae-slicked cement, rushing to the bottom and frothing into foam before it sped downstream.

Alder took a deep breath and let it whoosh noisily out of her mouth. She leaned against Dana, who put an arm around her waist. They stood there watching the water plunge to the rocks below and continue on its way.

Dana gently put a finger to Alder's temple. "Reset," she said.

Alder pressed her own finger against Dana's head. "Reset to you, too."

CHAPTER
28

WHEN THEY GOT HOME, DANA BEGAN ASSEM-
bling the ingredients for turkey potpie. She planned to make
two—one for Mary Ellen McPherson and one to bring to Jack's
apartment.

"Let's have dinner at my place on Saturday," he'd said over
breakfast earlier in the week.

She'd found it annoying at first. *Might as well say, "Let's eat quick
and have sex,"* she'd grumbled inwardly.

But then he'd smiled so earnestly at her and said, "It'll be great
to just sit and talk without any distractions or rushing or anything."
And she'd softened and happily agreed.

Jet called. She'd changed her mind and wanted to go on the
hike with the Wilderness Club after all. Alder smirked—"She's gonna
hate it!"—and went to stay over at Jet's house to make sure she got
up on time and didn't leave the house wearing flip-flops.

When the meal was ready and the two steaming potpies sat in
cardboard boxes in the trunk of the minivan, Dana headed toward
the McPhersons' house. She regretted not checking the obituaries
to see if Dermott McPherson might have succumbed to his illness
by now. Once she had delivered a meal to an elderly woman whose
sister was sick with emphysema, only to find that the sister had died
the day before. Unmarried and without children, they'd quietly
lived together for over eighty years in the house where they'd been
born.

When Dana had arrived with her baked halibut, the woman had opened the door, revealing behind her a house teeming with relatives. Dana had asked brightly, "How's your sister feeling?" The woman had taken a quick look back into the crowded living room, stepped out onto her sloping front porch, and murmured, "She's free." Then she'd put a gnarled old hand up to cover her mouth and cried without a sound. It was one of the most desperate moments Dana had ever witnessed. And she'd been unprepared with any words or gestures, and so she'd said nothing more than, "I'm so sorry . . . I'm really sorry . . ." After a minute the old woman had collected herself, taken the foil pan of fish, and gone back into the house.

Now as Dana turned onto the narrow street where the McPhersons lived, she tried to come up with something to say to Mary Ellen if her husband had in fact passed on, but it all sounded trite and hackneyed. *Sorry for your loss . . . You're in my prayers . . . He's out of pain now . . .* Dana snorted in frustration.

By the time she was standing on the front stoop with the boxed turkey potpie and the bag of side dishes hanging from her arm, she'd almost convinced herself that Dermott McPherson had actually died. So it was doubly surprising when a man answered the door.

"You must be the Good Witch of Cotters Rock," he said warmly, though his face seemed cold and bloodless, as if his chin and brow and cheekbones were pressing too hard against his skin. He was probably no older than forty. Dana opened her mouth to answer, but nothing came out. He held the screen door for her, chuckling. "It's okay. Mellie says no one gets my jokes."

"Mellie?" Dana wondered for a moment if she'd come to the wrong house.

"My wife, Mary Ellen." He took the box from her and set it on a small table by the door. "She said she'd met you."

"Oh! Yes, of course."

"I'm Dermott." He held out his hand to shake. "It's cold," he warned her, "but it still works." And true to his word, the hand was icy. Dermott compensated for this by gripping hard and giving her hand a pump that sent tremors up her arm. He glanced at the pot-pie as if to size up an adversary. Then he gave a resigned sigh. "Do you mind carrying that for me?" His sweatpants dangled precariously around his hips, and he hitched them up to his waist before he turned. "I'm a little wobbly these days."

Dana followed him through the cramped living room to the kitchen. "How're you feeling?" Immediately she pinched her lips together. Her mother had hated that question in her last days as she lay trapped in her bed, adrift like a tiny iceberg on an endless sea. Dana knew better and accepted his clipped response—"Upright and breathing"—as an appropriate rebuke.

Dermott turned to see if he'd insulted her, and she met his gaze with a knowing nod. He gave his own head a brief, penitent shake. "What can I get you?" he asked. "Tea? Juice? Shot of tequila?"

She laughed, knowing he needed her to, and accepted his implicit apology. "Well, that tequila sounds good, but I'll be asleep by eight if I start now, won't I?" She unpacked the bag of food and laid it out on the counter. "But you go right ahead without me, if you want."

"Yeah." He grinned. "Like I don't have enough toxic waste swimming around in my veins." He lit the burner under the teakettle and sank onto one of the scratched wooden chairs. He ran his finger slowly over a line of green Magic Marker on the blond wood of the table.

"Where is everyone?" asked Dana, turning to lean against the counter. "Usually this place is pretty busy."

"She took the kids over to a friend's for a couple of hours." He slid an elbow onto the table and propped his head against his palm. "Wanted me to rest."

"And here I am, keeping you from it." Dana hastily gathered up the plastic bag.

"No, stop," he said. "I didn't mean for you . . . I only . . . Would you please just sit?"

Dana stopped shoving the plastic bag into her purse. The tea-kettle whistled. She looked at him, but he didn't get up. She raised her eyebrows in question. He smiled back at her, relieved. "There's lemon wedges in the fridge. Just put one in hot water for me, please." He added quickly, "There's real tea in that cabinet by the stove, if you like."

She was wearing her new blouse, the one Nora had given her, and didn't want to chance spilling tea on it. When she'd assembled two mugs with hot water and lemon wedges and sat down, she asked, "Now, why are we drinking this?"

He laughed. "Some Eastern-medicine crap about cleansing the liver. Mellie spends half the night on the Internet looking for mira-cle cures."

Of course she does, thought Dana. His face changed, went darker, and she could see him regret making a joke at his wife's expense. He glanced up at Dana, let his eyes linger uncomfortably on hers. She felt as if she were being visually vetted for the Secret Service. Then he looked down into the steaming water of his teacup and poked at the floating lemon wedge with the tip of his finger. "I miss her al-ready," he murmured. Dana knew he didn't mean today. "It's like I'm already gone," he went on, "facing a lifetime of missing them."

Dana felt her eyes sting—his words were so utterly hopeless it was all she could do not to weep. He looked up at her, and she wanted to apologize, to say, *You must be so sick of sad faces.* But her throat closed up, pulled tight like the cords around the mouth of a string bag.

"Why do you do this?" Dermott asked her, apparently uncon-cerned by the sorrow she was trying so desperately to hide. "I mean, I *have* to be here, and so does Mellie, and I suppose my friends and family members feel some obligation. But you're a stranger. Are you really so nice that you'd keep showing up to a family you don't even know, who's this deep in the weeds?"

Still not trusting herself to speak, Dana shrugged and at-tempted a weak smile.

"I'm sorry," he said, as if he had just noticed her state. "For some bizarre reason, I find myself accosting strangers with—"

Dana shook her head at him. "My mother," she said, speaking softly, testing her voice as if she were stepping out onto an icy pond. "My mother had lung cancer. She was old, and most of her friends had passed on or retired somewhere. No one came. No one helped. It was *exhausting*. My sister was there sometimes, but she works, so she couldn't come every day. Mostly weekends." The stinging behind Dana's eyes intensified. "I miss my mother," she said, "but I never thought about *her* missing *me*. I guess I assumed that wherever she is, she's just . . . happy."

Dermott gave a bitter little smile. "That's what the brochure says." He ran his finger along the Magic Marker streak again and said, "But how could I be happy without them? I mean, how could that be *me*?"

When Dana saw his eyes go glassy with tears, she reached across the table and took his hand very lightly in her own, and he allowed this. They sat for maybe a minute or so, but it seemed like the longest, quietest moment of her life.

"Jeez," Dermott said finally, reclaiming his hand and giving his eyes a quick swipe, "You'd think I wouldn't have a drop left after all the puking I've been doing."

"Pretty bad, huh?"

"Well, it's experimental. I've run through all the normal stuff, so now I think they're secretly trying out household cleaning products. Pretty sure this last batch is either Tilex or Drano."

She smiled at the dark humor. "Maybe they think you're made of enameled porcelain."

"And this is just a *really* bad case of soap scum." He grinned.

Almost recovered now from their shared sorrow, they chatted for a few minutes longer. When the hot lemon water was gone, Dana took the mugs to the sink.

"Hey," he said, standing to walk her to the door. "Um, I know this is kind of a huge favor, and possibly against the rules or something . . . but could you keep bringing meals for a little while . . . after? Maybe just for a couple of weeks? You're like the Queen of Yum around here, and I think they're probably going to need it."

"Of course," said Dana as they reached the front door.

"Also . . ." He glanced away, embarrassed, then forced himself to continue. "Could you tell Mellie what I said . . . about missing them? I just think she'll want to know that she's not the only one, you know . . . feeling the loss."

"Absolutely," she murmured.

He nodded his thanks, and opened the door. "Well, off you go, Good Witch. You must have a hot date or something." He laughed at her startled reaction and added, "Hey, with a blouse like that, I *know* you're not running out for groceries."

As she drove over to Jack's, Dana tried not to think about Dermott McPherson missing his young wife from the grave. But no matter what she turned her attention to—the upcoming Veterans Day school holiday, the new bra that poked against her ribs just a little, her first husbandless Thanksgiving in fifteen years—her thoughts veered back to Dermott and the requests he'd made on his wife's behalf. Food and the assurance that, though dead, he would be just as miserable as the living.

Jack lived at Velvet Mill, an old textile factory in Manchester that had been converted to apartments in the early 1990s. It was considered a very hip place to live when it first opened its doors, he'd told her, and he'd been one of the first to sign a rental agreement, securing a "primo spot" on the top floor. He met her at the apartment door, curled her into an enormous, smothering hug, and murmured, "How come you're late?"

She didn't really know why she chose to lie, saying a road was closed and she'd had to find a different route. All she knew was she didn't want to talk about it.

In fact, after putting the turkey potpie into the oven to warm and seeing his contributions to the meal—a bag of frozen corn, a bowl of Ruffles potato chips, and an elongated loaf of white bread with the words "French Bag-ette!" written on the paper wrapper—it was she who set the evening's activity in motion. She turned away from the sight of embedded grease around the stove burners and pressed herself against his chest, which was as solid and toasty as a sun-warmed stone wall.

She leaned up on her toes, because even wearing boots with heels she was not nearly tall enough to square her face to his. But when he curved down to her and she felt his full lips on hers, she could finally settle the vision of Dermott's bloodless face and cold hands into a distant corner of her awareness. Her lips parted, and so did Jack's, the tip of his tongue slipping in just as far as the edge of her teeth, then retreating, then penetrating a little deeper until she wanted to climb him like a tree and cling to the safety of his branches. He was a good kisser, the best she'd ever kissed, and that's all she wanted to think about just now.

CHAPTER

29

O N SUNDAY EVENING WHEN KENNETH BROUGHT the kids home, he came into the house with them instead of saying his good-byes in the driveway. He stood just inside the mudroom door, watching them drop their overnight bags and jackets onto the floor as if he were studying the migratory patterns of a nomadic tribe.

Morgan's cell phone beeped; she tugged it out of her jacket pocket and squinted at the screen. "Kimmi's sleeping over tomorrow night," she announced.

"But it's a—"

"No it's not, Mom," Morgan corrected. "We don't have school on Tuesday. It's Soldier Day, or whatever."

"Duh, Morgan, it's Veterinarians Day," said Grady. "They get it off so they don't have to deal with pelican guts and goat poop and junk like that."

"*Ew.*" Morgan registered her disgust without looking up from texting Kimmi.

"Actually, it's *Veterans* Day," said Kenneth, trying to stifle a laugh. "It's when we remember all the people who fought for our country."

"Remember?" said Grady. "I didn't even know any to begin with." He grabbed Kenneth's hands. "Mom, look. I can still do that spinny thing."

As he walked his feet up Kenneth's legs and pushed off to flip over, Kenneth let out a grunt of exertion. "You're getting too big for this, buddy."

"You just need to work out more," said Grady. "Hey! Maybe I can stay over tomorrow night and we can go to the gym again!"

"I can't," he told Grady. "Even though it's Veterans Day, I still have to go in to the office."

"I could just hang around with Tina until you get home." He took Kenneth's hands again to do another climb and flip.

"Tina has to work, too," said Kenneth, disengaging his hands and patting Grady on the shoulder. "But, hey, I'll see you in two weeks, and we'll definitely go to the gym, I promise."

Grady stopped trying to grab at Kenneth's hands. "Two weeks?" he said, staring up at his father, his voice muted by surprise. "Two *weeks*?"

"Grady, you know it's every other weekend," said Kenneth defensively. "That means there are two weeks in between."

The boy looked to his mother for a denial of this wholly unbelievable calculation.

"More like twelve days," she said.

"Oh." Grady stared down at his overnight bag for a moment. "Well, bye," he muttered, then turned toward the kitchen, dragging his sock-clad feet across the floor tiles.

"Bye, Dad," said Morgan. She gave him an awkward hug and followed Grady out. Kenneth watched them go.

"Everything okay?" asked Dana, suspicious now that the kids were gone and he was still standing there.

"Absolutely." He zipped his jacket up another inch and yanked the waist down over his hips. Dana waited, annoyed by his fidgeting and his failure to leave. "I might stop in on Wednesday while you're working late," he said. "Depends on a couple of account reps. I'll let you know."

"Thanks," she said.

"Okay." His hand gripped the door handle for a moment, and then he left.

Dana padded through the house later that night, turning off lights and slipping the sticky ice-cream bowls into the dishwasher. Suddenly there was a buzzing sound. Searching around, she saw Morgan's cell phone on the counter and picked it up. There was a text from Kimmi: OK BUT ITS FUNNER IF ITS MORE KIDS.

What's funner? Dana wasn't a big texter. She could reply to Morgan's occasional messages to BRING SNEAKERS FORGOT GYM or CAN U GET CELLO AFTER SCHOOL. But it took her a minute to figure out how to see the entire text thread. She was also slowed by a momentary qualm about snooping at a private conversation. But what *exactly* was so much "funner" with more kids?

WANNA SLEEP OVR MONDAY NITE? Kimmi had begun six hours earlier.

WHOS HOUS, Morgan replied.

MINE.

HOW BOUT MINE I HAV TRIPL CHOC BROWNIE MIX, Morgan offered.

YUM.

The texting veered off toward a debate over triple-chocolate brownies versus maple-frosted sugar cookies, randomly interspersed with updates on each one's activity of the moment (from UGH HATE STUPD ENGLSH to SRRY BACK NOW NAILS DRY to IDIOT BROTHR TOOK PHN).

Then Kimmi suggested, WE CUD SNEAK OVR TO DEVYNNES.

YEAH FUN, replied Morgan. But this was quickly followed with MY MOM WANTS ME HOME CUZ ITS R TURN TO HOST.

Kimmi asked, U LIKE DEVYNNE?

YAH DEF, responded Morgan. VRY COOL.

CAN DEVYNNE SLEEP OVR TOO?

MY MOM SEZ ONLY 1 KID. They bemoaned their mothers' lack of understanding for a few rounds, and then Morgan suggested

Devynne come over on Tuesday morning. The three of them would still have the whole day together. SO JUST U AND ME FOR MONDAY NITE, she concluded.

OK BUT ITS FUNNER WITH MORE KIDS.

Why had Morgan declined to invite Devynne over, too? Dana had hosted plenty of three- and four-girl sleepovers. And why had Morgan doggedly asserted her right to host, despite Kimmi's obvious preference for her own house? A pinprick feeling went down Dana's spine.

Slow down, she told herself. *How bad could it be? They're twelve, for Pete's sake!*

Morgan had lived a fairly sheltered life (until recently anyway, when Kenneth left and the roof blew off their shelter), and this Devynne sounded a bit more worldly; possibly Morgan was intimidated by that. Or maybe it was Nora's occasional brusqueness—she had come down pretty hard on Kimmi about baking treats and was obviously concerned about Kimmi's weight (though the girl was ballerina thin). The implications about Morgan's own more rounded tummy were certainly enough to make her worry.

It's just a jumpy time for her, Dana assured herself, turning off the lights and going to bed.

The next day her concerns about the texts ebbed to nothing as her mind took up the task of obsessing over every emergency that could possibly arise from leaving the kids home while she went to work on Tuesday. Veterans Day being one of the lesser holidays, Cotters Rock Dental was very much open for business. Alder would be home, but Dana still felt vaguely anxious.

"Come a little late, leave a little early," Tony suggested. "I'll even give up the pleasure of your company if you want to go home for lunch. Don't worry about me—I'll just hum to myself and try not to whimper," he teased.

"You don't think I'm a negligent parent, letting them stay home alone?"

"No, I think you adore your kids and you're a little bit of a wor-rywart, which is a recipe for an excellent parent, in my humble opinion."

I just love this guy, she thought, allowing herself to believe him for the moment.

The boy who had tackled Grady at school drop-off the previous week came over that afternoon. His name was Javier, "But everyone calls me Jav, like javelin, 'cause I'm like a spear flying through the air," he told Dana matter-of-factly.

"They call you that because you *tell* them to," corrected Grady.

"So?" said Jav.

They skittered from one activity to the next, leaving a trail of sweaty socks, elastic bands, Yu-Gi-Oh! cards, dirt-encrusted stones, and Monopoly money. At five o'clock Jav's mother called about picking him up. "Lemme talk to her, can I talk to her, when you're done I have to talk to her," chanted Jav as both boys wiggled impa-tiently. A sleepover at Jav's house was quickly arranged. Dana felt funny letting Grady go to a stranger's house overnight, but the lure of adult supervision while she worked the next day clouded out fears that Jav's family might be members of a sacrificial cult.

Alder and Jet worked on a poster for the Wilderness Club. Ac-tually, Alder worked, her head bobbing close to the paper to add detail to the elaborate landscape. Jet ate peanut butter out of the jar and made comments like, "Not gonna lie, that squirrel looks really freakin' vicious." After dinner they went to the club treasur-er's house for a fund-raising meeting. "We have to, like, *meet* and talk about raising, like, *funds*?" Jet explained carefully to Dana.

Alder rolled her eyes. "I'm sleeping over at Jet's," she said. "I'll be home before you leave for work."

Morgan and Kimmi emerged occasionally from Morgan's room to get a snack, go on the computer, and once to take a walk around the block. "I disgust myself if I don't exercise," Dana heard Kimmi tell Morgan as they pulled on their boots. After dinner they made brownies and ate them with scoops of ice cream while watching *Dirty Jobs,* shrieking and hiding against each other, as sewer sludge spattered the host's face.

At ten o'clock Dana herded them up to bed. They were tucked into sleeping bags on the floor, heads sharing the same pillow in the cozy darkness, when Dana returned to the office to pay bills. Short of a massive and immediate turnaround in Kenneth's prospects, Dana wouldn't be an at-home mom again anytime soon. In fact, it was now clear the cushion had been getting slowly unstuffed ever since Kenneth had left. Two homes were a strain on even a healthy paycheck, and belts that should've been tightened hadn't been. And yet there was no way she could have told her kids, "Not only is Dad moving out, but you won't be able to do all the things you used to do and have all the things you used to have. The cloud has no lining, silver or otherwise."

Dana stared at the wall of drawings that Morgan and Grady had made for Kenneth. *Daddy still lives here with us,* the pictures seemed to say. *You don't have to worry about anything.* She rose and carefully, lovingly, slid her finger under the taped corners of each picture and laid them on the end of the desk. *No more lies,* she thought.

Then she went to the kitchen to console herself with the brownies and ice cream she had so carefully avoided the entire evening. But there were none. She checked every cupboard and found nothing. She did, however, find that the pan in which they were baked had been washed and shoved to the back of the pots cabinet. The ice cream was also gone, the box buried in the garbage bin, shrouded with newspapers and an empty cereal box.

The pins and needles along her spine rose up again. Her brain scrambled for plausible explanations, and she knew that if she wanted to, she could make herself believe any one of them. Or she could simply stop thinking about it and go to bed, which was almost as tempting as those brownies had been.

No, she would have to do something. She would start by asking

Morgan about it tomorrow, after Kimmi had gone home. When she got to the top of the stairs, however, it was clear the girls were not asleep. They were in the bathroom. The light streamed out into the darkened hallway from the not-quite-closed door, and Dana could hear Kimmi's voice.

"See?" she was saying. "I don't even have to use my finger anymore. My stomach just knows what to do."

CHAPTER

30

THERE WAS A MOMENT, AS SHE STOOD THERE IN the dark quiet of the hallway, when Dana's mind went completely blank, as if the plug had been pulled in her cortex. When her brain reluctantly powered back up seconds later, she questioned whether she had really heard what she'd heard.

But she had. And as the sounds of muted gagging from behind the bathroom door crackled in the air around her, she knew she had a decision to make. *Do I respond now or come up with a plan and respond later?*

Dana was completely dumbstruck by the situation before her. She wondered how she could possibly handle it without making a scene. If Morgan had been alone, that would've been one thing; with Kimmi involved it was so much more complicated. But there was a notion poking at her, prodding her to act. It said, *Morgan needs to know that I know. And if I don't do something now, I might chicken out.*

She pushed open the door. Kimmi was rising from her knees by the toilet. Morgan was lowering herself into a crouch, index finger jammed to the knuckle into her mouth. Startled mid-motion, the two girls turned to stare at her. Then Kimmi blurted out, "Mrs. Stellgarten, we're not feeling well, and we think maybe that chicken you made for dinner wasn't cooked all the way through and we might have blotchy-ism."

Botulism, Dana thought. *If you're going to lie to me, at least get the word right.*

"It's time to go to bed," she said quietly.

"Mom . . ." whispered Morgan.

"Bedtime," said Dana firmly.

The girls scurried back to Morgan's room. Dana stood for a moment in the hallway, listening to them settle into their sleeping bags, wondering if she'd handled it properly. She padded to her bedroom, realizing ruefully that she would have the whole night to obsess about it.

Not the whole night after all. Sometime before dawn Morgan floated wraithlike into the room and silently slid under the covers. She did not touch Dana, as she usually did when she crawled into the bed, didn't tug gently at Dana's hair or at the skin on her elbow. She simply lay there, meekly waiting to be thrown a scrap of her mother's attention.

"Did you sleep at all?" Dana murmured.

"No."

"Are you upset?"

A tiny gasp from the opposite pillow and a shuddering against the mattress let Dana know she was crying. "Morgan," whispered Dana, her hand smoothing along the skin of her daughter's clenched forearm. "Morgan, honey." Bit by bit, Morgan let her hand slide forward, so that Dana's caresses could reach all the way up to her shoulder. Then suddenly she surged forward, pressing herself into the curve of her mother's body. Dana wrapped her arms around her and breathed the still-childlike smell of Morgan's prepubescent skin. She felt terribly sad for Morgan—for the pain of the divorce, and the pressure to be perfect, and the worry that kept her awake night after night.

The crying slowed. "I didn't lie," sniffled Morgan.

"About what?"

"I really did stop for a long time," she insisted. "Like weeks."

"When did you start again?"

"When we started eating all those cookies and brownies and stuff."

"With Kimmi." Morgan didn't respond, and Dana suspected she didn't want to implicate her new best friend. "How about if you stop baking and find something else to do when you're together?"

"I tried that," Morgan said. "But Kimmi really likes to."

"I see. It's that host problem again. Except you did it here, too, where *you're* the host."

"It's hard, Mom, you don't even know how hard! Some people arc just, likc . . . in *charge,* no mattcr whcrc thcy arc."

The truth of it rippled through her. So many people in her own life seemed to fit that description. "You're right," she said. "And I *do* know how hard it is. Some people just seem to get their way no matter what you do, don't they?"

"Yes! Like Devynne! It's like a superpower or something."

Dana restrained herself from demanding to be told what bad behavior Devynne had instigated. "I don't know her," she said, hoping to sound only mildly curious. "What's she like?"

"She's *so* popular—you know, like Kimmi?—but she's not afraid of anything. She tries stuff. She has two big brothers, and they're in high school, so she knows all about it."

Dana worked to keep her breathing steady and tried to sound casual, "So . . . like pot or drinking? Stuff like that?"

"Yeah!" Morgan was excited now, half horrified and half thrilled to be telling the story. "Her brothers were high on Halloween when we went over there, and they kept laughing at our costumes like they were watching some hilarious show or something! And they said we could try it, and Devynne did, but then she started coughing really bad and they laughed even harder!"

Dana's heart banged angrily against her chest. Her Morgan, *her baby,* being offered drugs! She hoped her next question wouldn't stanch the flow of information. "Did you try it?"

"Mom!" said Morgan, jerking away from her momentarily. "That stuff is stupid!"

"Okay, sorry," said Dana. "But you see why I had to ask."

"I guess," said Morgan. "But I'm not *that* dumb."

You'd let Kimmi lead you back to bingeing and purging, but pot smoking is stupid, thought Dana. *At least I know where you stand.*

"I better get back," Morgan murmured. "Case she wakes up and thinks I'm telling."

The door opened and closed, disturbing the air in the room, making the sheers seem suddenly to throw themselves against the window glass before swinging back again. Dana lay awash in this new information. Only a few weeks ago, Kimmi had seemed like the antidote to Morgan's insecurity—but clearly she had serious problems of her own.

I have to warn Nora about this. The thought made Dana wince. She had no idea of how to broach the subject. *I can't just walk up to her and say, "I caught our daughters making themselves vomit, and Kimmi seems pretty well versed in the procedure, and oh, by the way, she may also have smoked pot."*

More important, what about Morgan? How had she been drawn so quickly back into the self-destruction of bingeing and purging? Of one thing Dana was sure: she was in over her head with Morgan's food issues.

Unable to sleep, Dana went downstairs to the office to look up child therapists online. The Multiservice Eating Disorders Association had a "Get Help" button with lists of professionals by town. She chose a few with kind-sounding names and cross-referenced them with her health insurance's "Find a Healthcare Provider" resource. Bethany Sweet showed up on both lists.

With a name like that, she's either the best person for the job, thought Dana, *or the worst.*

She was leaving a message on Ms. Sweet's voice mail when she heard movement in the hallway and wondered who could be up so early. She followed the sound of footsteps out to the mudroom, where Kimmi was waiting by the door, fully dressed, packed bag hanging from her narrow shoulder. Glancing furtively behind her, she caught sight of Dana and flinched. "I . . . I called my mom," she murmured breathlessly. "I don't feel good, and she's coming to get me." She searched desperately out the little window next to the door. "She's here!"

"I'll walk you out," said Dana.

"No!" said Kimmi. "You don't have to." She twisted the door handle, and when she opened it, Nora was standing on the front step, about to knock. Her sleek mahogany hair was dull and disheveled. She wore a green velour hoodie that barely covered what looked to be a pajama top. "You said you'd be waiting outside," she growled. Then she saw Dana. "Get in the car," she ordered Kimmi. The girl didn't wait to be told twice.

"It would probably be a good idea for us to talk," Dana suggested. "Maybe later on today."

Nora ran a hand through her hair. "No," she said. "Let's just get this out now."

"Oh, well . . . if you want—"

Nora cut her off. "I know about Morgan's eating disorder. I've known about it for weeks, but I decided to let the friendship run its course. We aren't the kind of people to steer our daughter away from a child who could benefit from her friendship. But now that Kimmi's told me what they've been up to, as a responsible parent I have to put a stop to it. I can't let her get dragged down by another girl's misfortune."

Dana's face went wide with shock. *Kimmi dragged down? KIMMI?*

"Nora, you certainly have every right to do what's best for your daughter, but I think you should know what I saw and heard last night."

Nora huffed an impatient sigh. "I *know* what you saw and heard. Kimmi told me all about it. Morgan made those awful brownies and pressured Kimmi into eating them with her, then showed her how to throw them up."

"I'm sorry, but that is *not* what happened, Nora. I heard them. Kimmi was saying . . . Well, to be quite honest she was bragging about how good she is at making herself vomit. It sounded to me like Kimmi's been doing it for some time now, and I—"

Nora's eyes narrowed into beads of fury. "Don't you *dare* blame this on my daughter! Kimmi was perfectly fine until she befriended Morgan. Polly told me about Morgan's problem, and I felt sorry for her—to be 'quite honest,' as you say"—Nora's fingers sliced quote marks into the air—"I felt sorry for *you*, too! And this is the thanks I get. I should have known—"

"Hold on," Dana said, finally picking out the strangest detail from this barrage. "*Polly* told you?"

Nora backhanded the air, swatting away the admission. "My poor daughter is waiting in the car, probably traumatized, and *I'm* standing here dealing with *you*. All I can say is, I hope you've learned something and you'll finally take responsibility!"

She swung around, yanked the door open, and whipped herself through it as if propelled by a slingshot. It was clear her intention was to slam it, but she'd inadvertently kicked one of Grady's cleats toward the doorsill on her way, and the door bounced open again. For the briefest instant she stopped, as if uncertain whether she should go back for a second try, but then she continued down the steps. Through the open doorway, Dana could hear her bark something at Kimmi as she got into the car. Then she gunned the motor, threw the car into reverse, and sped backward down the driveway, narrowly missing the mailbox post.

It was another moment or two before Dana's skin, flushed to a near boil, registered the wintry air infiltrating the house through the open door. She pushed her stunned limbs forward to dislodge the cleat and secure the entryway. When she turned around, Morgan was standing at the other end of the mudroom, her eyes wide with horror.

BY LUNCHTIME DANA KNEW SHE HAD MADE mistakes—from forgetting to input appointments to using incorrect billing codes on claim forms. Weeks and months from now, Tony would face double-booked slots, fussy claim reps, and irate patients from the many errors she'd made just in this one four-hour period.

But all she could think about was Morgan . . . who'd overheard the entire bizarre conversation with Nora and rightly concluded that her ex-best-friend-forever had been using her for cover . . . who'd realized that the lies Kimmi had told her mother would soon spread like pinkeye through the whole sixth grade . . . and who had wept in childish fright and ancient shame.

Dana had spent several hours attempting to console her inconsolable daughter, managing only to see her through to a sniffly, hiccupping exhaustion. When Alder got home from Jet's, she had quietly included herself in Dana's efforts and had eventually guided poor Morgan to the TV room to watch a movie with her. They'd been lying under the pink fleece blanket with the opening credits of *Little Women* rolling as Dana reluctantly left the house, promising to be home for lunch at the latest. Alder called around nine to say that Morgan had fallen asleep watching Susan Sarandon give the speech about wanting her daughters to value themselves for more than just their "decorativeness."

At lunchtime Dana popped her head into Tony's office. "I'll try to be back by one," she said, feeling suddenly so tired she was unsure if her legs would carry her all the way to the parking lot.

Tony nodded, watching her intently, inviting further explanation. It was that same look he'd given her over lunch at Keeney's that day, and its intimacy unnerved her. But all he said was, "Take as long as you need." She retreated before the last word was out of his mouth.

On the drive home, she called Kenneth and told him what had happened, to which his irritable response was, "Why did you let them make the brownies in the first place?"

"What am I supposed to do—*outlaw baking*?" she yelled back. Her phone beeped, indicating another caller. "I have to go," she said, and switched calls. "Hello?"

"Hi, this is Bethany Sweet!" said a high, perky voice. "Is this Mrs. Stellgarten?"

How old *is she?* Dana thought desperately. *A teenage therapist is not what we need right now!* She was tempted to hang up, but instead she sighed and said, "This is she."

"Great!" chirped Bethany. "So glad I caught you! Is this a good time?"

No, it's a positively awful time, Dana thought, pulling in to her driveway. *But it's as good as any.*

Over the next ten minutes, Bethany Sweet asked a series of questions, from "What's Morgan like?" to "Is there anything particularly stressful going on right now?" to "How often do you suspect she's purging?" It was hard to take her seriously with her high, singsong voice, but she seemed professional enough, and she made sure to mention her eight years of experience as a child and family therapist. She had a cancellation on Thursday; would that fit Morgan's schedule?

Yes, it would. And though Dana still had doubts, it seemed as if she'd been thrown a lifeline, thread-slender though it might be, and she let herself take a deep breath for the first time all day. As she turned to open the car door, Polly's face, pinched in an apprehensive smile, bobbed into view on the other side of the glass.

There was the briefest moment when all Dana wanted to do was step out of the car and into the possessive embrace of Polly's friendship. If there was ever a time when she needed the compact solidity of Polly, her intractable certainty and loud, intemperate love, it was now. But that worried smile, staining her features like an ill-considered tattoo, served to remind Dana of Polly's crime.

Dana got out of the car. "I can't talk to you now," she said as she strode toward the house.

"Let's go for a walk." The tension in Polly's voice made it sound like a question.

Dana started up the steps to the porch. "Morgan's waiting for me."

"Dana," called Polly, and then more insistently, "Dana!"

She stopped and turned to face her neighbor. "What."

Stance wide, arms taut at her sides, Polly's pixielike body was braced for an assault. "How is she?"

Dana could see now that Polly knew. Nora must have called her to vent about the morning's altercation and spilled the beans about repeating what Polly had said. Dana had never wanted to slap someone so much in her life. "She's just been thrown to the sharks by her best friend," she said tightly. "She's heartbroken."

Polly's chest registered a quick intake of air. "Can I . . . Would you let me talk to her? Maybe I can—"

Dana could feel fireworks going off in her major arteries, tiny explosions that burned the back of her throat, making her words come out in a violent hiss. "Are you *joking*? You betrayed her! I told you something in strictest confidence, and you blabbed about it—to someone in your *book group,* for godsake! Maybe the whole group for all I know—maybe the whole damn town!" Dana came down the steps, her finger shooting out in front of her. "She's *miserable* and *mortified,* and *no,* you cannot see her, and no, I will not take a walk with you. So you just *go home!*"

She went back up the steps into the house and closed the door behind her. Her legs went loose and quivery as her purse flopped to the floor. *That's the second friend I've lost,* she thought, *and the day's not even half over.*

She never did go back to work. Text messages were crisscrossing Cotters Rock like hungry locusts looking for their next rumor-laden meal. Those that flew Morgan's way were generally along the lines of Y DID U LIE ABOUT KIMMI?

Darby counseled, MAYBE U SHUD STAY HOME SICK TOMORO.

Devynne got straight to the point: U HAV NO FRIENDS NOW LOSR.

Morgan was wild with shame and worry and was only able to calm herself late in the afternoon by working on her "Timber Wolf: Predator or Prey?" report. Dana called Tony to say there was a bit of an emergency and she wasn't going to be able to finish out the day.

"No problem," he said. He didn't ask the nature of the emergency.

Going to bed that night should have been a relief. Contrary to Dana's every expectation, Morgan fell asleep almost as soon as she lay down, the receding tide of adrenaline that had crashed over her all day sapping her last sliver of resistance. Dana worried momentarily that Morgan had slipped into a shame-induced coma.

It was Dana who couldn't sleep, knowing as she did how bad tomorrow would be. It was tempting to let Morgan stay home, let the locusts gnaw at the juicy tidbit of scandal for a day in hopes that they'd be bored of it by Thursday. That's what her own mother had done after her father was gone: she'd let Dana and Connie stay home. And Dana had stayed, curled under her ballerina comforter, with David Cassidy setting his interminably sultry eyes on her from the poster tacked to her ceiling. She lay there spinning stories in her head that might account for her father's actions, wanting so desperately for some happier—or at least less drastically tragic—explanation to be revealed. She almost made herself believe that someday there might be. Almost.

The next day she had dressed so carefully in her best corduroy gauchos and Qiana shirt, working the hair dryer till it burned her scalp as she curled her hair into unwiltable Farrah Fawcett wings. Maybe the entire seventh grade wouldn't avoid her if she looked normal—better than average but not noticeably different.

It hadn't worked. Even her best friends hadn't known what to do, letting her sit with them at lunch but never actually speaking to her. She would've given anything to crawl back home and into that poster, into the tan, soulful arms of David Cassidy.

Connie declined their mother's offer of temporary sanctuary and went to school. "It's third grade," she'd said. "They probably won't even know." When Dana grilled her that afternoon, the only one who said anything was "Patsy McCarthy, who seriously thinks she's gonna be a saint someday," Connie had sneered. "Like *that's* a real job."

Better for Morgan to get it over with, Dana decided, lying tense in her bed. *Better not to seem weak or culpable.* But the thought of sending her fragile daughter into battle the next day, armed with nothing more than her mother's belief in her—which amounted to zero in the primitive world of preteen girls—made Dana's muscles twitch with sympathy pain. Unable to keep her eyes closed for more than a minute, she flung the covers off, went downstairs to the kitchen, poured a tall glass of sugar-free lemonade, and ripped open a bag of potatoes.

It was a bigger pile than she'd ever made before, and it glimmered on the plate, Yukon-gold nuggets sprinkled with oil as if by benediction. Each mouthful was a seductive distraction from her worries, and it wasn't until she was pressing the back of the fork onto the last crispy brown remnants that she noticed how heavy and overloaded her stomach felt, as if she'd eaten ball bearings in Pennzoil instead of home fries. No longer distracting, this new sensation amplified her anxiety.

This is bingeing, came the horrifying thought. *I do it, too.* Dana let the fork clatter to the plate and swatted it across the kitchen table so it slid to the very edge. Finally she cried the spine-wrenching sobs that had threatened to burst loose all day.

After the tears subsided, she laid her head on the table, her cheek pressed against the hard, cool wood. Her thoughts slowed, and she felt a blankness come over her that verged on relief but was also mildly frightening. She wondered if she knew anything anymore, or whether everything she'd previously believed had merely been lies she'd told herself so she could feel normal—her children's happiness, Polly's loyalty, Kenneth's love, her own self-control. All gone.

A strange thought came to her then, a willingness—a need, even—to know what was real and to understand how what had been true before had changed into what was true now. She'd always been more comfortable dealing in surface realities, she realized, a strategy that had served to protect her from the bleaker aspects of her life. But that wasn't working anymore. It was time to dig down to the deeper truths.

For instance, she'd always been an attentive mother, but did that make her a truly *good* mother? *Am I giving Morgan what she needs?* she wondered. *Do I really understand her?* She certainly didn't understand this need Morgan had to violently force food from her body. It made no sense to Dana, and yet she wanted desperately to understand it. How could something so disgusting possibly feel good?

She went to the basement, far away from the sleeping children, and into the little half bath by the boiler room. She knelt down in front of the old, rust-stained toilet, lifted the seat, and stared into the bowl. She touched the back of her throat with her finger and immediately gagged, stomach lurching, tongue rising up reflexively to repel the invasion. It felt awful, but she jammed her finger back again and again, each time her abdominal muscles seizing like an overheated engine. Finally some fluid came up and shot into the bowl.

Okay, enough. I've done it. But her gag reflex had been tripped by the rising liquid, and masticated potatoes erupted from her mouth in uncontrollable bursts, plopping into the toilet water and splashing up into her face. The smell, like something that had once been a vegetable but now resembled rancid cheese, assaulted her nostrils. She clutched the spattered rim of the bowl to keep the spasms from propelling her farther toward the water. *Stop! My God, stop!*

Eventually the clenching in her stomach subsided, and she sucked in air, letting her hair drip into the mess below her. She clawed blindly for the roll of toilet paper and yanked off a long ribbon to wipe her face. Exhausted, she rose slowly and went to the sink to wash herself.

I still don't understand this, she thought. *But at least now I know what it is.*

Though she'd given her teeth a punishing brushing before going back to bed that night, the taste in Dana's mouth when she woke up was like a thick sauce that had curdled. Through the fog that veiled her sleep-deprived brain, she struggled to recall the cleansing tea she'd had with Dermott McPherson. Was that only five days ago? *Lemons,* she remembered, and she dragged herself downstairs.

"We're making French toast!" Grady called as she entered the kitchen. "Look, Mom, look at this. Watch me, I can do it now!" He picked an egg out of the box, raised his hand high, and sent it smashing down onto the lip of the bowl. The egg exploded, shells flying, shiny whites slithering down onto the counter. "Dang," he muttered.

"Easy, G," said Alder admiringly. "What are you, Iron Man or something?" As she reached for the paper towels, she said to Dana, "I think Morgan's in bed."

Dana found Morgan fully dressed, covers pulled up to her chin. "I can't do it," she said. And though Dana tried to convince her that it might be even harder tomorrow, Morgan wouldn't budge. "I just can't." And she rolled over to face the wall.

Dana saw Grady and Alder off to school. There were no lemons in the house, so she made herself some scalding black tea, which burned going down but helped to clear the curdled hollandaise taste in her throat. Her Wednesday List, a running tab of all the household tasks she planned to accomplish on Wednesday mornings before going to work at noon, stared back at her from its place on the fridge, held captive by a plastic BLESS THIS MESS! magnet.

The phone rang. "It's me," said Kenneth. "I moved a meeting so I can come this afternoon while you're at work."

"Thanks," said Dana. "I left at lunch yesterday and never went back, so I should try to be there for the whole shift today."

"I don't think it's good to leave them unsupervised," he said stiffly.

"Kenneth, if you think for one minute—"

"Wait," he cut her off. "I didn't mean to sound . . . I'm just telling you that I'll be there."

The call-waiting tone beeped. "Fine," she said. "I have to go. Someone's beeping in."

"I think we should try not to fight," he announced.

"Agreed. I have to go." She hit the "flash" button on the phone.

"Hey there, gorgeous girl."

Who the . . . ? thought Dana for the briefest second. Then she remembered. "Hi, Jack."

"So the heck with Hebron Diner today. I say let's do it up and go to the Sheraton!"

Oh, for Pete's sake! thought Dana. *Like I have time for daytime sex.*

"For breakfast," he added quickly. "Not to get a room or anything . . . Unless you want to . . ."

She closed her eyes, willing herself not to snap at him. "That is *such* a nice idea, Jack, but I've got a bunch of stuff going on here, and I'm afraid I can't do breakfast at all. Morgan's home from school—she's, uh . . . she's not feeling well—and I have about a million things to do."

"Oh." Disappointment wafted through the phone line.

"But we'll see each other this weekend," she said, guilt squeezing at her. "Oh, wait. I've got the kids this weekend . . . Let's shoot for next Wednesday, okay?"

"Next *Wednesday*?" His tone was like Grady's, incredulous that it would be two weeks until he saw Kenneth again.

"I wish things weren't so complicated. But it's beyond my control—you can see that, right?" He didn't answer immediately, and the guilt pinched harder. "Jack, I would *really* like to have breakfast with you. Honestly. I wish we could just book a room and spend the whole day together."

"Really?"

"Absolutely."

And he seemed satisfied, she thought. *At least there's one person who doesn't think I'm failing miserably.*

The Wednesday List remained a prisoner to its magnet on the fridge, and absolutely nothing got done. Dana sat at the kitchen table in her pajamas drinking hot tea, feeling anxious and angry by turns. What she really needed was someone to talk to, but there was no one to confide in without fear of judgment, or feeding the rumor mill, or both.

There was one person, though, who would certainly judge her but who would be far more disgusted with all the *other* characters in this horrible drama, who would happily voice the fury that Dana could barely find words for. She reached for the phone. "Connie, it's me."

"Christ, it's about time. So much for keeping me up to date on my kid."

Dana smiled despite herself. Not calling Connie was the least of the mistakes she'd made. "I'm thinking of taking up smoking," she said.

"Wicked," said Connie. "Marlboro Lights, I hope."

"What do you want to hear about first—Alder or my disaster of a life?"

"Tough one," said Connie. "Alder being the child of my womb, your disastrous life sounding like an episode of *Desperate Cupcakers*."

Dana clamped down hard on her molars. "You're my sister, for godsake. Can you please not act like a rabid bobcat for *one stinking phone call*?"

There was a brief silence on the other end of the line—the only time Dana could ever remember her chronic smart-ass of a sister apparently nonplussed.

"Well," Connie said finally. "I suppose I could give it the ol' *Peyton Place* try. What's up?"

Dana told her everything, starting with Morgan's purging.

"Poor kid," said Connie. "She turned the gun on herself."

"My God, what's *that* supposed to mean!"

"Hey," said Connie. "We're all armed—even *you*. All I'm saying is, it's not always easy to keep the safety lock on. Especially for young girls."

Dana recounted finding Morgan and Kimmi in the bathroom, Kimmi's lie, and Nora's reaction.

"Holy shit!" yelled Connie. "She's a fucking rottweiler with a Prada bag! You should seriously kick her ass!" Her curse-strewn indignation was a balm to Dana's wounds.

About Polly's defection all Connie said was, "Wow, I didn't see that one coming."

"Me either," said Dana, feeling her chest tighten. "She's my closest friend."

"I always kinda liked Polly, but that's a hell of a screwup." Connie asked about Grady, and Dana told her about his trouble with friends and his desperate bids for Kenneth's attention. "Fucking Ken," muttered Connie. "Guy's a total numbnuts."

"I know you never liked him, but—"

"Of *course* I never liked him. Jesus, Day, could you have *picked* a less imaginative guy?"

Day, thought Dana. *She hasn't called me that in years.* "Oh, imagination. I didn't realize *that* was your big beef with him," she teased.

"Biggest, maybe, but certainly not only."

"Well, my list has grown some, too. I met his girlfriend— complete bimbo. That's what he left me for, a hairdo in a puffy coat." It felt good to snarl about Tina. But it also made Tina more real. Dana blew an aggravated sigh. "I think they're getting serious."

"Bound to happen," said Connie. "He finally sank to his rightful level."

A companionable silence fell between them. After a moment Connie said, "Okay, can we talk about my kid now, or did you have any other assholes to tell me about?"

Dana hesitated.

"Christ," said Connie. "How bad is it?"

"Well . . . it was bad, but I think she's doing better now. Connie, you have to promise you won't flip out. She's handling it, but she has to heal at her own pace." When Dana finished recounting Ethan's cruel abuse of Alder's friendship, Connie let out a string of expletives that was almost poetic in its lush, descriptive imagery.

"True," said Dana. "But, honestly, I think she's turning the corner. She's made some friends, and she's been incredible with Morgan and Grady." The thought of Alder's kindness toward her beleaguered cousins lifted Dana. "You've got quite a girl there, Con. She's something special."

Dana could hear the pride in Connie's response. "You have no idea," she murmured.

"Yes," said Dana, "I actually do."

CHAPTER

32

"*PLEASE,*" BEGGED MORGAN AT THE CURB OF COTters Rock Middle School the next morning. A bell rang, and kids moved into the building, some scurrying with their backpacks thumping against their backs, some trudging as if on a forced march.

"Morgan, honey, you can't miss any more school. I know it's going to be tough, but if you need me, I'm just a phone call away, I promise." She tried to sound positive, but it was all she could do not to pull away with Morgan still in the car, sparing her from the imminent nastiness.

Finally Morgan zipped up her jacket, her face rising pale as an iceberg from a fleecy sea. Dana smoothed her hair. "You're seeing the therapist tonight. I think that'll help."

Morgan rolled her eyes. "I am such a freak," she muttered, and got out of the car.

Tears rolled down Dana's cheeks all the way to work. Dabbing her face with a napkin she found in the glove box, she ordered herself to pull it together. She'd worked hard the day before—there was a lot of catching up to do, and it had been a welcome relief to think of nothing other than claim forms and billing statements. *Work,* she told herself now. *Just focus on that.*

She was so focused that by eleven-thirty she had done everything but vacuum the reception area and rearrange the posters on teeth whitening. Her cell phone rang "Ode to Joy."

"It's lunch," whispered Morgan. Cell phone use was strictly prohibited at school.

"How's it going?" asked Dana anxiously.

"No one would sit with me," she muttered. "No one. Then a couple of boys—Kimmi worshippers—started fake-puking, so I left."

"Oh, honey." Dana sighed. "Where are you now?"

"The back stairs by the gym."

"Can you hang in there till the end of school?"

Morgan's voice trembled. "I have to go to science now."

"I love you, sweetie."

But Morgan was already gone.

When Tony's vegetarian sub and iced tea arrived, he came out to pay the deliveryman. He gave Dana a quick glance. "Coming?" he asked.

With no projects left to complete, she gathered up her yogurt and carrot sticks and walked back toward the little kitchen. Marie passed in her running gear. She had a new tattoo on her wrist, a little blackbird carrying a pentagram in its feet. "Have a nice run," said Dana.

"Have a nice lunch," Marie replied with a quick smile, which, while not exactly friendly, seemed to bear no malice.

Tony and Dana sat at the small round table, their conversation mild and impersonal. At first this was exactly what Dana wanted, to steer clear of anything that would trip off her hair-trigger emotions. But after a while it seemed shallow—heartless, even—to be talking about fresh snowfall in Vermont with so many more relevant topics pulsing beneath the surface of their conversation. "How's your daughter?" Dana asked suddenly. "The one in med school."

Tony's tan cheeks rounded into a grin. "Much better!" he said, apparently just as relieved as she was to stop talking about distant weather patterns. "She got a day or two off, and she—"

"Hello?" called a man's voice from the reception area. "Anyone home?"

"I'll go," said Tony, laying his sub down on the butcher paper.

"No, I will," Dana insisted, as they both walked toward the front of the office. "I forgot to throw the bolt after Marie left."

Tony was a step ahead of her and told the man, "I'm sorry, we're closed for lunch."

A second later, when Dana came into view, the man said, "There's my girl!"

It was Jack, filling up the waiting area with his oversize shoulders and loud voice. He was wearing a maroon tie with a dizzying pattern of little brown footballs. He saw Dana catch sight of it and said, "Like it? My team gave it to me last year. Excellent conversation piece with car buyers. Unless they're women or foreign, or whatever."

Dana hoped her cringe wasn't visible as she introduced him to Tony.

"Nice to meet you, Dr. Sakimoto." Jack pronounced it "Sacky-moe-toe," as if he were a cast member from *McHale's Navy* and Tony were Fuji, the diminutive cook. He gave Tony's hand a perfunctory pump and turned to Dana. "Let's go!" He grinned.

"Go?"

"I'm kidnapping you for lunch. There's *no way* I'm waiting a week to see you."

"That's so thoughtful," she said quickly. "But my break's almost over. Tony and I were just about to get back to work." She looked at Tony, and he nodded convincingly. "Let's talk tonight, okay?" She took Jack's arm and started to walk him toward the door.

But Jack was not ready to admit defeat. He turned to Tony. "Hey, Dr. Sakimoto, my friend. Can't you let this pretty lady off the hook for an hour? I'm sure she'll work extra hard when she gets back." And then he actually winked.

Tony put on a look of pleasant bafflement. "Well, she works pretty hard as it is there, Jack."

"And I'm sure she does, but at the moment she needs some lunch." He swiveled back to Dana. "Dontcha, honey?"

Dana was mortified. Who did Jack think he was, showing up at her workplace and trying to steamroll her employer like that? "I really can't go, Jack," she said. "I already had to take time off this week, and I'm swamped with the catch-up."

"Aw, come on." He fake-pouted. "I came all the way over here and everything."

"I know, and I'm so flattered, but unfortunately I just can't."

The boyish pout faded, and she saw a flash of anger behind his eyes. "I was just trying to be, you know, romantic," he muttered. He shot Tony an annoyed look and let Dana steer him to the door.

She walked him to his muscular black truck and let him kiss her deeply and with too much gyrating, making her worry that early patients might see them. Wiping her mouth as she went back inside, she thought, *He's not really the world's best kisser. My standards are just low.*

It was so embarrassing to face Tony, who was still in the reception area, plucking the older magazines out of the pile fanned out across a side table. "All set?" he asked innocently as he tossed the armload into her recycle bin behind the counter.

"Tony. I can't apologize enough."

He gave a shrugging head shake, as if to say it was nothing.

"No, really, I don't know what he was thinking!" Dana followed him back to the kitchenette. "He can't just come in here and . . . and just assume I would . . ."

Tony sat down and took up his sub. "You could have gone if you wanted to. You're not a hostage here."

"After the way he talked to you? He was so"—Dana swatted her hand around, as if the word were a fly she could catch—"just *embarrassing*. He mispronounced your name! On purpose!"

Tony sat back, tapped a paper napkin to his lips. He stretched his short legs out in front of him and folded his arms across his middle. "Some guys are like that."

"Like *what,* for goodness' sake?"

"Like they have to—if you'll pardon the language—piss in a circle around everything they think is theirs. He was just making the point that he has a claim on you."

"A *claim* on me! We've only been dating for a few weeks!"

Tony shrugged. She could tell he was thinking things he wasn't saying. "Some women like that," he said after a moment. "A guy who calls the shots. They like that caveman stuff."

"Well, *I* don't." She gave her yogurt a vigorous stir. "I don't appreciate it at all."

Tony scratched his chin. "How come you told him your lunch hour was over? And your work is already organized within an inch of its life, so I'm not sure what you meant about 'catch-up.'"

She gave the spoon a few more turns. "I just . . . I just didn't want to."

"Fair enough," he said, and sat forward to work on his sub again.

The motor of the half-size fridge cycled on, and its low, whining hum filled the kitchenette. The phone rang at the front desk but then stopped when the answering service picked up.

"He's not much of a talker," said Dana.

"No?" Tony took a swig of his iced tea. "He seems pretty outgoing."

"No, he is. He just . . . Well, we talk about things that are . . . lighter, I guess."

Tony nodded. "Like . . . ?"

"Oh, you know." *Like what?* And why was she getting into this with Tony? "Fun stuff," she said, with a lighthearted shrug. "Sports, because he coached Grady's team. He was so good with them." She nibbled at a pretzel. *What the heck else did they talk about?* "Also, he's a really hard worker—he sets up challenges with the other guys about who can sell the most cars."

Tony inhaled and held it for a second, then let the air out.

"What?" she said.

"Hmm?"

"You were about to say something." Dana felt a ping of aggravation.

He wadded up the butcher paper and tossed it in the trash. "Just that it seems he's more of a talker than a listener. I mean, all that with the sports and the cars—that's *his* subject matter, right?"

The pings of irritation came faster now, like someone hitting a stone with a flint. "We talk about things I'm interested in, too." She hated the indignant sound of her voice and tried to dial it back. "But we can't talk about dental appointments all the time, now, can we?" she said with a thin little laugh. "That would just be boring."

His eyebrows went up. "Definitely." He nodded. "A real buzzkill."

Dana let out a huff of frustration. "I'm not trying to insult you. But I don't know why you have to pick at things."

"I don't—"

"Yes. You do. You ask these probing questions, and I end up feeling like an idiot." She shut her eyes and gave her head a quick shake. *Now I'm angry, and I don't even know why.*

He leaned forward, put his elbows on the table. "Hey," he murmured. "You are *not* an idiot, by any stretch. And if I made you feel that way, then *I'm* the idiot."

She exhaled. The sparking inside her chest dissipated. Speechless, she offered a silent apology. He accepted, a hint of a smile deepening the crow's-feet around his eyes. "You know," he said slyly, "you're gonna think I'm nuts, but the way you get mad at me—I'm honored. Like when I offered you this job, remember? I'm guessing you don't let your anger out too often." His grin widened. "Makes me feel kind of special."

"I don't know about that," she said. "I get pretty mad at my ex-husband these days."

"Yeah, but he doesn't score points for that."

"Why not?"

"Because *he* deserves it."

⟞⟝

BETHANY SWEET'S OFFICE WAS ON A SIDE STREET near East Hartford Center, in an old Victorian house with a mansard roof. "Great," muttered Morgan as they trudged up the walk. "My therapist lives with the Addams Family."

"It's just an old house converted to office space, sweetie," said Dana. "Try to keep positive."

"Right . . ."

They waited in what was originally the foyer of the house, now lined with wooden chairs and a love seat upholstered in faded blue toile. A metal box the shape of an oversize doughnut sat on the floor emitting a shushing hum that sounded like distant highway traffic. "For privacy," murmured Dana. "So no one has to worry about anyone else hearing them."

A door opened. Out stepped a short, young-looking woman with bobbed brown hair corralled by a headband. Below her stretchy leaf-print shirt, a black skirt belled out around her ample hips. She made a beeline for Morgan. "I'm Bethany Sweet," she chirped, smiling professionally. "You must be Morgan." When she offered her hand to shake, her shirt crept up above the skirt's waist, revealing a narrow shoreline of pale flesh.

Morgan sat up as if she'd been cold-called in class. "Uh . . . hi," she muttered, glancing quickly to her mother for the correct answer. Dana shot a pointed look to Bethany's extended hand, and Morgan reached out and rested her own in it briefly before withdrawing.

"And you're Mrs. Stellgarten," said Bethany, the childlike voice distracting Dana, making her wonder momentarily if she should have brought goldfish crackers and juice boxes. They followed Bethany into her office. The room seemed purposely nondescript, with a beige couch and a matching chair. Dana noticed a photo taken inside Fenway Park looking down to a swarm of players coalesced into a red-and-white amoeba against the bright green infield.

"Game Five of the 2004 playoffs against the Yankees," said Bethany proudly. "I was so glad I brought my camera. Do you follow any sports teams?" she asked Morgan.

Morgan glanced to her mother again, as if this were a trick question on a substitute teacher's quiz. Dana gave her a micro-nod, urging her to answer. "Um . . . not really . . ." Morgan's voice went up at the end, making it sound like a question.

Morgan and Dana sat a body width apart on the beige couch, Morgan clutching a brown throw pillow onto her lap.

Bethany settled into a leather swivel chair. "So maybe we could just get to know each other for a few minutes?" She addressed these comments to Morgan, as if Morgan were the teacher and Bethany needed a hall pass. "And then maybe Mom could go read a magazine or text her girlfriends or something?" She held up an imaginary BlackBerry and poked at it with her thumbs. Morgan's face softened at the ludicrous image. Bethany went on. "And then if we feel like it, we'll call her back in here, okay?" Morgan nodded her consent.

While Dana was in the room, Bethany chatted amiably with Morgan, who slowly loosened her grip on the pillow. What was Morgan's favorite of all her activities? "Cello," said Morgan. "Except I really suck at it." She blinked, horrified at having used the word "suck" in front of a stranger.

"Oh?" said Bethany. "How bad do you suck?"

Morgan's eyes shot sideways toward her mother, then back to Bethany. "Um, like really bad?"

"So why do you like it, if you suck so bad?"

Morgan thought for a moment, her finger trailing up and down the pillow's piping. "I guess I like how it sounds. It's not high and squeaky like a violin. It sounds more like a person's voice."

"Huh," said Bethany. "I never thought of that, but you're right. It does sound sort of like a low voice."

"Yeah," said Morgan with a hint of enthusiasm. "Like, maybe a man's. Except the way I play, it's like the guy's got strep throat." The corners of her mouth inched up at this little joke.

It's the first time I've seen her smile since Monday night, thought Dana.

Soon Dana was invited to go back out to the waiting room. She glanced at the magazines: *Psychology Today, Redbook,* and a few others. But she didn't want to read about archetypal themes in geriatric psychology or decorating for a more festive Thanksgiving. She sat staring at the unadorned wall. It was off-white. The metal doughnut made its shushing sound.

Her mind seemed to pull back from its tight focus on the immediate situation. It zoomed out until she couldn't quite see Morgan or Grady or Alder, or all of the misery they seemed to have soaked up like sponges to dirty water. It felt as if she were floating in space, looking down on the town of Cotters Rock, in the state of Connecticut, some of its inhabitants momentarily happy, some momentarily angry or sad. *There's no such thing as perfect,* she could hear her mother saying, *and if there were, it wouldn't stay that way for long.*

And a sense came over her that maybe it would all be okay eventually. It was hard right now, and messy. But the shushing sound echoed the air flowing in and out of her lungs, and for those few moments it seemed that the expansion and contraction of her chest was all she really needed to keep going.

The door to Bethany's office opened. "Want to join us for the last few minutes?" Dana followed her into the office, wondering how nearly an hour had flown by so quickly. "I have Morgan's permission to tell you some of what we've talked about today," said Bethany, sinking down into her chair. "Mostly we've talked about what stress is and how it can be good sometimes but how it can also make us think and do things that aren't so healthy. For instance, bingeing and purging."

Bethany didn't waste any time getting straight to the point, did she? Dana glanced at Morgan, but she seemed okay, if not quite relaxed.

"Divorce can be a pretty big stressor for kids—just like it is for parents, right, Mom?" Bethany aimed an empathetic smile at Dana. "It makes everyone feel off-kilter, like they used to know what to expect and now they don't. Knowledge is powerful, and when you feel like you don't have that power anymore, sometimes you do things that *feel* like power but aren't really. Like putting things in your body that it doesn't need and then forcing them back out again."

Bethany went on to say that they had talked about some ideas to help Morgan take control in healthy ways, nodding confidently at Morgan. "So why don't you talk it over with Mom, and if you'd like to come back, I'd be very happy to see you again."

When they walked out to the car, flakes of snow were swirling in the early-evening darkness. The sidewalk was slick with the melted remains. "Was it okay?" Dana asked.

Morgan shrugged. "I guess."

"Do you want me to make another appointment?"

"Might as well."

"It went okay," Dana reported to Kenneth once the kids were settled in bed. She sat in the office with the door closed, promising herself that once she completed this final task, she could finally put on her pajamas and go to bed.

"Meaning?" said Kenneth.

"Meaning it went okay." Exhaustion nibbled at her temper. "Morgan seemed to like her. She seemed to know what she was doing."

"Seemed to," muttered Kenneth. "Where did she get her de-gree? Where did she train?"

"Oh, for Pete's sake, I can't remember, and I don't care. Morgan agreed to go back—that's what's important."

"I just want to make sure she's not some quack who's going to light incense, hang a crystal around Morgan's neck, and call her cured."

"Well, thanks very much for that vote of confidence in my ability to find a reputable therapist. If this is your idea of us not fighting, it isn't going very well."

Kenneth inhaled noisily and let his breath out into the mouth-piece. "Okay," he grumbled. "Please just tell me she's board-certified."

Dana had no idea. "She's board-certified," she said.

"Okay then." He let out a little cough. "Well, there's something else I'd like to discuss with you if this is a good time."

Something else? thought Dana. *Our daughter's in therapy, our son can barely keep his temper in check, our finances are a mess—and you've got something ELSE?*

He didn't wait for her answer. "Tina likes to enter contests."

"Okay . . ." said Dana, wondering what that had to do with the price of tea in China.

Tina's salon played a radio station that did contests and give-aways, he told her. While a customer sat reading magazines and waiting for her dye to set, Tina would slip into the office and try to be the right caller. "Last week she won a hundred-dollar gift cer-tificate to Perfectua—that pricey boutique at the Evergreen Mall? Barely covered the cost of a sweatshirt," he muttered. Dana flinched at the name of Nora's employer. "Anyway," he continued, "she was automatically entered to win the grand prize." He hesitated then, as if what followed would be bad news. "And today we were notified that she won."

Couldn't possibly care less, thought Dana.

"It's an all-expenses-paid trip to Disney World. For four." There was silence on the line, as if he were holding his breath, and then the words rushed out. "It's for the week of Thanksgiving."

Dana almost said, *So?* But then the pieces of Kenneth's little puzzle came together in her mind. He wanted the kids for a whole week. Including Thanksgiving.

"Absolutely not."

"You can't just dismiss it out of hand!" Kenneth fumed. "You have to at least *consider* it."

"It's not an option."

"Dana, for godsake—"

"I can't talk anymore," she said. "It's been a long day. I'm going to bed." And she hung up.

On Saturday, Dana awoke to the sounds of long low wails, punctuated by quick, scratchy groans. At first she thought a coyote had gotten hold of some poor animal in the woods behind the house. Then she realized the animal's death cries had a tune to them. Either there was a rabbit out there who knew the melody to Pachelbel's Canon or Morgan was practicing her cello.

Dana moved her sluggish body toward Morgan's room. "You're up early," she said.

"I was up a long time ago." Morgan squinted at the sheet music as if it were written in disappearing ink.

Dana sank down onto the bed. "But it's not a school day."

"Exactly."

Dana nodded. "And you were so happy you didn't have to go to school that it woke you up."

Morgan leaned the cello against her desk. "Can you take me to Peshawaug?"

It was a town way out in northwestern Connecticut. "What's in Peshawaug?"

"It's this place called the Wolves' Den. They have real wolves there, and all this stuff about how they live. I have to do research for my paper."

"Can't you get that on the Internet?" Dana had been looking forward to a relaxing day of catching up on laundry, making pancakes, and letting the kids watch too much TV.

"It's not that good. Some of it looks made up. Plus, we're supposed to have primary sources. Real wolves is totally primary." She twisted her hair back and forth. "Um . . . and that Bethany lady says I should do stuff that makes me feel better."

By noon all four of them were in the minivan headed west to Peshawaug. They ate sandwiches in the car, Grady growling and gnashing at a peanut-butter-and-ketchup sandwich. "See this?" He snarled, holding up a sandwich half. "This is Little Red Riding Hood's arm!"

"You're more like a disgusting little pig than a big bad wolf," said Morgan.

"Here, piggy." Alder handed him a napkin. "You have Red Riding Hood guts on your cheek."

They arrived as the tour was about to start and followed the crowd to the wooden benches by a chain-link fence that surrounded the wolves' expansive habitat. A young woman staff member stood in front of the fence and began to talk as two wolves paced behind her. Wolves were born afraid of humans, she told them. The only way staff members were able to interact with them was by taking them into the building as pups, feeding and playing with them, so they would imprint onto humans. "We don't train them," she said. "Wolves aren't trainable or tamable. In order to be accepted, we must live as the lowest in the wolves' very strict social order."

She explained that in every wolf pack there were an alpha male and female who ruled the group. They were responsible for the pack's safety and were the first to eat at every meal. If a lower-ranked wolf tried to eat before an alpha, it would be threatened and nipped. She demonstrated this with chunks of cheese she threw over the fence to them. The alpha always ate first. She went on to say that only alphas could mate. The other wolves were called "celibate subordinates" and served as hunters, nannies, and teachers to the pups. If they wanted to mate, they would become "dispersers," leaving to start their own pack with other dispersers.

Morgan scribbled furiously. At the end of the presentation, the staff member invited visitors to send up a "social howl." Grady howled with gusto, his little tenor heard above the voices of the more hesitant adults and older kids. The wolves obliged by howling back, which sent Grady hopping up and down with enthusiasm.

"Was that helpful?" Dana asked Morgan as they filed out.

"Yeah," said Morgan. "It was just what I needed."

Dana had turned off her cell phone during the presentation. When they got back into the car, she turned it on and the "Missed Call" message flashed. In fact, there had been several missed calls.

"Dana, we have joint custody—*joint,* not you making the decisions and me just rolling over. I don't know when you turned into someone who thinks she's entitled to make unilateral policies, but I'm not going to stand for it. Call me back as soon as possible." Dana deleted it.

"Hey there, beauty! I know you've got the kiddos this weekend, but there's this new invention called a baby-sitter . . . Just kidding, but you know what I'm saying, right? I miss my girl! Call me, okay?" She deleted it, reminding herself to return the call when she was alone.

"I know you hate me for telling Nora about Morgan's problem, and frankly I hate myself. Victor thinks I should have my head examined. But I can't stand this silent treatment, Dana, and I think I deserve a chance to explain and apologize. I think you owe me that, so please call."

OWE you? thought Dana. She deleted the message.

"Yeah, uh, this is Manchester Tire and Service. We got your Volkswagen Rabbit on the back lot, and it's been sitting here for a couple months. You gotta either give us the thumbs-up to fix it or get it outta here by Thanksgiving." She'd have to call Connie and see how she wanted to handle the car. She glanced at Alder, who was playing the license-plate game with Grady.

"Maine!" Alder called out. "On that green SUV over there."

"I saw that first!" said Grady.

"Liar, liar pants on fire," she retorted. "Get your own Maine."

There was one last message. "Hi Dana. I don't mean to intrude on your family time, but I was thinking about what you told me at lunch yesterday. You know, with Morgan's issues and the Disney trip and everything. It's a lot. And I just wanted to say if you need a little time off to sort things out, I'm fine with that. Honestly, you're the best receptionist I've ever had, and I figure it's in my interest to keep you happy—plus, you deserve it. Hope you're having a great weekend. See you Monday."

Dana sighed and felt the tension ebb from her neck. She saved the message, as if its mere existence could serve as a protection against whatever troubles might lurk in the days to come.

"Bath time," she told Grady that night before bed.

"I took one yesterday!" He put the television remote behind his back.

"Well, that's good for yesterday, but it doesn't count for today." She went over to the TV and pressed the "off" button.

"But I'm clean, I swear—smell me! Smell how good I smell!"

Dana took this rare opportunity to gather Grady onto her lap. At seven he barely fit, so she had to squeeze him up into a ball, one arm behind his back and the other under his knees. He giggled and protested, but he didn't try to escape. She stuck her nose into his neck, and he laughed even harder. "Swiss cheese!" she declared.

"No way!"

She sniffed toward his feet. "Rotten eggs. Forget the bath—you're going straight into the washing machine!"

They straggled up the two flights of stairs to the bathroom on the second floor, and she ran a bubble bath. When he got in, she collected his clothes to put in the hamper. The pants had something round and hard in them, and when she reached into the pocket, she pulled out a golf ball. Written in black marker across the tiny dimples were the words "You rock, Dude!"

"Where'd this come from?" she asked him.

"That's mine!"

"I'm not taking it," she assured him. "I just asked where you got it."

He sank under the bubbles until only a thatch of his hair was visible. Dana waited. When he surfaced, he seemed surprised she was still there. "Dad said I could keep it," he grumbled.

"Dad gave this to you?"

"Yeah." Grady let out a resigned huff, as if he'd been caught with contraband. "We call each other 'dude' sometimes. Dad said I could carry it around when I miss him. Okay? So don't lose it."

She looked at him there in the tub, soap bubbles clinging to his hair, and he seemed so small. With most of his body underwater, he looked much as he had when he was two or three.

How did this happen? How did my baby grow into a boy with a golf ball standing in for his father?

"I'll put it on your dresser so you'll know where to find it." And she left him there bobbing a plastic shark in and out of the suds. She pulled a sock out of his drawer to set the golf ball on so it wouldn't roll onto the floor.

She remembered finding a shirt of her father's in the back of her mother's closet years after he was gone. Her mother had shrugged. "I still loved him," she said. "Even after what he did." When she died, Dana and Connie cleared out her apartment and Dana looked for the shirt, half afraid to find it. But it wasn't there. Their mother was a purposeful person; she wouldn't have thrown it out by accident. Dana remembered thinking, *She must have been ready to let it go.*

Clearly, Grady wasn't ready to let anything go, nor fully accept his father's reduced presence in his life. And it occurred to her that the desperation Grady felt might also be shared by Kenneth himself. How must Kenneth have felt searching for something to soothe his sad little boy and then writing these words to remind him of their private joke? How does it feel to hand your child an inanimate object and say, "Pretend this is me"?

Dana had never had to do such a thing, and she hoped she never would. But standing there looking at the golf ball, she had a moment of sympathy for Kenneth.

Later, when Grady had put on his pajamas and gotten into bed, she came back in to say good night to him. The golf ball was not on the dresser, and she knew without a doubt that it was with him, possibly under the pillow or more likely held tightly in the safe harbor of his hand.

"GOSH, THAT WAS NICE OF YOU," SHE SAID TO TONY as he unlocked the big glass door on Monday morning. "Calling to offer me some time off."

"Yeah?" he said, an uncharacteristic note of uncertainty in his tone. "After I hung up, I was worried you'd think it was over the top, calling you on the weekend like that. But I figured you'd need some time to figure out the logistics. Otherwise I could've just told you when you came in this morning . . ." He trailed off.

"Not at all," she assured him. "In fact, after the other messages I got, it was like when you open the mail and you think it's going to be a bill and it ends up being a check instead."

"Good," he said with a little sigh of relief, as they hung their coats in the closet. Tony unwound the scarf from his neck and tugged on the fringe. "So . . . you think you'll do it?"

"You're going to think I'm crazy," she said with a chuckle. "But I *like* being here. This is the easy part. What I really need is a break from everything *else*."

He smiled back at her. "All right. Well, the offer stands."

She reached out and gave his arm a pat. "You are the best boss, Tony. Honestly, no one could ask for better."

At lunch she told him about the golf ball, and he nodded knowingly. "Ingrid picked out things for the girls," he said. "When she went to the hospital all those times, and then at the end . . ."

"Oh, Tony," Dana murmured.

"Yeah, heartbreaking." He shook his head. "She tried to do the same for me, and I got so mad."

"Mad? Why?"

"Because I'm not a child, for godsake. I know the difference between a lifeless object and my wife! Besides, the whole world reminded me of her. Everything was a symbol of what I'd lost."

"Is it still that way?"

He thought for a moment. "Yes and no. I've had experiences since then, taken trips, made new friends. It's not all about her anymore, which is a good thing, I think. A healthy thing. I mean, how the hell could I have gone on like that? I'd be in the loony bin by now. But I look at my beautiful girls . . . and there she is." He sighed. "There she is, and right where she should be."

He looked back up at her, the warm brown of his eyes calling her into his loss, his survival, and she felt a surge of pride that he would share it with her. She found herself reaching out and giving his hand a squeeze. His face changed, a fleeting reaction—surprise, she thought. Or maybe panic? She was his employee, after all. She shouldn't be holding his hand across the chipped tabletop as if this were a lunch date at some Parisian café. She slid her hand back and made an excuse about needing to make some phone calls before her lunch break was over.

Actually, she did need to make another appointment for Morgan. She left a message on Bethany Sweet's voice mail. She called Connie and left a message about Alder's car. There were still ten minutes left—who else could she call?

"Hi, Jack, it's Dana."

"Ohhh," he said, his voice rising and falling like a taunt. "You finally had time to call back."

"I'm sorry, it's just that the kids have had some . . . trouble. I hope you understand."

He let out a little grunt of appeasement. "I suppose," he conceded. "I'm not the kind of guy to get in the way of a mom and her kids. I just didn't think you'd forget about, you know . . . *us.*"

"No, I didn't forget. But you have to understand they're my priority. Also, I know you meant well, but you can't show up at my office like that. It makes me look unprofessional." *Especially when you're disrespectful to my boss,* she thought.

"Well, *that* guy, he's on some sort of power trip," insisted Jack. "He couldn't let you off for *one hour?* I mean, come on! Who does he think you are—his slave?"

A fury came over Dana so fast she felt as if she could hit something. "That's a horrible thing to say, and it couldn't be further from the truth," she said tightly. "Tony Sakimoto is one of the kindest, most understanding guys in the world."

"Well, *excuse me!* I didn't know he was the Second Coming, or I would've knelt and kissed his ring!"

Dana narrowed her eyes at the phone. "You know what?" she said. "I'm not talking to you anymore!"

"Well, neither am I!" he yelled, and the phone went dead.

There's another friend I've lost, she told herself. But she couldn't seem to feel bad about it. In fact, she realized with surprise, what she felt most was relief.

The sight of the first patient to come in after lunch nearly knocked her out of her chair.

"Hey, Good Witch!" he teased, leaning on the counter. "I didn't know you worked here."

"Dermott! Is . . . is everything okay?" She had this strange notion that maybe something had happened to Mary Ellen or one of the children. But why would he come here? And tell her?

"Everything but my dental hygiene, apparently." She stared at him. He stared back, perplexed. "Did my appointment get canceled? Mellie made such a big deal about dropping me off on time."

She looked down at the day's schedule. There was his name. "Oh, yes, I'm sorry. I just didn't know you were a patient here."

"Nah, it's okay. I really wasn't planning on coming, but Mellie insisted."

"Why weren't you going to come?"

"Well"—he smiled at her—"you know." She hadn't a clue, and it must have showed, because he added, "It's kind of like getting your car washed before you junk it."

His eyes locked onto hers for a moment in that way he had, and she felt herself blanch. "Jeez," he muttered, "I'm always doing this to you."

And then Tony was there in the doorway, saying, "Dermott, how goes it?"

"Shitty," said Dermott. "And whatever you do, don't ask me about changes in my health status."

"Deal." Tony clasped a hand on Dermott's shoulder, and they went into the operatory.

When he came back out, Dermott showed her his teeth. "You practically need sunglasses, don't you?"

"Marie's the best," said Dana nodding. *What a beautiful face,* she thought. Gaunt and pale as he was, Dermott's humor and kindness still shone through. "I need to ask you," she said hesitantly. "It's a standard question."

"Next appointment?" He considered for a moment. "No. I wouldn't want one of those reminder cards going out. I'm trying to make it easy on her. Well, as easy as I can anyway."

"I'm glad you came today," Dana ventured. "It sounds like it means a lot to her."

"She's not ready." He stared into space for a brief moment, then focused on Dana again. "Thanks for everything, Good Witch. My chauffeur should be here any minute." And he walked gingerly out the door.

———

Bethany Sweet called back while Dana was helping Grady with his homework. The slightly epileptic strains of Morgan's cello practice drifted down from her room. Dana left Grady with his double-digit addition problems and went into the office. They set the next appointment, and she told Bethany about the Disney trip. "I just don't think this is the right time," Dana concluded. "Morgan needs stability, and I don't want her to miss a weekly appointment with you."

"I see your point," said Bethany. "And it's important for Morgan not to feel she's being forced to go if she doesn't want to. So many things feel out of her control right now—I wouldn't want to add to that pile. However . . ." There was a little pause, and Dana could feel her neck muscles tighten. "It could be a very good thing for her."

No! thought Dana, but what she said was, "Why?"

"First of all, because she's missing her dad. Kids this age often don't express it—sometimes they don't even know it themselves. But I got a little clue when she said her favorite activity is cello, even though she doesn't think she's very good. Why would she enjoy it? But then she said it reminds her of a man's voice. So we chatted about that, and in fact she does miss her father very much."

The cello is her golf ball. Oh, dear God.

"Also, school is pretty tough right now," Bethany continued. "They love a good drama at this age, and unfortunately The Morgan Show seems to be the main attraction. They'll get bored of it soon enough, or something else will come along. But until then, it's hard. Knowing that she only has to make it through one more week before going on a fun trip could be a real lifeline for her."

Of course it would, thought Dana with growing despair. *This is exactly what she needs.*

"I hadn't thought of it quite like that," she said quietly. "And it won't be a problem to have her miss an appointment? I thought consistency was so important in therapy."

"It's really about how it feels for Morgan. Missing one appointment is a small price to pay for a week of relief." Bethany let out a little bird-size cough. "It must be hard to think about having her gone for Thanksgiving. Morgan says the two of you are close."

Gone for Thanksgiving. Both of them.

"I just want what's best for Morgan," said Dana, hearing the dullness in her voice.

"Good parents always do."

"I thought you were done with your wolf paper," said Dana. By nine o'clock it had already been dark for so long that it felt like the middle of the night. She was surprised to find Morgan still fully dressed and sitting at her desk writing in a notebook.

"I am," she said. "This isn't schoolwork. It's, um . . . it's an assignment. From Bethany. I'm supposed to write about my life and stuff."

An assignment, thought Dana, impressed once again with Bethany's powers of observation. If she had simply suggested Morgan keep a journal, it probably wouldn't have worked. But an assignment—it was like a balm for Morgan.

"Okay," she said. "Well, you'll have to work on it tomorrow, because it's time for bed."

Morgan groaned and put the notebook away. She grabbed her pajamas from the end of her bed and began to change. Dana picked up an abandoned shirt from the floor and hung it in the closet. When she turned back, Morgan's pajama top was still hiked up above her shoulder blades. Dana marveled at the smoothness of her skin and the straightness of her back, like the stem of a flower about to bud. Morgan tugged down the pajama top and nestled into her mess of covers.

"Teeth," said Dana.

"Already brushed."

"Really?"

"I'm not five," grumbled Morgan. "I understand the importance of dental hygiene. Otherwise your teeth get all yellow and nasty-looking."

It's all about how it looks, thought Dana, straightening the silky edge of the blanket.

"Um," said Morgan, squinting in indecision. She pulled her Hershey pillow close.

"Yeah?"

"Um, I think Tina . . . I think Tina might be . . . you know, doing it."

With the pall of the Disney trip hanging over her, the mention of Tina's name made Dana flinch. "Doing what?"

Morgan stuck her tongue out and motioned toward it with her finger. The horror on Dana's face made the girl recoil. "I could be wrong," she said quickly. "I only heard her once!"

"Was she sick?" asked Dana, trying to recover. "Did she have some sort of a bug?"

"Maybe . . . but I don't think so. She ate some pretzels, and then we went shopping. I don't think she knows I heard her." Morgan's hand ran up and down the Hershey pillow. "What are you going to do?"

"Well, I'm not really sure just yet, sweetie," Dana said, trying to wipe the dismay off her face. "But this is not your problem. I'm glad you told me, and now it's up to the grown-ups to figure it out." She gave Morgan a quick kiss, impatient to lock herself in the office and pick up the phone.

"Kenneth, I've made a final decision about that little trip, and it's definitely no, after what Morgan just told me." She relayed the conversation, awaiting his humbled response.

Kenneth let out a weary groan.

"So you knew about this!" she exploded. "And you were willing to expose our children to—"

"It's not what you think."

"Right," said Dana, her voice salted with sarcasm. "She only did it that one time, or it's some exotic medical condition, or—"

He chuckled humorlessly, and the sound went up Dana's spine like an army of red ants. "Actually, it *is* a medical condition," he said. "Called pregnancy."

Dana closed her eyes. She wasn't sure she could stay upright in the swivel chair. "Oh. My. God," she breathed. "How *could* you?"

"How *could* I? Well, the usual way, I guess, if you have to know."

Dana wanted to hang up, but her limbs seemed to have frozen and she felt as if she might faint.

"Wait," he said, as if she had any choice, as if she might be capable of action. "I need to . . . Not that it's any of your business, but I just want you to know I didn't plan this. Really, I'm as stunned as . . . And I mean, this is a lousy time to have someone else to take care of, with the company in the crapper, and the kids . . . the kids *needing* so much." His voice broke then, and desperation leaked out. "But, God, what can I *do*? I love her, and I can't ask her to . . . And she wouldn't anyway, so what's the point of even going there?" He let out a long, hard breath. "It is what it is, and I just have to deal."

A tear fell down her face, and though she pitied herself and her children far more than she did her philandering ex-husband, still, she couldn't help but feel for him. She knew all too well that he had never wanted more children. In the past whenever she'd brought it up, he'd always said two was quite enough for him. By the heaving sound of his breath in the receiver, she could tell he was crying, too.

"I know I don't owe you an apology for this. I don't owe anyone any apologies," he insisted, a hint of self-righteousness coming into his voice before deflating completely. "But, Dana . . . I am *sorry*. For all of it. You know I never meant . . ." He couldn't finish.

"You're getting remarried, aren't you?" she asked numbly.

"Yeah. I'm not one of those guys who—"

"I know."

"We were going to tell the kids on the trip."

She'd never heard him sound so defeated, and she realized there was no way to stop it—no way for any of them to evade this fast-approaching storm. Morgan and Grady needed fair warning, and finding out during a fun-filled trip might lessen the blow. "That's probably the best way," she said, wiping salty tears from her chin with the back of her hand.

"Really? You'll let them go?"

"It is what it is," she said. "We all just have to deal."

"I'M GOING TO THE GALAXY WITH RITA!" MORGAN yelled into her cell phone, the cacophony of the school bus obliterating pieces of her words. "She's got money! I'll call when I need a ride!"

Who's Rita? wondered Dana. But it was the first time in over a week that Morgan had had any plans after school, and besides, she sounded happy. Or at least not beaten down, which was the way every other phone call had sounded since the blowout with Kimmi Kinnear.

Grady invited Jav over, and they made chocolate-chip cookies, mixing the chips into the stiff batter, groaning and making faces for effect. Then they went into the backyard to toss a football against the pitchback while Dana spooned the dough onto cookie sheets and put them in the oven. She was waiting for the last batch to cool, watching the boys leap for the erratic flight of the ball, when the mudroom door burst open and girls' voices erupted into the quiet.

"Those kids are wicked pigs," said one, familiar to Dana but not quite placeable.

"Especially Calvin Ridger. He's got those eyes that get all shiny and weird when he's hyper!" This from a twittery voice she didn't recognize at all.

"Thank God you came, Jet," said Morgan. "I was about to freak." And then the three of them swarmed into the kitchen, oohing over the cookies. Jet took one without being offered. "Way good!" she announced, melted chocolate like an oil slick across her lower lip.

Morgan introduced her new friend, Rita, who had crazy wild red hair and battalions of freckles marching up her neck and across her face. Her pale eyes seemed to burst forward in a look of constant surprise.

Alder came in and retrieved the gallon of milk to which Jet had just helped herself. "What happened?" she asked. She got a cup and poured the milk for Jet.

"Oh, my God, it was, like, shocking!" gushed Rita. "These boys? They came into Galaxy like they, legit, owned the place!"

"Kimmi slaves," said Morgan. "Kimmi doesn't actually like them, but they're hoping she will someday. Like maybe when they're elderly." The girls said the four boys had rolled into Galaxy Pizza, placed their order, and looked around for something to do while they waited. They locked in on Morgan and Rita, each with a slice of pizza and sharing a Fresca. The taunts began: fake puking and eye bugging and words like "titless wonder."

"So then, um, she . . ." Rita motioned toward the older girls.

"It's Jet," said Alder. Jet gave a toothy smile, revealing another stolen cookie.

"Yeah, Jet came in and saw what they were doing? And she sat with them! She slid right into the booth with them! And they were, like, freaking!"

Alder looked at Jet, who gave an amused shrug. "It was fun," she said.

"She started drinking their drinks and asking their names and where they live and stuff." Morgan grinned. "Oh, my God, Calvin Ridger looked like he was gonna have a seizure."

Jet had ordered her slice and taken the girls with her when she left. "Didn't seem like too brilliant of an idea to leave them there," she explained.

Dana's eyes met Alder's, and Alder raised her eyebrows as if to say, *Told you*. Dana nodded. Alder had been right about Jet. Under-neath the sooty makeup and bad manners, the girl had quite a heart. "Jet, honey," Dana said, "would you like another cookie?"

At lunch on Friday, Dana stared at her yogurt. The gelatinous pink mass nauseated her. "They're leaving tomorrow," she told Tony.

"I know," he said.

Of course he did. She'd already told him everything. But the quiet sympathy she now heard in his voice was exactly what she craved. "I'm coming to work all day next week, okay?" she said. "You don't have to pay me for the extra hours, I just need to be out of the house."

"It'll be my pleasure, and of course I'll pay you."

"No, don't." He started to object, but she cut him off. "Tony, I'm serious. I'd feel like it was charity wages."

"Okay, I get it," he said. "But look at it from my perspective. In an ideal world, you'd be working here full-time to begin with. How much of a slimeball would I be if I benefited from your unhappi-ness and *didn't even pay you*?" He waved away the very notion. "No chance." The look of intractability he gave her made her slump in grateful defeat.

There was banging at the front door, and they both startled in their seats and then strode quickly to answer it. There behind the glass was Jack Roburtin, his expression an odd combination of anger and hope. For a moment Tony and Dana just stood there. "I'll take care of it," she muttered.

"I'll be in my office," he said. "Listening."

Dana unlocked the door. "Hi," said Jack in an oddly unsettled way, as if he didn't know which character he was playing in his own little movie.

"Hi," she said.

He squared his shoulders and narrowed his already narrowly set eyes. "I've got a few minutes before my shift starts, and I figured we better clear the air before the weekend."

"Okay," she said, though she hadn't had even a fleeting thought of him since their fractious phone call earlier in the week.

"So I guess you have stuff on your mind," he offered.

"Yes, I do."

"Well, I am very sympathetic to that. As a matter of fact, so do I." Attempting a casual stance, he crossed his arms and shifted his weight, one side of his torso going out too far. He looked like a Ken doll in need of a hip replacement. Dana bit her lip to keep from laughing.

"What's so funny about that?" he demanded. "You think you're the only one with stuff? For crying out loud, sales are down! Not for me, really, but for a lot of guys. And I'm going to Florida to see my mother for Thanksgiving, and I hate to fly! What am I supposed to do—*drive*?"

"No, no, I'm sorry!" she insisted, though she couldn't seem to control the chuckle in her throat. She put her hand over her mouth, but that made it worse.

"Okay, I am *definitely* getting the impression you're not interested in making up," he warned.

"Making up?" she said. "I thought you just wanted to clear the air."

"Why would I want to clear the air if we aren't getting back together?"

Together. With Jack. Is that what she wanted? Dana hadn't even considered whether they'd broken up after their little verbal skirmish. And now it appeared there were peace offerings to be made. Her limbs seemed to fill with lead at the very thought.

"Oh," she said.

"Oh? *Oh?*" The awkwardness left him as his biceps tensed and his rib cage expanded. "I come here ready to take you back and you give me 'Oh'? I don't think so!" He looked around the tiny waiting room as if there were an audience only he could see. "Can you *believe* this?" he demanded of his invisible viewership.

"Jack, I'm sorry," she began, but couldn't think of what she was sorry for. She heard noise behind her, drawers thumping closed and throat clearing. Tony was making his presence known.

"I didn't realize you were that type, Dana. The kind who toys with a guy and just uses him for dates and sex!"

Oh, God, thought Dana, knowing that Tony was listening. *This is so embarrassing.*

"I thought we were building something," his tantrum continued, "and you were . . . you were just knitting mittens! Screwing around, having your fun!"

She'd intended to let him blow off steam, wear himself out with his yelling and posturing, the way she always had with her kids when they were little. But he seemed to be ramping up rather than winding down. "Jack, I'm sorry, but I have to get back to work now. You'll have to go."

"You're *chucking* me? You think you can just *chuck* me? Well, let me tell YOU something!" His massive arms flew out in front of him, thick fingers poking the air toward her shoulders. "*You aren't worth it!* You aren't *pretty* enough or *nice* enough or ANYTHING enough! I hope you plan to be alone for a *long time,* because no guy worth a good goddamn would want you!"

In that moment she felt as if he had thrown a bucket of acid at her, as if he had disfigured her with his words. And when he saw that his assault had hit its mark, he gave a vengeful little smile and strode out the door.

Dana was still standing there when Tony came in and stood next to her, resting a hand on her shoulder. "Nice work," he murmured. "Never heard the word 'Oh' used with such satisfying results." She continued to stare out the glass door. Tony went on. "He was getting a little scary toward the end there," he said. "Seemed like you were holding your own. But maybe I should have come out."

"Would've made him madder."

"That's what I figured. I was getting ready to call 911. Are you scared of him? Should we look into a restraining order?"

She shook her head. She wasn't scared of him. He had already done the damage he'd wanted to do. "I don't think he'll be back."

"Listen to me," he said. "All that baloney about you not being good enough—you know that's complete crap, right?"

"I guess."

"Don't guess," he said quietly. "Be sure. Because you are one in a million, Dana Stellgarten."

She didn't feel like one in a million. At the moment she felt like *none* in a million. If Tony's hand hadn't remained firmly on her shoulder, it seemed like she might fade into nothing.

"Hey," he said, giving her a gentle shake.

When she glanced up at him, his face was kind and concerned, and evidently she hadn't disappeared, because he was looking right at her. "Okay," she said.

They walked back to the kitchenette. "And what's this business about knitting mittens?" he asked her. "The idiot's got a yarn fetish?"

A laugh came out of her so suddenly that when she inhaled again, her nose made an embarrassing snorting sound.

"Nice!" He nodded admiringly. And she laughed even harder.

TWO DAYS LATER, ON SUNDAY MORNING, ALDER asked, "When's the last time you went for a walk?" She peered over a bowl of Bran 'N Flax cereal, eating quickly as if to minimize the time it spent with her taste buds. She had poured it for Dana, but Dana wasn't hungry.

"I don't know . . . weeks." Dana cradled a cup of black tea against her chest. Except for the one spot where the heat from the mug penetrated her flannel pajama top, she felt cold and dull.

"Maybe you should go."

I'm being pathetic, thought Dana, *and she doesn't want to watch.* She looked out the window. If it had been a blue-sky, zip-a-dee-doo-dah kind of day, she would have gone back into hibernation. But it was hazy and gray, the late-autumn fog creating a lather of mist against the shrubbery. Good hiding weather. For Alder's sake she thought she could manage a walk. A short one.

She did not go past Polly's house, certain that Polly would somehow sense Dana's nearness and come out and demand to talk to her. No talking. Not today. She trudged up the street in the opposite direction, skirting the long way around the edge of their neighborhood to get over to Nipmuc Pond.

Today is Sunday, she reminded herself, as if the past forty-eight hours had reduced her short-term memory to that of an Alzheimer patient's. *Six more days.*

———————

Dana had helped them pack Friday afternoon. Morgan had wanted some spending money to buy Rita a Disney memento. "How did you two become friends?" Dana asked her.

"She didn't make the basketball team." This was expected to be self-explanatory, and Dana had had to prod for details. "She was on the soccer team, and all those girls were her friends, but when she didn't make the basketball team, she wasn't part of the group anymore."

"Just like that?"

"I don't know," said Morgan. "I guess. Also, she's got those froggy eyes and crazy hair, and boys make fun of her. The soccer girls had to stick up for her a lot. That gets kind of tiring."

Dana was incensed. "They dropped her because *other* kids' behavior was tiring?"

"Jeez, Mom, I don't know. One minute she was with the group, the next minute she wasn't. The tiring part was just a guess, okay?"

They rooted through the bin of Morgan's summer clothes, pulling out mismatched tankinis and wrinkled shorts. "But how did *you* get to be friends with her?"

Morgan hesitated, a secret mirth playing around her lips. "Okay, but you can't repeat this!" She'd been sitting in earth science, pretending to work on her already completed wolf paper, trying not to make eye contact, so as to avoid any possible attention. "Rita's seat is right next to mine, and since I was looking down, I saw it before anyone else."

"What?"

Morgan started to giggle. "Her undies!" Hanging out from the hem of Rita's jeans had been a pair of underwear. When she slumped into her seat, feet splayed out into the aisle, the brightly colored garment had flown clear of her pant leg and landed beside Morgan's chair. "They had little pink pandas all over them. But the worst part was the tag! It said her name—like her mother had labeled them for camp or something!"

"Oh, my gosh! What did you do?"

Morgan had quickly set her backpack over them. At the end of class she convinced Rita to stay until the other kids left. Then she lifted the backpack. "At first she didn't get it, and she was mad, like how did I get her undies and stuff. But then she remembered she wore those same jeans the day before, and picked them off the floor to wear that morning. The old undies must've still been in them, and slid down her leg until they came out in science."

"Did she thank you?"

"Um, kinda. She called me her savior and hugged me till she nearly broke my neck. So I sat with her at lunch."

Dana had given Morgan a twenty-dollar bill. "Get Rita something really nice," she'd said, "like a stuffed Minnie Mouse or something."

"Ew, no!"

Maybe she's in a gift store right now, mused Dana as the pond came into view, veiled in a somber drizzle. Maybe she was happily tormenting Kenneth as she took hours to make up her mind. Dana dearly hoped so.

Dana had also offered Grady money to buy a gift for Jav.

"No way, he's a jerk."

"What happened?"

Grady's face went sulky. "Took my golf ball," he muttered. That day, Friday, Grady had shown his private treasure to Jav on the playground. Jav had pronounced it "killer."

"That's not very nice," Dana had commiserated.

"No, 'killer' is good. It's like 'sick.'" But then Jav had wanted to play with it. "I kept telling him to give it back, but he just kept saying 'Why?'"

"Did you tell him it was special to you, that it's from your father?"

Grady's face squinched up in annoyance. "I'm not gonna tell him *that!*"

They'd been standing on the pavement next to the school, a

sprawling, one-story, flat-topped building, when Jav had thrown it into the air. It had landed on the roof and never come down. "Now it's there *forever*," muttered Grady. "Jerk."

Dana had given the twenty to Kenneth when he'd arrived to pick them up, in case Grady changed his mind. "I have money," he'd grumbled, insulted by the gesture.

"Oh, for Pete's sake, just take it!" she'd told him.

And then the kids were hauling their duffel bags out to the car, scrambling back in for a forgotten cap or book, giving her one more extra squeeze, and scrambling back out again.

And then they were gone.

Later that night Jet had come over with Thai takeout and a DVD of *Young Frankenstein*. "This is one of the weirdest, funniest movies ever made," she told Dana. "Couldn't possibly remind you of *anything*." Alder had given Jet a look. "What?" said Jet. "Like it's not *obvious* she's missing her kids?"

"Can you just zip it?" Alder muttered under her breath.

"It's okay," Dana told her.

"See?" said Jet. "Besides, her kids are lucky."

It was true, and Dana knew she would do well to keep that in perspective. "A free trip to Disney World doesn't come along every day," she conceded.

"Not *Disney* World," Jet responded with mild disgust. "They're lucky they have a mother who likes having them around so much. My mother would be psyched if I *moved* to Disney World."

Dana suddenly embraced the surprised teenager and murmured, "I still can't thank you enough for rescuing Morgan and her friend the other day."

Once released, Jet responded with a half-embarrassed, half-proud little grin. "Good times." She nodded. "I might be thinking of a career in law enforcement."

"You'd be wonderful."

On Saturday, Dana had run errands and taken the girls to REI in West Hartford to research gear for winter camping with the Wilderness Club, and it hadn't been hard to pretend it was just another weekend when the kids were at Kenneth's. The day had passed. And after a call from Morgan and Grady to say they'd already found eight hidden Mickey ears designed into the decor of the hotel lobby, Dana had gone to bed—at seven-fifteen.

Now, as she rounded the opposite shore of Nipmuc Pond, she saw a boy, shaggy hair whipped into a tangle by the breeze, throwing a tennis ball to a beagle along the sandy spit of shoreline. *I should get them a dog,* she thought. A gust of wind raced off the water, and she burrowed her hands into her pockets, fingers balled against the cold and the unseemliness of her own desperation. Her empty stomach gurgled for food. She veered off course, away from the lake and out toward the main street. Maybe she could choke down a doughnut with a cup of tea.

She pulled open the door to Village Donuts and was met with a comforting blast of warm, sweet-smelling air. People sat in booths reading the *Hartford Sunday Courant,* tapping away at laptops, or chatting amiably with each other. Two women with graying hair tucked back under knit hats burst into melodious laughter. Dana wondered if her friendship with Polly would ever be so seamlessly mended that they could come here in ten years and giggle together like sisters.

The line moved quickly, and just as it was Dana's turn to order, she realized that the five-dollar bill she usually kept in the little pocket of her exercise pants was gone. "Oh," she said to the proprietor behind the cash register. "I thought I had money, but I . . . Could I just have a cup of hot water, please?"

"Unquestionably," he said with an amused grin. "And as luck would have it, we've got a special going at the moment—with every order of hot water, we're offering a free tea bag."

Dana stared at him for a second. *A kindness,* she realized. She thanked him wholeheartedly when he handed her the tea. As she turned to go, she heard the man behind her say, "Hiya, Richie. I guess I'll get in on that free-tea-bag offer."

"Ahh, too late, my friend," the proprietor said, guffawing. "Special's over!"

When Dana got home, the dishwasher was running and Alder was wiping the kitchen counters.

"Uh, listen," Alder said, face tense with apprehension. "I called my mother."

"About your car?" asked Dana.

"Not specifically."

"Then what, specifically?"

Alder scrubbed at a speck of hardened pad thai noodle.

"Alder?"

The girl gave her aunt a worried glance.

"Oh," said Dana. "About me."

Alder winced apologetically. "I was just worried, and I didn't know who to talk to. I didn't expect her to actually *come* here . . . But she's coming . . . tonight."

CHAPTER
37

WHEN CONNIE'S AGED VW VANAGON ROLLED
up the street and into the driveway that evening, sputtering like an angry lawn mower, the entire neighborhood was effectively put on notice. Dana was dusting the dining room. She had started cleaning shortly after Alder's announcement.

"Not like she'll notice," Alder had said as Dana tugged the vacuum from the hall closet.

"I know." Dana had witnessed far too many battles between Connie and their mother over the "war-torn pigsty" that was Connie's side of the bedroom she and Dana had shared. "Why does it *matter*?" Connie would moan at their mother. "I'm just gonna trash it again!"

Dana was cleaning because it felt good to do something so quintessentially normal. Tidying up for guests—wasn't it the cornerstone of civilized society? Now, where would Connie stay?

"She's not sleeping with me!" said Alder. But she agreed to move to Morgan's room so her mother could take over the pullout couch in the TV room. By the time Dana had stashed the Lemon Pledge under the sink, Connie was clomping up the mudroom steps in her wooden clogs.

She looked different. Her dark hair had been blunt-cut just below her ears, and it bushed out from the sides of her head like the points of graying triangles. Her favorite batik-print quilted jacket with the Chinese-coin buttons hung loosely from her frame. Connie had always been lanky, but her narrow face now seemed almost gaunt. Dana reached for the coarse-woven bag hanging from Connie's shoulder. "Here, let me take that."

"Still polite." Connie smiled. "Must not be so bad." Her glance shifted past Dana to Alder, and it seemed to Dana that she was controlling herself, pedaling backward against her own tendency toward temerity. "Hi," she said.

"Hi," said Alder.

Connie's self-control ebbed, and she reached out to touch Alder's two-toned hair. The black at the bottom had continued to grow out, revealing more of the natural ginger brown. Connie lifted a hank from the ends and slowly let it cascade down across her daughter's shoulder. "Haircut, maybe?" she murmured.

"Maybe," said Alder.

The three of them turned in concert like a small flock of birds and headed into the kitchen. Dana had made cornbread, a salad, and vegetarian chili; the smell of simmering tomatoes, cumin, and cayenne gave them a focal point around which to orient themselves. They served one another, poured drinks, passed the butter. They settled into the people they knew one another to be.

"Dana says you've got new pals," Connie said to Alder. "How 'bout some details?"

"It's no big deal," said Alder.

Dana reached over and jiggled Alder's elbow. "You're making a liar out of me!"

Alder smiled despite herself. "You tell her, then."

"Well, there's the Wilderness Club . . ."

"Makes sense." Connie nodded. "You'd *need* a booster shot of nature in the middle of all this—"

"And there's Jet," Dana interrupted, shooting Connie a warning look. Alder's smile had dissipated, and she began pushing an errant kidney bean around her bowl with a spoon.

"Nice name," said Connie, making a show of interest. "What's his story?"

"She's a *girl*," Alder muttered at the bean.

"She's quite a . . ." Dana began, not entirely sure where she was going. "Well, she's not completely housebroken . . ." Alder let out a quick laugh. "But she's a good soul, right?"

Alder nodded, her gaze rising to meet her mother's, daring her to comment. The parental ache in Connie's eyes was so familiar to Dana that she could feel it in her own. *Her daughter's got a friend with a good soul who she's never met,* thought Dana. *She's grateful and heartbroken all at the same time.* Connie's lips pressed ever so slightly against each other. Dana could almost hear the zipping sound.

Alder retreated to Morgan's room early, claiming a need to get in some last-minute studying for a history test the next morning. She took the pink fleece blanket with her. Dana set Connie up in the TV room and got another blanket from the linen closet.

"So," said Dana, "not to be too direct, but . . . how long are you staying?"

Connie laughed. "Counting the minutes?"

"No." Dana smirked. "Just trying to plan how many more vegetarian meals I'll be making. Doesn't Nine Muses expect you back at some point?"

"I'm the manager now. I make the schedule." Connie shrugged. "So how long do I get?"

"Long as you want."

"I'll get back to you."

Dana had just sailed off into a creamy blackness when she felt a presence in her bedroom. *Morgan?* The mattress lurched as someone descended onto it, bouncing Dana into full alert. "Oh, for Pete's sake," she said when she saw her new bedmate. "You're about as subtle as a Mack truck."

"That pullout couch is torture," grumbled Connie. "You should sell it to the CIA." She punched the pillow and yanked the covers. "I tried Grady's bed, but it smells like a wet dog."

"Does not," muttered Dana.

"Totally does."

"Stop bouncing around, will you?"

Connie's movements slowed as she nestled into the big bed. Dana had begun to drift again when Connie said, "If Ethan's the one who treated her like shit, why's she so pissed at *me*?"

Dana sighed, sleep almost within arm's reach. "She's hasn't said much."

"Yeah, but you have an opinion."

An opinion about someone's parenting—was there any surer way to invite trouble? Dana wanted to slide back into the satiny swirl of unconsciousness. "Can we talk about it tomorrow?"

"No," said Connie. "We can't."

Dana groaned inwardly, knowing Connie would harass her until she answered. "It's not an opinion," she said finally, "only a guess."

"Fine. Guess."

"Well . . . it just seems like kids get mad at their mothers for one reason or another. Sometimes it makes sense, and sometimes they're just mad and we're the easy target."

Connie's silence communicated her utter dissatisfaction.

Dana struggled to organize her thoughts. "You know, we tell them from the minute they're born, 'I'll take care of you.' Then when something bad happens, it's our fault, even when they're old enough to know we don't control everything. We told them we'd always protect them, and then we can't live up to the promise."

"Maybe *you* made that promise, but *I* never did. You always try to fix everything for everyone; I raised Alder to know her *own* power."

Now it was Dana's turn to go silent.

"All right, I'm sorry," Connie said without remorse. "But, hey, it's no secret that you and I are different kinds of mothers." She reached out and shook Dana's shoulder. "Come on. Talk."

"Fine, you want me to talk? Then I'll tell you that giving up your virginity to a guy you worship, who won't speak to you afterward and then leaves the state, does not feel like *power,* Connie. It feels like abuse. She's sixteen, and she's trying to handle it herself, but she can't. It's too big. And she can't talk to you about it, because you're so insistent on not overprotecting her—or too busy throwing tantrums at her school about trigonometry!"

Connie didn't say anything for a moment. Then she got up and left. Dana felt terrible. Though Connie was often overbearing and sarcastic, her devotion to her daughter was unimpeachable. She had taught Alder the things she felt were important in life, and for the most part that had worked out. Letting her live with Dana for two months had required an act of extreme restraint. Despite this sacrifice, Dana had placed the blame squarely on her sister's shoulders. Guilt fended off sleep for another hour before Dana was rescued by her own exhaustion.

When she woke in the morning, she stretched her arm and her fingers slid into a mass of thick, coarse hair. She turned to find Connie's eyelids testing the brightness in the room. They blinked at each other for a moment. "That was really bitchy," Connie murmured.

"I know," said Dana. "Sorry."

"It's not like you."

"It kind of is, these days."

Connie's sleep-wrinkled cheeks shifted into a sly smile. "Wish Ma was here," she said. "She'd never believe it. Perfect Dana, bitching someone out."

Ma, thought Dana, and she could almost smell the Charlie cologne that didn't quite cover the residual cigarette smoke. She had died in August, and last Thanksgiving had been the first holiday without her. *Another holiday without Ma.*

"Stay for Thanksgiving," she told Connie.

An uncharacteristic uncertainty rippled across Connie's face. "We'll see how it goes."

"DON'T FORGET YOUR PERMISSION SLIP," DANA reminded Alder, who was slathering peanut butter onto chunks of banana. Connie came into the kitchen wearing a T-shirt silk-screened with a group of ethereal-looking women in flowing dresses. NINE MUSES BOOKS & ART was written under their sandal-clad feet.

"What permission slip?" Alder asked.

"Wadsworth Atheneum. It's for tomorrow, so you need to get it in today."

"Or you could blow it off," said Connie, opening and closing cabinet doors. "Most of that crap's so derivative anyway."

Alder shot Dana a look that could have meant anything from "Maybe she's right" to "I may have to hit her." Dana chose to believe it meant "Help."

"The whole art class is going," Dana said. "It's mandatory."

"She could *teach* the class," grumbled Connie. "And not by dragging them past dusty portraits of dead rich people." She turned to level a suspicious eye at her sister. "You don't have any green tea?"

"Oh. I guess maybe I don't."

"They have it at Whole Foods," Alder told her mother as she rose to put her plate in the dishwasher. "It's right in Glastonbury." To Dana she asked, "Where's that slip?"

"On the table in the mudroom. Have a great day, sweetie!"

"Bye," said Alder. "Bye, Connie."

"*Whole Foods,*" Connie muttered derisively after the door slammed.

"Now, what's wrong with Whole Foods? I thought you liked all that organic, unprocessed—"

"It's just so corporate and well lit. Might as well be McDonald's, for godsake." Her face was pinched in annoyance, as if whatever she was looking for was purposely hiding.

"Are you still mad about last night?" Dana asked.

"No." Connie's expression burst open like a hand grenade. "I'm mad about *this morning.* How is it that *my* kid is going on some bullshit expedition to a so-called art museum and *you're* the one signing the permission slip!"

"Oh, Connie," Dana murmured sympathetically. "I'm sorry." She reached out from her seat at the table and slipped her hand into Connie's.

"And don't hold my hand!" But Connie did nothing to rid herself of the warm fingers in her palm, and Dana made no move to withdraw them. After a moment Connie rolled her eyes and made a show of pulling her hand away. But her face had softened, and she sank into the chair next to her sister. "You need anything at *Whole Foods*?" She gave a little sneer. "An organic Happy Meal, maybe?"

"I'll be working till five. Feel like making dinner?"

Connie shrugged a confirmation, then looked out the window and watched the curled brown leaves blow across the yard. "How come we haven't seen each other since Ma died?" she said.

"I don't know." Dana sighed. "We don't always . . . click."

Connie let out a laugh and raised her eyebrows as if to say, *Isn't that the truth.* "Milkweed and skunk cabbage for dinner," she said. "Just to warn you."

Dana waited at the big glass office door. *I should ask him for a key,* she thought. But for all she knew, his real receptionist would get over her morning sickness and return to work tomorrow. The realization made Dana flinch. She could find another job, she told herself. Her skills were up to date, and Tony would give her a good reference. *Oh, but . . .*

"I should have a key made for you," Tony called out as he came around the corner of the building. There he was, the best boss she'd ever had. And she would lose him. Probably sooner rather than later. How long could an unmarried, pregnant woman afford to stay out of work? Not very long. And then Dana would be the unmarried, unemployed one.

"Sorry to keep you waiting." He slid the key into the bolt. "I had to deal with a little holiday drama that's been playing out over the weekend."

"Oh?"

"Thanksgiving." He held the door open for her. "Total nightmare. Lizzie—the one at Brown—was supposed to be in New Jersey with her boyfriend. Zack." Tony made a face as if he had just tasted mud.

"We don't like Zack?"

"No," said Tony, hanging his coat in the closet and holding out a hand for hers. "We don't. Especially after they had a screaming fight this weekend in which he told her he thought the whole 'meeting-the-parents thing is such a cliché.'"

"Commitment issues."

"Of the epic variety." He pulled his white lab coat from the closet and put it on. "So there's one daughter at loose ends. Then Abby, the doctor—assuming she can stick with it—Abby is supposed to be working and having a quick midshift slice of processed deli meat with a couple of her med-school friends. She was planning to come home next weekend for about half a day just to see the old man."

"You were going to be alone for the holiday? Why didn't you tell me? You could have—"

He held up a finger. "I was *supposed* to go to New York to spend it with my . . . girlfriend? That sounds childish, but it's better than 'lady friend,' which makes me sound like Wilford Brimley."

Girlfriend? Dana had a vague memory of Tony's mentioning a relationship. Something about her being there when one of his daughters had come home unexpectedly. But he'd never spoken of her since, which seemed strange, since he was so open about everything else.

"Anyway," Tony continued, leaning in the doorway, "a psych patient started a fire in Abby's hospital by knocking two pebbles together near an oxygen tank—"

Dana let out a little gasp and Tony nodded. "I know, can you beat that? So they started shipping patients to other hospitals and handing out days off to the staff. Abby won the lottery and got Thanksgiving. So now I have not one but *two* daughters who want to come home, and I'm not even supposed to be there!"

"But then why doesn't your . . ."

"Martine."

"Why doesn't Martine just come here?"

"Because she kind of went overboard and invited a bunch of friends, and it got sort of . . . enormous. Like fourteen people. But more than that, I think it got enormous in her head." Tony stared into middle space for a moment, then shifted his gaze back to Dana. "You know when something suddenly takes on grander proportions than it normally would?"

Dana nodded. It had happened to her with Kenneth from time to time, usually because she was imagining that whatever was so important to her was also important to him. It was always an embarrassment to find out it wasn't. "So did she invite the girls, too?"

He gave an odd, almost melancholy smile. "Eventually. When she called back. It took her a little while to come up with it."

"Does she have children?"

"Yes, she does," he said, pointing at Dana as if she'd figured out the answer to a riddle. "One son. Got a job in Singapore when he graduated last year. She describes him as 'studious.'"

"Studious? That's all?" What kind of mother had only one adjective to describe her child? Dana had hundreds for Grady and Morgan. Which, she realized, might be excessive.

"Uh, I think I've also heard the word 'independent.'"

Well, he'd have to be, wouldn't he? Dana thought. "So are the girls going to New York with you?"

"Okay, that was this *morning's* series of phone calls. Abby's exhausted, and Lizzie's furious-slash-heartbroken, and they want to sleep in their own beds and not play the pride-inducing daughters of Tony Sakimoto for two straight days." His hands went up in a "there you have it" gesture.

Dana laughed.

"Oh, sure," he said, grinning back at her, "easy for you! Just go right ahead and enjoy the entertainment!"

Her smile dimmed. Easy for her—but not really. In the happy distraction of Tony's story, Dana had forgotten that her own children would not be in their beds. They would be a thousand miles away with her adulterous ex-husband and his home-wrecking, pregnant girlfriend. And with no confirmation that Connie and Alder would be there for Thanksgiving, it was actually possible that Dana would be alone. She couldn't even beg an invitation to Polly's.

"Oh . . . hey," Tony said apologetically.

"My sister Connie showed up unexpectedly last night." She gave a little eye roll to wrench herself from a descent into self-pity.

"Yeah? Alder's mom?"

She nodded. "If there's anyone out there who's more my opposite, I have yet to meet her."

"No kidding!" said Tony. "This I've gotta see. Hey, is she around still? Invite her for lunch!"

"Oh, I don't know . . ." Connie in an enclosed space with her boss? Dana wasn't sure she was up to the potential for disaster that would present.

"Seriously," Tony said as Dana went to greet a patient coming in the door. "Think about it."

As it turned out, it was just as well she didn't call Connie; Tony spent the better part of the lunch hour in his office placing and fielding phone calls from Nashville, Providence, and New York. By the time he was able to get to his veggie sub, he was irritable and exhausted.

"So?" Dana hazarded to ask.

"Cranky daughters coming home, angry girlfriend *definitely* staying in New York," he said around bites. "*Ohhh,* it's gonna be one happy Thanksgiving." He took a swig of his iced tea. "Okay, tell me about this polar-opposite sister of yours."

All too soon the next patient arrived, but throughout the afternoon he popped his head into her work area between appointments and murmured things like, "What about Alder's father?" and "If she weren't your sister, would you like her?"

He couldn't possibly be so interested in this, Dana told herself. *He's just trying to keep his mind off his own problems.* Enjoying the distraction of someone else's drama, as she herself had been doing, though she really did want to know about Abby and Lizzie. She found herself hoping she'd get a chance to meet them. And Martine . . . well, maybe not. Dana knew she was hearing only one side of this one incident with Martine. She was very likely a nice person if Tony had chosen her to love. Assuming it *was* love. He hadn't ever ascribed that particular word to it. Hadn't really given any words to it at all. Nonetheless, Dana had a less-than-positive impression.

"If Connie weren't my sister?" Dana had to think about that. Her instinctive response was, *Yes, of course.* But would she really? "Well, I hate to admit it," she told Tony, "but Connie wouldn't be the kind of person I'd gravitate toward."

"No kidding," he teased. "And you two being such peas in a pod. What I meant was, knowing who she is down deep, would you be friends with her?"

Down deep, she mused. Leave it to Tony to want to know everything down deep.

Later, as they were locking up the office, he said, "Well, keep me posted."

"I'll see you tomorrow morning," she reminded him.

"Yeah," he said vaguely. "But if . . . you know, if things went completely haywire and you wanted someone to bounce things off of, you could call me at home."

"Okay, thanks," she said, squinting into her purse as she rooted for her keys, knowing she would never call her boss *at home* with a personal problem.

"Though I don't think I ever gave you the number." He patted the pockets of his bomber jacket, looking for a pen and paper, she supposed. "Well, here," he said, holding out his hand. "Give me your cell phone, and I'll program it in."

As she handed over the cell phone, she couldn't decide whether the buzzing in her head meant she was appalled or—even worse— *happy* that he was taking such liberties with her personal items. Either way it was a bad sign.

He's just being his usual kind self, she told herself. Something he would do for any half-broke employee who had been dumped by her husband, invaded by her overbearing sister, and was facing a major holiday without her children, possibly completely alone. In fact, who *wouldn't* take pity on such a sad sack?

But the look on his face bore no signs of charity as he handed back her cell phone. "Hope that wasn't out of line," he muttered. "Next I'll be telling you my health problems."

"You have health problems?" she asked, suddenly worried that he had some undisclosed condition.

"Fit as a fiddle." He gave an embarrassed chuckle. "I just meant I hope I wasn't being intrusive . . . or presumptuous . . ."

"Not at all," she assured him. "And I promise not to use it except for emergencies."

"Use it anytime," he said. "Really."

CHAPTER

39

⁂

POSSIBLY IT WAS THE CURRIED LENTILS WITH TEX-tured soy protcin. Didn't their mother always say spicy food before bed made for a night of wandering with the hobgoblins? And having Connie sleeping next to her, in almost constant motion—twitching her toes or grinding her teeth—didn't help either. Whatever the source, Dana found herself drifting in the long-gone Paragon Park of her youth.

Where are they?

It was dark, and the place seemed abandoned, though the rides still lurched along. She darted from attraction to attraction, certain that Morgan and Grady were there somewhere, waiting for her, needing her. They weren't on the carousel, which screamed its warbling organ music at her. Not on the Wild Mouse or the Congo Cruise. She kept searching, desperate to find them.

"Mom!" It was Grady's voice, and she darted toward it, past the smell of burning sugar—cotton candy, she realized, left to spin too long in the heat of its enormous Bundt pan. Grady was the lone rider on the Matterhorn, cars wagging wildly as they sped over a circular track, into a building painted with cartoon mountains, and back out again. His car was filled with golf balls, which he raised one by one, looking for identifying marks. "Jump!" Dana called to him.

"I have to find it!" he yelled. His car swept into the darkened building, and she waited, but it never came back out.

"Mom!" A cry from the opposite direction. She ran toward it.

Then she was on the platform of the Comet, screaming to Morgan, who was clamped into the front car beside her cello. The panic on Morgan's face turned grotesque as the ride took off, shaking and grinding up the track to the top of the roller coaster's peeling white latticework. Dana lunged for the last car. In the dream she was screaming, but when she opened her eyes, she knew it had been a whimper.

Connie groaned. "Y'all right?"

"They're gone," she breathed before her throat closed around the words. *They're never coming back.* In the wake of the dream's terror, the possibility seemed very real.

"What's gone?" muttered Connie, scratching her neck. "The kids? They're just in Plasticland with their idiot father."

This was true. But there was a goneness that defied geography, and Dana couldn't ward off the sense that something essential was changing, that they were now separated from her by more than just distance. "I miss them," she choked out. "I feel like they're dead."

"It's Disney World," said Connie. "They'll recover."

Dana gave her a shove. "You make fun of everything! I'm *sick* of it! Go sleep somewhere else."

"Oh, all right. Y-ross."

It jiggled something in the back of Dana's brain, and she turned to squint at Connie in the waning darkness.

Connie said, "Come on. You made me say it to you about every other night when we were kids."

Growing up, they had shared a room the size of a closet that accommodated only two twin beds separated by a tiny bedside table. *Y-ross.* Dana remembered. "Sorry" spelled backward—sort of. "You can't just say Y-ross and think it makes everything okay."

Connie considered this for a moment. "Double Y-ross," she said. "Best I can do."

Wholly unsatisfied, Dana lay there sulking, nerves still pulsing staccato from the terror of the dream.

"I do know a little bit about this, by the way," Connie said after a while. "You've had my kid for almost two months now."

"Yes, but I'm not going to *keep* her, am I? I'm not going to go marry some thirty-year-old and have more babies and kidnap her into my new life without a backward glance."

"What if she likes your life better than mine?" Connie said quietly. "What if she chooses you?"

Dana stared at the ceiling, predawn beginning to wear the edges off the darkness. What if Alder wanted to stay—needed to? And if she left, what would it be like without her comforting presence? "I would never take Alder away from you," Dana said.

"Yeah, but what if it happens anyway?"

By noon Dana could barely keep her eyes open. It seemed that whatever little sleep she'd gotten had been erased by the nightmare and the disconcerting conversation with Connie. The day's schedule had been full, but several patients had canceled, citing the holiday, incoming relatives, and grocery-store trips that had taken on the magnitude of preparations to climb Mount Everest. With no patients in the office, Marie had left early for her lunchtime run, and Dana took a moment to lay her head in the crook of her arm on her desk and close her eyes.

Misplaced children, she thought as she drifted. It was as if Morgan, Grady, and Alder had been playing a game of musical chairs and had each ended up in the wrong seats. Or the seats themselves had changed.

She knew that the delivery boy from Nelly's Deli would be here soon, but she told herself she would hear the tinkle of the bell on the door and be upright before anyone saw. A clump of hair slid across her face, but she was too sluggish to push it back. *Haircut,* she thought. It had been months.

Would they be different when they got home from Plasticland?

Would they be so full of thrill rides and restaurant food and care-free laughter with their father and soon-to-be-stepmother that they could barely remember the boring life with their cash-strapped working mom? There was a sound, and she wanted to rise from the comfort of her arm, sleeved in knit cotton, but her head disobeyed her. And there were voices, one mid-toned and anonymous, one deep and sonorous, a rumble like distant thunder. Voices!

"Oh, my gosh!" she muttered apologetically, not entirely sure to whom. When her vision stabilized, she saw Tony holding a white bag and sliding money into the breast pocket of his lab coat. "The door's locked," he murmured. "Put your head down and go back to sleep."

"Oh . . . no, I . . ." She ran her fingers back through her hair to subdue it. "I just . . . I woke up so early this morning . . ." A strand stuck to her lip, and she swiped her face several times but couldn't quite locate it. "And then my sister—"

"Okay, Rapunzel," he teased, "pull yourself together." He reached out and drew a finger across her forehead, capturing the rogue hair and tucking it back behind her ear, his fingers sliding down along the strands to the end, brushing lightly against her shoulder. She could still feel the trail they'd traced across her skin, and a flush came into her cheeks. He was staring at her with an intensity tinged with surprise that made her wonder if he'd regretted his action. Mortified, she turned away quickly and said, "I'll just get my lunch."

He left, and she snatched the brush from her purse and raked it through her hair. *For godsake, settle down!* she told herself. *He's probably done that for his daughters a million times.*

When they were seated at the little table with their lunch items spread across it like chess pieces, he asked about her bad night's sleep and she told him about the lentils and the nightmare and sharing her bed with Connie. "We slept in the same room our whole childhood, and I always sleep with her when I go to her place. Her house is small, and she doesn't have extra beds. It's only when she comes to Cotters Rock that she sleeps in a separate room." Dana considered this. "I think she must have been holding that against Kenneth for fifteen years now."

"I didn't get the impression you two were that close."

"We're not." Dana thought for a moment. "But in some ways . . . We don't like each other that much, but we're—I don't know—attached."

"Lizzie and Abby are like that. Very different. They got closer after Ingrid died. By the way, the late-breaking news is Lizzie's going to the boyfriend's for Thanksgiving after all." He let out an annoyed snort. "Miss Thing throws a conniption about how much she *needs* to be *home*. I change my plans, and she gets back together with Joe Cool."

Dana smiled. "She's the one to the left of your wife in that picture on your desk."

Tony nodded. "Smirking, as usual." He reached into his back pocket for his wallet and withdrew a small photo. "This one's recent." Their arms were hung around each other's shoulders, wind blowing the taller one's auburn hair out to the side. She was laughing, mouth open, teeth white behind bright lipstick. The shorter one grinned modestly. Her skin was a darker olive shade, like Tony's, and her wavy black hair hung just below her ears.

"Abby got the Italian looks from my mother," he said, his head leaning close to Dana's to gaze at the photo with her. "Lizzie takes after Ingrid, except her hair's darker. My father used to say, 'Where's mine? Where's the Japanese granddaughter?' And my mother would say, '*Madonne!* They have your last name—you got them both!'"

"They're beautiful," said Dana. "No wonder Joe Cool wants Miss Thing back."

Tony nodded in appreciation, but then his expression turned pensive. "Why do girls go out with jerks? Honestly, I've never been able to figure it out."

"I've wondered about that myself," said Dana. *Billy the pothead, Kenneth the adulterer, Jack the twelve-year-old,* she ticked them off in her head. *What's my excuse?*

Tony glanced over at her, "I didn't mean—"

"No, it's okay. I've never gotten it right."

"Dana . . ."

She shrugged, gave a halfhearted smile. From the front of the office, her cell phone rang, and she got up to answer it.

"This is Maureen from Comfort Food. There's a situation, and I have a favor to ask."

Oh, dear God! thought Dana. It was Dermott, she was certain.

"The McPhersons were hoping to have Thanksgiving with family in New Jersey, but Mr. McPherson is too sick to travel. When I offered to have one of the volunteers bring over a turkey dinner . . . well, they specifically asked for you. I know this is late notice—"

"Of course!" said Dana. "I'd be happy to."

"Polly came by." Alder was sitting at the kitchen table hunched over her math book. She squinted up at Dana, unaccountably apologetic. "Connie dealt with her."

Poor Polly, Dana thought instinctively. "How'd it go?"

"Uh, really awkward."

Dana sighed apprehensively. "How awkward?"

"Stuff like 'piss-poor big-mouth friend' and 'get your skinny ass out of here.'"

"How did Polly react?"

A sly grin bloomed on Alder's face. "She can dish it out pretty good. Called Connie a hemp-wearing freak and asked where the hell's she been all these months while your life was falling apart. They both got what they had coming."

Dana began to smile, but something brushed back the humor. *Connie got what she had coming?* It hadn't occurred to Dana to be angry with Connie for keeping her distance. In fact, if she'd stopped to think about it, she might have been relieved. Connie's irascibility would have caused more tension than Dana could have withstood, even though it would have been aimed at Kenneth (and his lawyer, his girlfriend, his landlord—anyone remotely connected to him, including, eventually, Dana herself). Dana wondered if Connie had considered this. Had Connie purposely done her a kindness by staying away? She sat down at the table next to Alder. "Your mother didn't do anything wrong."

The humor slipped off Alder's face. "She didn't show up."

"Sweetie, that's between me and her. *I* get to decide if she let me down, not you."

Alder's face tensed in disbelief. "How can you just . . . let her off like that?"

Dana shrugged. "Because I can. It's my decision." And choosing to assume the best of intentions wasn't always such a liability, she thought, even though Connie herself would have accused her of permanent residence in fairyland. "Alder, is this why you're so mad at her? Because you think she didn't do enough for me when Kenneth left?"

"Well . . ." The girl's eyebrows shot up. *"Partly,* yeah."

"Oh, honey. Thank you. But I'll tell you what—your services are no longer needed. You can be angry at her for *you* if you feel like it, but you don't have to be angry for me anymore, okay?"

Alder's eyebrows downshifted. "You don't see what I see," she said quietly.

"True," said Dana. "But you don't always see what I see either. And sometimes it's the people closest to us that we don't see as clearly as we see other things. Even for you." She reached out to give Alder's two-toned hair a little tug. "If you cut the black off, it'd be really cute short. Maybe you'll let her take you tomorrow?"

Alder shrugged, but she didn't say no.

That night, waiting for sleep, trying to ignore Connie's toe twitching and blanket yanking, Dana wished for the millionth time that the kids were there to tuck into bed. There was something about getting them settled under the secret security of blankets that defused her own worry. Watching their small bodies release the day and latch onto sleep had the beauty of a ballet some nights.

Did they miss her? They called every night, brief flurries of conversation about rides ("Space Mountain three times in a row!") and the hotel ("Mickey Mouse soap—I saved some for you"). Tonight Dana had murmured a furtive, "How *are* you?" to Morgan. "Are you getting any sleep?"

"Yeah, it's weird. I guess I'm really tired. Good tired, not like freaked-out tired," she'd said. "How are *you*?"

"I'm just fine, honey," Dana had lied. "Aunt Connie's here, and we're all going to have Thanksgiving together." She hoped this last part was true.

"Aunt Connie? Will she be there when we get back? She's so funny!"

Connie was punching her pillow as if it were punching back when Dana said, "Morgan's hoping you'll be here when she gets home."

"Huh," said Connie, plopping her head on the conquered pillow. "I always thought I kind of scared her." The hallway light sifted in around the bedroom door, casting a muted glow onto one side of her face. They lay there easily in the soft darkness, and their stillness leaned toward sleep. But then Connie murmured, "Do you ever think about Dad?"

Dana felt as if she had brushed up against an invisible electric fence. "Uh, Dad? A little . . ." She faltered. "Do you?"

"All the time these days. Mostly I think about how to keep from turning into him."

"What? Connie, you're nothing like him! The only time I've seen you low was when you came home from Europe pregnant with Alder. And you snapped out of that as soon as she was born."

"Mmm." A tenuous agreement. "But what if it happens again? There sure as hell won't be another baby to throw me a lifeline." Connie rolled onto her back, and Dana scrutinized her sharp profile from the safety of shadow. "Besides, kids aren't supposed to be our security blankets." Connie's eye slid sideways toward Dana, making a point.

"I just don't see you as . . . like that."

"Yeah, but it's in there, maybe waiting around a bend in my DNA. In yours, too." After a moment Connie shook her head. "Probably not, though. If anything, you're terminally upbeat."

"I don't think *either* of us is liable to end up like him."

Connie chuckled. "Know what I thought of the other day? Mom adding water to things. Empty tomato-sauce jars, shampoo containers—remember that? She hated to leave anything in the bottle. There was always something left, she said, even when it seemed like there was nothing. She could wash pots for days on those last diluted drops of dish soap."

Dana remembered it clearly. "She'd hand you a jar and say, 'Give this a sprinkle.'"

"You're like that," said Connie. "You're a rehydrator."

This sounded insulting, but half of everything out of Connie's mouth seemed like a dig, so Dana couldn't be sure. "You think I'm cheap?"

The eye that Dana could see rolled in mild annoyance. "You're the *opposite* of cheap, for godsake. You could find the last drop of good in anything." It was possibly the nicest thing Connie had ever said to her. "Don't get all sappy," warned Connie. "It's not always an asset. Being kind to a fault is an actual *fault*."

Dana couldn't help it. She reached over and patted her sister's cheek. "Connie," she cooed.

"Cut it out."

Dana heard something, as if her brain were creating background music. "Love you, Con."

"Blah, blah, blah." But she didn't turn away. Dana felt Connie's cheek swell into an unintended smile under her hand. The music got louder. *In your eyes, the light, the heat . . .*

"What in the hell is that?" Connie groused.

It was coming from outside. The two of them got up to look

out the window and saw a figure in the darkened front yard that seemed to loom like a giant beside the driveway. It stepped into the light, and they could see it was a man raising something above his head.

In your eyes, I am complete . . .

It was Jack Roburtin. He was holding up two rectangles connected by a cord. An iPod and a speaker.

"Oh, my God!" Connie burst out. "*Please* tell me that's the moron you were dating!"

"Good Lord," breathed Dana. "He's lost his mind."

"Don't you *get it*?" Connie gave Dana's shoulder a little shove. "It's from that movie! About the loser who goes out with the smart girl from high school. He plays their song in her window." Her eyes were wide with delight. "*It's how he gets her back.*"

"Oh, no." Dana looked out the window in horror.

"After all that crap he pulled, coming to your office, talking to you like that, this is his idea of roses and a box of chocolates!" Connie was bouncing on her toes like a little girl.

"No way." It was too absurd to be true.

"Serious as a heart attack! Can I handle it? Oh, *please* let me." Without waiting for an answer, Connie slid the window open and lifted the screen. "Hey!" she called, sticking the upper half of her body through the opening. Dana was watching from the other window. Jack's large head jerked up toward them. "Listen up!" yelled Connie. "This is NOT the EIGHTIES, and YOU are NO JOHN CUSACK, so you can just GO the HELL HOME!"

"*Dana?*" Jack's voice cracked a little at the end, sending Connie into spasms of laughter.

"Connie?" Alder was in the doorway behind them. Connie pulled her head back into the room.

"It's okay, honey," said Dana. "It's just . . ." *It's just what?* The situation defied description.

"DANA?" yelled Jack.

Dana put her head out the window. "Go home, Jack," she called to him.

He pulled the cord, disconnecting the iPod from the speaker. "I'll call you tomorrow?"

"No, Jack. Please don't call me anymore."

"I'm sorry about the other day." His voice was loud. She would have to apologize to the neighbors in the morning. "I was just . . . I really missed you!"

"Well, that's very nice and all—"

"Rehydrating," hissed Connie. "Kind to a *fault.*"

"Shut *up!*" Dana hissed back. "Jack," she called out the window. "It's over. I don't want to see you anymore."

Jack's fist clenched in front of him momentarily, as if his team had narrowly missed a touchdown. He looked up at the window again. "You sure?"

"Yes," she told him. "I'm *really sure.*"

The three of them watched him slump back to his truck and pull away. Connie took Dana's hand and thrust it into the air. "The champ!" she said, and they all laughed. Too giggly to sleep, they went down to the kitchen and made hot chocolate.

Alder said, "We're staying for Thanksgiving."

Dana looked to Connie, who shrugged. "I didn't want to promise," she said. "I wasn't sure how we'd get along."

"I think we're doing fine."

Connie raised her hands over her head in an imitation of Jack and gave a wicked little grin. "The entertainment definitely helps."

CHAPTER
40

I CAN'T WAIT TO TELL TONY, SHE REMEMBERED THINK-ing as she'd slid into the comfort of well-earned sleep. Then the alarm had gone off, and she must have hit it, or Connie did, because now she was racing well above the speed limit in hopes of getting to work no more than half an hour late. When she arrived, coat misbuttoned, one end of her scarf dangling by her knees, Marie gave her a look.

"I'm *sorry,*" Dana said, and she meant it. But there was an edge to her voice, a warning that elicited a shrug of innocence from Marie, as if to say it made no difference to her.

Tony was in one of the operatories. Dana peeked in, behind the balding head of a reclined patient, and Tony glanced up, a smile igniting behind his eyes. *Sorry,* she mouthed.

He furrowed his eyebrows and shook his head, as if to say, *For what?*

Patients streamed through the morning, blustering in from the cold, agitated about long-standing billing questions they'd never bothered with before. It was as if they were getting their affairs in order, preparing for the advance of peevish in-laws and socially challenged cousins, awaiting their last supper. For every patient who canceled or came late, there was another who felt the need to haunt the reception desk, fretting about his insurance coverage, or irritable because the patient before her was taking too long. Dana barely had a minute to catch Tony's eye, much less regale him with the victory of the night before, which annoyed her beyond reason. Once when he brought a chart up to her, she whispered, "Do I have a story for you!"

"Tell me," he murmured back.

But then Mrs. Prezewski-Griff and her gold vinyl purse approached the counter and launched into a stream of vitriol about her insurance company's refusal to cover teeth whitening, and Tony had to take another patient. After that, Dana thought briefly of writing him a note. *You're not in middle school,* she chided inwardly. *Get a grip!*

Finally the last patient of the morning was gone, and the delivery guy from Nelly's Deli had been paid, and Tony was saying, "Come on—gimme the goods!"

"Oh, my gosh," she breathed. "You aren't going to believe it!" She got all the way to the part with Jack saying, "You *sure?*" when the bell on the front door rang. In their hurry to sit and talk, she had forgotten to lock it. She started to rise, and Tony, still laughing, said, "Wait! What did you say?"

"I said, 'I'm *really sure.*'"

Tony guffawed and slapped the table. "Good girl!"

Dana grinned broadly, the satisfaction of her victory compounded immeasurably by his reaction.

"Dad?"

Startled, they looked up to see a tall young woman with auburn hair tied back in a messy bun. She had a strange smile on her face, as if she had happened upon something surprising and illogical, like finding a baby elephant happily grazing in her father's dental office.

"Lizzie!" Tony jumped up. "I thought you were going to—"

Her expression switched quickly to exasperation. "Yeah, *no,*" she snorted. "He's a jackass." She glanced quickly at Dana and muttered, "Sorry."

Dana waved away the apology. Didn't she know as well as anyone about jackass boyfriends? She stood and offered her hand. "I'm Dana Stellgarten. I'm temping for Kendra while she's out."

Lizzie shook the hand but looked at her father. "Dad's mentioned you."

"Yes, well . . ." Tony said. "Abby's flight lands at seven-thirty."

"I know," she said.

"All right, then." He looked at her for a moment like he wasn't sure what to do with her. "Are you heading back to the house?"

She glanced over at Dana, then at his sandwich. "Actually, I'm kinda hungry." She pulled over a stool, sat down. "Can I have a bite?"

Tony gave Lizzie half of his sub, and Dana shared her pretzels and baby carrots. They talked about Zack.

"Loser," muttered Lizzie.

Tony said, "Needs a beating, that boy."

"Oh, yeah, Dad." Lizzie gave him a knowing smile. "Like you're the butt-kicking type." She turned to Dana. "You've probably noticed by now that my father is the world's biggest sweetie pie. Vin Diesel—not so much."

"He's very kind," agreed Dana, surreptitiously watching a tide of pink rise up Tony's neck. It was so cute, his daughter's effect on him. "But he's no pushover."

Lizzie's eyes rested on hers for an extra half second—an assessment, Dana realized. She'd made similar evaluations of Morgan's and Grady's friends countless times, to determine if they were nice enough and reasonably well behaved. To guess whether they might lead her children toward trouble or trampled feelings.

"Hey," Tony said. "I'm sitting right here. At least have the decency to talk behind my back."

"Huh. Like we couldn't think up more intriguing subject matter," Lizzie teased.

They finished lunch, and Lizzie left for her childhood home, "to sleep for, like, a million hours."

"She's wonderful, Tony," Dana said after she'd gone. "What a smart, funny, lovely girl."

He looked away, and she could tell he was suppressing a surge

of visible pride. "She's a pip," he said. He shook his head, but a bliss-
ful grin surfaced all the same.

Cotters Rock Dental was closing at three o'clock that day, in obser-
vance of the Thanksgiving break. At five minutes to three, a woman
walked in and waited while Dana scheduled an appointment with
an outgoing patient. The woman was tall, maybe five foot nine,
Dana gauged, and attractive, with short blond hair.

"I'll be right with you," said Dana. The woman answered with
a short-lived smile and glanced away. She rooted in a shallow red
clutch and pulled out lipstick, squinting into a compact mirror as
she applied it. She smoothed an eyebrow.

Dana finished with the patient and said to the tall blond
woman, "Thanks for your patience. What can I do for you?"

"Mm," said the woman, a tiny noise that seemed to serve the
dual purpose of giving the shortest possible response and generating an extra second for her to compose an answer. "I am here to see
Dr. Sakimoto." There was a barely perceptible accent, but Dana
couldn't place it.

"Well, we're just about to close up for the holiday. Would you
like to make an appointment?"

Another brief, manufactured smile. "No, I'd like to see him now.
Would you get him, please?"

"Uh, okay. Can I tell him your name?"

The woman seemed to find this mildly impertinent and said,
"He'll know when he sees me."

Dana didn't like this. She sensed a surprise attack of some kind.
But Tony would know how to handle it. Besides, there was an uncertainty that underlay the woman's haughtiness, as she flicked a
finger to smooth the other eyebrow. She seemed to have a case to
make.

Dana went to get Tony and found him reviewing a chart with

Marie. "There's someone here to see you," she told him. "Says you know her. Tall, bobbed blond hair, little bit of an accent?"

Tony looked startled for a moment. Then he handed the chart to Marie and took a breath. "Make a note to keep an eye on nineteen," he said. "Please."

They watched him walk down the hall to the waiting room. He meant to close the door behind him, but it didn't latch properly. Slowly the door swung open again, and when it did, he was coming back down from tiptoes and the tall woman's head was rising, her long neck uncurling itself back to its natural position.

"Is that . . . ?" Dana murmured.

"Yeah," said Marie, writing on the chart. "She came in once before a couple of months ago. They met at a conference and hit it off. Tooth talk," she said dryly. "*So* romantic."

Martine. She was reaching out to hold his hands, speaking quickly. Dana couldn't hear anything but a few emphasized words. ". . . want *so* much . . . would *never* . . . the *thought* of . . ." Tony nodded—in acquiescence? Dana wondered. *Or is he humoring her?* Tony nodded again and lifted her hand to his lips.

Dana's chest felt strangely tight. Attempting to ignore it, she turned to Marie. "Have a happy Thanksgiving! Any plans?"

Marie handed Dana the chart. "I don't celebrate Thanksgiving," she said, and went down the hall to sterilize instruments.

Dana couldn't stand there in the hallway anymore, but neither could she intrude upon their personal moment by walking toward them to her desk. She sidestepped into Tony's office and leaned her back against the wall. *He's got his girlfriend and his daughters for Thanksgiving. That's nice.* She was not a person to begrudge the good fortune of others, even in the face of her own privations. But the hard press of self-pity against her chest would not subside, and she hated herself for it. Voices approached, and she slipped from the office before they could overrun her.

"Dana," said Tony, catching up before she made it to the safety of her reception area. "I want you to meet someone."

"Oh, of course!" she said, and set the dial to deferential-friendly. Tony introduced them, and they shook hands, Martine firing off one of her now-signature transient smiles.

"You are the single mother," she said offhandedly, and Dana couldn't help but recoil. Evidently Tony had told Martine about her, had indicated her marital status, and perhaps her dire financial straits as well. She couldn't even look at him.

Propping the smile back onto her face, she said, "Yes, I suppose I am. You two have a really terrific Thanksgiving. Great to meet you!" And she practically dove toward her desk. There wasn't much to do other than file the chart that Marie had handed her, shut down her computer, and put the answering service on. She didn't bother to button her coat, and she jammed the scarf in her purse as she made for the door. Marie was just behind her.

"Doesn't add up, does it?" said Marie as they emerged into the sallow late-afternoon light.

"Pardon me?"

"Tony and the French orthodontist. The Sophie Marceau of the dental set."

"I didn't really . . ." Dana was flustered by this unexpected verbosity from the chronically taciturn Marie. "I only met her for a minute."

"Still, you can tell. There's no balance." Marie went to her car. She wasn't given to parting pleasantries. Or, for that matter, any pleasantries at all.

When Dana got home, Alder's VW Rabbit sat in the driveway behind her mother's Vanagon, as battered as a returning war veteran. She found Connie and Alder at the kitchen table, shelling and eating pistachios. Jet was sitting on the counter, banging the backs of her Chuck Taylors against the cabinets below and eating Bran 'N Flax cereal from the box.

"Hi there, sweetie," Dana said to Jet, giving her knee a pat. She took the box from Jet, poured some cereal into a bowl, and handed it to her.

"My mom's in rehab," said Jet between handfuls of cereal.

"What?"

"Yeah, she's been waiting for a spot, and one finally came open."

"Oh, my gosh! Well, that's a good thing, now, isn't it?"

"Not gonna lie," Jet muttered.

"Can she have Thanksgiving with us?" Alder asked. "She's supposed to stay with her mom's cousin, but he's going to Buffalo to spend it with his wife's relatives."

"Of course she can." Dana turned to answer her niece and noticed her hair—short and spiky, her original gingerbread color with the faintest hint of darkness at the tips. "Alder, you did it!"

"Yeah, it was getting kind of annoying. The ends were all split." As if that were the reason. The old Alder! Dana had to hug her. She sat down at the table with them to make a shopping list for Thanksgiving dinner. It did not include a turkey.

"We do the traditional eggplant parmesan," said Connie. "With soy cheese."

"Fine," said Dana, because she really didn't care. There would be four of them for Thanksgiving. Not the same four who'd been there last year—Morgan, Grady, and Kenneth would be at Liberty Tavern in the Magic Kingdom, eating their turkey with Tina and Goofy.

Still, she thought. *It's a good group.* And for that she was thankful.

A LONG WITH THE SOY CHEESE AND EGGPLANTS, Dana bought a turkey for the McPhersons, as well as ingredients for all the other holiday-appropriate foods she could think of. She wished she knew what the McPhersons' traditions were. Did they eat their sweet potatoes with marshmallows baked on top, as she had her whole life? Or would they find that utterly disgusting? She thought of calling, but didn't want to bother them.

She got up early to put the turkey in the oven, and there was a facade of normalcy to it. This was what she did every Thanksgiving. She found herself pretending it was Morgan and Grady sleeping late instead of Alder and Jet.

Then Connie came down. "All you need is a cigarette hanging from your lip and bobby pins in your hair and you're mom," she said, slumping into a kitchen chair.

"I'll take that as a compliment."

"That turkey stinks. How can you stand the smell of roasting flesh?"

"Because I can, Connie," Dana said, holding the baster. "And this isn't even for me, so let's just change the subject before we get into a fight on Thanksgiving."

"Whatever," said Connie. Dana chose to believe it was conciliatory.

"I had a nightmare about Dad," Connie said. "Do you ever get those? Like, you see him stepping in front of a speeding car or jumping off something really high?"

Dana opened the oven and slid the tip of the baster under the turkey, squeezed and released, letting the tube fill with juices. "Sometimes," she said.

"Like what?"

"I don't know." She basted the turkey slowly to keep from spattering the oven.

"Come on."

"I said I don't know."

"You do too—you just don't want to talk about it."

Dana closed the oven door and stood up. "No. I don't want to discuss nightmares about our absent father, or the fact that my kids aren't here, or that my finances are in the toilet, or that I'll probably be out of a job soon." She tossed the baster into the sink with a clatter. "For *godsake,* Connie, will you give me one huge break—just for today!"

At noon Jet and Alder went with Dana to deliver dinner to the McPhersons.

"We've got a bunch of items here, so I brought some helpers with me," she told Mary Ellen when she answered the door. Dana introduced the girls, and they began ferrying things back and forth from the car. "Also, I broke the rules just a little. We're supposed to deliver everything in disposable containers, but I knew you'd want it to look nice, so I just plated it myself. And don't you dare wash anything! I'll come back later today to gather everything up."

The McPherson kids sat in the living room, watching a movie. The older boy and Laura, the four-year-old, sat in the opposite corners of the couch, gazing intently at the TV. Dana said, "Hi," and Laura gave a shy wave. The toddling boy who had tried to open the door for her about a month ago lay on his back between them, sucking his thumb. They were all dressed up—ties and jackets, a frilly dress for Laura. The older boy's jacket was too short at the wrists.

"Isn't that a handsome bunch! You all look beautiful," Dana said to Mary Ellen, who was wearing a dress. A seam was beginning to pop at the shoulder.

"I just felt I had to," said Mary Ellen with a little catch in her voice. "To celebrate."

"Of course you did," said Dana. "It's Thanksgiving."

Mary Ellen gave a tenuous little laugh. "Not much in the way of fancy clothes to choose from, though. I haven't gone shopping in a while."

Dermott shuffled into the room then, wearing a jacket and tie and a belt cinched tight, creating pleats in his pants where formerly there weren't any. "Hey, it's the Good Witch of Cotters Rock," he said with a pallid grin.

"I was just telling your wife how wonderful you all look."

Having finished setting up the platters in the kitchen, Alder and Jet came to stand with Dana. "Way better than us," said Jet. "No lie."

Alder was gazing at Mary Ellen. "Maybe you'd like a picture?" she asked.

"Oh, yes! We need a picture!" Mary Ellen left to find a camera.

Dermott continued his forward progression until he reached Dana and leaned over to kiss her on the cheek. "Blame me for this," he murmured. "I'm the one who requested you."

"I'm honored," she said. "And it was pure pleasure, believe me."

Mary Ellen came back and held out the camera to Alder. Then she arranged the children in front of the fireplace, with the toddler on her hip and Dermott next to her. "Say 'Gobble, gobble,'" said Dana. But the older boy and Laura began to fuss with each other, and the toddler reached down and grabbed a handful of Laura's hair. A look of despair came over Mary Ellen's face as she tried to quiet them.

It could be the last picture of them all together, thought Dana, wondering desperately how to help.

"Hey!" yelled Jet, a bit more loudly than necessary, but it caught the children's attention. "Say 'Barbecued monkey guts'!"

The kids burst out in giggles, and Dermott with his arm around his wife's waist gave her a quick tug toward him. Her chin went up as she laughed. The camera made its synthesized snapping sound over and over as Alder held down the button.

When the three of them returned home, Connie was taking the eggplant out of the oven, and though the soy cheese on top had browned in an unnaturally uniform manner, it smelled wonderful. "That's it," she said. "Everything else is already out." She rested the pan on top of the stove for a moment, and Alder hugged her.

"Whoa!" Jet called from the dining room. "What the f—!"

"What's the matter?" Dana hurried into the dining room with Connie and Alder close behind.

"There's freaking marshmallows all over this orange stuff—it's awesome! What twisted mind thought of *that*?"

By midafternoon the meal had long been over, but the four of them still sat around the table, slouching back in their chairs. They sipped decaffeinated coffee until it grew tepid and cream circles formed on the surface. Connie and Dana laughed about holiday meals of years past, when the kids were little and ruled by uncontrollable impulses to tip over the gravy boat, stand on their chairs, mold their food like Play-Doh, or strip down to their diapers during dessert. Jet was uncharacteristically quiet, sitting sideways with her legs over one arm of her chair, occasionally fingering the last vestiges of sweet potato from the casserole dish. She listened with a surreptitious intensity, as if she could somehow absorb these stories into her own history.

The doorbell rang, and they all looked at each other for clues. It rang again, and Dana got up to answer it. On the front porch stood a young man in khakis and a slightly wrinkled button-down shirt with a brown spot on the breast pocket. His hair was dark and shaggy, and he flipped the bangs away from his forehead when he saw her coming through the window beside the door.

"Uh, hi . . ." he said when she opened the door. "Is Alder here? Happy Thanksgiving, by the way," he added quickly. "Hope I'm not . . . Are you still . . . like, eating?"

At first Dana thought he might be a member of the Wilderness Club—maybe a boy who was just full enough of warm holiday feelings to get up the nerve to approach her niece. But the voice was familiar somehow.

"Happy Thanksgiving to you, too!" she said, holding the door open for him to enter. "We're just finishing up—come on in." She followed him through the mudroom, and it wasn't until they were in the hallway by the dining room that the realization hit her like a sucker punch. She wanted to reach out and grab him, to yank him by his stained shirt right back out the front door. *No!* she wanted to say. *Not one more step!*

By then he was standing in the archway to the dining room, and all sound stopped. Then Jet said, "Who's *that*?" and Connie said, "Ethan, you little shit," and Ethan said, "Alder, *please*. Can we *please* just go somewhere and talk?"

Alder's gaze was fixed on Ethan. "Why would I *ever* want to be alone with *you*?"

His eyes darted to the other women, then back to Alder. *"Please,"* he whispered.

Alder crossed her arms. She glanced at Connie and Jet. "Is it okay if you guys go?" she asked. "Dana can stay." It was the slightest possible concession to him—one onlooker instead of three.

Connie stared at Dana momentarily, and there was anger at not being chosen and a sort of pleading to keep on top of things. *"Don't rehydrate,"* she muttered as she rose. She took Jet by the arm and led her toward the living room. Dana was fairly certain they would listen in and just as certain that Alder didn't care. She took a seat by her niece.

The girl looked at her former best friend. "How did you even know where I was?"

"Your, uh . . . your mom gave me the number. And when you weren't home, I figured maybe you were still . . . You talk about your aunt sometimes, and I remembered her name, and—"

"You *Googled* my *aunt*?" Her lip curled in disgust. "All right, whatever you came for, just get it over with."

He took a breath and held it, as if he were about to leap from a high dive into a kiddie pool right there in the dining room. "First off, I am totally and maximally *sorry*." The air came out of him then, his apology staggering him just a little. "Everywhere I go," he continued miserably, "I, like, *reek* of regret."

Dana glanced at Alder. The stress around her eyes had lessened, and her jaw had unclenched. "Why," she said.

"I know, right?" he concurred. "Why would I screw things up so badly with the *one person* . . . Christ, Alder, I barely even get it *myself*."

She looked away, eyes half lidded in dissatisfaction.

"Wait," he said, anxiously. "I think it's . . . I couldn't get, like, normal after that. It was so . . . *much*. . . . All these feelings that totally freaked me out. I almost didn't want to go to college anymore! I just wanted to stay and be with you every second and be, like, *married* or something. I'm eighteen years old, for chrissake—I'm not ready for that. Developmentally, I'm an idiot!"

There was a subtle snort of air from Alder, an agreement, a softening.

"Also," he ventured warily, "you know me so well . . . It's, like, *too* well."

Her eyes narrowed.

"It kinda spooked me out sometimes, like you could almost read my mind—and believe me, most guys do *not* want girls to know what they're thinking." He stopped for a moment, his eyes softening with remorse. "I knew I owed you an explanation for leaving without . . . But I just kind of figured . . . you knew."

"Well, I *didn't* know!" Alder flew forward in her seat, pointing at him. "I don't read your mind like a freaking *comic book,* like all I have to do is flip the page to know you're going to screw me and take off!" Hot tears sprouted from her eyelids. "I trusted you more than *anyone,* and you *used me for sex*! I thought you were good, but I was wrong, wasn't I? You're just a *user!*"

A groan came out of him, and the muscles around his spine seemed to disengage. Dana wondered if he might collapse. "Alder," he said, "if there's one thing in my life I wish I could take back, it's *that.*"

Alder closed her eyes and turned her head, tears flowing freely down her face. Dana took her hand. It was loose and weak in her own.

"I miss you *so much,*" Ethan murmured. "College sucks. There's no you. I thought that would be a good thing—like, it'd be a relief to be anonymous. And it was. For about a week." He slumped against the doorway. "But then I got so lonely. I kept waiting for it to pass, like a sinus headache or something." He gave a listless shrug. "Got a little better after I made some friends. But, Christ, I forgot how much *talking* you have to do. So much *explaining* about who you are and what you're into.

"It used to make me nervous how well you got me—but I never realized how exhausting it is to have to *tell* people stuff! To have to say out loud that you hate ham and have everybody *comment.* Like, they agree and they have to tell you what nasty thing *they* think it tastes like, or they disagree and have to make some lame joke about it. Who fucking *cares*! It's all this tidal wave of stupid words, and I just keep thinking, 'Alder doesn't talk like this. She just paints, and we hang out, and it's all good.' It's all so good, it, like, *hurts.*"

Alder was crying silently, shoulders shaking. Dana pressed a dinner napkin into her free hand, and she used it to wipe her chin.

"I just wanted to tell you . . ." Ethan sounded so weary that he might actually lie down on the shiny oak boards of the dining-room floor and slip into unconsciousness. "I just want you to know that I know what I did. I know how much it hurt you. And I'm so sorry."

After a moment Alder's shoulders went still, and she inhaled a sniffle, pressing the napkin against her eyes to dam her tears. "Okay," she breathed.

Ethan revived a little. "Yeah?" he said, only half believing.

Alder shrugged. She gave Dana's hand a squeeze, released it, and stood up. She walked toward Ethan and motioned him into the hallway, following him out. The front door opened and shut. Dana went to the kitchen window to watch, deputized as she was to monitor the situation. They stood there talking for five minutes or so, each with their arms crossed tightly over their chests to keep out the cold, eyes cast down mostly, but blinking up at each other from time to time. They never touched. Then Ethan walked down the driveway and drove off.

"YOU WERE GREAT THIS AFTERNOON, CONNIE," Dana said as they settled into bed that night.

"What's your point?" Connie rolled over, yanking blankets and sheets with her as she went.

"You let Alder talk about Ethan when she was ready—it was just what she needed." Dana tugged back a few inches of covers and sighed. "Before I had kids, I never realized how much self-restraint it takes to be a mother."

Connie punched her pillow once or twice and burrowed down like a bear getting ready to hibernate. Her breathing slowed, and Dana thought she might have fallen asleep, but then she said, "Why'd you call Dad 'absent'?"

"What are you talking about?" Dana grumbled, hoping to sound sleepy.

"This morning when I asked you if you'd ever had nightmares about Dad, you called him an 'absent father.'"

"Well, he is. I don't see him around, do you?"

"Don't get touchy."

"I'm not *touchy*, I'm *tired*. It's been a long day, and I don't need to dredge up ancient issues when I've got plenty of current ones to deal with."

Connie was quiet. After a moment she said, "You know Dad's dead, right? Tell me you're not still cutting out those articles on amnesia and international kidnapping like you did when we were teenagers."

"Oh, my *God,* Connie, can you just zip it? I have to work tomorrow—I need sleep!"

"You think he's still out there," Connie murmured. "Don't you?"

Dana sat up in bed. She'd had it with Connie—she always knew what bothered you most, and poked at it until you couldn't stand it anymore. Anger crackled across Dana's brain like heat lightning. "Well, we aren't absolutely sure *where* he is, *are* we!"

Connie propped her head on her hand. "We know he went to Swampscott and left his clothes and wallet on the beach."

"Right! So a guy can't go back to his hometown and take a swim?"

"In the middle of the night," said Connie. "He got up in the dead of night, drove twenty miles, and left everything he owned in the sand."

"He was low! He needed to take a drive!" It suddenly felt important to defend him, to hang tightly on to the remote possibility, however irrational, that he hadn't . . .

"He was clinically depressed," said Connie quietly. "And he killed himself. His body was probably washed out to sea, they said. Or he could have weighted himself down with something. Suicides do that sometimes."

Dana grabbed for the closest thing at hand—a pillow—and threw it at Connie. "Why do you do this!" she hissed between clenched teeth. "Why do you have to be so fucking mean!"

"Well," said Connie, "I guess because 'fucking nice' was already taken."

"GODDAMN IT! I really HATE you sometimes!"

She sat there, chest heaving in and out, the pulse in her neck throbbing as if it might burst. *Dad.* The word skipped over and over in her mind, like a flat stone out to sea. *Dad, swim back!* she wanted to say. *Get your wallet and put your clothes back on and drive home!*

But he hadn't. And he never would. He'd never seen her children, hadn't held their faces in his hands, hadn't marveled at their wondrousness like grandpas were supposed to do. He might have held her own face when she was little, but it was quite possible that in her desperation to matter to him she had concocted the image, cut and pasted it from a TV show or a magazine.

Dad killed himself. He had a choice between life with a family who loved him, and death . . . and he chose death. Of course she knew this—always had. It was only that she wanted so much to *un*know it.

"I don't think you ever told me you hated me before," remarked Connie. Dana rolled her eyes in annoyance. "It's kinda weird," Connie continued, "coming from you, I mean."

Dana slid down into the covers, yanking them from Connie and tugging them up over her shoulders. Of course Connie had never heard her say "I hate you." Dana had never actually said it before, to anyone. She took a deep breath and let it slide out slowly.

"You know, the thing about you is," said Connie, "you seem so normal, nobody gets how screwed up you are."

"Just shut it, Connie."

"You should embrace your own psychosis more."

"How about if I embrace my own violence and sock you one? Will that shut you up?"

"Shutting," said Connie in mock sweetness, and Dana was tempted to lash out, but Connie put a hand on her shoulder. "Love you, Day," she murmured.

"Blah, blah, blah."

Connie burst out laughing.

Dana left them all sleeping on Friday morning. She put a note on the kitchen table: "Went to work, back at five. Love, D." They knew this, but she wrote it anyway. She preferred to have her whereabouts confirmed.

The patients were as genially languid today as they had been frenzied on Wednesday. They seemed to be still full of turkey and the relief that comes of having mounted a successful holiday campaign, or at least survived it. The schedule was light. There were no cleanings, only lesser procedures that Tony could handle without an assistant, since Marie had put in for a personal day. Tony confided that he'd heard her on her cell phone during a break between patients, booking a flight to Canada.

"Wow," said Dana. "She really meant it when she said she didn't celebrate Thanksgiving."

"I'm thinking she's on an alternative spiritual path," he mused, leaning in the doorway to the reception area, waiting for the next patient to show.

"Aren't we all," she muttered. She looked up to see him gazing at her in amusement. It was the look he'd given Lizzie when she said they had better things to talk about than him. A kind of thinly concealed admiration.

Such a nice face, she thought. The graceful lines of his nose and eyes. The smoothness of his skin peppered by closely shaved whiskers. There was a strange contentment in just looking at him that dusted away drama and disappointment. But after a moment it felt strange to stare at her boss as he stared back, and she blinked and said, "So how did it go? Did all your girls get along?"

His expression turned wry. "They got along some of the time. The rest of the time they acted like hens at a pecking party." He described a twenty-four-hour period—from Martine's arrival on Wednesday to her dramatic departure on Thursday, shortly after her fig tart had gotten burned because Lizzie had shoved it to the back of the oven rather than placed it at the front as had been requested. "They fussed at each other like five-year-olds," he said. "It was hell."

"And where was Abby in all this?"

He chuckled. "Flying under the radar, as usual. Holed up in her room, studying for the clinical-skills exam of her medical boards. It was the only thing Lizzie and Martine agreed on—that Abby wasn't helping enough."

"Sounds awful," she commiserated. "Have you talked to Martine since?"

"Yeah . . ." His expression went flat, and he looked away. "It didn't go well."

"She broke up with you over a *pie*?"

"Well, yes and no. I think it was because I didn't really try hard enough to talk her out of ending it." He shrugged. "Hey, the girls weren't on their best behavior, and I told them so. I was pissed. But Martine wasn't exactly behaving like a grown-up either." He looked perplexed. "I'd never seen her act like that. She's usually so smart and self-possessed."

"Some situations don't bring out the best in people," said Dana.

"Yeah, I thought of that. But then I was taking Abby to the airport last night, and she said, 'Dad. Really. Her?'" He shook his head, then glanced at Dana. "What did you think of her?"

"Oh, um, she's very . . . tall, isn't she?"

Apparently it wasn't the kind of answer he was looking for. "Uh, yeah, I guess."

"Does that . . . did it bother you? Dating someone so tall?"

"You mean taller than me? Nah. It could, I suppose. But at my height it'd really reduce the options." He flashed a quick grin, "And where's the fun in that?" Then he dialed down the light in his eyes. "Seriously," he said, pursuing his earlier question. "What did you think?"

She treated me like an orphaned handmaid. Dana jiggled her computer mouse and watched the cursor flick across the screen. "She seemed nice."

Tony studied her for a moment. "You're lying, aren't you?"

"Okay," said Dana. "I didn't like the way she said, 'You are the single mother.' As if it's a role I play on some TV show." She returned his gaze. "Is that how you talk about me?"

"Dana," he said, shame coloring his smooth features. "I never—"

The bell on the door jingled, and Mr. Kranefus came in, removing his fedora and fingering the brim as he made his way to the coatrack.

"Hi there, Mr. Kranefus," said Dana. "How was your Thanksgiving?"

"Endless." He slid off his overcoat and hung it on a hook. "But now it's over."

Dana was just finishing a call with a claim rep when she heard Tony's drill whine down to silence. A moment later he came into her reception area and pulled down his mask. "I want you to know I never called you that. I talked about you from time to time, and I guess I mentioned you had kids and were divorced, but I would never identify you as The Single Mother."

"Okay," she said.

"I don't think of you that way. And I'm very sorry she said it." He put his mask up and went back to Mr. Kranefus.

At lunch she told him about Jet's inspired contribution at the McPhersons' house, the surprisingly pleasant substitution of eggplant parmesan for turkey, and Ethan's bid for forgiveness.

"But what happened out in the driveway?" he asked. "Did she ever tell you?"

"A little. She said she partly forgave him and that the rest of it might come over time. They have no plans to see each other again, but I think they'll touch base at some point. The most important thing is she's not walking around with all that pain and rage. Or not as much anyway."

"Do you think she'll go home now?"

It was a startling thought. But the way had been paved, hadn't it? Hamptonfield, Massachusetts, was no longer quite so much of a crime scene to Alder, and relations with Connie had definitely improved. Dana stared at him as she contemplated the days ahead without Alder.

"She's pretty lucky to have you for an aunt," Tony said gently. "Giving her a safe harbor while she figured all this out and helping your sister reconnect—that's a heck of a contribution."

"It would just be nice if things could stay the same for more than five minutes in a row."

"What planet does *that* happen on?" He smiled. "My passport's current, I'm ready anytime."

Dana was sitting at her desk, with Tony looking for a patient chart on the shelves behind her, when Connie came in. "It's colder than a pile of poop on Pluto out there," she grumbled.

"Connie!" said Dana, putting on a smile as her heart thumped out an alarm. "This is my boss, Tony Sakimoto. Tony—my sister, Connie Garrett."

Connie gave him a transparently appraising look.

"Nice to meet you, Connie." Tony smiled. "I hear you make a mean vegan eggplant parm."

"And I hear you're the best boss since Santa," Connie replied dryly. "She hurries off to work every morning like there's sleigh rides and free candy canes."

Dana's face went hot. Tony let loose a deep, rumbling laugh and said, "My secret's out. I said the heck with health benefits, let's get some reindeer in here!"

Connie raised her eyebrows at Dana, a look that meant, *He's weird, but entertaining.*

"So listen," she said, leaning on the reception counter. "I think the girls and I will head home for the weekend. I've got a friend at Hamptonfield Auto Service who'll give me a break on fixing the rest of what's wrong with Alder's car, and I really ought to show up for a shift at Nine Muses. Also, I think Jet needs a change of scenery.

She's starting to eat the condiments, and that much soy sauce can't be good for you."

"Oh . . . okay," said Dana, trying to absorb it all. "When are you thinking of leaving?"

"Now, pretty much. The girls swung over to Jet's house to grab some extra clothes. They're meeting me at the Hebron Ave Shell station, and we'll caravan, in case her car gives her trouble."

"So you'll be back on Sunday?" Dana's panic over Connie's presence was quickly morphing into panic over her absence. It was still another thirty-six hours before the kids got home. And she realized she would genuinely miss Connie.

"Sunday?" Connie squinched up her face in thought. "Probably not. I mean, some subset of us will be, but I can't really afford to take off any more time. I'll call you, though. Maybe tomorrow night." She gave the counter two little slaps. "Gotta go."

But she didn't move right away. Some thought came to her, and she smiled at it and looked up at Dana. It was almost a thank-you. Then she turned to Tony, said, "See ya, Santa," and left.

D ANA PULLED INTO THE DRIVEWAY AFTER WORK
and looked up at her darkened house. *No one home,* she thought.
She flicked on lights as she made her way from the garage up to her
bedroom, but it only seemed to confirm her aloneness.

It's temporary, she chided herself. *They'll be home tomorrow night.*
She pulled off her slacks, unbuttoned her blouse, and hung them
both on hangers to avert an unnecessary trip to the dry cleaners.

It wasn't the empty house. *It's me,* she thought as she tugged on
a T-shirt and a battered pair of jeans. *Everything's changing, and I'm
not keeping up.*

A swirling, nauseating sense of exhaustion swept over her, and
she lay back on her bed, legs dangling over the edge. The swirling
and a hopelessly dislocated feeling reminded her of the miscarriage
she'd had before Grady. She had lain in that very bed when she'd
gotten home from the hospital after "the procedure." That's how
Kenneth had repeatedly referred to it. "Do you need me to drive you
to the procedure? . . . How long will the procedure take? . . . Thank
God the procedure's covered under our insurance."

"Yes!" she'd finally yelled at him. "Let's thank God for that!"

And he'd looked at her as if her unseemliness affronted him,
but that he would disregard it given the circumstances. She had
read that in his face and knew it was true. He would grant her the
favor of disregarding her. And so she knew she was alone in it. The
loss would be hers to carry by herself for the rest of her life. She still

missed that baby from time to time, but she never told anyone. Not after the look he'd given her.

I miss all my babies. It seemed so weak—to yearn for two children who'd been gone only six days and for another who'd never even arrived. And Alder, a child who wasn't hers to begin with. She thought of calling Connie to see how Alder was doing, back in the town she'd fled two months earlier. And had Jet stopped eating condiments? *Poor thing. Missing her mother,* Dana realized.

She thought of calling Polly—making up just to have someone to talk to. She even thought of using the home number that Tony had programmed into her cell phone. But she didn't make any calls, partly out of exhaustion, partly out of not wanting to put her weakness on display. And because, most important, in the end she knew it wouldn't help. It might anesthetize the wound for a short time, but it would not suture it. Things were changing, and the life she'd had with her children constantly and happily tangled around her was shifting into the past.

Not like it wouldn't have shifted eventually anyway, she reminded herself. If the parenting books were right, Morgan and Grady would soon become secretive teenagers with social lives she'd only glimpse from the driveways of their friends' houses. She wasn't ready for them to have whole pieces of their existence that didn't revolve around her, that she wasn't even privy to. But what choice did she have? She could hear her mother saying, *You play the hand you're dealt.*

Ma, she thought. A woman with vastly different daughters to raise and a husband who couldn't get up off the couch—until he got up and drove to Swampscott and left his life on the beach. Mary Ellen McPherson came to mind, and Dermott with his gallows humor and wasting body. And three little children.

A mismatched thread shot through the fabric of her pondering, a memory of something she'd neglected—dishes. The serving platters she had instructed Mary Ellen not to wash, that she would retrieve on Thanksgiving night. But then Ethan had shown up and the dishes had slipped her mind. They were probably clogging the counters, plastered with the remnants of yesterday's meal, annoying Mary Ellen when she had bigger issues to deal with. Dana reached for the phone.

"I haven't given them a thought," Mary Ellen told her. "Isn't that awful? I should have washed them, but we had such a nice time—the kids went crazy for the marshmallowed sweet potatoes. And Dermott is feeling . . . well, not great, exactly, but pretty good! He's finally starting to get his strength back." She was elated. "We're going out tonight, just the two of us."

"That's wonderful! And you have a baby-sitter?"

"My neighbor's daughter is coming over. It's perfect. Well"—she laughed—"if I can find anything remotely decent to wear. Everything I own is so tired and ugly."

"I have something." Dana sat up. "It's not right on me, but it would look *fantastic* on you."

Dana got home from the McPhersons' with an armload of crusty platters and a satisfied grin she couldn't seem to get off her face. The perfect blouse, the perfect recipient. Mary Ellen had looked amazing in it. And Dermott had smiled the half-dazed, half-hungry smile of a man in love with his wife.

Dana was filling the sink with soap suds when Morgan called. "Tina's pregnant," she murmured tightly. "They're getting *married*." And she broke into gasping sobs.

"Oh, honey," Dana soothed. "I know it's hard. This isn't what you expected."

"You *knew*?"

"Dad told me just before you left."

"I can't believe this! You knew they were . . . and this was all . . . and you didn't *tell* me?"

"Sweetie, it wasn't mine to tell."

"Oh, my God! Are you, like, *happy* about this? You don't care at all!"

"Of course I care. This is a big adjustment for all of us, but—"

"Mom, he used to be your husband! How can you be so *cold*?"

Cold! Dana wanted to say. *I nearly erupted into flames when he told me! I wouldn't mind if they both vanished into thin Orlando air!*

"Morgan," she said firmly, "I know this is hard, and it's not what any of us—and I mean *any* of us—planned on. But you cannot go accusing me of not caring. You have no idea how I feel, and it's not your business to know. But trust me, I *care*." Morgan fired off another round of sobs. "Sweetie, where are you?"

"In the bathroom," she choked.

"Does Dad know where you are?"

"Sort of. Him and Tina told us, and then I tried to, like, smile and sound happy and stuff, but it was really hard. And then Tina said, 'Maybe you want to talk to your mom,' and I started to cry a little—I couldn't help it. And Tina gave me the phone, and she told Dad they should go down to the restaurant by the lobby and he could have a beverage. That's what she called it—a *beverage*! Like I don't know it's beer or alcohol or something!"

Poor Morgan, trying to hold it together. And Tina saying call your mom. It was either a complete cop-out or remarkably sensitive—Dana wasn't sure which. And had she taken Kenneth to the bar for his sake or to give Morgan privacy for a good weep?

Dana swallowed, pressing against the tension in her throat, hoping she could sound normal. "Morgan, I really think this is going to be okay. I know it's a lot to handle, honey, but we'll manage. Dad and I—and Tina—we'll all do our best to make it work. And you'll do your best, too, right?"

"Yeah." She sniffled. "Mom? Are you mad at Dad?"

Dana almost laughed. *Oh, just a little*. But that was only part of her. Another part knew he just wasn't her business anymore. "You know," she told Morgan. "It kind of caught me off guard. But Dad and I talked about it, and we think it'll be okay. We'll all have to get used to it at first, but then it will just be normal."

Morgan inhaled—a damp but valiant effort—and let it out. "Okay," she said.

"Honey, where's Grady?"

"Watching TV."

"Can you get him?"

Dana could hear them fussing with each other. "Take the phone . . . Why? . . . Just *take* it . . . No. I like this show . . . It's Mom! . . . Can she call back? . . . You're such a— . . . Ow! You don't have to throw it . . ."

Grady put the receiver to his ear. "Hello?"

"Hi, honey. How are you?"

"Okay."

"I guess you got some big news, huh?"

"What big news?"

"About Dad and Tina getting married and having a baby?"

"Oh, yeah."

"How's that sound to you?"

"Okay, I guess." He turned away from the receiver and said, "Hey, I was watching that!" Morgan's distant voice responded, "Well, now you're not."

"Grady," said Dana, "we can talk about this another time, but I just wanted to make sure you were okay with it."

"Well, it doesn't sound too different. Except for the baby part. That'll be kinda weird. But he'll be little, so he'll mostly be with Tina. Dad and I can still do stuff."

"That's true. In the beginning babies mostly sleep and eat. And maybe when it gets older, you might even want to play with it."

"Yeah, maybe." His breath whooshed across the mouthpiece for a moment. "Mom? Did anyone call you from school?"

Dana had a sinking feeling. Had he been getting into fights again? "No, why would your teacher call me?"

"Not my teacher. The custodian. I thought maybe he found my golf ball. He goes up on the roof sometimes. We were watching the Weather Channel, and it says it's going to snow in Connecticut on Sunday. So I was hoping he found it."

"I haven't heard anything, but you can ask when you get back to school."

"But the snow's on *Sunday*. I really need it."

Why? she wanted to ask. *You have your father right there with you. You've been together all week.*

"Well," she said, "we'll see what we can do."

When Dana woke early in the morning, she knew she'd been dreaming of Ma. She could smell her perfume, like roses and fresh-mown grass. *What did she do after Dad died?* It was difficult to conjure a clear picture, limited as she was by the long distance of the memory and the self-absorption of adolescence. She couldn't remember her mother saying anything. The clichés and platitudes stopped for a while—Ma seemed to smoke more and talk less. This unexpected silence was disorienting, and Dana remembered making plans to be elsewhere every day, even trying out for a small part in the school play so she would have practices to go to. She'd had only one line: "As you wish, Dr. Wallenquack." Connie had taunted her with it for months. Anytime Dana asked her for something—a barrette, a dish towel, a lick of her ice cream—Connie had answered with that line. ("Pass the salt." "As you wish, Dr. Wallenquack." Dana had wanted to kill her.)

Eventually Ma's friends had convinced her to join their card night, rotating from home to home every Tuesday, playing pinochle and euchre. "We just don't have the attention span for bridge!" Dana remembered a woman saying when her mother hosted one night. The rest of the ladies had laughed as if she were Lucille Ball.

Then Ma started waitressing the lunch shift at Friendly's, and her daughters got used to seeing her in her polyester uniform when they came home from school. Ma would be sitting sideways in the kitchen nook, her ice-cream sticky sneakers hanging off the end of the bench, smoking a cigarette and turning her head to blow the smoke out the window behind her. She'd be tired, but a purposeful kind of tired. And that became normal, the new normal without Dad.

Dana lay in her bed a while longer, plans forming and dissolving like sugar crystals in water. It was a sharply sunny day; she could tell by the way the light knifed in around the edges of the drapes. She wasn't sure she was up to the challenge of such brightness, but she rose and put on the jeans and long-sleeved T-shirt she'd taken off and thrown over a chair the night before.

An idea came to her, and she followed it blindly, willing herself not to think too much. She got onto I-84, then the Massachusetts Turnpike, and drove toward Watertown. Soon she was parked in front of what used to be Friendly's. It was a Starbucks now, and she went in to see if there were any vestiges left of her mother's former workplace. There weren't. The spattered chrome shake machines, the vinyl-clad booths, the hanging sign that looked like a window shutter listing the ice-cream flavors were all gone. She bought a latte and got back into the car.

Then she was driving down Belmont Street, past the Oakley Country Club and the Armenian markets, merging onto Mount Auburn and turning right into the protective shade of the cemetery. The last time she'd glided slowly down these winding, narrow lanes, a little over a year ago, Kenneth had been driving, hands clenched at ten and two on the steering wheel. They'd sat in their somber clothes, the kids staring unhappily out the windows.

"Is this where Grandma's gonna live now?" six-year-old Grady had asked.

"She's not alive anymore," Morgan had reminded him.

"Yeah, but is this gonna be her address?"

Now it was Dana driving to her mother's new address. CATHERINE GARRETT, BELOVED MOTHER. It had been Connie's job to order the stone after the funeral. Dana had never returned to see it installed, so it was a surprise to see engraved below her mother's name JAMES GARRETT, BELOVED DAD. There had never been a marker for him, because there had never been a body over which to place it. There'd been no funeral or burial. He was just gone.

Beloved dad. Connie had opted for "dad" instead of "father," a role he'd filled solely by virtue of his DNA toward the end. It was a kindness toward him, Dana realized. Connie's kindness was rarely so obvious; Dana would call and thank her.

She knelt on the grass, still frosted with ice crystals, and ran her fingers across the chiseled names. So many memories of Ma—her smell and her words of advice, her utter delight in each grandchild, her bravery at the end. And almost no clear memories of him.

A golf ball would come in really handy about now, Dad.

At a stoplight on the way home, she flicked through the contacts on her cell phone and hit the "send" button. "You don't happen to have a really long ladder, do you?" she asked when he answered the phone.

DANA WAS WAITING ON THE FRONT STEP WHEN Tony pulled in to her driveway with a metal ladder tied to the top of his Toyota RAV4. She got in on the passenger side. "Okay, now you know for sure I'm nuts," she said.

"Just a little," he said. "But it's the quirky, harmless kind, so I'm not afraid for my life or anything."

On the way to the elementary school, she told him about her trip to Watertown. "I guess I have a new appreciation for the little meaningless things that mean something." They pulled in to the empty parking lot, and she asked him, "Did you keep anything special of your wife's?"

"Well, I still live in the same house, so there's lots of stuff she picked out—furniture and things. But I tried not to make a shrine of it. At first I couldn't help it, but then I started letting things go." His fingers, resting on the steering wheel, began to tap a little tattoo. "There is one thing, though—a scarf she made for our first Christmas together. It's just awful—she never knit another thing, and if you saw it, you'd understand why." He shut off the engine and looked out over the playground. "I don't wear it anymore. But it's the one thing I'd never give up."

They got out and hoisted the ladder down off the roof of the car. From Grady's description they picked a spot in back of the school where Jav might have stood when the golf ball went flying, and they set up the ladder. Tony went first and held it from the top as Dana climbed. Their quarry was nowhere in sight.

The wind coursed across the top of the flat building, making it hard to talk if they wandered too far from each other, so they kept within hearing range. He told her about Lizzie's apology for being catty and unwelcoming to Martine. Much to Dana's surprise, she found herself telling him about how the kids' being gone and all the changes that were happening had reminded her of the miscarriage.

"I once had a patient come in for a cleaning," Tony said, "and when I asked her that standard question about health changes, she burst into tears. She told me she'd just lost a baby."

"*Ohh,*" said Dana. "What did you do?"

"I sat there with her while she cried. She was in no shape to have anyone poking at her, so we rescheduled. And, you know, when she came back, she acted like nothing happened. I asked her how she was feeling, and she put on a smile and said, 'Perfectly fine.'"

"It's so personal," explained Dana. "Such a dark, empty feeling. It's really hard to talk about." And yet here she was talking about it with him as they scoured the rooftop of a public building for a critically important golf ball . . .

She felt such affection for this man, such gratitude. And when he found the treasure they'd been looking for wedged between a vent pipe and a generator of some kind, she couldn't help but put her arms around his shoulders and kiss his wind-reddened cheek.

He slipped an arm around her waist and raised the ball high with the other hand, and they stood there for a moment grinning success at each other. The breeze blew a wisp of hair across her eyes, and he brushed it back behind her head, his hand resting at the nape of her neck. And then, slowly, his face came closer and pressed gently against hers, the faintly minty smell of his breath penetrating her own as he kissed her, lips traveling across each other until she didn't know where his ended and hers began. Her chest flooded with warmth, and her heart started to pound, and she had a sort of unbuckled feeling, as if she were careening through space at warp speed without benefit of an air bag or a passive-restraint system. It was terrifying.

When his lips came away from hers, he kissed her on the cheek, then pulled back a little. "Wow. That was completely inappropriate," he murmured, without a hint of regret. He had that same dazed/ hungry look she'd seen the night before on the face of Dermott McPherson.

"We'd better go back down before someone sees us," she said. And he released her.

With no more conversation than was necessary to descend the ladder, carry it to the parking lot, and tie it to the roof, they were soon seated in his car.

"You okay?" he asked, glancing intermittently at her, as if sharp focus might cause her to disappear altogether. "You seemed a little terrified up there."

"Well . . . I guess I was a little."

"And now?"

"Still slightly terrified," she admitted worriedly.

"Okay," he said, starting the motor. "Good to know." He let the motor idle a moment as he stared out at the barren trees. "Feel like grabbing a bite at Keeney's?"

"Yes," she said, desperately thankful that her fear hadn't driven him away. "I'm starving."

They ordered burgers and fries and each had a beer. He asked her more about her childhood in Watertown, and she told him anything she could remember that was the least bit interesting. Thanks to Connie, she even talked about her father's suicide.

He told her about growing up in Cranston, Rhode Island, the only child of Dorotea Consilina Sakimoto and Takashi Sakimoto— also the only European-Asian kid anyone in his neighborhood had ever met. "Not so easy. I got called 'half-breed' or—my personal favorite—'half-Chink' quite a bit," he said wryly. "But then I could also make you a damn good pasta e fagioli or miso soup, depending on your mood. Unusual situations have their benefits."

Feathers of light dusted across Nipmuc Pond as the sun descended behind the evergreens on the far shore. He took her home. She was afraid that he would kiss her again, then not sure if she was disappointed when he didn't.

About an hour later, the kids arrived—travel-weary, tripping over each other to tell her the highlights of the week, slightly sunburned yet needing to press themselves against her, tugging at her elbows, leaning into her as if she were the only source of heat in the blustery chill of the night. Kenneth hauled their bags in, kissed and hugged them with more familiarity than he had in months, and gave her a weary nod. "Thanks," he murmured. "It was a great trip."

"Good."

"I'll call you tomorrow." And he went out to the idling car where Tina was waiting.

On Sunday, Alder and Jet returned, driving Connie's Vanagon. "My car's not done yet," Alder explained. "And we needed to get back."

They stood in the mudroom. Jet wore a denim jacket over her sweatshirt—the warmest outerwear she seemed to own. Her backpack still hung from her shoulders. Without the black eyeliner, she looked pale and very young. Dana put her hands on Jet's cool cheeks. "Should we ask your mom's cousin if you can stay with us for a while?" she said. The girl's eyes went wide and shiny, and she let the backpack slip to the floor with a thunk.

Later, when Morgan and Grady were in bed and Jet was taking a bubble bath, Alder came looking for Dana. She was in the office, squinting at the computer spreadsheet she had devised to track her budget.

"How's it look?" Alder asked.

"Actually, it looks a little better than I thought it would. Not by much, but I'll take it."

"I just wanted to say thanks about Jet and everything. She's a little freaked right now."

"Of course she is. And I'm very happy to have her." Dana gave a little smirk. "But you knew I would be."

Alder shrugged. "You have a thing for strays. You're like . . . adoptive."

"I don't know about that. I wasn't so sure about taking *you* in."

"Oh, please. That was a slam dunk. You just didn't feel like going up against Connie."

Dana laughed out loud and wagged a finger at her niece. "Alder Garrett, you are . . . I don't know, but you're *some*thing!"

Alder grinned and leaned up against the desk. "Okay, so I think I have a plan."

A wisp of anxiety stirred in Dana's chest. "Let's hear it," she said.

"Well, Jet's mom is in rehab for four weeks, so she gets out a couple days before Christmas. The last week or so, she's supposed to have visits and stuff, and Jet's a little, you know . . ."

"Unsure."

"Yeah, she's seriously unsure. So I thought I'd stay and hang with her till she gets through it."

"You talked to your mother about this?"

"Yeah, she wasn't exactly psyched, but I negotiated pretty hard."

"What does she get in return for letting you stay here another month?"

Alder wound her finger around the string on her hoodie. "Home by New Year's," she said. "For good. No bullshit."

"That sounds like a direct quote."

"Very direct."

Dana sighed. It was hard to think about losing Alder, but then again, a whole additional month was really more than she could have expected. The tip of Alder's finger was turning purple from the tightly wound hoodie string, and Dana reached up and tugged at her hand to loosen the tourniquet. "She's very lucky to have you," she told Alder. "And very generous to share you with me."

Alder gave a sheepish smile. "I didn't tell her about Christmas, yet."

"Where's Christmas going to be?"

"Here."

THE HEAVY GLASS DOOR WAS ALREADY UNLOCKED when Dana got to work on Monday morning just before eight. She let herself in and peeked into Tony's office. "Hi," she said.

He looked up from the paperwork on his desk, and his fingers reached for one another and laced, as if they were fencing in some untamed creature hiding there among the patient charts and professional journals. "Hi," he said, his eyes taking in every inch of her.

"You're in early."

"Just trying to keep ahead of the curve," he said lightly. "Practically more paperwork than dentistry for me to do around here."

"Thanks again for helping me out on Saturday. You should have seen Grady's face."

"Yeah?"

"He kept saying, 'You were up on the *roof*? Of my *school*? With a *ladder*?' As if I had gone to the Arctic Circle on foot or something."

Tony smiled, and she watched the smooth skin around his eyes press itself into perfect little folds. "He'll be telling that story for the rest of his life."

She loved the thought of that. After a moment their mutual delight began to feel silly, and she said, "I guess I better get to work."

"Okeydoke." He turned back to his papers.

Okeydoke? she thought as she booted up her computer. That doesn't sound like him. She didn't have long to ponder, though, because at that moment Marie came in with a walking cast on her foot. Dana jumped up to help her with the door. "What happened?" she asked.

"Don't ask," said Marie. And apparently she meant it, because the question never did get answered, even at lunchtime, with the three of them sitting around the tiny table coming up with nothing better to talk about than current events and possible enhancements to the waiting area. After about twenty minutes, they all found reasons to return to their work.

"Can I talk to you?" Tony said, appearing in the doorway as she reached up to file a chart.

A faint chord of worry chimed in Dana's head. It sounded serious—maybe about the kiss?—but she still hadn't worked out how she felt about that and wasn't ready for a confrontation. "Well, okay, but patients should be arriving any minute . . ."

"This won't take too long."

She followed him into his office, and he sat down in the wooden Windsor chair, leaving her the upholstered one. *Oh, Lord,* she thought, *the bad-news chair.*

"I just got a phone call from Kendra," he said. "She's in her second trimester now, and the nausea's gone. She wants to come back to work starting next week." His expression softened into regret. "Dana, I'd like to keep you on staff forever, but legally I'm obligated to take her back."

"Oh," she murmured, feeling as if she'd been pushed off a cliff with no assurance of water in the river below. "Well, that's good for her, I guess. I never had morning sickness, but I hear it's awful. Must be such a relief to have that behind her . . ."

A hint of amusement warmed Tony's face. It was that toddler-doing-something-adorable look that Alder gave her sometimes. "That's a very Dana reaction," he said. "But I know you must be worried about your income."

Dana let out a breath. "I'm doing okay at the moment—and hoping things will pick up for Kenneth after the New Year."

And what if they did? He had a new family to support now.

He'd called the night before and given her the news. They would be married on Saturday, December 13—less than two weeks away—and Polly's husband, Victor, would be his best man. Kenneth had all but asked her permission about that last part. "He's your best friend," Dana had answered. But it stung.

The kids were invited to be bridesmaid and groomsman, but that hadn't been confirmed yet. Tina insisted that they have time to think about it, that it would be fine either way. "Despite the fact that I'm pretty sure Polly hates me, she offered to take the kids shopping for wedding clothes," Kenneth had told Dana. "She knew we wouldn't have them again until the wedding, and she was worried you'd end up doing it." Dana found the gesture both touching and infuriating.

She focused on Tony again. "I'll start looking for another position. Maybe a department store—they need extra salesclerks for Christmas." *Presents,* she thought. *I'll have to do some serious bargain shopping.* For the first time since she'd had children to shower with holiday gifts, the idea of it depressed her.

And there would be no chatty lunches, no one to commiserate with or tell stories to. No Tony.

"Department stores don't pay that much," he said. "I put some calls out to friends who might have office-manager positions—couple of dentists and a buddy of mine who has a small construction company. Let's see what we can come up with." He reached over and gave her hand a tentative pat. "I really think it's going to work out just fine," he said. It was exactly what she'd told Morgan about Kenneth and Tina's getting married. And she'd been bluffing.

On the way home, Dana stopped to pick up a *Hartford Courant*. Tony would help her find another position if he could. But she knew how the best of intentions didn't always work out. Her life was littered with proof of that. Besides, he didn't seem all that unhappy about losing her, which burrowed into her skin like a rash and made her doubt him.

That afternoon was Grady's first basketball practice of the season, and though she had some errands to run, she decided to stay. She wanted to take stock of the coach, and Grady would feel more confident with her there watching him. It was the one thing Jack Roburtin had told her that made any sense.

In the beginning the boys ran around chasing the basketballs as if they'd never seen one before, though most had been on Grady's team last year. It was as if someone had given them pumpkins to play with. But soon the coach had them doing simple drills, and their limbs began to respond to internal cues they barely remembered but somehow knew how to follow.

"Excuse me," said a man who'd taken a spot near her on the bleachers. "This is embarrassing, but does this say, 'We made it to basketball'?" He held out his BlackBerry to her. "I can't find my reading glasses, and I promised his mother I'd send a confirmation on arrival."

Dana took the device. "I have to admit, I can't tell you until I find *my* reading glasses." She rummaged in her purse and put them on. "Actually, it says, 'We mace it ro nasketall.'"

She smiled over at him as she handed it back, and he laughed at himself, hazel eyes crinkling. "Well, that's good enough for government work, I guess," he said, hitting "send" and putting the phone back in his pocket. "She'll just have to translate."

"Did she think you wouldn't get here?"

"No, she's a worrywart. Since the divorce she's gotten a little obsessive about knowing where he is every minute."

"It's hard to give up the control when you're used to being with them all the time."

He studied her for a moment, his face growing thoughtful. "Sounds like you know."

Dana gave a little shrug that said she did. They chatted amiably, eventually introducing themselves and pointing out their sons to each other. His name was Ben Fortin, and he guessed that she was in sales from the work clothes she still had on, but she told him no, she was a soon-to-be-unemployed office manager. "Maybe you should try sales," he said with a grin. "With that nice, honest face, I bet you could sell sand in the desert."

Is he flirting with me? she wondered. *Please tell me he's not flirting with me.*

When practice was over, they stood and shook hands. He was taller than she expected him to be and handsome in a rangy, high-cheekbone sort of way. "Very nice to meet you, Dana Stellgarten," he said. She was impressed that he remembered her full name. It was her experience that some dads didn't focus too hard when they dropped into the mom-dominated world of kids' activities.

On Wednesday she worked late, as usual, and Kenneth went to the house to give the kids dinner and supervise homework. He was gone by the time she got home at eight-fifteen.

Jet told Dana, "You should've seen his face when he realized he had four kids for the price of two. See if you can pick up a couple more kids by next Wednesday—that'll *totally* put a twist in his panties!"

Dana burst out laughing. The humor went flat, though, when she realized that Kenneth wouldn't be coming next Wednesday. She'd be out of work by then.

After the kids were in bed, she walked through the house turning off lights and retrieving stray objects that had migrated from their homes during the day. A cordless phone lay on the living-room rug; she picked it up and checked her voice mail. "Hi, Dana? This is Ben Fortin. We met at basketball—I'm the guy who couldn't read his own text message. I really enjoyed talking with you, and I'm wondering if you'd give me a call when you get a minute." Dana nearly dropped the phone. Then she took it up to her bedroom, closed the door, and called Connie.

"What should I do?" she said after relaying the encounter and the ensuing phone message.

"Who cares?" Connie yawned. "Call him, don't call him. What's the diff?"

"You're no help, you know that?"

"Seriously, Day, I don't get the question. He's cute, he's nice . . . So he takes you out for dinner at some overdecorated steak restaurant where illegal immigrants bus the tables for leftovers. So what?"

"Oh, all right," muttered Dana. "What I didn't tell you is, something happened last weekend. With Tony."

"Ohh," said Connie. "Santa."

"Don't call him that!" But despite her irritation, Dana told Connie about the high-altitude golf-ball search and Tony's passionate kiss.

"Huh," said Connie.

"For Pete's sake, what's *that* supposed to mean?"

"Nothing. It's just rare that people are surprising. Mostly they're so predictable it makes you want to light them on fire."

Dana groaned. "Forget it. I'm going to bed."

"No, think about it. The guy's clearly got a thing for you, and if he were like most guys, he'd wait about a day and a half and then he'd be hounding you for a date or some other lame affirmation to his ego. But not Santa—he's laying back, giving you a chance to come to your own conclusions on your own timetable. It's impressive, really."

Dana considered this for a moment. *That's exactly what he's doing,* she realized. *He's waiting.*

"This is a total no-brainer," said Connie. "And thanks for waking me out of a sound sleep, by the way—I thought it was an actual emergency, possibly involving my kid."

"I'm sorry. I didn't mean to scare you. She's absolutely fine."

"I figured that out when we spent fifteen minutes talking about your love life. Or I should say your *potential* love life."

Dana didn't respond. She was thinking about Tony and his im-pressive show of patience, and wondering how long it could hold.

"What," said Connie.

"I don't know . . . I guess I'm not a hundred-percent sure I'm attracted to him."

Connie let out an annoyed huff. "Does he have some disgusting phlegm-hawking habit or a ceramic-angel collection I'm unaware of? Because the guy looks perfectly fine to me."

"Well . . ." Dana was loath to admit it. "He's kind of . . . short. And just a tiny bit pudgy."

"And the half-blind texter is tall and thin. Great, there's your answer. Can I go to bed now?"

"No, wait. I'm not trying to be superficial. But don't you have to be attracted to someone to go out with him? I mean, otherwise you'd just be friends, right?"

"Cripes, you're asking me? You're the one who was married for fifteen years."

And look what that had amounted to. How was it possible to be forty-five years old and still not know what you wanted—still make huge mistakes like Jack Roburtin?

"What about the guy in Europe?" Dana ventured, knowing she was testing the bounds of their newfound closeness. "Alder's father. What was that like?"

There was no answer, and for a moment Dana wondered if they'd been disconnected—or if Connie had hung up. But then she heard the faint whoosh of Connie's breath. "It was amazing," she said finally. "He was a phenomenally talented artist, and we had unbelievable adventures . . . and then it was over. And it didn't sur-prise me, because I knew he wasn't durable goods. I knew that from day one. Didn't make it any easier, though."

"Did he know you were pregnant?"

"I found out after we broke up. But I told him."

"What did he say?"

"Nothing memorable. It wasn't that. It was the look on his face. Like I was pressing a loaded gun to his chest."

"Did you ever think about . . ."

"An abortion? No, not really." She was quiet for a moment. "It was the only piece of him I could keep. And as it turns out, it was the best piece."

DANA WAS WORRIED ABOUT MORGAN. THE HIGH of the Disney trip had dissipated, and she was attacking her homework and practicing her cello more than ever. Rita had called several times, but Morgan had declined offers to get together after school. She'd had an appointment with Bethany earlier in the week, and Dana hoped it had helped. Morgan wouldn't say.

On Thursday afternoon Grady had a play date at Jav's. Their friendship had mended with the return of the golf ball and Jav's satisfying response to the story of its retrieval: "That's so sick! My mom would never do that—she'd probably call the police if she saw your mom up there! Then the cops would come and chase your mom all over the roof, and she'd be like—*BAM, BAM, BAM*—knocking them over the edge!"

Dana secretly enjoyed the idea that anyone could think of her as an outlaw. But she said, "Police officers are the good guys. I would never try to hurt them."

"Whatever," said Grady.

Now, with Grady at Jav's house and the older girls at a Wilderness Club meeting, Dana hoped Morgan would open up a little. She made her some toast and sat with her at the kitchen table while she ate. "How are things at school?"

"Okay."

"Who are you sitting with at lunch?"

"Rita and some other girls."

"Is Kimmi bothering you anymore?"

"No, she's going out with Jason Dalton-Gomez now. He's the most popular kid in sixth grade, so that takes up all her attention."

"Going out?" They were twelve—what could that possibly entail? "Do they actually *go* anywhere?"

Morgan looked at her as if she'd just asked if they had run away to join the circus together. "It's just *called* going out," she said. "They sit together at lunch and text each other a lot."

The conversation was starting to feel more like an interrogation, and Dana didn't want to scare Morgan off. She got up to make herself a cup of tea.

"Why don't you drink that fake lemonade anymore?" Morgan asked.

Dana was startled—she'd drunk the stuff for so many years and hadn't even noticed she'd stopped. The last time she'd had it was when she'd made herself vomit, and the memory of its coming back up made her grimace. "I guess I just stopped liking it," she said.

Morgan made a face. "It tastes like that stuff you spray when you dust."

Dana chuckled. "It *does,* kind of!" She poured hot water into her mug and returned to the table. Morgan took a bite of her toast, watching as her mother dunked the tea bag in and out.

"When tea leaves are growing," Morgan said, "do you think they have any idea that they're only born so someone can pour boiling water on them?"

Several answers came to Dana, all of them completely wrong. *Tea leaves don't have thoughts . . . The hot water doesn't hurt them . . . I'm not a tea-leaf killer . . .* "That's an interesting question," she said. "What do you think?"

Morgan popped the last piece of toast into her mouth and shrugged. "I have to work on my paper."

"I thought you already handed that in."

"We got an extension because half the class had a stomach bug last week. He said if we already finished, we could compare it to some other endangered animal for extra credit." She rose from the table, but before she got to the doorway, she turned back momentarily. "Thanks for the toast," she said. "It was really good."

Dana had left a message for Bethany soon thereafter and requested a return call on her cell phone during her lunch hour the next day, Friday. She hadn't anticipated that Tony and Marie would have a little good-bye party for her, complete with a tiny round cake Tony had picked up at a supermarket. It said simply DANA, being too small to accommodate a sentiment like GOOD LUCK or WE'LL MISS YOU or HOPEFULLY, YOU'LL FIND WORK AND NOT END UP BURIED IN CREDIT-CARD DEBT WITH A REPOSSESSION CREW AT YOUR DOOR.

Marie sat with her boot-casted foot propped on a case of exam gloves, her disdain for such silliness peeking out from behind an obligatory smile. Tony's face kept changing, smiling one moment, slightly anxious, almost melancholy the next.

Waiting, Dana thought. *It's driving him crazy.* But she had no answer for him. She wasn't even entirely sure of the question. He hadn't asked her out or told her his feelings. She had the strange sense he was happy she was leaving. *What do men want anyway?* she wondered. *Besides the obvious.*

She was slicing the cake and handing out pieces when she heard her cell phone jingle on her desk and ran to answer it. As she had hoped, it was Bethany. Dana told her about Morgan's obsessive studying, cello practicing, and lack of interest in friends.

"I'm glad you called," said Bethany. "It really helps to be working with a parent who's so observant. And your concern makes sense. Shutting people out, compulsive studying—those are some of Morgan's coping skills, and she's leaning on them a lot these days."

"It's the wedding and the new baby, isn't it?" said Dana. Rage toward Kenneth bubbled up like molten lava inside her. Morgan needed another thing to worry about like a hole in the head.

"Those things are hard on kids, that's for sure," said Bethany.

"But plenty of kids go through worse without developing eating disorders. No one factor is enough to cause self-destructive behavior. She seems to have a tendency toward anxiety and perfectionism, and then there's the hormonal and physical changes of puberty. And middle school isn't easy—kids are socially primitive at that age. If you're hard on yourself to begin with, feeling guilty about something and dealing with changing family dynamics on top of that, preteens are a pretty tough crowd."

Feeling guilty? wondered Dana. "What does she have to feel guilty about?"

"I don't really like to get into specifics about what clients tell me unless it's a danger to them or someone else. It's not good for trust building."

The hell with trust building! Dana wanted to yell. "It would really help me to know," she said, trying not to clench her teeth. "Otherwise I might accidentally make her feel worse."

Bethany was quiet for a moment. "I think you could be right," she murmured, but she didn't say anything right away. Dana racked her brain. *Stealing,* she thought, *maybe shoplifting . . . or spreading rumors—some sort of retribution against Kimmi Kinnear . . .*

"She worries about you," said Bethany.

"About *me?*"

"She knows her father initiated the divorce and it hit you hard. She also heard the whole interaction between you and her friend's mother, so she knows that you lost two friends over her—the girl's mother and the woman down the street."

"Polly," breathed Dana. "But Morgan didn't do anything wrong—the adults caused the problem, not her."

"It's one of those strange psychological phenomena—sometimes kids think they're to blame for their parents' misfortune. And they're often very aware of their parents' feelings. More so than they let on. She knows you're not . . . that you've got a lot on your shoulders."

"She knows you're not happy," thought Dana. *That's what she was about to say.*

She needed more time to think about this. Was she an unhappy person? Connie had always accused her of being a Pollyanna, finding the last drop of good in anything. How was it that her daughter saw her as the opposite?

She thanked Bethany, and they scheduled the next appointment. Bethany said, "I'd like to have you come in with her sometime in the next month or so. It's always good to bring parents into ongoing therapy, once trust has been established. Would you be comfortable having Morgan's dad here, too, at some point?"

Kenneth in therapy. Dana almost laughed. He'd had quite a year: divorce, work troubles, his children needing him more than ever, an unanticipated baby on the way, a new marriage... He probably could use a little therapy. "Yes, of course," she said. "I'd be fine with that."

She was tucking the cell phone in her purse when she heard the *step-thump* of Marie approaching.

"Here," said Marie, unceremoniously handing her a little muslin pouch.

Dana took it and loosened the strings. Out spilled a silver charm—a circle with a tiny purple stone embedded in the middle, two crescents facing outward on either side.

"Marie!" said Dana. "This is beautiful! You didn't have to get me a going-away present."

"It's not a going-away present," said Marie.

"Oh, okay . . . Well, it's very thoughtful. I think I have the perfect silver chain for it at home."

Marie stood there frowning. "You know what it is? That symbol?"

Dana studied the charm. It looked vaguely familiar. She seemed to remember seeing something like it at a medieval fair years ago.

"It's a triple goddess," said Marie impatiently. "I made it."

"You made this? Marie, I didn't know you were a jeweler. What does it symbolize?"

"Maiden, mother, and crone," Marie said, as if it were obvious.

"When I made it, I kept thinking of you for some reason, so now I have to give it to you."

Maiden, mother, and crone . . . It shook loose a vague memory of a documentary she'd seen on the History Channel. Witchcraft. Druids. She looked up at Marie.

Marie rolled her eyes. "It's Wiccan, okay? You're not a religious bigot, are you?"

"No!" said Dana, without a moment's speculation as to whether she might or might not be. "Of course not. It seems very interesting—I'd like to learn more about it."

Marie gave her a skeptical look. "Anyway," she said, "it's about the power of each stage of life and how they integrate together." She picked up the little muslin pouch. "Can I have this back? It's my last one."

"Sure," said Dana. "And thanks so much. I can't wait to wear it."

"See you at your next cleaning," she said, and *step-thumped* down the hall.

At three o'clock Dana gathered up her things. There wasn't much—no pictures of her kids or postcards co-workers had sent her from their vacations, as she had at her last job. She put on her coat and took one last look around at what once had been hers and no longer was. Just like that. Things come and go. No one knew that better than she did.

Tony and Marie were in with a patient—root canal, poor Mrs. Jameson. Dana walked back and peeked into the operatory. "Heading out now," she whispered. "Thanks for everything."

Marie looked at Tony expectantly. "We're pretty much done here," she told him.

"Would you mind . . . ?" he asked her. She took the package of gauze from his hand. "I'll walk you out," he said to Dana, and pulled off his exam gloves.

They crossed the parking lot, and when they got to her car, she made herself turn and look him in the eye, even though it was hard and she would have preferred to pretend that this was any other Friday. If she looked at him, she knew she would see the truth of it, that he was no longer her boss, the best boss she'd ever had and likely ever *would* have.

And there it was, written across his face, the reality of something—yet another thing—ending. "When will I see you again?" she asked.

"Up to you." He reached out and straightened her scarf, tucking it more snuggly against her throat. Then he retreated, crossing his arms tightly around his thin scrubs.

The sight of him shivering against the cold in the frost-speckled parking lot just to be with her brought on a wave of guilt. She couldn't stand what she was doing to him, but she didn't know how to stop. She put her arms around him and hugged him, and his arms circled her waist, pulling her in, but not too tight. He was controlling himself.

"I'm not sure," she whispered. "I don't know yet."

"Okay," he murmured, kissing her cheek. "You know where to find me."

"I'm sorry," she said.

"No," he insisted, though she could feel the pain that seemed to radiate out from his body and into hers. "Don't be." And he let her go and went back inside.

SATURDAY WAS WARM BY DECEMBER IN NEW England standards, the high predicted to be a near-tropical fifty degrees. Dana awoke with a need to move, motion seeming like the only thing that might quiet her worry for Morgan and her indecision about Tony. And Kenneth's marriage to his ever-expanding girlfriend was one week away.

I have to get out of here, she thought.

But an idea occurred to her as she passed Morgan's room and saw her curled over her notebooks at eight in the morning, then went down to the basement and found Grady in front of the TV, his body strewn across the couch as if he'd been flung there by his ankle, a prisoner to the flashing lights and whining cartoon voices before him.

We ALL have to get out of here.

She went to the TV room, where Alder lay wrapped around a pillow on her side of the pullout couch. Jet was facedown, drooling, a leg dangling off the far side. "Girls," Dana whispered.

"Buh," breathed Alder.

"Girls," Dana insisted.

"Fuck off," muttered Jet, still half asleep.

"This is my house!" said Dana. "Do *not* tell me to fuck off!"

Both girls jumped. Jet rolled off the bed and crawled around the end toward Dana. "Sorrysorrysorry," she muttered. When she reached Dana, she hugged her knee. "Seriouslysorry."

"Okay," said Dana, patting Jet's head. "Now, let me ask you two something." Jet released her and climbed back onto the pullout. "Where is there a nice little mountain with a good view?"

And so, after putting her foot down with Morgan that while hiking might not be her first choice of activities, she would give it a try nonetheless, and after attending a tutorial by Jet and Alder about the proper layering of clothing, and after convincing Grady that water shoes were not appropriate footwear despite their "totally killer grip" . . . Dana finally had them all in the car and on their way to Talcott Mountain State Park.

At first Morgan hiked as if she had a cinder block tied to each foot. Grady tended to sprint ahead, then stop for extended periods to climb on a fallen log or check out what he invariably thought were bear caves but were actually just piles of rocks.

"Shit," Dana overheard Jet mutter to Alder. "It's like hiking with Eeyore and Tigger."

"Shut up," murmured Alder. "You used to think Under Armour was a video game."

About halfway up, however, Morgan apparently decided she might as well make the best of it, and Grady settled in to hiking with the group. By the time they got to Heublein Tower, a beautiful old house built on the mountain, Jet was racing Grady to the top, and Morgan was chatting with Alder about what art classes she might take in high school. At the summit they ate their squished sandwiches, bruised fruit, and broken cookies, and no one complained.

"What was the best part of today?" Dana asked Morgan at bedtime.

"Going to that ice-cream place on the way home." They had stopped at Friendly's in Avon for a bathroom break and ended up all jammed into a booth, ordering cones.

"*Ohhh,*" said Dana tugging a lock of Morgan's hair. "The ice cream . . ."

"No, I liked the stories you told about Grandma. I never knew she was a waitress."

"Yeah, it's funny the things you might not know about people, even though you're related."

Morgan gazed at Dana as if she were speculating on the secrets she might uncover about her own mother one day.

"Hey," said Dana. "Remember when you told me that thing about Bubble Wrap? How all the hard things that happen and the mean things that people do pop our bubbles?" Dana stroked the wheat-colored hair, fanning it out around the pillow. "I've been thinking about that. You're right. That's just how it feels. Like you're deflating."

Morgan nodded almost imperceptibly.

"But then," said Dana, "I was thinking . . . it's just wrap. It's on the outside. And it's really awful when it gets popped, but at least it's not the only thing you're made of."

"Feels like it," Morgan murmured.

"Yeah, but it's not. I mean, it's part of you, but it's not the deep down true part." She watched Morgan's eyes, the pupils spreading wider into the flecked brown irises as she pondered this possibility. "Also," Dana continued, "the popping—it's temporary. The bubbles reinflate."

"How do you know?"

"Because I've felt it. Maybe somebody helps you out, or laughs at your joke, or just gives you a look like they're on your side . . ."

"But then you have to wait around for someone to feel like being nice to you," said Morgan bitterly. "Some days *nothing* good happens."

"Unless you make it happen."

"Like how?"

"Like doing something nice for someone else." Dana hesitated, not sure if she should keep going in the direction she intended. *You're afraid to state the obvious,* she told herself, and forged ahead. "As you know, it's been kind of a tough year for me. The divorce, going back to work, not being home as much. But when I take a meal over to that family with the sick dad or I solve some problem at work"—she gave a sly smile—"or I make you try something new, and you like it even though you won't admit it . . . I feel good. And no one can pop those bubbles. They're permanent."

Morgan looked doubtful.

"Trust me," whispered Dana, leaning down to kiss Morgan's forehead. "I'm forty-five years old. I know a few things."

On Monday morning the kids went off to school, and for the first time in a month and a half Dana stayed home. *It should be a relief!* she told herself. But it wasn't, and not just because of the money. She missed it. She'd been good at it. And she wondered how Tony was.

By the time the kids got home, she had scoured the house, re-organized all the kitchen drawers, made a batch of chili for the McPhersons, and baked three loaves of zucchini bread. She took Grady to basketball, and it wasn't until Ben Fortin was hiking up the bleachers toward her that she remembered his phone message. She'd returned his call, not wanting to be rude, and knowing she'd have to face him again at basketball anyway. But the message she'd left was so brief it couldn't be construed as anything remotely like interest.

He sat down next to her. "Hope you don't think I'm some stray dog you can't get rid of now because you took a thorn out of my paw."

"Not at all," she said. It was exactly what she was thinking.

"You're a friendly face for a poor dad in a sea of mommitude." He grinned. "Sorry I didn't get back to you, by the way. Work's been so crazy, and the week got away from me. I was hoping to make my case before someone else snapped you up."

Good Lord, thought Dana, *here it comes.*

"You haven't found a new position, have you?" Ben asked.

New POSITION? What in the world was he talking about?

Confusion must have shown on her face, because he added, "Last week you said you were about to be laid off . . ."

"Oh! Yes, I was—am! Today was my first day off, in fact, and I thought it would be a relief, but I kind of missed it."

"So you're interested in finding something again? Because I was talking with my partner, and we think it's time to get some help. Business is going well, but we both hate to answer the phone—got into a real tiff about it a couple of days ago . . . Anyway, it's a renewable-energy company, very start-up. The job is office-manager stuff. Ordering supplies, keeping track of things, dealing with clients when we're out. We aren't ready to take on someone full-time yet—maybe twenty, twenty-five hours a week." He looked doubtful. "That's not enough, is it?"

"Actually," Dana said, "that's plenty."

She was feeling hopeful as she drove to the McPhersons' a few hours later with the chili dinner tucked snugly in a shopping bag in the backseat. Ben had called his partner right there from the bleachers to set up a formal interview for Wednesday. There was a teasing affection in his voice that seemed to go beyond the bounds of business partnership or male friendship. Dana wondered if that had been the reason for his divorce.

As she drove, the sky was blue-black and the streetlights were already lit at five-thirty. The feel of Tony's arms around her waist and his lips on her cheek came to her again, as it had all weekend. Despite the uncertainty between them, it had felt so . . . good.

Maybe too good. Unlike the kiss on the rooftop, which had made her feel scared and disoriented, their embrace in the parking lot—the tenderness with which he'd adjusted her scarf and kissed her cheek—had felt utterly natural. It lacked the push and pull, the unspoken negotiation she was used to with Kenneth and other men.

Had the embrace been brotherly? She tested this possibility in her mind, but it didn't fit. Familiar, maybe, but not familial.

When Dana pulled up in front of the McPhersons' house, there were two extra cars in the driveway. She wondered if the visitors were staying for dinner. She'd made extra, as usual, but it could be stretched only so far. A stranger answered the door.

"I'm Dana Stellgarten. I'm here with dinner."

The woman squinted at Dana as if she didn't understand English.

"Comfort Food?" Dana said. "Is Mary Ellen or Dermott here?"

"Oh, God," the woman murmured. She glanced behind her, opened the door a little wider, and reached for the shopping bag. "Here, just give it to me."

"Who's that?" came a voice.

"Just a delivery person," the woman called back.

"Wait!" Mary Ellen appeared in the doorway, her eyes red-rimmed, tendrils of hair loose from her ponytail. "Dana!" she said. "I knew it was you," and she began to cry. Dana stepped toward her, and she reached for Dana, clutching at her and sobbing in seizurelike spasms. Dana looked to the woman behind them and made eye contact, silently begging for an explanation. The woman mouthed, *Dermott died today.*

They stood in the doorway with their arms wrapped around each other, crying for what could have been moments or hours. Dana felt as if her insides had turned liquid, and every concern she had, every wish for herself and her life, had gone seeping out through the bottom of her feet, pressed as she was in the frantic embrace of a newborn widow.

It had happened just an hour or so before. He had lain down for a nap earlier in the afternoon and died in his sleep. Mary Ellen went in to check on him and was able to scoot the kids over to a neighbor's house before they figured it out. Minutes later the paramedics arrived.

"I told the dispatcher, 'For godsake, don't put the siren or lights on—it's the only chance I have that they won't notice,'" she told Dana later when they were sitting at the Magic Marker–stained kitchen table. Two other women were there, friends she'd called who lived nearby. One had Mary Ellen's address book and was making phone calls; the other was tidying up the house in preparation for the tides of friends and relatives who would arrive shortly to cry and comfort her and cry some more.

"I just wish I'd been with him," Mary Ellen said to Dana, her voice hoarse with emotion. "I could have lain down, too. I was tired. Why didn't I lie down with him? Maybe he would've said something. But I just didn't think . . . I really believed he would make it!"

"You couldn't have known," Dana soothed. "And what could he have said that you don't already know? That he loves you? That you're a good wife? You know these things."

Mary Ellen's chin trembled. "When we went out on that date last week, he said it all . . ." Tears began to spill down her cheeks. "Do you think he knows I'm sorry I wasn't with him?"

"I think," said Dana, biting the inside of her lip to keep from crying again, "I think he knows you would've done anything for him. Because you *did* everything—everything you could do. I need to tell you something now, before a million people show up. Something he asked me to tell you." Her throat clenched, and it was hard to get the words out. "He wanted you to know he's missing you. Right now. Just as you're missing him, wherever he is, he's missing you, too."

Mary Ellen laid her head down on the table and sobbed. Dana rubbed her back, brushed her hair off her cheek as she would have done for Morgan or Alder or Connie. As she would've done for anyone who was so sad she couldn't hold her head up anymore.

When Mary Ellen quieted a little, Dana put her own head down on the table to talk to her. "One more thing," she whispered. "He said I should keep cooking for you."

A sound burst out of Mary Ellen then, and it took Dana a second to recognize it as a laugh. "Demanding son of a gun, isn't he?" she said, a smile breaking across the tearstained cheeks.

"I would have done it anyway," Dana confided. "He just gave me an excuse."

Relatives and close friends started arriving. Dana let herself out and walked to her car. She sat there in the front seat, mind awash with Mary Ellen's sorrow and the image of Dermott's face as he had gazed at his wife only a week before, when Dana had brought over the silk blouse. As sick and diminished as he was, he looked as if he felt lucky.

I am such an idiot, thought Dana. She called home and told Alder what had happened. "I'm going to go see a friend," she said. "Can you hold down the fort?"

"Gotcha covered," said Alder.

———————————————

TONY OPENED THE DOOR AND LET HER IN TO THE warm light of his house. "Is everything okay?"

"Remember that family I cook for sometimes?" she said. "Dermott McPherson—he's a patient of yours."

"Of course." He helped her off with her coat and tossed it over the varnished wooden banister. "You gave his wife that blouse."

"He died today. I went to bring them dinner, and he had just died." She didn't think it was possible to produce any more tears, but her eyes filled nevertheless. Then his arms were around her. "I thought I was all cried out," she whispered.

"All right," he soothed, his hand stroking her hair. "Okay." She felt as if she'd arrived at someplace perfect, as if this were the only comfort that would do.

After a moment she pulled back. "Do you have a tissue?" she said, sniffling.

"Sure thing." He stepped into a doorway behind the stairs, a half bath, she guessed. When he came back with a box of tissues, he led her into the living room and they sat on a brown leather couch. Two hardwood lamps on either side spread their pools of light across the room.

She blew her nose, self-conscious because she knew he was waiting. "I didn't come here to cry," she said, stuffing the tissue into her pocket, "I came because . . . I miss you."

"I miss you, too."

"Yes, but you *know* that. I mean, you know how you feel. Not that I'm making any presumptions . . ."

"It's not presumptuous," he said. "Marie actually came right out and told me to knock it off."

"Knock what off?"

"Being irritable because you weren't there today. Kendra's a good receptionist, but she's got nothing on you for lunch conversation. Or anything else, for that matter."

"How's she feeling?"

"Fine," he said, making it clear he had no intention of pursuing that tangent.

"Marie's a Wiccan, by the way," she told him.

"Great."

"Did you already know?"

"No, but I'm not really interested in Marie right now." He leaned back against the couch and crossed his arms.

She gazed at him for a moment and remembered her initial impression of him: a birdbath—short and squat, his essential goodness an open reservoir. She took a breath and released it. "Okay," she said. "I'm a little freaked out."

"Because . . ."

"Because I'm not really sure how I feel. Part of me is so comfortable with you, it's like I've known you my whole life. And I trust you. A lot."

"Maybe too much," he speculated.

"Yes! And that scares the hell out of me. You're a terrific person, but you're not perfect."

"Well," he said, "I'd like to think I've got a little more under the hood than the last guy you were with."

A laugh burst out of her. "*That's* a pretty safe bet."

He uncrossed his arms and allowed himself a smile.

"The thing is," she said, "sometimes less under the hood is easier to deal with. You don't get so . . . attached."

"Which comes in handy if they leave you."

"Wow," she breathed, looking down at her hands, the truth of it hitting her like a rogue wave. "That's really messed up."

"We've all got our issues," he said.

"Connie says the problem with me is I seem too normal. I should 'embrace my psychosis.'" She made quote marks with her fingers.

"Sounds like Connie's on to you."

"She says *you're* on to me."

"I'm liking her better and better."

"She still refers to you as Santa," Dana admitted.

His eyes narrowed. "That part not so much."

They sat there in silence for a moment, the brown-and-cranberry coziness of the room insulating them from the bitter cold. "This is a lovely house," she said. "I can see why you didn't move."

He nodded agreement and thanks. "Dana," he said. "Why are you here?"

I miss you, she thought, but she knew it wasn't enough. "I'd like . . . I'd like to try."

"Really?"

"Yes."

"Not just because you saw something incredibly sad and needed a safe shoulder to cry on?"

"Well . . . to be honest, I was already thinking about you all the time, and that sort of tipped the scales. Not the safe-shoulder part so much as not wanting to lose you."

"What makes you think you'd lose me?"

"Tony," she said, "you're a very understanding guy and all, but you don't put up with much. You wouldn't go for the whole 'let's just be friends' thing."

A hint of a smile crossed his face. "Sounds like *you're* on to *me*."

"I hope I am . . . I want to be."

He slipped his arm under hers and clasped her hand. She slid over next to him, rested her head against the back of the couch and felt the muscles in her shoulders release their grip on her neck. He put his feet up on the oak coffee table, and she did the same. They talked or sat silent, listening to the gurgles and pops of the heat cycling on and off and the wind making the trees brush up against the house. At eleven-thirty she said, "I should probably get home."

He walked her to the door, helped her on with her coat. Just as he reached for the doorknob, she slid her arms around him and kissed him. She had meant it to be more than a peck, but not much more—and yet it went on, an exploration, a confirmation, her heart rate rising, her arms tightening around him, pressing toward him, allowing him to pull her closer. When they began to separate, he kissed her cheek and her chin and her nose, then rested his forehead against hers.

"*Oh,*" she sighed.

"*Mm,*" he said.

Yes, she thought as she drove home. *A little more under the hood than the last guy.*

POLLY RANG THE DOORBELL AT A QUARTER TO three, just before the kids were due home. She never rang the doorbell, not since the early days of their friendship. She'd yell, "It's me!" and walk in.

When Dana opened the door, Polly said, "Should I wait out here?" It had a tone to it, but Dana suspected that Polly truly needed to know, and held the door open for her. They stood in the mudroom, not looking at each other until Polly blurted out, "I quit that book group. They're a bunch of gossips, and I let myself sink to that level. Nora thinks she's permanent prom queen or something, but she's just a manipulative bitch." She gave her head a hard, frustrated little shake. "I'm not making excuses—it's all on me. But I just want you to know it's not a mistake I'll ever make again."

Dana nodded. "Good," she said.

"Also, Victor's practically ready to divorce me over this." An exaggeration, but Dana understood her point. "He keeps saying, 'You threw Dana under the bus for what—that snotty Nora Kinnear? What's the matter with you?' And he's right, but can you believe the nerve of him, after the crush he had on her? And then he says to me every day, 'Don't you go up there to the Stellgartens'. Don't you hound her till she takes you back from sheer exhaustion. You let her come to you when she's ready.' Like he's got a Ph.D. in human relationships or something. Let me tell you, he *doesn't*."

Dana looked her in the eye. "It's not what you did to me, Polly, though that's bad enough. It's what you did to Morgan."

Polly blanched. "God, I know," she breathed. "I'm sick over it. I *never thought—*"

"No one ever thinks gossip will go very far. But it's gossip, that's what it does. She overheard Nora say you were the one who told her. She knows you did it."

"I could kill myself." Her pixielike stature seemed to diminish even further, and Dana thought of that line from *Peter Pan*. *"Clap if you believe in fairies."*

"And now she feels bad because she thinks she ruined our friendship."

"That's crazy! She didn't do a thing!"

"I wish you'd tell her that. Today, if possible. Don't let on that you know she feels responsible. Just apologize and let her see she's not to blame. Please."

"It's a done deal."

"How'd it go?" Tony asked when he called that night around ten, just as Dana was getting into bed and wondering if it was too late to call him.

"Okay, I think." She told him about her conversation with Polly.

"Did she do it?"

"I think she must have. Morgan seemed calmer tonight. But I didn't want to ask her—then she'd know I set it up."

"Good thinking," he said. "You're a heck of a mom."

Dana groaned. "You know that saying, 'It's not rocket science'? It's not—it's harder."

"Tell me about it." Tony chuckled. "I talked to Lizzie tonight. She's all happy because—wait for it—"

"She got back together with Zack!"

"No, Zack *tried* to get back together, and she told him to go jump in a lake. Actually, I'm sure the phrasing was much more current than that, but you get the gist."

"Good girl!"

"Also, I told her about you."

Dana's breath caught in her chest for a second. She hadn't told anyone yet. It seemed too fragile, still, to expose to public scrutiny. "And?"

"I believe that her exact words were, '*That's* what I'm talking about!' Something along those lines. I always sound ridiculous when I use their lingo. Which has been confirmed by them, of course."

He asked about the funeral arrangements for Dermott. Dana had stopped by with a suit jacket for the oldest boy, remembering how the sleeves were too short on the one he owned. She had learned that there would be no wake or funeral. Dermott had requested that his ashes be spread over Nipmuc Pond, and since it was currently frozen, Mary Ellen had decided to do a memorial service in the spring.

They talked a while longer, and Tony gave her pointers for her job interview the following day. Finally he said, "Good night, sweetheart."

Dana grinned. "You're calling me sweetheart?"

"Your heart is very sweet," he said. "I couldn't help but mention it."

Dana changed her clothes twice before the job interview. The first outfit was too boring, and she didn't want to look like some sad sack who'd be so grateful for the job that she'd agree to low pay or put up with disrespect. The second outfit was too synthetic—a polyester print blouse and tan rayon slacks. *It's a renewable-energy company,* she chided herself. *You need to look green!*

Finally she got into the car, dressed in wool pants, a cotton sweater, and Marie's triple-goddess necklace. She hoped the sheep-farming and cotton-growing industries were environmentally friendly. And if her potential employers were aware of the charm's symbolism, she hoped they weren't, in Marie's words, "religious bigots."

The office was in a small industrial park in the nearby town of Glastonbury, and when she arrived a few minutes early, she could see the need for her services. Files splayed out on tables, office supplies piled haphazardly in a corner, and the phone ringing and ringing.

"I'm not getting it!" she heard a man call from an office in the back. "I got it the last time!"

"And I made you breakfast, walked the dog, and did the laundry," Ben's voice called from another direction. "Payback's a bitch!"

The next day she met Tony for lunch at Keeney's. She couldn't wait to tell him about the new job. "It's not a ton of money, but they did give me a tiny bit of stock in the company."

"They decided that fast? You just interviewed yesterday."

"I already started! They're paying me under the table until they get the paperwork filed. God, it's a mess, but they seem really nice."

Their conversation wandered from Marie's new tattoo to Kendra's enormous lunches to the pair of polypropylene walking socks that Polly bought her and sent home with the kids.

"She really wants you back," said Tony.

"I'm thinking about it," said Dana. "She was a really good friend before she totally betrayed me. Plus, at the moment she's in my life whether I want her or not—she'll be with my kids for most of the weekend. The rehearsal dinner's on Friday night, the wedding's on Saturday, and her husband's the best man."

"Speaking of this weekend . . . I'd like to take you out on Friday. On a date."

A date. "That sounds very official."

"As official as you want it to be."

She didn't let herself think for more than a moment before she said, "As official as you can make it."

All too soon he had to get back to work. In the parking lot by the edge of the pond, he kissed her like he meant it, his body pressing her against the minivan. She didn't want it to end, but there was a cough not far from them, and they turned to see its source. Two fishermen stood a little ways down the shore, lines reaching into one of the few parts of the pond that wasn't frozen. The men were grinning appreciatively in their direction.

"How's it going," Tony called wryly.

"Good," one of the guys called back. "You?"

The other guy burst out laughing.

Polly's apology seemed to settle something for Morgan, and for the next day or two she was more relaxed. She even went to Rita's house after school on Thursday. But on Friday she came home and went right to her studies. She played her cello for an hour and stalled when Dana told her it was time to put it away and get dressed for the rehearsal dinner.

"Can I bring it?" Morgan asked. "I have to practice for the concert."

"Oh, sweetie, I'm not sure. It's kind of a busy weekend, don't you think?"

"I could practice tomorrow morning. The wedding's not till noon."

When Polly came to pick up the kids and take them to the dinner, Dana pulled her aside. "I think Morgan's pretty stressed about all of this. She's not saying much, but it shows," she said. "Polly, I need you to keep an eye on her. Just make sure you're with her, if you can."

"Of course!" said Polly. "I'd do anything for that kid."

"Thank you. I'm so worried about her."

A month or a year or ten years ago, this would have precipitated a full-body, vice-tight, ten-second hug from Polly. Maybe longer, if Dana had started to cry. But now she only reached out and squeezed Dana's wrist. "I'm on it," she said.

Dana took a shower and was standing in front of her open closet with a towel wrapped around her, wondering what to wear for her very official date with Tony. There was a moment—albeit brief—when she wished she still had the beautiful silk blouse Nora had given her. *Even for free,* she reminded herself, *it wasn't worth the price.*

There was a knock on the door. "Come in," she said.

"Hey," said Alder.

"Nice towel," said Jet.

"Hi, girls. What are your plans tonight?"

"Um . . ." said Alder.

"We thought we'd get high, steal some airsoft guns, and shoot each other without protective gear," said Jet. "Okay by you?"

Dana gave her cheek a little pinch and said, "You are *soooo* funny."

"Actually," said Alder, "Connie's putting on massive pressure for me to go home for the weekend. But I said no way, except maybe for Sunday. Morgan and G come back Saturday night, right?"

Protective gear, thought Dana. *She thinks she's my armor.*

"Honey," she said, "your mom deserves more than a day. She misses you, and I'm fine here." Alder looked skeptical. "Really," said Dana. "With the new job, I have a million little catch-up tasks. I'll be going pillar to post tomorrow. And tonight"—she grinned proudly—"I have a date."

Alder and Jet looked at each other. "With *who*?" Jet demanded.

"Not the iPod guy!" Alder was horrified.

"Oh, *please.* Give me a little credit, will you?" said Dana. "No, this one is pretty special. Maybe I'll tell you about it when you get home. On Sunday."

So the girls had gone to up Hamptonfield, and Dana had gotten dressed. She didn't come up with anything so spectacular as that blouse, but she felt she looked pretty good. Tony arrived at seven-thirty carrying a Stargazer lily tied with a dark pink bow. The rich smell filled the room when he came in. "I was going with a rose," he explained, following her into the kitchen. "But Lizzie made snoring noises over the phone when I mentioned it, and Abby suggested this."

"You're getting dating tips from your kids," Dana teased, reaching for a bud vase.

"Hey, if the advice is sound, I'll take it where I can get it." He took the vase from her and began to fill it with water. "Follow the one with the working compass."

"Your compass works fine."

He took the lily from her hand and slid it into the vase. "I'm glad you think so," he said, and kissed her lightly, then more urgently, his arms slipping across the silkiness of her dress, her hands sliding beneath his sport jacket to press at the muscles of his back. They almost missed their dinner reservation.

The restaurant was beautiful and the meal delicious, but Dana didn't focus on that. As Tony told her a story or asked her a question or guessed—often quite accurately—about her opinions, she watched him. The way he looked at her, eyes glinting above the light of the candle, happy and longing at the same time. The way his tan fingers slid cross the tablecloth to connect briefly with hers when she said something particularly astute or funny or endearing.

"Hey," she said as they shared a chocolate dessert torte. "How come you seemed just the tiniest bit happy when you told me Kendra was coming back and you had to let me go?"

"Because I was. I knew I had it bad for you, and either you

would go out with me or you wouldn't. Either way it was going to get very difficult to be your boss for much longer."

As they walked out to the parking lot afterward, she said, "Remember when I broke my tooth and you told me that story about wearing the dead husband's suit jacket?"

"I certainly do," he said. "It was the most embarrassing thing I could think of."

"It was so generous," she said, tucking her arm under his. "Taking the time to make me feel less pathetic. It really impressed me."

He opened the car door for her, then let himself in on the driver's side. "Good to know my worst date was impressive," he said. "Leaves a generous margin for improvement." He started the car but didn't put it in gear. He glanced over at her. "You're in the driver's seat," he said.

She looked at him, taking him in—all of him, not just what was visible. "I'd like to see your house again," she said quietly.

"Buckle up," he told her, and the engine roared to life.

S HE HALF HOPED THEY WOULD GO STRAIGHT TO bed. There was a tiny part of her that wondered, *What if he doesn't like my body? What if I don't like his? What if we really love each other but the sex is bad and it ruins everything?* She had heard about that—couples who should have just stayed friends. If she were ever going to know, it was best to speed straight ahead without a chance to chicken out.

Unfortunately, Tony seemed to be of an opposite mind. He opened a bottle of wine. Poured it. Gave her a tour of the house while they sipped. This was Abby's room, with the geometric bedspread and the framed calligraphic rendering of the periodic table. This was Lizzie's, with the animal-print curtains and the poster of a bunch of mud-spattered boys called Tokio Hotel, whatever that was. A half hour went by as they chatted and sipped and reviewed the artifacts of his life, her anxiety rising as quietly and relentlessly as the tide.

She stared out the window in the guest bedroom. *Relax,* she ordered herself. *For Pete's sake, RELAX!*

"What's going on?" he asked her. "You look funny."

"Nothing," she said, focusing on him. "No, I, um . . ."

He waited.

"Do you . . . um . . . do you think we'll . . . sleep together?"

His eyebrows went up.

"God," she breathed. "That was unbelievably tactless."

He scratched the back of his neck. "I was trying not to rush things."

"Yes, I could tell. And I really appreciate it—you're always so thoughtful. But I . . . uh . . . It's just starting to drive me a little crazy. Not knowing."

"Well," he said, "what did you have in mind?" His mouth trembled just a little, and at first she thought he was getting emotional. *Oh, God!* she thought. *I've shocked him!*

But then he bit the inside of his lip, and she could tell that he was trying desperately to contain himself. She frowned at him, and his face broke open with laughter. "I could prepare an agenda." He grinned. "With a timeline."

"Shut up."

"Maybe a flowchart?"

She let out an aggravated sigh and leaned against one of the bedposts. He tried to put a conciliatory arm around her, but she shrugged him off.

"Sweetheart," he said gently. "Do you think I'm not thinking the same thing? Do you think I'm not wondering, 'Now? Is this the right moment? Or even the right day?'"

Anger ebbing, but not completely gone, she flashed a look at him. He put a hand to her face, brushed his thumb across her cheekbone. "Dana . . ." He kissed the other cheek. "Sweetheart," he whispered against her skin. Her jaw unclenched, and her neck loosened, and she turned her lips toward his. They stood there kissing and holding each other, and then his hand slid up her spine, his fingers dipping into the neckline of her dress.

He's in, she thought. The boundary of her clothing had been breached. And she wondered how it was that she could disrobe so easily with Jack Roburtin, a man she'd thought so little of, and yet Tony's finger inside her collar felt like the first step toward bliss or misery. She wouldn't know which until she got there.

His lips moved along her jaw and down her neck and onto the

span of shoulder he had revealed with his finger, as if he knew it was tender, a wound beginning to heal. Then he covered it back up and murmured, "Let's just lie down together and see how that feels."

"Yes," she said. And they lay on the pale blue cotton quilt of the guest bed, facing each other, not touching until she leaned forward and kissed him. And then waiting became unbearable, so she undid the buttons of his shirt. He watched her do this, not moving except for the quick, shallow breaths that made his rib cage rise and fall. His tan chest was smooth except for a sprinkling of fine black hair across his pectorals. Another sprinkle ran from his navel down into his pants. She ran the palm of her hand down from his collarbone, following the trail to his belly, and he let out a sound, half groan, half sigh. The sound reverberated in her brain, and she slid closer, kissing him, wanting to feel that sound in her body. No longer able to restrain himself, he reached for her.

He unzipped her dress and pulled it forward, tugging at the sleeves to help her out of it. She undid his pants and slid her hand inside, down the warm, smooth length of his thigh. Soon all the clothing had been tossed off the bed like unneeded ballast.

"You are amazingly beautiful," he said, and let his hand glide across her shoulder and breast and hip. Then they were pressing against each other, arms and legs intertwining, the kisses deeper, more urgent. That unbuckled, speeding-headlong feeling she'd had on the school roof came back to her, but it felt right this time. No passive restraint necessary.

They must have slept. The light in the room was different, the darkness less thick. But it seemed she'd dozed for only a matter of minutes, that his hand had only just stopped running lightly up and down her arm, as she nestled her cheek into the flat spot by his collarbone. He had been saying something to her, and she had answered, but now his breath came in even, rumbling passes, as if he'd been asleep a long time.

Then a gauzy light was spilling into the room, and his chest was pressed against her back, his thighs tucked behind hers, his arm curled around in front of her. Her breast was cupped in his hand as if it had settled there like a bird into its nest.

The next time she woke, he was coming into the room wearing blue-striped boxers. As he slid back under the covers, she asked, "Where did you go?"

"Just to put on some coffee. I didn't know if you were a coffee person."

"Not really," she told him. "Tea sometimes."

"Duly noted." And then he was kissing her again, and the coffee was overcooked before they got down to the kitchen to drink it. He gave her a pair of sweatpants that she kept hitching up to keep from sliding off her hips, and a Brown University T-shirt. "Lizzie brought that home for me, Christmas freshman year. Never fit me. Looks fantastic on you, though."

He made spinach-and-feta omelets, and they ate and talked and smiled lazy, satisfied smiles at each other. She let out a spacious yawn, and he took her hand and led her back upstairs.

At four-thirty she told him, "I should go. The kids will be back in a couple of hours." But by the time she actually got up and got dressed, she had to hurry if she wanted to get home, shower and change her clothes before they arrived.

Tony threw on jeans and a T-shirt and drove her home.

When they pulled into her driveway, he took her hand, interlacing their fingers. "So," he said, gazing at her, "that seemed pretty official."

"It was practically an inauguration."

"Took about as long." He grinned. "Not that I'm complaining."

She raised his hand to her lips and whispered, "I love you." For a moment she worried that she'd been too forward. But then he slid his arms around her and murmured, "I love you, too, sweetheart. Call me when the kids are in bed."

Victor carried Grady in and kissed Dana on the cheek as she removed the sleeping boy's shoes. Then he went upstairs to put Grady into bed. Polly came in with Morgan, both weary, arms around each other. Morgan slid away from Polly, then slumped against her mother and let herself be kissed and hugged. Her hair was arranged in elaborate curls and ringlets. Dana could feel the lattice of bobby pins along her scalp. "You hair looks very fancy," Dana murmured.

"Tina did it." She could barely keep her eyes open. "I'm going up to change," she said, and then, glancing at Polly, she told her mother, "Come with me."

You're not my armor, Dana thought for the second time in as many days. "I'll be up in a minute." When Morgan had gone, she looked at Polly.

"She did okay for most of it," said Polly. "Really held it together. Has to be hard seeing your dad marry someone else, when last year it was your mother in all the family pictures."

"You stuck with her?"

"Like white on rice." She glanced away. "It was hard for me, too. You and I and Kenneth and Victor were so close. Now everything's in the toilet."

"Tina doesn't seem that bad."

"Who gives a shit about Tina!" Polly flared. "I don't want Tina!"

Victor came back from tucking Grady in. He took Polly's arm, said, "Good night, Dana," and muscled his wife out the door. "Time and space," he muttered at her before the door closed.

Dana went up to Morgan's room. She was under the covers, her dress in a heap on the floor. From habit Dana put it on a hanger. "Don't bother," said Morgan. "I'm never wearing it again."

"Never say never." *Boy, that sounded just like Ma,* she thought.

"Okay, I'll wear it when the Jonas Brothers ask me to play cello on tour with them."

"Fair enough." Dana scooted her over and lay down beside her. "How'd it go?"

"Terrible."

"Details, please."

"I did good," Morgan said, "up till the vows. Up till the 'death do us part' part. And I thought, 'He said this same thing to Mom, and he didn't mean it. How come anyone believes him now?'"

"He did mean it."

"Yeah, right," she snorted. "And look where *that* got us."

"Morgan, I'm not going to start defending your father," Dana said quietly. "But I was there fifteen years ago when he said it the first time, and I know he meant it. He had every intention, and so did I. But sometimes the best of intentions just don't work out. A lot of times they do, but sometimes they don't. And I'm sorry you had to learn that so early in life, sweetie, I really am. But hating Dad is no help to you."

"How do you know? Maybe it helps a lot."

"Because I've tried it. It's like eating a quart of ice cream. Makes you feel better for a little while, but eventually it makes you feel worse."

Morgan didn't say anything after that. Dana could hear the tiny Styrofoam beads squeaking against one another inside the Hershey pillow as Morgan's fingers pressed at it.

"Sweetie, what happened when you heard the vows? Did you get upset?"

"I cried—not loud or anything. No one could hear me. But Polly was sitting next to me, and she slid right up close and put her arm around me."

"Was that good?"

"Well . . . you know Polly. She grabs you so tight you can hardly breathe. But yeah, it felt kinda good. I thought I was going to freak out and be, like, embarrassing. But she's so strong—I think she's been lifting weights. It was like having a superhero right there in the pew."

Thank you, Polly, Dana thought. *Thank God for you.*

"Are you and her friends again?" Morgan asked.

"We're getting there," said Dana. "Sometimes when somebody

really lets you down, you need a break, no matter how much they apologize. But I think the break's about over." She gave Morgan a squeeze and kissed her forehead. "Sleep late tomorrow, okay?"

She was almost to the doorway when Morgan said, "Wait, I forgot to tell you. I got that wolf paper back. My teacher really liked it, and I got all the extra-credit points."

"That's wonderful, honey! Can I read it?"

"It's in my backpack downstairs."

Dana went down to the mudroom and finally found it, stuffed behind books, a water bottle, a damp hoodie, and one gym sock. Dana brought the paper into the office to get her reading glasses and sat down at her desk.

"The North American Timber Wolf: Predator or Prey?" she read. "By Morgan Stellgarten." The teacher had marked it with "A+, 105/100, Beautiful job, Morgan!" The first section detailed the history, hunting and communication skills, social hierarchy, and endangered status of the timber wolf. It had no predators other than humans, who had almost completely exterminated the species. "In a couple of states, wolves can still be killed anytime, even though they're endangered. Those people must really hate wolves."

The last section was titled "Extra Credit, Comparing Wolves to Another Endangered Species, Humans."

Humans? thought Dana. *That's a hard case to make.*

"Most people do not consider humans endangered," wrote Morgan. "Maybe nobody does. But being human is very dangerous. No other animals hold grudges against each other, or build bombs, or think about hurting each other a lot of the time like people do. There's a lot of us, so no one thinks we're in trouble. But we are.

"Wolves are unlike humans in many ways. If you're a wolf instead of a human, you always know where you stand. You're either an alpha or a celibate subordinate, and either way your job is clear. It is very strict, but that makes it safer. Wolf cubs don't have to worry who is going to take care of them. No one loses their job or worries about money or being pretty enough."

"Wolves are like humans in some ways, too. Middle school is like a really big wolf pack, only the jobs switch a lot for no real reason. Everyone knows who the alphas are, but tomorrow that could change. The celibate subordinates get bitten if they are acting too cool, or too awkward, or just because the alphas feel like it. That is called bullying, and the guidance counselors talk about it a lot, but it never really goes away. Maybe it is just part of being in the pack. It is more dangerous to be a disperser, a person who gets kicked out or goes off and tries to start their own pack, because in the time between leaving your pack and starting a new one, you get attacked a lot.

"A family is like a wolf pack, too, except for the changing-jobs part. In my family my father was the alpha male. I'm not sure what my mother was. She wasn't a celibate subordinate, because she had the cubs (my brother and me). But she didn't act too alpha. Then my dad turned into a disperser (even though alphas are not supposed to do that) and went to start a new pack. So then we had no alpha for a while. My mother had some trouble getting bitten by wolves from other packs. But she must be pretty smart, because she figured out how to be an alpha pretty quick. She nips back a little now, too. It is safer in our pack now, and mostly I believe her when she says, Everything is going to be okay."

A PENGUIN READERS GUIDE TO

DEEP DOWN TRUE

Juliette Fay

An Introduction to
Deep Down True

Fortysomething Dana Stellgarten has always been nice to everyone, to a fault. These days, however, she's got her hands full and her patience is wearing thin. She's fresh out of a divorce—in a move that even she found painfully predictable, her husband left her for a younger woman—and trying to raise two children on increasingly limited funds in suburban Connecticut. Dana must essentially start over, make some new friends, learn how to date again, and find a job after being at home with her children for years.

If all that weren't enough, her ex, Kenneth, continues to make her life miserable with his insensitive demands, and both of their children seem to be internalizing the pain of the divorce. Twelve-year-old Morgan is starting to exhibit some suspicious behavior, and Dana suspects that she might be in the early stages of an eating disorder. Her once happy-go-lucky seven-year-old, Grady, is acting out in school, alienating his friends and irking his teachers. Determined to provide a better home life than she had growing up with her hapless mother and depressed father, Dana will do everything she can to make her kids feel safe, secure, and loved.

Then one day Dana's sixteen-year-old niece, Alder, arrives unannounced: She's running away from home, though she won't say why, and needs somewhere to stay, far away from her contradictorily controlling bohemian mother, Dana's sister, Connie. Dana, kindhearted as always, can only say yes, hoping that she can somehow make the new arrangement work while finding a way to keep her infuriated sister at bay.

Even with all these moving parts, Dana eventually starts to settle into post-divorce life. She volunteers delivering meals to a local family in need. She starts dating Grady's enthusiastic football coach. Nora, the popular and glamorous mother of Morgan's new BFF, befriends her, and Dana feels flattered. But it's when she begins working as a temporary receptionist for her dentist, Dr. Tony Sakimoto, that Dana finally finds a real connection, one that will teach her that nothing is more important than being true to your own heart.

Juliette Fay's second book is a tender, often humorous, story of rising above the unexpected, sometimes disappointing, circumstances of life. Dana is the quintessential everywoman, finding her own voice and inner strength just when she needs it most. Fay has a knack for creating authentic characters whom readers will come to love. With savvy dialogue and compelling emotional insight, *Deep Down True* is a novel with intelligence and soul.

ABOUT JULIETTE FAY

Juliette Fay received a bachelor's degree from Boston College and a master's degree from Harvard University. She lives in Massachusetts with her husband and four children. Her debut novel, *Shelter Me*, was on the Indie Next List, was chosen as a Target Bookmarked Pick for 2009, and was a 2009 Massachusetts Book Award Book of the Year. *Deep Down True* is her second novel.

A CONVERSATION WITH JULIETTE FAY

While Dana and Kenneth's divorce is a central event in this novel, it has mostly happened before the story begins. What inspired you to write this book and why did you decide to start the narrative where you have?

I was inspired by the fascinating crucible of the middle school experience, and how sometimes we as adults can be thrown back into those feelings of desperately wanting to belong, while also trying to follow our hearts. At any age these two things—belonging and being true to ourselves—can sometimes be hard to accomplish simultaneously.

The narrative starts after the divorce because the divorce itself isn't as interesting as the way it shatters Dana's complacency with the life she knows—a barely lukewarm marriage and an existence that revolves around everyone but her. It challenges her to stop settling for so little and start building a life that is worthy of her.

The kids' dialogue—from Morgan's explanation of "emo" to Grady's request for muscle-building pancakes—is pitch-perfect. How much of it comes from your own life as a mother? Do your children read your books?

I guess it's kind of like moving to another country— eventually you learn the lingo. And for the stuff I don't get right, I have a native speaker in my teenaged daughter, Brianna, who corrects my drafts. She's the oldest and the only one of my four children who's read my novels. The boys have never asked to. Maybe if I were writing thrillers or fantasy they'd be more interested.

I rarely if ever quote my children—or anyone's children—in my books. I have too much fun making it up myself. But I do use little common phrases, mannerisms and reactions. As a writer I'm lucky to have such ready access.

The theme of Dana's volunteer work with the McPherson family provides an interesting point of contrast throughout the story, in some senses keeping Dana's own troubles in perspective. What function did it serve for you as the author?

Making the dinners for the McPhersons is emblematic of Dana, who is such a selfless giver that even as her own life is falling apart, she never stops doing for others. The flip side of that coin is that it also serves as a self-soothing behavior. Her rituals of kindness keep at bay the harshness of a world where people kill themselves and husbands leave and kids are cruel. And hey, it's food, Dana's drug of choice.

The dinners are more than just food, though. They serve as an entrance ticket into the life of another family in the throes of even greater adversity than Dana's. And it's a way for her to tap into her true self, which is not about what she can *do*—she cannot fix anything for the McPhersons. But she can offer her particularly wonderful brand of compassion, which is one of her essential strengths.

Your portrayal of bulimia is quite nuanced and believable, particularly the ways adults unwittingly reinforce kids' negative behaviors. Did you research this topic or come to it more organically?

I did a lot of research, read reports, talked to experts, poured over Web sites, went to a conference. The Web sites that anorexic and bulimic girls themselves put up about what they do and how and why are absolutely haunting. I also interviewed a couple of adult friends who'd been bulimic. Ultimately I kept thinking back to a friend from my younger years who was anorexic. I confronted her and begged her to stop starving herself and she told me, "I want my mother to make me stop." I'll never forget it because it was then that I knew she was in for a long haul. Her mother was utterly checked out. It made me see that even as we are leaving childhood behind and insisting that we don't need help, we want our parents' guidance and leadership.

Alder is a really compelling personality—a smart, surly teen with a truly compassionate heart and a natural way with metaphors—and in many ways she is the lynchpin of the novel. Was she an important character in the book's conception, or did she come to be more prominent in later drafts?

Alder was there right from the start—even before Dana! I had originally envisioned her for my first novel, *Shelter Me*, but there wasn't a spot that was quite right for her. So I knew I would include her in my next story, which turned out to be *Deep Down True*.

I'm glad I waited, because in her offhanded, teenagery way, Alder is the perfect role model for Dana. As they both struggle for healing and repair, Alder is willing to be alone or hang out with the very unpopular Jet. Refusing to cave to her domineering mother, she goes to Dana, who, Alder knows, will give her the support she needs without making her concede to outside expectations. And Alder quietly demonstrates for Dana how not to be such a doormat—from getting Grady to help clear the table, to standing up for herself in the final showdown with Ethan. Everyone should be lucky enough to have an old soul like Alder in her life.

Early on, you write, "The story of Dana's divorce bored even her." Was it a challenge to take on the all-too-familiar trope of a middle-aged husband leaving his wife for a younger woman?

Not really. While it's familiar, it's no less dramatic because of the tsunami it can create in its wake. And I don't really see this as a divorce story so much as an awakening that happens to have been launched by a divorce.

*Dana's lack of assertiveness has gotten her into lots of trouble—
in her marriage, in her social life, with her own family—and her
journey in this book is to find her own voice amid the many forceful
personalities in her life. Ironically, the less she seems to care about
other people's opinions, the more these people ultimately seem to like
or at least respect the new Dana. Can you elaborate on this dynamic?*

I think that in each one of us there is what some would
call the True Self, or the Divine Self, or the Center. We get
pulled out of that center all the time—by stress or disrespect
or hormones or any one of a million things. And if we pay
attention, we can feel when we're in and when we're out. There's
something very appealing about being with someone who knows
her True Self and can be that self a lot of the time, because it
helps us discover and love our own. Dana's growing self-respect
is ultimately a stronger draw than her relentless niceness.

*By being let into Dana's head, the reader becomes acutely aware
of the millions of decisions that must be processed on the fly in an
average parent's day. To your mind, what makes a good parent, and
where do Dana and Kenneth fit in on that scale?*

Oh my gosh, is there a harder question than what makes
a good parent? Loving but not indulgent, attentive but not
hovering, strict but not controlling . . . I can say all these things,
but they hold different meanings for every parent and each kid
may need a different balance of each.

Dana and Kenneth are well-intentioned parents. They
love their children. But while Dana is a bit of a hoverer, Kenneth
is fairly disengaged—just like in their marriage. They both learn
to correct for that more by the end of the story. And they learn

to parent better *together* as they do, which is tricky enough for married couples, and even harder—and more important—when there's a divorce.

The scene where Dana purges to feel closer to her daughter is both harrowing and poignant. Was this a difficult scene to write?

Absolutely. I never thought I'd ever write such a detailed account of vomiting, of all things! But while there are many examples of Dana's failings, I wanted to show one of her great strengths, which is the length to which she will go to understand fully and be compassionate toward the people she loves.

The notion of "deep down true" is a wonderful one—that we all have some essential truth of who we are and what we want inside. Did the title drive the story or did you arrive at the title in the writing process?

For my first novel, *Shelter Me*, I had a title in mind as I wrote that ultimately didn't work out. This time, I decided not to title it until the end, and see what the story offered up as a suitable name, which I think it did in *Deep Down True*. There was, however, a phrase that I kept in the forefront of my mind as I wrote to hold me on course. That phrase was "the tension between being true to yourself and being liked," which, while not a good title, was a very helpful compass for the journey.

QUESTIONS FOR DISCUSSION

1. Dana's husband tells her that the divorce is his "best chance for happiness." What does this statement say about him? What is Dana's best chance for happiness?

2. Throughout the book, Dana struggles to allow herself to feel anger. Is this emotion productive for her, and if so, how?

3. Sometimes Dana learns about herself through her children's observations. How do her children perceive her and how are their insights helpful to her?

4. In times of stress, Dana turns to food to comfort herself. How might her behaviors have directly or indirectly influenced Morgan?

5. For Grady, his dad's golf ball is a precious gift. What does it represent and how does it comfort him?

6. There are many parallels between Dana's social life and her daughter Morgan's middle school lunchroom as they jockey for position among the seemingly popular, more powerful people. How do the Kimmis and Noras of the world shape who we are?

7. Dana must eventually confront the unspoken truth of her past and what really happened to her father. How has this event affected her and her sister? How are they similar or different as a result?

8. Dana eventually begins to regain her sympathies for her ex-husband, even as she continues to cope with her own disappointment and anger. Why does she start to see his point of view, and how does this change her behavior?

9. As Dana's relationship with Tony blossoms, it becomes clear that he is giving her something that she doesn't get from other people in her life. What is this quality, and how does it bring out the best in her?

10. By the end of the book, Dana's life has changed significantly. How is it different and which of these changes surprised you?

For more information about or to order other Penguin
Readers Guides, please e-mail the Penguin Marketing
Department at reading@us.penguingroup.com or write to us at:

Penguin Books Marketing Dept.
Readers Guides
375 Hudson Street
New York, NY 10014-3657

Please allow 4–6 weeks for delivery.
To access Penguin Readers Guides online, visit the
Penguin Group (USA) Inc. Web site at www.penguin.com, or
www.vpbookclub.com.